MW01516345

WE

Douglas S. Kirkland

PublishAmerica
Baltimore

© 2003 by Douglas S. Kirkland.
All rights reserved. No part of this book may be reproduced in any form without written permission from the publishers, except by a reviewer who may quote brief passages in a review to be printed in a newspaper or magazine.

First printing

ISBN: 1-59286-932-7
PUBLISHED BY PUBLISHAMERICA, LLLP
www.publishamerica.com
Baltimore

Printed in the United States of America

To all of us, from whence

WE was created.

PREFACE

Dawson Kohler and Ashton Smyth were strangers until the paths of their lives crossed during an afternoon of trauma for them both. They were caught in the midst of turmoil created by sinister forces bent on changing the complexion of America through terrorism and fear.

In his job as an agent of the Secret Service, and her job as a brilliant young research scientist at the Lawrence Livermore National Laboratory in California, they were both very much aware of anticipated terrorist threats to the U.S. homeland by rogue groups and nations. The methods of attack could include nuclear, biological and chemical attacks using various means of delivery as well as attacks using airplanes such as the 9-11-01 events, explosives and any number of other deadly methods of mayhem.

What their combined knowledge chanced to reveal, though, was an even more deadly threat involving the use of a giant laser. The technology to produce such a weapon and deliver its deadly effect on critical targets was both simple and complex. The two of them, with their unique knowledge and resources, became the front line of defense to discover and neutralize the source of this developing capability by an equally resourceful adversary.

They, along with six other select people, became a team whose sole objective was to prevent this weapon from ever threatening the United States. Once perfected, there was no currently known defense against its use, so it was critical that it never reach the deployment stage.

Dawson and the beautiful and perky young girl, Ashton, who would become co-leader of the team with him, fall in love with each other in the course of their joint quest to find the potential perpetrator of the laser attack.

As their professional and personal lives become entwined with each other, they find that they would never be able to refer to each other as merely you and me. The bond formed between them required that they become "we".

At the conclusion of their journey together they each have to make a critical choice as to whether or not they would go forward into the future as "we". Events transpire that would make that decision as inevitable as it would prove to be startling for both of them.

You and me,
we are we,
joined together
forever and ever.
And if we part,
in our heart
we'll still be we
you and me.

Douglas S. Kirkland

CHAPTER ONE

I stood out in the cold misty rain outside the Peachtree Centre in downtown Atlanta. I had been standing there over an hour, shifting my position back and forth from one corner to the other across from the Centre. I was watching, waiting, observing the people and activities around me. It was Tuesday, December 17th, 2002. The crowd of late Christmas shoppers bustled by, unaware of my presence.

The President of the United States was to be in Atlanta the next day, with his motorcade stopping at the Centre so he could make a speech from the plaza between the four buildings, before going back to Hartsfield International Airport to board Air Force One and return to the White House. As a lead agent in the Secret Service, I was there in advance of the President's visit with no specific assignment other than to map in my mind the surrounding area, determine the best exit route in the event of a problem, and be alert to any unusual activity on the day prior to the President's visit. Others were taking care of the more mundane security provisions. I had a free rein to just do what my instincts told me to do in preparation for the short presidential visit. It was a hell of a way to spend my 36th birthday.

I was there for another reason, also. There had been a disturbing report in recent days of a new weapon that could be in the hands of potential sponsors of terrorist activities. The information the CIA, FBI and Secret Service had was vague. All they knew was that a significant technological breakthrough had been made at the Lawrence Livermore Laboratory on an enhanced laser beam, that could be combined with other magnified light emissions to create a destructive force never before imagined. Through an intercepted transmission from a fanatical group in the Middle East to a suspected terrorist cell in Sudan, it appeared some or all of this technology had been passed on to this group. The message indicated that work had to be done on developing a strategically effective delivery technique.

In checking with the Laboratory, it had been learned just this morning that one of the lead scientists who had been involved in developing this laser was to be in Atlanta today visiting their parents, and was scheduled to give a scientific review on new laser applications for medical uses at the Peachtree Centre today at 1:30 PM. I didn't even know what the scientist looked like. All I had been given on the hurried cell phone call a few minutes ago was a name, Ashton Smyth. It was after 2:30 PM now, so the conference should be breaking up soon. I would like to meet this Ashton Smyth, if I could identify that person. The information desk had told me the building in which the conference was to be conducted and I was watching the exit from that building. When I saw a group exit the building, I would enquire of one of them as to which one was Ashton Smyth.

There was a group exiting the conference now! The meeting must be over. I started crossing the street. There were about a dozen people, a beautiful young girl who must have been taking notes on the presentation, four or five definite scientist looking types and a half dozen non-descript people.

"Excuse me ma'am," I said to the girl I thought must be the secretary. "Could you tell me if a Mr. Ashton Smyth is in this group?"

She looked at me quizzically with a hint of a smile on her face. "I'm afraid there is no Mr. Ashton Smyth in this group," she replied. I noticed she had beautiful blue-green eyes and her pretty face was outlined by long, dark brown hair that cascaded over her shoulders with a wisp blowing in the slight breeze across her face. Without staring, I also noticed she had an exquisite figure that was evident in a skirt that stopped just above her knees and clung nicely around a firm and shapely rear. Her waist was tiny and she was moderately endowed on top.

Before I could recover from the encounter with this beautiful girl and her response that Smyth wasn't in the group, she laughed a musical laugh and tossed her hair back over her shoulder with a twinkle in her eyes.

"There is, however a Ms. Ashton Smyth," she said with amusement showing in her eyes, as I blushed from my mistake.

"I'm sorry," I stammered. "I didn't know — I just assumed —you know..."
She nodded knowingly, still smiling.

"I don't see any ladies in your group. Can you tell me where I might locate Ms. Smyth?" I continued, recovering slightly.

"Oh," she said teasingly. "You don't see any females in our group?"

"Well, only you of course. I believe Ms. Smyth is a scientist and I hardly think you resemble that type," I replied, fully recovered now from my embarrassment of a moment before.

"And what type might that be?" she asked. I sensed she was still having fun with me.

"Well, you know. Thick glasses. Middle aged or older. Hair in a bun. That sort of thing. Please, do you know where I might find her!?" I asked urgently, getting impatient now.

"Yes, I know her. And you did," she replied.

"I did what?"

"You found her. I'm Dr. Ashton Smyth and I'm sorry I don't fit your prototype. May I ask who you are and what you want with me?" She smiled again as she extended her hand.

Now I was crimson again. "I guess I've really botched this introduction up big time," I laughed. "My name is Dawson Kohler and I am with the Secret Service," I replied as I shook her hand and offered her my identification.

"Let's get out of the rain if you want to talk," she smiled. The continuing mist had made her hair cling damply to her face, making her look distractingly cute and disheveled.

"Do you have time to spend about fifteen minutes with me? We can go down the street to the McDonald's," I suggested.

"Sure!" She began to turn in that direction just as I caught out of the corner of my eye a car approaching at relatively high speed for a city street. We were standing on the sidewalk right next to the curb.

All of a sudden the car veered sharply in our direction, heading right towards us!

"Look out!!" I shouted as I violently shoved her to the other side of the sidewalk and threw myself across her, just barely dodging the oncoming car at the last second.

The car careened sharply to the right, plowing into a section of the building behind and to the right of us. Suddenly there was a huge explosion! Scattered glass, bricks and soot began to fall down on and around us. People were screaming and running away, fearing another explosion. It was all over in a few seconds. A suicidal driver with a car bomb had tried to run us down! Failing that, he had driven into the building behind us. Miraculously, we both had escaped serious injury or death.

"Are you alright!?" I asked, looking down to see her frightened face with a smudge of soot on her cheek.

"Yes. I'm scared," she said, trembling slightly as we staggered to our feet.

"I could have expected and been prepared for something like this if it had happened tomorrow with the President's visit. I really don't understand. It was as if we were the target," I said thoughtfully.

By now sirens were sounding all around us with police cars, fire trucks and ambulances. There was quite a lot of building damage from the car bomb but, fortunately, no apparent serious injuries.

"I may have been the target," she replied.

A police captain approached us, inquiring if we were okay and asking us to describe the attack. We told him what happened without mentioning Ashton's last comment. After satisfying him that we had told him all we knew about the incident and giving our names in case they had future questions, we proceeded to McDonald's. We ordered coffee and found a quiet table away from the other patrons.

"What did you mean about you being the target?" I asked when we got settled in our seats.

"Well, first maybe you should tell me why you wanted to meet me," she said.

"Fair enough. As you know, I'm with the Secret Service. My primary reason for being here is to assist in the security preparations for the President's visit tomorrow. However, our agency, along with the FBI and CIA have been made aware in the past few weeks of your lab's breakthrough in laser technology, and the potential for this technology to be developed into a weapon for the U.S. or other parties who might not have our welfare in their interests. I was informed a couple of hours ago that you were one of the lead scientists on this project and that you were to be here today. I wanted to meet you and ask you about the security for the project's information."

"Yes. There have already been agents from the FBI talking to us about some of the technology getting outside the lab," she replied.

"Are you aware that this did happen?" I asked.

"I'm not aware that it didn't. You see, our work was not classified because we were just continuing work on advanced laser applications and configurations to benefit private industry and medical use. It was only after the experimental combination of light transmissions resulted in a beam that had heretofore unknown potential, that we realized that what we had discovered had highly potential destructive applications. But at that point we had run out of funding on the project and had not perfected the system. All of us were very disappointed because we felt like we had done something, like inventing the light bulb, but had to stop before discovering how to make the switch that would turn it on."

"So what happened then?"

"Well, we got funding to continue about two months later and went on to perfect the technology, informed the government of our findings, conclusions, and the success of our experimental work that by accident produced something that could have enormous military use. At that point the work became classified and, with the controls on access and security, I doubt that any information got out after that. But it's very possible that information on the project could have gotten out prior to the funding freeze. The technology at that point would have been fairly easy to conclude for anyone who had more than basic laser knowledge."

"Now, back to my first question. Why do you think you could have been a target for the car bomber?" I asked.

"Well, maybe I'm paranoid. But after our discussions with the FBI, if someone does have the technology, they would not want the U.S. to have it for two reasons. It would mean there could be a retaliatory strike on an aggressor with the same weapon, much like the Cold War nuclear capability that both the U. S. and the Soviet Union had. It was a deterrent for use by either country. A more likely reason for the groups who might use this weapon would be that the only effective defense from a laser attack would probably be a laser with similar capabilities. It would be like a missile defense capability against rocket attack. If all of that presumption is correct, these people would benefit from all of us who worked closely on the project being wiped out."

"I see. Your argument makes some sense. They certainly weren't after me, and it did appear we were the target for the driver, unless he was just trying to bomb the building and our being in his path presented an opportunity to take out a couple of people on the way in," I responded.

"I would like to stay in touch with you if I may," I said, noticing that she had finished her coffee.

"Here's my card. I will be returning to San Francisco tomorrow after staying at my parent's house tonight. It's my birthday. You can contact me any time," she said, handing me her card.

For some reason, I didn't want the conversation to end and wanted very much to stay in touch with her. I had married when I was thirty to a pretty reporter I had met at a Presidential cocktail party, and divorced four years later when I discovered she was seeing the TV anchor on her station while I was traveling with the President. I had stayed busy and not really noticed or been attracted to other females until I met Ashton. She was not only beautiful, but smart and had a good sense of humor. I liked her. And today was her birthday, too! What a coincidence!

"You won't believe this without me showing you my driver's license," I said, pulling my license out to show her. "Today is my birthday, too!"

"So we are both Sagittarius!" she smiled. "And I see you are 36 today. Congratulations!"

"Thank you. May I ask a personal question?" I asked as we rose to leave.

"Sure," she smiled. She was so cute that when she smiled with that little flash in her eyes and a look that seemed to invite further intimacy I almost forgot my question. "I may not answer, though," she quickly countered.

"Okay. Just how old are you today on your birthday? You don't look to be much beyond a teenager."

"Everyone says that! Actually, I'm 28 today. We'll, Mr. Kohler, it has been nice meeting you and thanks for saving my life. Call me any time if there is more I can do for you." She gave me that cute smile again, shook my hand and left.

I would definitely call her. I didn't realize at the time just how soon I would be making that call.

CHAPTER TWO

The next day the President's visit was uneventful from a security standpoint. I returned to my apartment in Bethesda, Maryland, that afternoon and reported to my section chief early the following morning.

"Hi, Dawson," Mike Reilly greeted me as I entered his office. "Tell me about the incident with Dr. Smyth."

Mike Reilly had been with the Service since graduating from college in 1976. He had a laid back personality, but had a reputation for quickly getting right to the heart of an issue. He was one of the most well respected people in the Service and had cultivated and maintained a close relationship with his counterparts at the FBI and CIA throughout his career. This sharing of information between the normally turf protective bureaucracies had served all the agencies well in the past several years. Mike's feeling had always been that in order to fulfill his most important responsibility, protecting the President, he needed to be proactive. Rather than just protect the President wherever he was, Mike felt he should be involved in finding what potential threats existed, where they existed and who the people were that represented the threat. He didn't care if a threat was only a possibility or even when it might surface. He wanted to stop the threat and the people involved before a threat became a probability, or a present concern.

In my eleven year stint with the agency, after the fifth year, Mike had pulled me out of personal security and given me a freewheeling responsibility to search out potential threats before they surfaced. Sometimes I was in the vicinity of the Presidential party, sometimes at a location in their future agenda, and sometimes in some far off corner of the country or the world seeking information or people who were, or could become, threats to our nation or its leaders. Most of the time these were secret missions, often being conducted in conjunction with some of my counterparts in the FBI or CIA. We had a good and open relationship built upon mutual trust and respect.

I carried an old Colt .38 caliber Cobra revolver. It was only accurate at relatively close range, but I preferred the light weight and ease-of-concealment characteristics of that weapon. I had used it numerous times. Some of those instances were only known to me and Mike and maybe one of the other agency people if they had been a part of the activity. When our national security or the security of our leadership was involved, and probable cause or strong evidence indicated the source, we never erred on the side of caution. We were expected to use good judgment, however, and I knew that I would always have to defend any action to Mike's satisfaction.

"Well, Mike, it was meant to just be an introduction on my part and a few questions about the laser information we had received. As it turned out, both of us almost got wiped out by a suicide bomber." I proceeded to tell him the whole story, including Ashton's thought that she may have been a target and why she felt that way. I mentioned she was young and very attractive without saying she was drop dead beautiful.

"Based on additional information the CIA has turned up, I think you better stay on this thing," Mike said. "From the top level of our agency as well as the CIA, we are very nervous about the apparent fact that the Lawrence Livermore technology has gotten in the hands of some dangerous characters. Their only deterrent to using it now is the lack of a delivery strategy and design."

"I guess I better go to California then," I said.

"I think so. But I need to give you a briefing first from information that is available to us. In addition to information we and the CIA have, the FBI have concluded their initial phase of the investigation at the lab in California. I don't have the results on that yet, but will some time tomorrow," Mike replied.

"Should I stop in tomorrow afternoon , then?" I asked.

"No, today is Thursday. Take tomorrow off because you might be gone quite a while, and we're not sure where this investigation might ultimately take you. Besides having all the information we have at this point Monday, I will be able to introduce you to the rest of your team," Mike responded.

"My team?"

"Yes. As I told you there is concern at the top levels of all our agencies and within the Administration on this potential threat. The Homeland Security Secretary insists that all the intelligence agencies be involved. You have been selected to lead the team, but you may need to recruit a co-leader who knows something about the technology," Mike answered.

"Who else will be on the team?" I asked.

"I will introduce you to them Monday, but you will have six other members assigned. Each of them have been selected as some of the best from their respective agencies. One will be from the FBI, one from the CIA, one from the State Department and one from the Army Delta Force. There will also be a NASA representative and a light research scientist. Plus the person you choose who would be available from the Lawrence Livermore lab who would know the specifics of this particular technology," Mike said.

"The State Department and Delta Force!? Why will they be involved? And why NASA and the scientist? That's eight people counting me and the one you want me to recruit! We'll get in each other's way. Well have to rent a bus to get around!" I exclaimed.

Mike laughed. "Dawson, you know how all of our activities are being coordinated now. You will probably see more of this kind of thing. And it's not all bad. We are sharing information and people more now and that part is good. Besides, I'm looking to you as team leader to utilize the resources without making it cumbersome to do so. You will be a team though, and will travel together and operate as a team."

"Mike, you didn't answer my question. I'm used to working with CIA and FBI types, but why the others?"

"Okay. The State Department because you may have to make some on-the-spot decisions regarding national sovereignty issues. That person will be authorized to evaluate your proposed action in terms of impact on international politics. If you violate a nation's sovereignty to pursue a suspect, the State Department person will tell you the international implications of that. It will still be your decision. The NASA person and the scientist, because you need people on the team that can recognize and evaluate effective delivery systems. The Delta Force guy because you may get into a dangerous situation and be glad to have another person in addition to yourself and the FBI and CIA people who can help out in tough situations. Any other questions?"

"I guess not." I was a little overwhelmed with the scope of this operation, but knew Mike well enough to know he had probably told me all he was going to tell me until Monday.

"Okay! See you Monday, then. Why don't you come in about 11:00. We'll make introductions, cater lunch in the conference room so you guys can chat a little and get to know each other, then we'll spend the afternoon briefing you on what we know."

My conversation with Mike had ended. I left, bewildered by the complexity of meshing such a divergent group of people into an effective investigative and, if necessary, fighting force.

I drove back to my apartment in Bethesda in deep thought. The top level of our government must consider this laser thing a really serious threat. Although there had been a lot more cooperation and communication between the various security agencies since the Homeland Security Office had been established and its Director made a cabinet level position, this team I was to lead was still unprecedented in its makeup and joint mission. My mind was still on Ashton who, I was sure, was back in California by now. We would need to start with her, I think. All of a sudden the seriousness of our mission had a pleasant aspect to it. I wanted to see Ashton again.

I pulled up in the drive and into the carport of my apartment. It was a nice, roomy, two bedroom apartment with a small kitchen and dining area, and a large living room with a fireplace. Located on a quiet, suburban street with shade trees along the walks, it reminded me of my hometown and the street I grew up on in a small town in Tennessee. The apartment was tastefully decorated and I was a pretty good housekeeper for a single male.

When I entered the front door, I took my revolver out of its holster and laid it on the little table by the front door, then went to the kitchen to pour a glass of gin over ice. Returning to the living room, I noticed the message light flashing on my phone. I pressed the play button.

"Hi Dawson! This is Ashton Smyth.." I suddenly remembered that I had given her my card when she offered me her's, and my card also had my home number on it. Her voice had that cute little girl sound.

"I arrived back in California a couple of hours ago," the message continued. "All the way out here on the plane I thought about how you pushed me out of the way and instantly threw yourself over me when you realized the car might hit us in Atlanta. I know I thanked you for saving my life. I just wanted to thank you again. If you are out this way any time, give me a call. I will take you to dinner. Bye, now! Hope to see you some time soon."

I stood there stunned. I had just been thinking of her as I walked in the door. I also picked up on her calling me Dawson and introducing the call as being from Ashton. When we met two days ago, it was Dr. Smyth and Mr. Kohler. This was her way of telling me that if we saw each other again we could be Ashton and Dawson to each other. That made me have a nice warm feeling. I finished my drink in great spirits. I would call her tomorrow when I found more about our mission. Already I knew we would probably need to start at Livermore and I was looking forward to the prospect of seeing Ashton again.

That night I went to sleep with thoughts of Ashton on my mind. As I fell asleep, though, the dream changed to a night of terror in a strange place with a bright beam of light flashing through the dream in an ominous manner. Perhaps the dream was a prediction of things to come.

16

CHAPTER THREE

I got to Mike's office about 10:45AM Monday, December 23rd. It was always a good idea to get to an appointment with Mike a little early, because he kept his watch about five minutes fast. Never be late though!

"Hi Dawson!" Mike greeted me cheerfully as I walked in. "Your team is gathered in the conference room. Let's go in and make the introductions and get started."

I walked towards the conference room with Mike with some trepidation. I still wasn't too sold on the idea of such a large team of divergent people. I would have preferred just a couple---the FBI and CIA people. As we walked in, the six people rose to greet us.

"Dawson, let me go around the room and introduce you to the rest of the team," Mike said.

"First, this is Steve Whitt with the FBI." We shook hands. Steve was medium height, solidly built, sandy headed and handsome in a rugged sort of way. He would be about my age, in his mid-thirties. We moved to the next person.

"And this is Dr. Thom Henson from NASA. He has prior experience with Boeing, and is very knowledgeable of rocket technology as well as satellites and fixed wing aircraft. He is also familiar with potential future designs and capabilities of equipment in space or within the earth's atmosphere." Thom was probably about forty-five years old, tall, slender with black hair flecked with gray that looked like it not been combed in a few days.

"Next, we have Darby Peters. He is a Lieutenant on loan to us from Delta Force." Darby was black, about six feet four inches, probably 240 pounds, all muscle. He had a pleasant, intelligent face and an easy smile, but your immediate impression was that you would want him on your side in any kind of fight.

"Then, here is Percy Thackett with the State Department." Percy was average height and build, very neatly and sharply dressed. He appeared to be in his early thirties, a very precise person with a somewhat studious demeanor.

"Now, let me introduce you to Dr. Ernest Brown. He is a scientist who has knowledge of light source delivery systems of all types. He has experience with lasers also, but not on the scale of the beam you will be investigating. As I mentioned last week, you should try to recruit someone from Livermore who is very knowledgeable of the technology of the specific product you will be looking at. We can help get that person released from their duties at the lab for the duration of your investigation." Dr. Brown was probably the oldest member of the team. He looked to be a very fit fifty year-old, wore glasses, a slight build and balding head. He looked like a scientist who probably jogged every morning.

"Lastly, here is Lawrence Childress. He goes by Larry, and is our CIA representative. He has several years of experience in almost every foreign country in the world." Larry was probably about forty years old, broad shouldered, stocky and about five feet eleven inches, 180 pounds. He had black hair and a mustache.

"That's it," Mike said as we all took our seats. "We have seven of what will become an eight person team, that will be engaged in this project until it comes to some kind of conclusion. Our mission is to learn about the recently developed laser technology at the Lawrence Livermore Lab, determine if all or part of that technology has fallen into potentially unfriendly hands and, if so, who has it. If you are able to progress to that point, then your mission will be to find and destroy the technology and the people who have access to it. Security going forward has already been taken care of and will be continued by members of some of your agencies outside of your group. Your mission is to find and destroy what might already be out there. Any questions so far?"

"Mike, it appears that each of us is a part of this team because of special expertise each of us has, that might come into play and be needed during certain phases of this quest. You have told us that Dawson is the team leader, and we understand the necessity for a chain of command. But who has the ultimate decision-making authority if there is a conflict within any of our special areas of expertise?" Larry asked.

"Give me an example," Mike said.

"Okay. Suppose, for example, we were about to take an action in a foreign country that would result in destruction of property, or loss of life to that nation or individuals who are citizens of or harbored by that nation. Further suppose that, due to potential adverse international political implications of that action, Percy opposed the action. Does his expertise rule or does the team leader's opinion rule?" Larry responded.

"Good question and good example," Mike said. "When possible, if there is strong disagreement within the team on a course of action, Dawson will be expected to review with me before implementing the action, and I will in turn discuss the pros and cons with the appropriate department head and with the Administration. But that will only be when time allows for that process to take place. Otherwise, after considering all of the information, Dawson's decision will be binding on the group. The person objecting will be expected to abide by that decision and to attempt to minimize in any way possible, without endangering the team ability to carry out that decision, the adverse consequence that is the root of the concern."

"Why is the Secret Service heading up this team?" Dr. Brown asked.

"Any one of the investigative agencies could probably have been chosen to head the project," Mike answered. "However, the information we received indicated that the laser threat was directed primarily towards the President and other top government officials. Obviously the threat could grow beyond that as the technology is refined but, as you know, the Secret Service is responsible for protection of our nation's elected and appointed officials. It was decided jointly by all of our agencies to have our department head the team with assistance from all the rest of you . As each of you know, this interagency work approach is being used more and more since the events of last fall."

"I might also mention that the Lawrence Livermore representative will be appointed as the co-team leader, at least in relation to methods of neutralizing the threat. None of you, nor do I, know the technology. And the best person to advise us and make decisions on means of destruction of knowledge or equipment if you find it would be that person," Mike continued.

"Mike," Steve interjected, "will we have any support to accomplish our mission from additional people from any of our agencies?"

"Certainly, all of the agencies will be available for support if needed. But, realistically, you will probably be on your own. I envision your activities to be fast moving and going a lot of places. When you reach your objective, it would probably be coincidence if you were at a time or place where any of us could help you," Mike answered. "Any more questions?" He asked. None were offered.

"Okay," he continued. "Lunch will be here soon. After lunch I will brief you on what we know about this threat. But let me close this session by saying to you that this super laser is the most dangerous threat we have to our nation and its citizens than anything since the development of nuclear fission. The danger exceeds that of nuclear attack because, as we understand it, it can be used strategically to pinpoint specific targets or to wipe out whole populations or cities. The greatest danger is that there is currently no known defense for this weapon. This investigation has absolute top priority for the security of our nation. The terrorist organization who may have attained this technology has to be stopped and the information and any hardware in their hands destroyed! Do you have any comments, Dawson, before we break for lunch?"

"Thanks, Mike. Yes, just a brief comment. I want to welcome everyone aboard our team. It is going to be difficult for me also to adjust to operating with a group of this size and diversity. I believe all of us understand the importance of what we are about to begin, though. I will benefit from your advice, assistance and expertise and I will listen and learn from each of you and any decisions I make will take into consideration each of your individual interests and inputs. We will be together like a family for perhaps quite a while. Mike tells me that when we get started, everywhere the team goes, we all go. I'm sure we will get to know each other, respect each other and, hopefully like each other."

"Knowing your backgrounds, the importance of our mission to our government and the fact that each of you represents the best that your experience or group has to offer, I'm proud to lead a team of this quality. Our goal will be to be successful. There will be danger involved and we will be on our own most of the time. I know each of you not only represent the best, but I am aware that you are all volunteers for this mission. Let's find out all we can this afternoon and be prepared to do what we have to do to accomplish our mission."

"Just one correction, Dawson," Mike interjected. "Percy can't be released from the State Department until the 4th of January because he has to finish a report to the Secretary of State before he leaves. As for the rest of you, take the Christmas--New Year week off then be prepared to leave together Wednesday, January 2nd. You will be going first to Livermore, California to see first hand and get a better understanding of the developmental work that has been done there, and to recruit the other team member from that facility if we can get someone there to volunteer to join this dangerous mission for the duration. Percy will join the rest of you wherever you are on the 4th. From that point forward, prepare to be on this project full time for as long as it takes you to get the job done. Now, let's eat!"

Sandwiches were brought in and we gathered around the conference table to eat and chat prior to Mike's briefing which would follow lunch. The informal meal gave us all an opportunity to know each other a little better.

"Dawson," Steve, the FBI agent, commented, "there will be eight of us on the team once we get the person from Livermore. It sounds like we could find ourselves almost anywhere in the world trying to accomplish our mission, and there will most likely be danger involved, requiring force at some point to capture or kill the people who have the information we want. I assume we will be armed, as some of us are anyway. What about the rest?"

"I was wondering the same thing," Larry, the CIA agent said. "You and I, Steve and Darby with Delta Force would be armed and trained in the use of firearms. That's only half the team."

"I was an Air Force pilot prior to going with Boeing and NASA. We were trained to use small arms and carried a sidearm on combat duty," Thom interjected.

"I want all members of the team armed at all times," I responded. "Those who are not trained in side arms or automatic rifles, which we might have with us if the situation dictates, will need to get some training and experience with firearms. Is there anyone here who doesn't know how to use a revolver, automatic pistol or assault rifle?"

Percy, the State Department representative and Ernest, the scientist raised their hands.

"Okay, so five of the seven of us are qualified in firearms. And we have to assume that the Livermore scientist might not be. Darby, I would like you to take the responsibility to take Percy and Ernest to the firing range and qualify them in the side arm of their choice and in the operation of an assault rifle. Maybe you can get started right away and you can continue to fine tune their skills, as we have time, after we get started on the 2nd. Okay with you guys?"

"I was selected to have the opportunity to be on this team due to my knowledge of the political implications of any action dealing with foreign countries. But prior to volunteering to serve, it was made clear that it would involve covert actions and most likely violence and danger. I'm sure they would have preferred to have had someone with my knowledge that was already trained in the use of firearms. But I agreed to learn what was necessary to contribute to all the team requirements. I have no problems learning from Darby," Percy quickly answered.

"I don't either," Ernest laughed. "But I may be a terrible student, Darby. I've never touched a gun in my life!"

"Okay. We'll worry about training the eighth member when we make that selection," I said.

"Okay guys. Everyone's through eating. Let's get started," Mike said.

"Here's all we know at this point," he continued. "The world's largest laser has been tested at the National Ignition Facility. Construction on this facility was completed this year. It is actually 192 lasers directed to collide with each other in a giant target chamber. You will find out much more about the specifics of this development when you get out there, and I'm sure Dr. Brown will understand it far better than I could. Let me just say that a recent discovery indicated that the new technology has enormous potential in domestic as well as military use. Smaller, mobile reproductions could be used to destroy individual targets much like a small laser can destroy a cataract in eye surgery. The NIF is now a maximum security agency."

"Is our concern then for any information that may have leaked out prior to NIF being locked down?" Larry asked.

"Yes. The project was actually stalled for a while due to insufficient funding. This was right after the discovery was made but before they had a chance to perfect it and fully understand its implications. Several months later funds were received to complete the project from anonymous sources and the project was completed. It was only then that it was discovered that a duplicate copy of all the work was missing."

"Do we know who the anonymous funding source was?" Steve asked.

"No we don't. As you may know, often scientific work is funded by private sources and sometimes those sources like to remain anonymous for various reasons. But someone knows where the generosity originated from. In this case, they receive a check for $2,000,000 indicating it was restricted funding for this specific project. Of course the NIF and Lawrence Livermore were very happy to get the contribution, but wanted to be able to at least privately thank the donor. The check was good, but was signed by an attorney who had power of attorney on a bank account owned by the estate of a postal worker in Los Angles. A large sum of money from somewhere had been wired to this account. The attorney disappeared and the wiring instructions followed a circuitous route through numbered accounts in the Bahamas. A tedious trace on those transactions begun after the FBI got involved found a probable original source to be Walid Alziddi"

"Walid Alziddi!! He's the guy who we think has masterminded and helped fund most of the terrorist acts in the world this past year. He seems to have taken over from Osama bin Laden as master of terrorism." Larry exclaimed.

"Right!" Mike agreed. "We have been trying without success to find his current whereabouts. We have ideas, but can't confirm his location. We know that if he used the funds to buy information, the technology is in extremely dangerous hands relative to U.S. security. He, like bin Laden, is a Saudi with access to money from his own fortune as well as contributions from others."

"If the information came from someone inside NIF, why did it go to NIF and not the person who gave the information to Alziddi's people?" I asked.

"We don't know the answer to that. We don't know that there was a source inside NIF. Security there was not stringent at the time, because the work they were doing was strictly experimental, and there was no indication that anything to come of it would have strategic military or terrorist importance. Someone from outside with an idea that the test might evolve into something useful may have just walked in and lifted the information. It would be unlikely though for an outsider to know what to take without some inside knowledge. We have run security checks on all present and former employees who had access to this information and have turned up nothing that would cause us to be suspicious. And none of those people have changed their lifestyle in terms of spending money," Mike answered.

"Sir, do we have any leads to follow up on or people to investigate other than what you have told us?" Darby asked.

"No. Your team will have to start with at least a cursory knowledge of what we are looking for and go find the people who have it. That will be your objective — to destroy the information and apprehend the people who got it. The FBI will continue to investigate the possible source of the leak of information. If you guys discover anything or have suspicions concerning anyone that will allow you to shortcut the accomplishment of your mission, then you can act on that in any manner you wish."

"Any other questions?" Mike asked. No one had any.

"Okay. I'm sorry the briefing was so devoid of information, but that's all we have at this point. The only other information we have comes from a contact within Alziddi's group, Infama. As Larry knows, in the past year we have tried to infiltrate these terrorist organizations. Previously we had relied too much on technology rather than people. Some of you may know that back during the civil rights unrest in the 1960s the FBI had infiltrated the Ku Klux Clan. They actually had agents in white robes burning crosses. This is how they found out what these people were doing, thinking and planning. We had gotten away from that kind of human resource utilization and have made some progress this past year in getting back to the basics of intelligence. You can't find everything from a satellite. You need people on the ground inside these organizations. Our man inside Infama is not anywhere close to the top. He certainly can't tell us where Alziddi is. But he did give us some startling information he had picked up."

"What was that?" Percy asked.

"That Infama does have the information and their intended use is to try to develop a means with it to assassinate the President. Although on a large scale, the laser could wipe out whole cities, that would prove to be too cumbersome for a covert assassination attempt. The equipment required would be huge and, unless an effective means of delivering such a beam such as a satellite could be developed, a smaller mobile version would better suit their purpose," Mike answered.

"In conclusion," Mike continued, "let me share some rudimentary information with you. I'm sure you will find this out when you visit Livermore. The laser at full strength is very powerful. To put it in perspective, the power is equivalent to 1,000 times the entire electric generating power of the U.S. And enough laser energy is generated to cause nuclear fusion simulating the power of a miniature star. NIF will produce more power in a one nanosecond pulse than all the power generated in the rest of the world at that moment."

There was complete silence as we all tried to comprehend the magnitude of what Mike had just told us.

"Impressive, huh?" Mike concluded. "Okay. Get to work. Time is of the essence. Plan on being on the job full time January 2nd and staying on the job until your mission is accomplished.

CHAPTER FOUR

"Hi! Did you get my message last night?" I had decided to call Ashton about 11:00 PM my time, which would be 8:00 her time. Apparently she had a caller ID because she answered cheerily on the second ring and obviously knew that I was the caller.

"Yes. You don't have to take me to dinner, but I would like to see you and I will be out there the 2nd of January. In fact, I will be bringing a team of people who would like to tour the lab and talk to you and the other scientists who worked on the super laser project."

"Great!! I'm glad you're coming!" she said enthusiastically. "I assume you will have no problem getting past our current stringent security."

"No," I laughed. "Our visit will be cleared in advance with the Administrator and I will have FBI and CIA agents with me in addition to a few other people."

"What kind of people?"

"A couple of scientist types, a Delta Force guy and a State Department representative will be joining us wherever we are on the 4th. We are forming a diversified team of eight people who will be trying to track down the missing technology on your laser and the people who have it. Counting myself, that is seven people. We need one more," I replied.

"Who will the other one be?" she asked.

"Someone from your NIF operation that understands the new technology needs to be with us, since we don't really know what we are looking for and what to do with it if we find it."

"Well, I will join your team if you let me," Ashton said in a teasing, coy tone. "And if they let me," she quickly added.

The thought of Ashton being with us had not crossed my mind because of the danger involved. For some reason, I felt protective of her and remembered the look of fear on her face when the car in Atlanta narrowly missed us. It would be nice though, to travel with her the next several weeks or months. She had a certain magnetism that drew me to her. Plus she was cute as a doll, and so natural and open. Maybe... No! As much as I would like to get to know her better, I could not think of putting her in that kind of jeopardy. Besides, she was a girl and the rest of the team would probably have some problems with that. Lots of reasons...

"Well, my section chief doesn't think getting the lab to release the person will be a problem, considering the interest of the Administration in our mission and the importance to our national interest. But no, Ashton. There will be a lot of danger involved and we could be on this thing for months. We'll get another scientist from your group. You were just kidding anyway, weren't you?"

"Dawson Kohler! You are a chauvinist! I am the most knowledgeable scientist on the development team. In fact, it was my idea as the newest and youngest member of the team, to try a fresh, new idea that led to the unexpected breakthrough!" She was angry in her response. I was shocked that she was, in fact, serious.

"What about the danger?" I countered.

"I grew up as an Army brat. I am familiar with living with danger. I'm not foolish, but I'm not a coward either. Please, Dawson---don't rule me out just because I'm female."

"Ashton, I would love to have you with us. I mean that. Yes, you are a girl, and a very beautiful girl. Some of my team members may have a problem with that, but I don't. I work with female agents all the time. But there is a real danger involved in trying to accomplish our mission. Based on the limited intelligence we have, we very likely will be dealing with Walid Alziddi and Infama. You know about them, I'm sure," I said.

"Yes. Dawson, I'm still not scared. Scientific research is interesting and exciting, but I guess I'm adventuresome. I would like to experience doing what you do for a while. I know there will be danger. I won't get in your way and you won't have to worry about trying to protect me. Besides, you said two other scientists were on the team. Why am I different from them?"

I was running out of arguments. "Ashton, we will all be armed. Even the two people on our team who are not familiar with firearms will be getting training over the next couple of weeks."

"Good! Maybe I can help train them!"

"What do you mean?"

"Well, Mr. Kohler, I was on the college rifle team at University of Georgia. I was the team leader because my skill with a rifle surpassed the others on my team. And, as I told you, my father was an Infantry officer. He taught me how to use handguns as well as rifles. I'll bet I could beat you at target firing!

Now what do you say?"

I could just picture her tossing her hair back, eyes flashing, challenging me to come up with another reason why she couldn't join us. What the hell!! I would love to make love to her and I could easily fall in love with her, I think. I had never met anyone quite like her. She would really be a distraction for me, the way I felt about her after such a short time knowing her. But she did have the talent we needed, seemed to want very much to be a part of our team, and didn't appear to scare easily.

"Let me think about it. We'll talk again when I get out there next week. Okay?" I said, trying to be noncommittal.

"Okay. Dawson, are you married, engaged or have a steady girlfriend?" she asked inquisitively.

That was exactly the question that I had wanted to ask her! I had been trying to figure out how to do that, but her straightforward openness had pre-empted me.

"No. I was married for about four years, but divorced two years ago. She found someone else. I have dated some since then, but not much. There is no one special in my life," I answered truthfully.

"I'm sorry about your wife, but I'm glad you are not attached," she said thoughtfully. "You think I'm forward, don't you?" she continued.

"No, uh---you know, I was going to ask you the same question," I stammered.

"Well, I usually say what I think. Sometimes it gets me in trouble. I do like you though, even though we only met once. Maybe we could like each other a lot if you gave us a chance, like include me on your team." I could almost see her smiling cutely after that comment.

"Oh! So you are just leading me on to get on the team, huh? And I was already looking forward to our getting to know each other better. Now I think I'll just look for some plain, middle aged lady with her hair in a bun when I get out there. You are a devious little devil!" I laughed.

"Maybe. I guess you will just have to get to know me better to know when I am serious," she said.

"I would like to do that. I was serious, even if you weren't. You're different, in a nice sort of way. You're pretty, sexy, cute, beautiful---all those things. Plus you are smart, have a good sense of humor and a daring attitude. You know, we just might be soul mates — whether you go with us on the team or not. Do you think that is possible?" I asked.

"Maybe. But if you go off for several months without me, then we may never know, will we?"

"Okay. I still don't know if you are kidding or not. But I think I will take you up on your dinner offer when we get out there. Is that offer still on the table?" I asked.

"Sure! I'll take you to John's Grill on Ellis Street in San Francisco. It's my favorite. You'll like it. And if you don't agree to give me a chance to be on your team, I will just leave you there and go home with someone else."

"That's blackmail! Do you mean that if I let you on the team you will let me go home with you?" We were playing word games now. I wanted to see how far she would go.

"You can take me home. We'll know if I should invite you in or not, I think. And if I do, it may not be for the reason you think. We probably won't go to bed together, if that's what you are thinking. That would be too soon to discover whether or not we could be soul mates. We might both want that to happen, but I don't think either of us would let that happen that soon. Do you? We would need to be sure, and we're not there yet. Okay?"

"You're right. You are different, and I wouldn't want to screw up our relationship by not treating us like something special. I'll see you on the 2nd. I'll let you know more when we complete our travel plans. And, Ashton...?"

"Yes?"

"I'm really glad you called. I was going to call you, but wanted to be able to be more specific as to when I might be on the west coast before getting in touch with you. No matter what, I do want to see you, as often as you will let me."

"Go to sleep now. It's almost midnight your time. We'll talk later. And think about what I said. Okay?" she said.

"I will. I will think about everything you said, before I go to sleep. Then I will probably still have thoughts of you after I fall asleep. Goodnight Ashton."

"Goodnight. And Dawson----"

"What?"

"I am not married, engaged or involved with a significant other. I haven't had time to date with all that has gone on in my life recently. I've had several ask me, but have not found one that would distract me enough from my work for me to want to go out with them. I do very much want to join the team you described, in spite of the danger. But I want to see you, too — no matter what. Call me when you find out what time you will arrive. I may be able to pick you up at the airport. For now, goodnight."

"Goodnight. I'll call." We hung up.

WE

I sat there by the phone for several minutes. It was late. I had not realized how long we had talked. I could have stayed on the phone the rest of the night.

As I went to sleep that night I had thoughts of having Ashton snuggling up beside me. She was a different and special person. She spoke her mind. I liked that, even though I was still trying to get over the shock of meeting a pretty girl that was able to confront thoughts and feelings as straightforward as Ashton did. I was elated that she seemed to have some of the same initial attraction that I did toward each other maybe some day becoming us.

Just as my sweet dream led to feeling her warmth close to me and initiating sex the bright beam of light in the strange place interrupted my exotic reverie and threw me into a state of terror in my subconscious state. As I tossed and turned through the rest of the night, I wondered---what combination of pleasure and fear lies ahead? Or was all of this just a dream?

CHAPTER FIVE

I called Ashton on Christmas Eve and wished her Merry Christmas. She was baking cookies when I called.

"You should see me now. There is no way you would want to go to dinner with me looking like this," she said.

"Well, I don't know. Describe yourself and I'll tell you if I would," I said.

"I have flour on my face, haven't brushed my hair and still have my jammies on. I've been making and baking these cookies all morning. I don't wear much makeup, but I don't have lipstick or anything on. I just look like a witch that just got out of bed. Is that enough? Would you take me out like this?"

"Well, I still don't know. You haven't told me enough. What do your jammies look like?"

"They're just plain white shortie jammies with a loose blouse-like top. Nothing special. Why?"

"I think I would take you then, just to see all the other patrons lust after you." I could see her in my mind standing there in her little shorts with her sexy little butt and legs and flour on her face. That would be a cute picture.

"Oh, Dawson! Get your mind out of the gutter! I look horrible."

"I doubt that. Who are you making cookies for?"

"Well, I have this neat little apartment. It's a stand alone on a shaded lot by itself that was built by a couple who moved away. It's real cute, but I don't have time to mow the yard, rake leaves and all the other little things that have to be done. So this real nice neighborhood boy, about sixteen years old, has been doing all that for me. I pay him of course, but I think he just likes me. He has a cute little brother and sister and they are around here all the time when I'm here. I'm baking them some Christmas cookies."

"That's sweet. Well I just called to wish you a great Christmas. I'm a little lonely myself. And I wanted to let you know when I will be arriving in San Francisco. My flight, United 409 from D.C., arrives at gate 10 at 2:10 PM on Wednesday the 2nd."

"Okay. I'll pick you up then. I'll meet you at the gate, then we can go on to the lab and I can introduce you to the Administrator, unless you want to check in at the hotel first."

"I appreciate that, but unless you have a big van, we all won't be able to get in. There will be six of us arriving at the same time. We will probably stop by the hotel and check in and get rid of our bags before coming to the lab. That first day, by the time we get there, we will probably just get the introductions out of the way and plan on spending the whole day, Thursday, the 3rd at the NIF lab. We better just rent a car and meet you at the lab."

"What hotel are you staying at?"

"I thought we would stay at the Hyatt on Union Square in San Francisco. I think its only a little over an hour from there to the lab, and it will be better to be there closer to the airport when we leave."

"Hey! That's great. The Hyatt is only about two blocks from that little restaurant I want to take you to. Tell you what. Why don't you go on to the hotel and I'll meet you there. You can ride with me and the others can follow us in the rental car. We can talk on the way over."

"Okay, we can do that. I'll call and let you know if we have any delays along the way. Well, I'll let you get back to your cookies. But first, did you get any Christmas presents?" I asked.

"Well, yes. I always get something from my parents and my little brother. He's 24. But I won't open them until tomorrow morning. I always get up early and turn the lights on the little tree I bought and open my presents Christmas morning. I'm like a little kid. But Dawson, I get lonely around Christmas, too. It's too bad you aren't out here now. Maybe we could have Christmas together since we are both lonely."

"That would be nice. I should have come out early. I wanted to and would like to be there to open presents with you. I really did think about coming early and let the others catch up later, but I would want to see you and didn't want to interfere with any plans you may have had for Christmas. I would have brought you a present, so you would have had another one under the tree," I said.

I really had thought about how nice it would be to be with her on Christmas morning. Maybe next Christmas, if she would let me. The thought of being with her made me ache with longing when I realized we were 3,000 miles away from each other. Just being able to talk to her closed the gap some.

"Maybe next year---" she repeated the thought that had just gone through my mind. "Oh!! My cookies are burning!!"

"Okay! Go take care of them. I'll see you on the second, little girl."

"Okay! Bye!" She hung up. The sound of her voice lingered in my mind. It just made me miss her more. The way she had captivated my thoughts after only meeting her that one time in Atlanta and talking to her a few times on the phone had pleasantly filled a void in my life. I looked forward to seeing her again in about a week.

That week went by pretty fast. I was in communication with the rest of the team constantly as we made our plans to leave. Darby had already started training Ernest and Percy on the firing range and he said they were progressing nicely. I had talked to Ashton a couple of nights also, just lingering conversations about nothing that seemed to draw us closer together. She had gotten a sweater from her brother and a Cusinart blender along with several little gifts from her parents.

Wednesday, January 2nd, 2001 the six of us arrived in San Francisco about six minutes later than scheduled. We all had business suits or slacks and sport jackets with our pistols or revolvers mostly hidden from view by the jackets in shoulder or belt holsters. I had my .38 on my left side in a belt holster with the butt to the front. Everyone was armed.

"Darby, why don't you and Ernest go down and pick up the rental car? We'll pick up your bags and meet you outside of baggage claim," I said.

"Sure. See you guys in about twenty minutes," Darby said.

"Any idea who we might get from here for our eighth team member?" Larry asked as we waited for our bags.

"There is someone who would like to join our team. Actually it's the lead scientist on the team that developed the super laser," I said.

"Hey! That would be great. Who is it?" he asked.

"Dr. Ashton Smyth who I met in Atlanta a couple of weeks ago," I replied.

"That's even better. You already know him," Larry said.

"It's not a him. She is going to meet us at the hotel," I said.

"A woman!? Dawson, are you sure we want a woman on our team? I mean, I have worked with a few female operatives at the CIA, but most all of the field jobs where covert action and danger exist are left to men."

"Well, this lady is pretty sharp. And tough, I think. We will need her knowledge," I said.

"I've worked with some pretty good females at the FBI. It was hard to get used to the first few times, but I found that they could handle the job as well as most of the males---all aspects of it," Steve volunteered.

"I don't know. I think a female will just get in the way. We'll have to worry about protecting her and I doubt if she could keep up with us if we have to move fast. I can just see us meeting up with Alziddi's people with a female in tow. And a scientist at that! What a combination!" Larry exclaimed.

"Wait just a minute!" Thom said. "I'm a scientist and I flew combat missions in Desert Storm! Some of us know how to take care of ourselves."

"Okay, okay. Sorry. But I bet you didn't have any female pilots in Desert Storm!" Larry countered.

By that time we had picked up the bags and were outside where Darby and Ernest picked us up in the van they had rented. The good natured but half-serious banter continued all the way during the twenty-five minute drive to the hotel. We went ahead and parked in the garage and carried our bags in to the check in desk in the lobby. Ashton was there waiting for us.

"Dawson! You got here sooner than I expected. Those flights are usually thirty minutes late. I just got here myself." I had forgotten just how vivacious she was. She had a black skirt and red sweater on that nicely set off her dark hair cascading over her shoulders. She came to me and squeezed my hand.

"Hi, Ashton. Thanks for meeting us. Let me introduce you to the rest of the team. This is Larry with the CIA. Larry Childress, this is Dr. Ashton Smyth."

Larry shook her hand and was speechless for a moment. "Uh---it's nice to meet you," he finally managed to say. I could tell by his look that he was astounded by her looks but probably even more firm in his thoughts that she would never fit with our team due to her youth and background as a scientist.

I then introduced her to Darby, Steve, Ernest and Thom, explaining that Percy, the missing member would be joining us on the 4th. I'm sure they all, in their shock, had some of the same thoughts Larry had.

"I'm parked out front. Why don't you go ahead and put your bags in your room, then you can follow me to the lab. Dawson you can ride with me," Ashton said cheerfully.

We did that and Darby pulled the van out of the garage and fell in behind Ashton's black Camry. After about forty minutes we were across the Oakland Bay bridge, through Oakland on a shortcut Ashton knew, and driving into the countryside on the way to Livermore. Ashton had chattered the whole time.

"Is there an out of the way place between here and Livermore that we can stop and do a few minutes of target practice?" I asked.

Ashton looked at me quizzically. "Well, there's an old sand pit about half a mile down on the left. Why?"

"Pull in there when we get to it."

"Dawson, I'm beginning to think you are missing some screws. What about the others?" she asked.

"They'll follow," I said.

"Oh. I thought you and I were just going to go parking by ourselves," she laughed facetiously.

"I wish. No, I want to test our team's marksmanship," I said.

She looked at me again like I had lost my mind, but dutifully turned onto a gravel road that led to a huge horseshoe shaped sand pit about a quarter mile on the left. The van pulled in behind us and, when we stopped and got out, they got out too, with puzzled looks on their faces.

I explained that, since we were only going to do introductions today, we had a little time and I wanted to test our proficiency with the firearms. They looked at me as if I were crazy, too, but we set up some beer cans about 50 feet away with the back of the horseshoe behind the cans. Darby wanted Ernest, who he had been working with, to lead off. We decided to each take three shots.

Blam!! Ernest had a .38 caliber revolver. He missed the can on the first shot, nicked it on the second and missed on the third. His missed shots were close.

"Not bad for only a week of training, Ernest. Congratulations to you and Darby!" I said.

"He's been a good student. He's learning fast. Percy's doing okay, too," Darby said.

Next, Thom with a 9mm automatic put the first shot right through the center of the can, but barely missed the other two shots. Not bad. Hitting a beer can from 50 feet with a handgun wasn't easy.

Steve followed Thom and nicked the can on the first shot, put the second through the center, sending the can flying and barely missed the third shot. Good shooting.

Then Darby shot, nicking all three cans.

I went next with my Cobra. A tough shot at that distance for a Cobra. I missed the first shot, put the second and third through the side of the can. I was very pleased.

Larry, our best marksman other than maybe Darby, went next with his 9mm automatic. Pop! Pop! Pop! He put the first two shots through the center of the first two cans and barely missed the third.

"Shit!!" he said. "Excuse me Ma'am," he said to Ashton, who just smiled. "I should have hit that third shot."

"Good shooting, everyone!" I said. "Let's let Ashton take three shots before we leave, just for the heck of it! Which firearm would you prefer to use?" I asked.

Ashton looked surprised. "Oh, I don't know, Dawson. I haven't fired a gun in a while. I guess Larry's automatic would be all right, but don't laugh if I miss the whole sand pit."

"We won't," I promised. "But first let me put three new cans out. Do you mind if she uses your automatic, Larry?"

"No, not at all," Larry smiled condescendingly and handed it to Ashton. His expression changed somewhat when I placed the three cans out about a foot apart 75 feet away, 50% further than the distance we had fired from.

"What are you doing, Dawson!?" Larry asked incredulously. "She won't come close from that distance! Give her a break!"

"You're probably right, Larry. I doubt any of us could hit from there. But us males are always giving the females a break, in golf and everything else. Let's make her show us if females can perform in a reverse situation where they are at a disadvantage!" I smiled as I walked back to the firing line.

"Do you mind if I take a shot into the back of the pit just to get the feel of the gun first?" Ashton asked. We all said fine and she squeezed off a shot into nowhere.

"Okay, I'm ready," she said hesitatingly. "Are you sure you want me to try this?"

"Yes, just do the best you can," I nodded.

Blam!! Blam!! Blam!! She fired three shots a second apart, sending all three cans flying in the air with holes in the center of each! Larry and the rest just stood there in silence, dumbfounded. Ashton handed the gun back to him.

"Larry, would you like to try from that distance?" I asked.

"Uh---no. The rest of my shells and clips are back in my room. I like to keep three or four shells in the gun. You never know when you might need it," he said.

"Okay. Let's go on to the lab for the introductions. I just wanted to check everybody out. I feel a lot better now. Everybody did pretty darn good!" I said as we got back in our cars.

"Why did you do that?" Ashton asked when we were back in the car.

"Well, if I consider you for the team, assuming you still want to be on it, I want all the members to accept you and Larry was a little hesitant when I broached the subject. He thought a female would be a liability. You did good,"

I said.

"What if I had lied to you about being on the rifle team in college and being familiar with firearms? What if I had not come close to the target? Larry's feelings would have been confirmed. You took a chance," she smiled.

"I know. But I believed you and I trust you," I smiled and reached over to squeeze her hand.

"That's nice to know. Well, here we are," she said as we turned into a paved road that led past a guard station manned by an armed guard. The sign said "Lawrence Livermore National Ignition Facility". Ashton showed her pass and each of us identified ourselves. Mike had cleared our visit beforehand.

None of us thought anything about the fact that the guard painstakingly recorded our names and affiliation twice, once on the log book and again on a separate sheet of paper. Neither did we take notice, as we were cleared and drove on through the gate, that the sheet of paper was handed to the driver of a black Buick who had been waiting in the large turnaround area in front of the guard shack.

Later, we would learn to be more alert.

CHAPTER SIX

Ashton motioned us into the visitors parking area, then proceeded to park in a secure parking area with her name designated on the curb in front of her space. We had to go through another checkpoint while the guard prepared to call to verify our appointment. Ashton walked over to where we were.

"Good afternoon, Dr. Smyth!" the guard greeted her as she walked up.

"Hello, Harry. These gentlemen have an appointment with Dr. Willoughby. I will escort them to his office," she said.

"Sure thing, Ashton. Are you sure you're safe with all these guys? A pretty girl like you needs to be careful, you know. Maybe I should go with you to protect you?" He joked.

"Well, I tell you what, Harry. Why don't you go with them to see Dr. Willoughby and I'll stay out here and take care of check-ins. Do you want to do that?" she asked with a smile.

"No way! In the mood Willoughby has been in since the security breakdown, I don't want to be near him for the next couple of months. Besides, I couldn't leave you out here all by yourself unprotected," Harry said.

"Go back to work Harry! I'll call you if I need help," Ashton laughed as we proceeded to the main lobby entrance.

We proceeded through a spacious lobby past a receptionist/telephone operator, who was on the phone but smiled and waved at Ashton, all the way to the back of the aisle leading from the lobby. On the right was the Administrator's office. We first entered a small reception area where his secretary was located. The open door behind her must be his office.

"Hi, Ashton! These must be the gentlemen who are here to meet Dr. Willoughby," the secretary greeted us cheerfully.

"Yes." Ashton replied. "Gentlemen, this is Sue. She keeps the bear in his den."

"I heard that!" A large, tall, sandy-headed man, who appeared to be in his late fifties emerged from the office. "So I'm a bear, huh? I'll remember that, Dr. Smyth, the next time you want some unbudgeted appropriation for your research work! Good afternoon, gentlemen! I'm Bob Willoughby. Come on in."

Bob Willoughby looked as if he could have been a professional football lineman and seemed genuinely good natured as he extended his huge hand to shake each of our hands when Ashton introduced us. Ashton would later tell us that he, in fact, was both an athletic and a scholastic All American at Southern Cal in 1967. He somewhat resembled a bear.

"Bob, I know you are busy today, but since they did not arrive until this afternoon, I thought it would be good to introduce you to them today before we get started on the tour and discussions tomorrow," Ashton said when the introductions were completed.

"Good! Well, gentlemen, I know your backgrounds and I know why you are here. Mr. Reilly called last week. Of course we have had the FBI here also. Mr. Reilly asked that we familiarize you with the super laser as best we can without getting too technical. It has also been requested that we release someone from the facility to work with you until the ongoing security problem is resolved. Since some danger will likely be involved if you are successful in your mission, that person needs to be a volunteer."

"The best person for that job is sitting here with us: Dr. Smyth. She was the lead scientist on this experiment and has also volunteered to join your group. I must say she is one of the very brightest people we have here and she will be sorely missed, but the national security implications of this development, and its apparent theft were made very clear to me. You obviously have met Ashton, so I guess I have the unpleasant, at least to me, task of telling you she will be assigned to your team for as long as you need her. I am concerned for her safety, but she assures me she can take care of herself."

"Yes Sir, we sort of found that out this afternoon," Larry interjected.

"We stopped a few minutes on the way here from the hotel to do a little target practice. Dr. Smyth showed us all up, I think," I explained.

"Oh? I didn't know you knew anything about firearms, Ashton. But that doesn't surprise me. As tenacious as she is, she can do anything she wants to, with excellence. I'm not sure I would want to challenge her in anything competitive," Dr. Willoughby said.

"Well, I know you are all tired after the long trip and have a busy day ahead of you tomorrow. So let me go over tomorrow's schedule with you, then you can be on your way this afternoon," Bob continued.

"Fine. We appreciate that," I said.

"Okay. We'll get started at 8:30 tomorrow morning. Ashton will take you on a quick tour of the facility and introduce you to others who worked on the project. Feel free to ask them any questions you like or ask to see any area or paperwork you want to. Ashton and the others will attempt to describe the basics of the system and related information you will be seeking. You can eat a quick lunch in our cafeteria, then continue your information gathering until 3:30 PM when I will meet with you along with Ashton in the conference room, to elaborate on our discovery that knowledge of this development has apparently been stolen by someone or some group. We can go over the information that has been shared with the FBI and try to answer any further questions you may have. That will conclude our preparations for your visit, but if you think any further information can be gained, you are welcome to stay as many additional days as you wish and we will be cooperative with your desires. Any questions?"

"No, we appreciate your cooperativeness, Dr. Willoughby. We will be here 8:30 in the morning," I said.

"Call me Bob. I'll see you tomorrow then."

"He seems like a nice guy, and very efficient, too," I said to Ashton as we were walking out to the cars.

"He is both. He tries to be a bear, but he's really very sweet," she said.

"I would hate for him to get me in a bear hug," Darby said.

"Yeah! He's strong as a bull. Dawson, we can go back to the hotel in my car and the rest of the guys can take the van again. I owe you that dinner for saving my life. Remember? If you're not too tired, I will pay the debt tonight. I can recommend a good place for you guys to eat, too. It looks like after we leave California, we will all be together most of the time when we eat or go anywhere. So you guys enjoy yourselves without me tonight," Ashton said.

"Well, we better get in all the girlie shows we can tonight, fellows," Ernest laughed as we got in the vehicles to go back to San Francisco.

On the ride back to San Francisco, Ashton was in a light-hearted mood. She seemed real happy as we talked about current events, the other members of the team and how we met was such a coincidence and the further turn of events that found ourselves joined together for the foreseeable future.

"Maybe we are soul mates, meant to be together," she smiled.

It was distracting being here in the car with her. The short skirt she wore was hiked up to the middle of her thighs as she drove, showing most of her shapely legs. And her pretty hair clinging haphazardly around her beautiful face made me glad to be fortunate enough to be sharing part of my life with this cute girl. She really could pass for a college coed, but her youthful looks and actions were misleading, knowing her background. I liked her a lot.

"I would like for that to be true, Ashton. I like you and I'm glad I met you, even under the bad circumstances of my bumbling introduction and the car bomb. I'm glad we will be together, too. But I am worried about your safety. It could get pretty scary, and I like you too much to take a chance on losing you or your getting hurt. Are you sure you want to do this?" I asked.

"I'm sure. Well, here we are at your hotel. It's almost 7:00 o'clock. Why don't we go up to your room to freshen up, then walk on down to John's," she said as she pulled into the parking lot.

"Okay, but I saw the other guys admiring you. If they see you going into my room, they will think we are more than acquaintances, and will worry that you will be my pet on the team. Besides, they will be very jealous," I laughed.

"Oh, come on," she grabbed my hand and led me to the lobby into the elevator. "Maybe I will be your pet. They will just have to live with that," she said defiantly with a squeeze of her hand which was still holding mine.

"Okay. I guess I'm just lucky and they will have to be jealous," I said. The elevator had stopped on the sixth floor and we went to my room, number 604. Just as I slid the key card in and we started to enter the room, Ernest came down the hall.

"Are you sure you don't want to go to the girlie shows with us tonight, Dawson? I can't blame you if you say no. Dr. Smyth, I'm not trying to be fresh, but you look stunning. That is meant as a compliment. I would have never thought you would be a scientist. And so young at that. I don't blame Dawson for preferring to be with you rather than us guys tonight!" Ernest smiled.

"Ernest, I'm not Doctor or Ms., just Ashton from now on. Dawson will be with you guys for a good while from now on. But just remember, I will be with you, too. And thank you for the compliment. And, no, I won't let Dawson go to the girlie show with you. He promised to join me for dinner," she laughed as we went in the room.

"You go ahead and do whatever you need to do. I'll go down the hall and get some ice and mix us a little drink before we go," I said.

"Okay! See you in a minute!" she replied.

When I returned with the ice, she was already coming out of the bathroom.

"Do I look pretty now?" she said, striking a model's pose.

"You were beautiful before you went in. What did you do?" I asked as I began to mix drinks.

"Just went to the bathroom and brushed my hair a little. I looked awful!"

"You couldn't look awful---ever! I hope you like gin. I put tonic in yours. I like mine on the rocks." I handed her a glass.

"That's fine. I don't ever drink much. I get silly, so I'll just sip this one." She was standing facing me as I handed her the drink and she looked up at me with her pretty blue-green eyes. I felt pulled to her closeness.

"Ashton—?" I said softly. I set my glass down and took hers from her hand setting it on the dresser also. Gently, I placed my hand on her cheek. Her lips parted when I tilted her head upward and bent slightly to meet her with my lips. Her eyes closed as we kissed, still standing slightly apart from each other. Her lips were soft and eager. We held our kiss and our bodies slowly came together. I felt the warmth and firmness of her as we embraced and could smell the sweetness of her soft hair against my cheek. As if we were one, we reclined on the bed, side by side and still embraced in our kiss. I could feel her passion and she moved her hand down to feel the part of me that throbbed with desire. My hand slid under her skirt that had gathered below her waist, exposing her white panties, as we fell to the bed.

"Dawson, no, not now---" she moaned slightly as my hand found the softness between her legs that was hot and moist under the panties. She placed her hand on my hand and arched her back and shuddered as she had an orgasm while at the same time pulling my hand away. I was on the verge of losing control myself.

"Dawson, I'm sorry. I want you and I know you want me, but I want us to wait until you are sure. I can't explain it, but I've been sure since the afternoon we met in Atlanta. I want you to be sure and I want it to be special when we make love. Please try to understand," she said through tears.

I kissed her softly. "I understand. I have felt the same way. Maybe we are soul mates. But I want it to be special, too, because when we make love that will change us and I will want to keep you, forever."

"Thank you. I'm sorry. I don't want to tease you. I want you as much as you want me. I want you to love me, with your heart as well as your body. Okay?" she kissed me lightly. We were still cuddled in each other's arms.

"Okay. Let me go in the bathroom a minute, we'll finish our drinks, then we will go to this John's Grill you told me about." I got up, squeezed her hand, kissed her on the back of her neck and went in the bathroom.

I returned quickly and sat on the bed with my drink, facing her seated on the chair in front of me. I was still aroused. She looked so cute sitting in the chair with her feet curled up under her.

"You're not mad at me are you?" she asked tentatively.

"No. I'm just glad you are with me. And I want to say something that I'm not sure I fully understand either, but I want to say it now so you won't just think I'm trying to get in your panties. I really mean what I want to say," I said, looking her in the eye.

"What is that?" she asked.

"I love you Ashton. I have wanted you since I first met you, not just to make love to, but to love. You are perfect. You are a combination of everything I have ever wanted. You are special. Now let's go to John's."

When I rose to set my glass down, she rose and threw her arms around me. "Those are the words I want to hear and want to be true. I love you, Dawson." We kissed, then left for John's.

We walked in the breezy and brisk San Francisco night air, holding hands. After a couple of blocks I saw John's Grill down the street on the right.

"This is the John's Grill of Sam Spade and Maltese Falcon fame. Do you read a lot?" Ashton asked.

"As much as I can. I like Clancy, Grisham and sometimes King and Koontz," I replied as we entered the restaurant.

We had a delicious steak dinner and a bottle of wine, then walked back to the hotel. This time I noticed the man who seemed to be following us.

"Ashton, I think we are being followed. Let's get your car out of the garage. I'll drive."

I gunned the car out of the garage and around the corner. The man I had noticed was standing on the corner as we went by. After a couple of blocks, I slowed.

"Will you stay with me tonight?" I asked.

"Don't tempt me. I want to, but not tonight. We have to get up early tomorrow and have a hard day at the lab. I'll be alright. I have my Baretta." She took it out of her purse and showed it to me.

"Okay. I'll get out here and walk back. I don't think we were followed, but be alert and be careful. I'll meet you at the lab tomorrow a little before 8:30."

"I'll wait for you at the gate house. You be careful, Dawson. I may be bringing danger to you, and I'm not even sure why. But I don't have but a night or two left in my apartment. Then I will be going with you ."

"I will. Call me on your cell phone if you have any trouble. Okay?" I got out and she quickly took the driver's seat.

"Dawson, remember. I will be with you soon. All of me. It will be nice. I love you," she said as she drove off.

"I love you, too," I said, but she didn't hear me. She was already gone. I walked back to the hotel. The man was nowhere to be seen. That night I went to sleep dreaming of being with Ashton. I didn't think about the man. I reasoned that I was probably paranoid. He was most likely just someone going back to the same hotel. I would prove to be wrong on that assumption.

CHAPTER SEVEN

8:25 the next morning, Thursday, January 3rd, we arrive at the external security gate at the entrance to the NIF. Ashton had already alerted the gatekeeper of our arrival. We merely had to show identification and we were motioned through to the guard shack leading to the parking lot and the huge facility beyond the fencing. Ashton was waiting there, chatting with Harry, the guard. She looked beautiful, as usual and was dressed in blue jeans and a navy blue sweater, explaining we would be spending most of the day in the plant. She looked like a college coed. I felt a warmth of closeness towards her after being with her last night in our intimacy.

"Hi guys!" she said as the six of us arrived. "You remember Harry? I've already cleared you to go in, but you still need to show him your identification, just as a double check for his records. Since we have been on maximum security, there is a lot of redundancy in our security measures."

"Hello again, gentlemen!" Harry said with a friendly smile as he checked our IDs. We then entered the building, following Ashton through the lobby on through that building into another large facility behind it. Evidence of the recent construction still remained.

"I am in charge, today. Do you guys think you can stand that for a little while? By the way, did you enjoy your girlie show last night?" she questioned the rest of the group with a hint of a smile.

"Yes, ma'am. But none of them was nearly as pretty as you are," Darby offered. Some of the others blushed.

"Okay, here we are. As you can see, this facility is as large as a sports stadium, but the target is very small---about the size of a BB pellet. You have been told that when the beam strikes the target, nuclear fusion occurs and releases more power in one nanosecond than all the power generated in the rest of the world at that moment. But each laser pulse only lasts a few billionths of a second."

I could tell by watching the other members of our team that they were dumbfounded by the information being presented to them. It was right out of a science fiction novel. And they were also astounded that this pretty little girl had played a major role in developing this technology.

"Actually the entire system is basically a target shooter," she continued as we moved towards the target chamber. "Each of the 192 laser beams must travel 450 meters, making four passes through a series of mirrors, lenses, amplifiers, switches and spatial filters. Without this multi-pass concept, the facility would have to be over a kilometer long for the pulses to gain the required energy."

We were now gazing into the 30 foot diameter target chamber. The portals gave it a dimpled surface that brought to mind an enormous golf ball from outer space. Ashton told us it weighed a million pounds and was perfectly aligned, vacuum, temperature controlled and vibration proof. The lasers must point at the target with extreme precision — on the equivalent of touching a single human hair from 90 meters away with the point of a needle. 1.8 megajoules of energy must be delivered to the target with a 50-micrometer pointing stability on the target. Fifty micrometers is about the thickness of a sheet of paper, so there can be no vibration in the system.

"After passing through a final optics assembly where the pulses are converted from infrared to ultraviolet light, they are focused on the target. The target is a gold plated cylinder with a gas filled pellet inside. The gases in the pellet, under the pressure of all this light, will compress to the point where they achieve nuclear fusion," Ashton concluded her initial run-through describing the basics of the process.

"Whew!! You lost me when we entered the building!" Steve said.

"Well, what I have done so far is just give you a brief overview of the components and the basic purpose of the system. The balance of the time before we meet with Bob this afternoon, I will try to explain some of the physics and technology involved in the project. We have just begun. Stop me if I lose you on anything and I will try clarify any of your questions. Are we okay so far?" Ashton laughed.

"Please, Dr. Smyth---uh---I mean Ashton. You are making me feel so dumb, I wouldn't dare ask a question for fear of further exhibiting my ignorance," Larry said.

"I promise I won't embarrass you. I can't expect anyone who has not studied this concept and been involved in its development, as I have, to understand the scientific theory behind the NIF experiment. I just want to explain the basics and demonstrate that it is very complex. If we find people who have the technology, we probably should look for people who have the knowledge to understand it and mold it to their purpose," she reassured him.

We spent the rest of the morning, broke for a quick lunch in the canteen, and the early part of the afternoon going over the mechanics of the super laser system. It would be obvious that a group or country that would be a threat to the U.S. could not duplicate this facility to deliver lethal force. Ashton tried to explain the concept, how it might be downsized, perhaps made portable and modified for terrorist purposes. Certain modifications of the concept of channeling lasers into one area so that the beams collided, could result in a beam that could destroy anything in its clear path, even on a small scale. A somewhat larger scale of the modification of this concept could result in a laser beam becoming the preferred weapon to zap missiles out of the sky. Ashton intimated that preliminary work has already started on this concept and she predicted that, within a decade, this defensive weapon would become a reality. Finally, it was 2:45 PM and we proceeded to the conference room to meet with Bob Willoughby.

"Well, gentlemen! Are you sufficiently confused now? If you understand everything Ashton has explained to you, we are taking applications," Bob greeted us cheerily in his booming voice as we entered the room.

"I know quite a lot about laser technology. But I must say that Ashton had me stumped on several occasions," Ernest responded.

"Well, let's get started. I won't try to add anything to what Ashton has shown you. Let me speak a little on the implications of this technology being in the wrong hands. It is possible to modify the concept and downsize it to the approximate size of one of the large TV cameras that you see carried by video crews with the major news networks. Although we have not done that here, anyone with the same kind of know-how that Ashton and a number of other of our scientists have could probably perfect a unit like that in six to nine months if working on it full time. It would be a very effective and portable weapon for someone whose mission it was to assassinate the President or any of the Western leaders," Bob let that comment sink in, then continued.

"The FBI has shared with me the information that there are very capable scientists who are either sympathetic to, our controlled by Infama as well as other terrorist groups or countries, such as Iraq. Funds to advance this research and development are not a problem to many of these organizations."

"Do we know specifically who these people might be?" Larry asked.

"We do know some of them. There are probably many more we don't know about. We have had international scientific meetings on the advancement of laser technology to support world energy needs. We have met some of the people who could possibly be players in any plot to threaten the U.S. One of those people who has adequate knowledge was trained at and worked for us at Livermore," Bob answered.

"Here!? Was that person employed here when the documents were discovered missing!?" I asked.

"Yes. As a matter of fact he was. Your boss, Mike Reilly was told about this when he called me last week. He asked me to reveal all the information I had on this individual to you when we met. The FBI was informed also and Mr. Reilly told me the FBI and CIA would be trying to locate him so they could give any leads they had on his whereabouts to you and your team."

"So this gentleman is no longer with you?" Thom asked.

"No. It's significant, I think, that he disappeared the same day we received the anonymous funds that allowed us to complete the project on schedule. He just didn't show up for work that day. The FBI later looked through his apartment, took prints and attempted to find other evidence that would indicate he had a hand in the theft. I'm sure they will inform you if they are able to find anything helpful," Bob responded.

"What is his name and nationality and how long was he with you?" I asked.

"His name is Abdul Mahmoud and he is a native Pakistani. He had come to this country originally on a student visa, then Immigration granted him residency when he showed promise in scientific research ability, and we offered him a job provided he could attain his residency status. He was quiet and never expressed any political thoughts. A background check did not reveal any problems in his past. Plus we were not then in a maximum security status, so we were not as thorough as we would be now in checking employee history. But neither did the Immigration Department find anything of concern. He had a rather non-descript background and was not on the FBI watch list. However, after a much more thorough check after he was determined missing, the FBI found through CIA contacts with informants in that part of the world, that his brother and father had been in bin Laden's Al Quaida organization. That, of course, was cause for great concern."

Just then the phone rang.

"Sue, I asked you to hold my calls until we finished our meeting," Bob spoke into the receiver.

"Oh. Okay, which line?" he said. "Dawson, it's Mike on line 2. He needs to talk to you. It's urgent."

"Hello Mike," I said as I took the phone. "What's up?"

"Dawson, we think we have located Mahmoud. He hasn't left the country yet. Reliable sources tell us he is in New York and is staying at the Salisbury Hotel on West 57th Street. It may be he didn't want to risk exiting the country if he is involved in this thing. He must surmise we would be on the lookout for him going through customs on a flight out of the country. Probably he plans to stay around in the U.S. until things blow over, or —more ominously, be a part of the delivery if the weapon is successfully developed. All this is speculation, of course, at this point. At any rate, we have a surveillance team on the way to the Salisbury right now. They have been instructed not to alert him or flush him from his current address or lifestyle. I want you and your group to take over when you get here."

"So our next stop will be New York, then?" I said.

"Yes. I think your entire group should take the redeye out of SFO tonight. I will give a list of the names to Percy and he can make reservations for all of you at the Salisbury and will meet you there. He's ready to join the team now."

"Fine. We'll head back tonight then and talk to you tomorrow morning. Bob Willoughby has been very cooperative and helpful. But I don't think we can gain much from staying here any longer. None of us will become competent laser geeks. Plus we have Ashton for that," I said. She stuck her tongue out at me.

Bob finished his briefing with no additional facts of significance. It looked like our best, and only, lead would be in New York. It was 4:30 PM. We decided to leave and stop by Ashton's apartment in Fremont so she could get her bag. She told us she had already packed, expecting we would be leaving today or tomorrow. We would then go on to the hotel, get our bags, check out and catch the first flight we could to go back to the East Coast.

"Hi Ashton!" Harry greeted her when we got to the interior guard shack to sign and record our exit times. "Give me your keys and I will get your car and bring it up while these guys finish signing out."

"Thanks, Harry. I appreciate that. I will be leaving tonight to go to the East Coast with these gentlemen and won't be back for a while. When I do come back, I'll bring you some of my homemade fudge you like so much," Ashton said as she handed her keys to Harry.

"Oh, I hate that you are leaving. Hurry back. We'll miss you," Harry said with sincerity.

"You're sweet, Harry," she gave him a peck on the cheek as he started to retrieve her car which was along the fence about fifty yards away.

Just as we finished signing out on the log book there was a huge explosion in the direction of the interior parking lot! We jerked our heads up just in time to see a huge orange flame burst from Ashton's car. Then the car just seemed to disintegrate with large pieces flying at least fifty yards in every direction. The cars that had been parked on either side of her's were heavily damaged. A cloud of black smoke rose from the shattered hull of what remained of her car, then there was deadly silence.

"Harry!!!" was the first sound. Ashton screamed and began running towards what had been her car. After a few steps, she stopped. It was clear there was nothing left of her car---or of Harry. She just kneeled to the ground, buried her face in her hands and began to sob uncontrollably.

"Jesus!!" Darby exclaimed. "Some son of a bitch planted a car bomb!"

People began running out of the building. Bob was in the lead. I went to Ashton and knelt beside her, placing my arms around her. She was trembling and still crying.

"What the hell?!! What happened!?" Bob asked, glancing towards the still burning wreckage.

"Ashton's car. Harry went to bring it to the gate for her," Larry told him.

"You mean—Harry was in there?" Bob said, looking again to the lot. About that time, the front gate guard arrived on the scene. Bob turned to him.

"Stanley, who has been through here!?" Bob demanded.

"Nobody, Mr. Willoughby."

"Nobody!!? Then how the hell did this happen!??"

"Well, uh, there was a garage truck that came in a couple of hours ago. They said Dr. Smyth had called them to replace her battery — that she had to have it jump started this morning."

"And you let them through without calling to confirm that!?" Willoughby asked, his face flushed with anger.

"Well, yes Sir. I figured Harry would check on that. Harry had told me Dr. Smyth would be in a meeting this afternoon with you, and I didn't want to disturb her. I figured Harry might call Sue."

"Stanley, you know that would be your job to verify the arrangements for entrance. I'm sure Harry assumed you had done that," Willoughby said sternly. "Who was the garage?"

"I didn't even notice, Sir. It was a pickup with a top on the cab and red and white letters. That's all I remember." About that time the police arrived. Someone had called 911.

"Chief, we have had a car bomb explode in one of our scientist's cars, and the gateman who went to retrieve it for her was killed. I want you to take this man in custody. He should have been a witness to and deterrent to the people who came in and did this. You will want to question him and hold him for the FBI who, I'm sure, would like to talk to him also," Willoughby said.

We all gave the Chief statements describing what we had seen. No motive was suggested and neither Ashton nor I mentioned the Atlanta incident in early December. We then left for Ashton's apartment in Fremont. She was still shaken, more for losing her friend Harry, it seemed, than for the near miss on her own life. She didn't take long to gather her things and we were on the way to the hotel where we got our belongings and checked out. It was 9:35 PM when we finally got to the airport and the quickest flight we could get booked on was the redeye which left at 11:20 PM. We got a bite to eat at one of the airport snack bars before boarding.

During the approximate five hour flight to New York, we all tried to sleep. Ashton didn't want to talk about the car incident. We were all tired from the long day and what we had gone through, knowing that the next day could be even more difficult.

Ashton, who had taken a seat by me, fell asleep on the way back, with her head resting on my shoulder. She was beautiful in her sleep in the dim cabin light, and I was glad that we were falling in love with each other. I was worried for her safety, though, and vowed to myself to watch out for her in the future. It was obvious that someone wanted her out of the way, maybe for the reasons she had surmised in Atlanta. Not too far in the future, I would find that all of us were targets for this unknown assailant.

CHAPTER EIGHT

The plane was 30 minutes delayed getting clearance to land, so the trip took about 5 ½ hours. Plus we lost three hours on the time change. By the time we got a couple of cabs to the hotel, we didn't arrive at the Salisbury until after 9:00 AM the morning of the 4th. Percy was waiting for us in the lobby.

"Hi, Dawson," he got up to greet us when we walked in. "I had a problem with the rooms. The city is still booked up with New Year people who came to the Times Square celebration and have stayed over. I couldn't get separate rooms. They only had four rooms left, all on the third floor, so I figured you would want me to get them. But that means us eight guys will have to bunk up together, two to a room."

He had not noticed Ashton.

"That's fine, Percy. It's the best you could do. But one of our members is not a guy." I then introduced him to Ashton.

Percy blushed fiercely. "Oh my gosh! Mike faxed me a list of the names so I could make the reservations and it included the new member, Dr. Smyth. He didn't indicate the Dr. was a, uh, female. I'm sorry. What can we do? I can call the Plaza to see if they have any rooms available. It's not too far away."

"No, I would rather us all stay together." I explained to him the attempt on Ashton's life yesterday.

"Well, I assigned Dr. Smyth to your room, Dawson, since Mike had mentioned that you had met the Dr. earlier in Atlanta. I guess three of us could squeeze into one room. I will sleep on the floor with a couple of the guys." Percy was still fumbling to find a solution.

"Hey, guys! I'm a big girl. I don't mind staying with Dawson. You don't need to sleep on the floor. I roomed with another girl and three guys in a crash pad while I was working my way through school. It worked out fine. Our beds were all in the same big room and we shared one bathroom. Besides, the places we may end up going together as a team may require that we all be together anyway. None of us should totally split up. I can handle it," she said, smiling.

Percy looked relieved. He felt better, but looked nervously at me to see if I would approve this arrangement.

"That's fine, Percy. By the way, Dr. Smyth prefers to be called Ashton by all of us. I---uh---should tell all of you guys that Ashton and I, since meeting in Atlanta a month ago, have talked numerous times on the phone since then. We spent time together, as you know, in San Francisco where we went to dinner together. We have a lot in common and there is, uh, an attraction between us that I would like to see grow into something special. I won't take advantage of the situation on the rooms and she knows that. But, I hope that by the time we finish our mission that Ashton and I will become "we". Whatever relationship we may or may not develop will not affect the conduct of our team's business. I guess I'm trying to say —I hope she, uh, learns to like me as I've begun to like her, but I know she's strong enough to say no if she doesn't." I was blushing and stumbling for words, but I felt the team needed to know that Ashton and I might become more than team members together. All the guys were smiling their understanding and approval, but Ashton broke the ice in what had been an awkward situation for me.

"What Dawson is trying to say is that in the month we have known each other, he has saved my life once in Atlanta and was present with most of you guys yesterday when my car was bombed. We have been with each other quite a lot by phone since then and share a common bond forged from the circumstances that threw us together. But there is more to it than that. We like each other —a lot! But both of us also share a desire to find the missing material and the people who have it. Doing that is imperative to our national security. And all of you share that goal with us. Nothing will detract us from trying to accomplish our mission. If Dawson and I can go forward together after that, that would be nice," she smiled and looked at me.

"I think that's great!" Thom said. "We sure need you, with the knowledge you have of what we are looking for. And after what you've gone through, it's nice to have someone like Dawson on the team who has a special interest in your not getting hurt, while trying to help us achieve what we all want."

"Thanks, Thom. Just don't look at us as newlyweds every time we come out of the room, or I'll tell all your girlfriends about your girlie show you went to in San Francisco!" Ashton laughed. None of the team were married. They may not have volunteered for this dangerous mission if they were.

From that point forward, Ashton and I were together everywhere we went. She would stay with me, and for protection and security reasons, we would stay two to a room with interconnecting rooms when possible.

"Let's go ahead and check into our rooms and meet in my room in thirty minutes. We'll call Mike to see if there have been further developments or if additional information has come to light. Then I suppose we will call on Mr. Mahmoud. After the redeye, is everyone sharp enough to go to work?" I asked.

"We're ready," Larry said. "See you in thirty minutes."

Percy gave everyone their room assignments. Larry was rooming with Ernest, Darby and Steve together and Thom and Percy would be together. As the team went forward, we would switch the room mates around at each location, except for me and Ashton, so that every team member was able to get better acquainted with each other.

"Is all this on the rooms okay with you?" I asked Ashton when we got in our room.

She came over to me and silently put her arms around my waist, laying her head on my shoulder and hugged me.

"Everything's okay," she said softly. "I want to be with you."

"I'm glad. I feel the same. I love you, little girl," I said, and turned her lips up to mine. We held our kiss until I felt we should pull away from each other. I could feel her closeness and the warmth of her firm body and smelled the faint smell of her perfume. She was so sexy and I ached for her, but we had work to do and the guys would be here soon. Reluctantly, I placed my hands on her shoulders and gently separated us.

"I know. We have to go to work," she said softly. Then she gave me a quick peck on the cheek and disappeared into the bathroom.

"Be back in a minute!" she said over her shoulder. "Go ahead and let them in if they get here. I won't be long."

She wasn't long— about five minutes. When she came out she had brushed her hair and pulled her blouse outside of the jeans she had not had an opportunity to change out of when we left California so hurriedly. Now she looked like a pretty little high school girl. And I loved her. Five minutes later there was a knock on the door. It was Darby.

"Okay to come in?" he grinned.

"Darby, remember what I told you! I'll have Steve get the FBI to find out who your girlfriend is!" Ashton laughed.

"Okay, okay Dr. Smyth. I didn't say a thing!" Darby feigned fear.

"Now I know I will find who your girlfriend is for calling me Dr.!" Ashton responded in a mock stern tone. About that time the rest of the crew arrived.

"Okay, I checked with the desk like you asked me to, Dawson, and there is an Abdul Mahmoud registered in room 612," Steve said.

"Any problem with the desk people?" I asked.

"No, I asked for the manager and he gave me the information after I identified myself as being with the FBI and explained that we were investigating Mr. Mahmoud on a matter of national security. I told him not to mention anything to anyone," Steve replied.

"Okay, let me call Mike before we get started to see if he has additional information," I said.

"Hi Dawson! Are all eight of you there and ready to get started?" Mike asked when he answered my call.

"Yeah, we're ready. I think we will start off interrogating him. If we get nothing, as I suspect, we can still hold him seven days under the terrorist suspect law. Right?" I questioned.

"Right. I don't have any new information other than the surveillance people say he has not ventured out of his room too often, and then only to get a sandwich around the corner or to get a newspaper. He has had two visitors who came together and stayed about an hour. One was bearded. Both dressed casually. As soon as we hang up, by the way, I will call the surveillance team and release them, so in fifteen minutes he will be all yours," Mike said.

"Okay. We know what room he's in. Anything else?" I asked.

"No, I'm afraid not. I wish I could tell you more. With his sudden disappearance from Livermore and his family terrorist background, it's a good bet he is behind the information theft, though. Just be careful, Dawson. If these people are who we suspect they are, they will be armed and dangerous when cornered," Mike replied before he hung up.

"Okay Steve, you and Larry go with me to Abdul's room. The three of us have the most experience in interrogation and something he might say may ring a bell with each of your department's information. Darby, you and Thom guard each end of the sixth floor hall and the elevator entrance. Ashton, you and Percy and Ernest go browse around the lobby. If any of you see two guys that might resemble the visitors he has had, call us on the cell phone, but don't stop them from entering the room if you have been able to warn us beforehand. It's 10:35. Go ahead and get in place. The three of us will wait here until 10:45, then go to room 612," I instructed. Everyone but the three of us left to take their positions.

At 10:48 AM we knocked on Mahmoud's door at room 612. We stood to the side so he could not view us though the peephole. Our weapons were drawn.

"Saeb, Mohammed!? Is that you? Why did you come back!?" we heard an agitated voice come from within the room.

"Abdul! Let us in!" Larry said, then shrugged at us. He had no idea whether he sounded like Saeb or Mohammed. We heard a rush to the door. There was hesitation. It didn't open immediately. I nodded to Steve.

"Mr. Mahmoud, this is the FBI. We want to talk to you. Let us in. Now!" Steve said. There was no immediate response. The door was sturdy and we didn't really want to shoot the lock off. Fortunately we didn't have to resort to that. Steve had attained a key to the room from the manager.

I nodded again and Steve, standing clear of the door, slid the plastic key card in and out of the slot quickly. When he saw the green light, he turned the knob and opened it a crack. Before Mahmoud had a chance to slam it shut again, I kicked it open. With me on one side and Steve on the other with weapons at the ready, Larry dashed in and immediately slammed his body against the right entrance wall with his pistol drawn while Steve and I covered him from each side of the door.

As we started to enter the room behind Steve with our handguns drawn, we froze. There was Mahmoud, sitting calmly in the chair at the back of the room in front of the window. There was no evidence that he was armed. His hands were folded in his lap. He just smiled at us. We lowered our firearms. I started to speak, but Mahmoud just held his hand up as if to silence me.

"Gentlemen, I've been expecting you. You must be Mr. Kohler. And if you are with the FBI, you must be Steve. I'm sorry, you will have to introduce yourself," he said to Larry. "I'm not sure which one you are. Perhaps Mr. Childress with the CIA, if I had to venture a guess."

We were taken aback. Before we could say anything, he continued.

"So where is the pretty girl, Ms.---or should I say Dr.---Smyth. I know her , you know. And the black guy, Darby Peters with your famous Delta Force? And surely Brown, Thackett and Henson are with you here also. Are you surprised that I know you all so intimately?" he asked.

"Well, yes. And I suppose you also know why we are here?" I asked, relaxing a little. He was very relaxed and cordial and did not seem to be a threat, at least for now.

"Yes, I can imagine. You have lost something and are trying to find it. You think I might can help you," Mahmoud responded, still smiling.

"Okay. Can you help us?" Larry asked.

"I can. But my main interest right now is to give you a message," Mahmoud replied.

"What is that?" Steve asked.

"Your government and its evil leadership will pay for your persecution of our people. We will triumph because God is with us. We are everywhere, and will strike when you least expect us, in ways you can't imagine. We have what you want, and will learn very quickly to use it to destroy you and the demons who run America. We are not afraid to die for our cause, because we will be rewarded in heaven as we become martyrs to destroy Zionists and the infidel Americans that defend them." He smiled benignly again.

"Okay. We get the message. Now tell us where we can find the information we are looking for," I said.

"Oh, look for the light!" Abdul laughed. "You know, we knew your government would come looking for the laser technology that your country was kind enough to develop, but too stupid to protect. The potential for this weapon is really quite amazing. We thank you. And it was not too hard to find the names and professions of the people who would be assigned to this task. But you are too late. We have it where you can't find it. And now that we know you, you are the target most likely to be hit, not us. You will die trying to serve your government's misguided attempts to find us. You will see."

"If you know us and knew we would be coming, why did you remain where we might find you?" I asked.

"You are quite right. Sometimes we are not as bright as we should be, also. I had no idea you would only remain a day in California. Actually, I had planed to leave tonight to join friends here where you could never find me. We have many friends in your country. Now it is too late. You have found me," he smiled wryly.

"Okay, let's go Mahmoud. We're going to have you locked up on suspicion of subversion. Steve will read your rights to you. In this country, you do still have rights, regardless of what you think of us or what we think of you. We will be over later this afternoon after you are booked to ask you a number of questions. You better get used to having us around," I said.

"Very well," he rose. "Let us go together. Allah-hu Akbar!"

As he rose from his chair, his jacket flared open slightly, just enough for me to see something dangling from his shoulder. I saw his hand move slowly to his side as he started to move towards us. We were all still standing close to the door.

"Look out!!!" I yelled and grabbed Larry's arm, diving to the floor trying to reach the door. I could feel Steve pushing himself out after us. When the explosion came an instant later, we were only half out the door, but all of us on the floor in the entrance and the hallway. There was a deafening sound and a hot blast of air that rushed out the door over our prone bodies. Splinters of debris blasted over us, some cutting into us. The windows in the back of the room blew out and black smoke billowed out of the room.

When we could recover our senses and finally see, Mahmoud had become a martyr and we were very fortunate to be alive.

CHAPTER NINE

Thom and Darby had come running down the hall when they saw us dive out of the room with the following explosion. Larry was bleeding across the eye where shrapnel had creased him. Steve and I were okay except for a few minor cuts. Soon the other three, along with the hotel manager arrived on the scene. They had heard the muffled explosion down in the lobby and some of the patrons had rushed down the stairs, not knowing what was going on. Fortunately, at that time of the late morning, very few of the guests had been in their room.

The curtains were burning and walls between the adjoining rooms were cracked. Someone had called 911 and we could hear sirens approaching. The fire was quickly doused and three rooms were vacated and cordoned off until repair crews could be scheduled to refurbish them. The manager was distraught.

"With all the activity going on, I doubt his two friends will return if they are still in the area, but for now, we should continue to stake out the lobby and the street corners leading to the hotel, just in case we sight them," I said.

"How do you think he knew about us?" Steve asked.

"I suspect the outside guard at Livermore. He recorded our names and could have passed them on to someone. We'll call later and see if they have made any progress in getting useful information from him," I replied.

"It was pretty common knowledge among a number of people at the lab that an investigative team sent by the Administration would be arriving. When he saw the FBI, CIA, Secret Service and the technical members of our team, they could very well surmise that we would be the group to hunt down the stolen information. Obviously, while we were all in the facility yesterday, someone wanted to be sure they got rid of me before I enlightened you too much," Ashton volunteered.

"But how did Mahmoud know you were with the team? He seemed to know all the members, including you," Thom asked.

"Probably because they saw us leave together---not just leave the NIF--- but the hotel. There may have been someone who followed us to the airport. Didn't you and Ashton say you thought you may have been shadowed last night?" Larry asked me.

"Yes, I thought so. Maybe you're right. At any rate, the Atlanta attempt on Ashton's life and the car bomb in her car at Livermore, along with Mahmoud's knowledge of the makeup of our entire team, and his threat that we all were now targets of his organization and would die, indicate from this point forward we need to be armed and alert wherever we go. We don't know where this thing will lead us, but we won't be able to accomplish our mission if we get killed. Tonight we will discuss the precautions we must take, as well as where we need to look now that our prime suspect is no longer with us," I said.

"Let's you and I sift through Mahmoud's room now that the smoke has cleared. I doubt we will find anything worthwhile that survived the blast, but you never know," Steve said.

"Good idea. The rest of you take positions on the street corners to see if his two friends are still around and curious enough to approach the hotel to see what's going on. Apprehend anyone you suspect, but be careful. Darby, why don't you stay in the lobby with Ashton. Steve and I will pick all of you up when we get done here, then we'll get a bite to eat and talk about our next move," I said. They all left to take their positions.

"Wow! This is a mess!" Steve said as we re-entered the room.

"Yeah! There's not much left," I responded.

The ambulance people had already removed what was left of Mahmoud, placing scattered pieces of his body that remained in a body bag. It was a gory scene with blood-spattered blackened walls, destroyed furniture, broken glass and water soaked carpets and bed where the firemen had put out the small fire that had resulted from the blast.

"Look, though! The blast went mostly out and upward. Lucky for us. But there are some papers and a little black appointment book on the floor by the desk and chair where Abdul was sitting. They are tattered and partially burned and water soaked, but some of what's there might still be legible," Steve said.

We picked the three single sheets of paper up gingerly. One was burned so badly that only a few letters could be made out on one margin. The second one had what looked to be a list of names. Several of our names were legible. This must be the list from which he had recorded or been given information on our team members. There did not appear to be anything else on that piece of paper. It had a fax number on the top. We would confirm later that he had picked up a fax last night at the desk. We recorded the number and saved the paper in a clean envelope we found still undamaged in the night stand.

The third piece of paper was also mostly illegible from the blast and water damage, but what could be made out was much more revealing.

"Look at this!!" Steve said. He was holding the third sheet we had recovered.

Although parts were scorched and missing, we could make out some of the words but could not tell where this fax came from. The phrases we could make out were:

"---in our --catio- -- Jakarta. --- --- close -- solving the mobility problem---range and power --- not sufficient for --- needs yet. Think ---- --- -olvable. Stay in N.Y. wit- Ga--- at --- ------- -ell. Will need your help to---- (At this place there was a large section torn away. Further down the sheet, the message picked up again in part.)

Cedric and --- LASER TEAM ---- -- eliminated. With resources available and makeup -- the ---- they can get in --- way -- ---------------- --- -ission. Stay on ---- --- -ake them out. Use Saeb and Mohammed to --- (more parts missing).

The last legible piece of information was at the bottom and was as clear as it was chilling.

Priority until we are able to get unit perfected and in place---The Smyth bitch and her seven associates must be eliminated. Without her they will be lost in trying to locate the device, the technical papers and our people who are working on it. She made a big mistake by joining the effort to locate where the info went and Alziddi wants to make her pay with her life. She will be the fool, not Infama, and we will succeed in eliminating the friends of the Zionists and their Laser Team one by one, when they least expect us to strike.

Allah-hu Akbar

Fazad

"Well, if I am reading this right, our team now has a name---the Laser Team. It has a nice sound to it," I said.

I glanced through the appointment book and did not immediately see anything of significance. Most of it was in some kind of code. I would look through it in more detail later and give the de-coding guys a shot at it. I placed it gently in the envelope with the three pages we had salvaged. A thorough search of the rest of the room did not turn up anything of interest. By this time it was 1:00 PM.

"Okay, Steve, let's get the others and go grab a bite to eat. Based on Mahmoud's apparent surprise that Saeb and Mohammed had returned, I doubt that it will be worthwhile to stake out the area looking for their return. We will give the limited description information we have to Mike and ask him to have the surveillance team return for a couple of days just in case," I said. I called Mike on my cell phone to report what had happened and he agreed to contact the surveillance people and have them return.

"Keep your Laser Team —I like that name," Mike laughed, "in New York and snoop around a little until we have a chance to examine the little riddle on that second page to see if our conclusions on what it means agree with what you come up with after you have a chance to study it. You can overnight the three pages and send the appointment book to me after you get a chance to look at it more carefully. If it is in code, I'll let the CIA guys take a look at it. I'll be back in touch. In the meantime, all of you be careful. It doesn't take a decoder to tell that your "Laser Team" is a target," Mike said before hanging up.

We went to a little café a couple of blocks away and ordered sandwiches.

"Well, what do you make of Mahmoud's messages?" Larry asked.

"The first one we looked at, I would say they have a location in Jakarta, Indonesia where they have people trying to translate the information they have and put together an effective mobile weapon. If I read between the lines correctly, they have made progress on developing a mobile unit using this technology, but it doesn't have the power and range sufficient for their intended purpose, which probably is to assassinate the President and/or other key Western leaders," I replied.

"If Dawson's correct, is this an insurmountable problem, in your opinion?" Thom asked Ashton.

"No," Ashton shuddered, "although we never attempted to do that, I would think enough series of mirrors configured correctly to duplicate what we had at Livermore would do the trick. Range and power would definitely be limited in comparison to what that unit could do. You would not come close to nuclear fusion. That would take a unit approaching the size of the one at NIF, although I think our continuing experiments will find we can duplicate that result with a much smaller unit. It would require more passes of the beams through optical configuration and a fixed weapon could be designed with the power to intercept and shoot down incoming missiles, for example. We are a few years away from that. But a mobile unit that would deliver a deadly beam with some limitation restrictions on range is definitely possible."

"What range would you think is feasible?" Darby asked.

"Without a lot of study and experimentation, I hesitate to guess at that. But, if you pressed me for an out of the air guess, I would say somewhere around a 100 meters would be the limit before it got too bulky for one person to handle. And that is probably stretching it a bit," she answered.

"But a bulkier unit that could be set in a window of an apartment building overlooking the route of a Presidential motorcade is possible with greater range?" Steve questioned.

"Perhaps. It would have to be assembled in parts, but would be mobile from the standpoint several trips with suitcase or trunk size loads and someone who knows how to assemble it could make a workable unit. But twice the size doesn't mean twice the range. A wild, uneducated guess is that 150 meters would be maximum range with anything that would not require pretty major construction and would be considered mobile by any definition," Ashton responded.

"Whew!! If Ashton is right, the 100 to 150 meters possible with a mobile or semi mobile unit is plenty to do what we think they have planned with this weapon," Ernest said.

"What do you make of the information on the other piece of paper?" Percy asked.

"Some of that is a little hard to speculate on, but the parts that seem clear is our "Laser Team" is a target, they obviously know who and where we are, Ashton is a principal target and Alziddi and Infama are definitely behind this thing. I don't know what the reference to "Cedric" might be. We will see what the spooks at the Company come up with. I didn't see anything in an initial scan on the appointment book, and a lot was in code, but I will send that to them after we look at it more closely ourselves," I volunteered.

When we finished lunch, we went back to the hotel and checked with the surveillance team. They had not seen anyone in the vicinity who resembled the description we had of Saeb and Mohammed. I looked through the appointment book more thoroughly, made a few notes, then sent everything to Mike by overnight express. We would wait to hear from him. Looking for Saeb and Mohammed, our only leads now, would be like looking for a needle in a haystack in Manhattan, especially with the limited information and description we had of them. We decided to stay around the hotel that day, hoping they would be sighted returning to see Mahmoud. No such luck.

Finally, at 6:00 PM we decided to have a light dinner together at an Italian restaurant just a few blocks from the hotel, then go to our rooms afterward. It had been an exhausting day coming from California on the redeye with the time change, and the events of the day adding to our state of tiredness. We were back at our rooms by 7:45 PM.

CHAPTER TEN

"I feel like I haven't had any sleep in ages. I'm numb. It's nice to be back in the room, knowing we don't have to go out for a while. Especially being with you," Ashton said as she came to me and hugged me. Actually she just leaned into me and laid her head on my shoulder. I held her there for a long moment.

"I know. I didn't sleep hardly any on the plane. You being beside me, looking so content, kept me awake," I said.

"Well, I'm going to hop in the shower. I feel grungy, too. That bed looks great. If I fall asleep in the shower and don't come out for a couple of hours, come in and get me," she pulled away, pecked me on the cheek and went to her suitcase to get something to put on after her shower.

"I'll be a while. You don't have to wait two hours to come get me though," she said as she disappeared in the bathroom.

She did take a while. I started to go in and check on her. I was looking for an excuse anyway. But after about fifteen minutes she came out. She had on the white shortie jammie bottoms and the little blouse top that I assume was the same outfit she had on when I called her on Christmas eve. I was stunned! She looked cuter and more sexy than I had even imagined that day.

"Why don't you take a quick shower? You will feel better. I do. I'm just going to crawl in bed. If I'm asleep when you get out, wake me up. Okay?" She hugged me lightly then pulled away quickly before I could react to the feeling that was rising within me. Then she got in bed and curled up, turning off the lights. Only the dim glow through the sheer curtains from the night lights outside illuminated the room. I got a clean set of boxer shorts out of my bag and headed to the bathroom.

"I'll be out soon," I said.

"I'll be here," she smiled as she curled up under the covers and turned her back to me. I could see the soft shape of her body under the sheet and light blanket. She was beautiful! I brushed my teeth, quickly shaved and jumped in the shower. The soothing warm stream of water did make me feel better.

I came out of the bathroom in my boxers. In the dim light I could see

Ashton, still curled up under the blanket, her long hair flowing loosely over the pillow. I thought she was asleep.

"Come to bed with me. I want you to cuddle me. And I want to make love with you. I'm ready now, Dawson, to let you have all of me, and I want all of you. I want to love you," she said without turning over. I could see the inviting contour of her body beneath the thin blanket.

I silently slid in beside her and snuggled up to her. She was still facing away from me and we fit together like two stacked spoons. I could feel her warmth and the sweet smell of her freshly washed hair. Without a word, she turned towards me and turned her lips up to mine. We met in a tentative kiss. Her tongue darted in and around my lips and she slid her leg between mine while pressing closer to me and sliding her hand around my waist. My hand slid under her blouse and the other hand went to the back of her leg just below her firm rounded little butt. I could feel the smooth, silky skin of her back and leg.

She applied pressure with her leg between mine. I was already hard and could sense that she felt that. I moved the hand that had been on her back around to her firm rounded breast and could feel the nipple harden as I did so. She slid her leg out from between my legs and rolled to her back. I could feel her arch her back slightly as she pulled off her little shortie pajamas. While I slid my boxers off, she loosened and removed the skimpy little blouse. Our naked bodies brushed each other as we unclothed.

"Dawson, put your hand down there," she whispered. At the same time she moved her hand between my legs and lightly stroked my already rigid shaft. I slid my hand up on the smooth inside of her thigh and let it rest in the soft center between her legs. She jumped slightly and spread her legs wider apart when my finger found the hot, moist little hole nestled between her legs. She let out a soft moan as I began to lightly move my finger up and down her hungry vagina, alternately stroking her clit and depressing slightly into the center of her hot and sticky opening.

"Ashton, I love you. I want to be inside you," I whispered.

She placed her hands on my hips and gently guided me into position over her outspread legs. She then took the part of me that was throbbing and aching to be inside her and placed it where I wanted to be. I hesitated a moment before entering her and glanced at her beautiful face. Her eyes were closed and her head tilted back slightly. She had a look of anticipation on her face that looked almost like pain.

"Come in me, Love! Fuck me!!" she said with an urgency that caused her to pull my hips downward so that I entered her steaming pussy. At first I only came into her a little, then I withdrew and pressed the full length of my dick into her. She gasped and thrust her hips into me with an energy that caused me to quickly withdraw, then thrust downward into her with force.

"Okay, little girl. I'm coming into you hard!" I said as I began to quickly withdraw and then thrust into her sharply, pausing once in a while at her opening, only to have her thrust her hips upward so she could receive the full length of me. We made love frantically and began to become sweaty as our bodies meshed together in quickening and arousing, synchronic movements with each other until we both exhausted our energies with explosive culmination. Afterwards, we just lay there cuddled together, holding on to each other as if letting go would erase the memory of the exhausting and exhilarating lovemaking we had just experienced. It felt so natural and nice for us to be together like this and there was a mutual contentment that did not require either of us saying anything for a while.

Finally, I brushed her damp hair back from her face and kissed her lips lightly. She responded with a full kiss. Her perfect body was still interlocked with mine as if we had merged into one.

"I love you. I have never made love like this before, with someone who is so pretty, and so good in bed and one that I cared about so much. You are sexy, Ashton. And you are real special to me. Thank you for sharing yourself with me," I said softly as her smooth body pressed even closer to mine and I could feel the softness and firmness of her. My right hand was rested on her butt in our embrace and my fingers extended down between her legs where I could feel the soft, warm, still moist furry part of her femininity that rested between her legs.

"I love you, too, Love. Please don't ever leave me. I'm scared, now that we have found each other," she said.

"What do you mean? I won't leave you. And I will give my life to protect you from Infama's people," I said.

"Oh, I wasn't talking about them. I recognize the danger there, but I'm not paranoid about it now that we are alert to the fact we are targets."

"What are you scared of, then?" I asked.

She didn't respond immediately. I thought I felt her convulse into a little sob. I looked at her face and, sure enough, there was a tear rolling down her cheek.

"What is it, Hon? Can I help?" I asked as I kissed the tear off her cheek.

"I don't know. What I'm scared of is that you will leave me. And if I tell you why I'm scared, you might leave me" she said. She was weeping earnestly now.

"Tell me---please. We are "we" now. And that won't change, no matter what," I reassured her.

"Oh, Love. I don't know how to start. But you have the right to know. I don't want you to find out later. You would hate me and you may not like me if I tell you. But I want to be fair with you. I don't want any deception to come between us. If we part, I don't want it to be because either of us has not been honest with the other."

"Go ahead. I'll listen. And it won't change anything with us. I promise," I said and I leaned over and kissed her softly. I began to feel aroused again. She was so pretty and sexy looking. But she was obviously distraught. I needed to listen to what she had to say.

"Okay. I told you a little about my family. But I didn't tell you the rest of the story, as Paul Harvey would say. The man who taught me to shoot was a career Army man. But he wasn't my father. He was my stepfather. And he abused me sexually when I was sixteen," she began, sobbing more as she recalled this part of her life. I squeezed her to me tenderly as she continued her story.

"My mother had to leave for a week to spend time with her sister who had just had a baby and had some problems with the delivery. My stepfather and I were alone in the house. The first couple of days, everything was fine. I would come home from school, we would warm frozen dinners or go out to a fast food place to eat. Afterwards, I would do homework or watch TV. I was a cheerleader and in the scholastic honor society in high school but didn't have a license to drive yet. I had a boyfriend who was eighteen, but we usually went to the movies together or just hung out with the rest of the kids. Once, when he brought me home, he kissed me and placed his hand on the inside of my thigh under my skirt before I got out of the car. His fingers brushed my panties and I could feel myself getting wet from the juices that flowed from me. I was turned on and might have gone all the way with him if we had been parking at some isolated place rather than right in front of my house. He didn't persist and I pulled away because I was scared my stepfather would see us. That was the first "sexual" experience I had," she continued, settling down now as she related her story.

"The third night we were alone together, it started out normal. We went out to eat and when we returned, I went ahead and took a shower and got my pajamas on and watched TV. I didn't have a date that night and there were no school functions to go to. I noticed, while I was watching TV, that my stepfather would look at me intently when he didn't think I was looking. It sort of gave me the creeps, but I didn't think much about it. I just felt like I was being watched and didn't understand why," she continued.

"Where was your little brother during this week," I asked.

"He's really my stepbrother. He's a nice kid. My real father was killed in an auto accident when I was two. My mother re-married about three years later. My brother left the second night for the rest of the week to go on a scout jamboree. He ultimately became an Eagle Scout," she replied.

"What happened then?" I asked.

"About 11:00 PM I decided to go to bed. About ten minutes after I turned the lights out, my stepfather came in my bedroom," she responded.

"Were you scared?" I asked.

"No, not at first. He often would open the door and say goodnight before he went to bed if I was still awake. This night, though, he came on in and sat on the bed beside me. He didn't say anything---just sat there a while. I was half asleep. I asked him if he was going to bed. He said yes. Then he quietly pulled the sheet away from me and slid into bed beside me. It was then that I noticed he was naked except for his boxer shorts. I didn't understand. I was confused and terrified."

"What happened then? You don't have to go through any more of this if it's too painful," I said.

"No. I need to talk about it. You are the only one I have ever said anything to about this." she said.

"What about your mother?" I asked.

"You are the only one I have ever told about what happened," she repeated.

"Before I could react," she picked up the story again, "he slid his hand under my pajamas and placed it between my legs while, at the same time, taking my hand and placing it forcefully inside his boxers. I had seen pictures and my friends and I had talked about sex and boy's private parts like most girls do, but I was still shocked at what I felt. I never imagined that it would be that big and hard. Now I was so frightened, I became nauseated and dizzy. It began to finally dawn on me what he had in mind and I was scared to death. I couldn't imagine anything like that being forced inside me without hurting terribly." Ashton began to cry again.

"That's okay. Stop now. I'm sorry. I love you very much," I tried to comfort her as I pulled her even closer to me.

"Well, that's about all of that story. He raped me. It did hurt. It was awful!

When he finally finished with me, it was almost a relief to feel the warm lubricant of his sperm. I felt like my insides had been ripped apart. And I felt so dirty."

"Did he say anything after it was over?" I asked.

"He just said I felt good and I would learn to enjoy it. And he threatened me. He said if I told Mom, my brother or anyone else, he would call me a liar and would tell them that I came on to him and that he had rejected my advance and I must be just trying to get back at him. And he told me to come home the next day right after school. He would have a surprise for me. He actually kissed me before leaving my room and told me goodnight when he closed the door behind him. I stayed awake, staring at the ceiling the rest of the night."

"Hon, I love you. Were you able to stay away from him after that?" I asked.

"Yes. But that's the rest of my story---and the part I'm afraid I will lose you when I tell you. But you have to know," she said with resolve.

"You won't lose me. Try me. No matter what you say, we start from now, and we have forever ahead of us," I said.

"I hope so," she said thoughtfully. "But you may change your mind when you hear the rest."

"Go ahead," I said, not realizing just how shocking and unreal the rest of her story would be.

CHAPTER ELEVEN

I quickly mixed a drink for both of us and Ashton continued her story.

"Okay. I got up about 4:00 AM that morning after he raped me. I had not slept, but I had formulated a plan. I packed two pairs of blue jeans, two changes of underwear, two sweaters and a jacket along with a few odds and ends in a big backpack I had. I had a bank account from some summer work I had done. It had about $450 in it. I knew where Mom kept some money in the house and found another almost $100. That morning, I ate cereal for breakfast, stuffed several candy bars in the backpack and left for school. It was only about four blocks so I usually walked. That morning my stepfather acted as if nothing had happened. He offered to take me to school. I took him up on that. When he asked why I had the backpack, I told him I was practicing for a play and had put some clothes in there that I would change into as part of the costumes for the play. When he let me out in front of the school, he told me with a knowing smile to remember to come home early that afternoon. He told me again that he had a surprise for me and that I would like it and he said we would just stay home and be together that night. He said everything would be better this time and that he would teach me some things, and I would like it."

"What happened when you went home that afternoon?" I asked.

"I didn't. I watched him drive out of sight, then I walked to the bus station and bought a ticket to Chattanooga. I wanted to get away and had decided to go to Atlanta, but didn't want to spend too much money. I would hitchhike from Chattanooga to Atlanta. A nice lady on the bus whose husband was picking her up in Chattanooga drove me from the bus station to a ramp leading to Interstate 75. I was only there thirty minutes when a man picked me up. He said he was going to Atlanta and I could ride with him."

"That was dangerous," I commented.

"I know. I was naïve and still in a state of shock from the night before. I just wanted to get away and disappear. We had not gotten down the road more than ten or fifteen miles when he took an exit onto a side road. He said he was going to get gas. He drove off on a little dirt road. I realized he was

69

not getting gas and tried to jump out, but he was going too fast. When he slowed, he smashed his fist against my cheek, knocking me almost unconscious. When I recovered enough from the blow to react, it was too late. He had already pulled into what looked like a farm road leading to a pasture. As soon as the car slammed to a halt, he was on me, ripping at my clothes and hitting me repeatedly when I screamed and tried to fight him. He raped me then hit me again, real hard, and shoved me out of the car. He started the car and rolled down his window and smiled at me. I was lying on the side of the road, bruised and bleeding. He tossed my backpack out and told me he should kill me, but that I was a good fuck. He then told me he would kill me if I said anything about this to anybody. Then he drove off in a cloud of dust. "

"Oh, Baby. You were innocent and only sixteen and brutally raped by two different men in the same 24 hours. You had to be devastated," I said, wiping the tears, that had begun to flow again, from her face.

"Do you want to hear more?" she asked.

"Only if you want to tell me. I know this is hard on you. But remember, I'm with you and I'll never leave you." I put my arms around her and wrapped the blanket around her shoulders. She was sitting up in the bed now. She was so beautiful. As she told her story, though, I felt close to her and wanted to give her comfort like I would a child in pain.

"I finally made it to Atlanta late that night. A truck driver picked me up. It was dark and he could not see my bruises and torn clothes when he stopped. He was nice and gave me some money to spend the night in a Day's Inn on the outskirts of Atlanta. He told me he had a daughter about my age and that, if I was running away from home, I should let my parents know I was okay. It had started to rain. He offered to buy my dinner, but I thanked him and said no. I went to my motel room, locked the door and ate one of my candy bars. I didn't even turn on the lights— just sat there in the dark room watching the rain through the open curtains."

I put my arms around her. She looked as desolate as I'm sure she felt that night, alone in that dark motel room, watching the rain, knowing she only had what was in her backpack and less than $500 with nowhere to go but too scared and hurt to return.

"What did you do the next day?" I asked.

"I had to be out of the room by noon, so I left about 11:30 with my backpack and just walked the neighborhood. I found a high school about six blocks away. After all that happened, I still wanted to graduate and get my degree. I went in and talked to the Principal's assistant and told her I had just moved to Atlanta and wanted to enter school. When she asked my address and information about my parents, I told her we had not found a house yet and were staying at the Day's Inn until we could find something in this neighborhood. I faked the rest of the information and the names of my parents and told her my dad had taken a job at a factory I had passed on my walk to the school. She asked me to have my school records from my home in Tennessee sent to her, gave me a class schedule and told me I could start the next day."

"That's amazing. After what you had been through, the first thing you do is pick up where you left off on your schooling," I commented.

"Yes, well I had excellent grades and was always motivated to succeed. I had always dreamed of being some kind of scientist and I didn't want to give up on that dream, especially not then," she replied.

"So did you find a place to live? And how did you survive financially?" I asked.

"Dawson, I had to get a job. And going to school during the day, it had to be a night job. Without a car, my world was about a ten block square area. I found a ratty little apartment not too far from the school and my work that only cost me $300 a month. I had enough money to cover the first month in advance. I started to work the next night."

"Where did you find a night job?"

"In a strip club. Now what do you think of me?"

"You had to survive," I answered.

"Yes. And I was good. I got good tips, along with minimum wage salary. We got $3 for every drink we sold for $6. They were watered down, so the club owner still made a good profit. Plus there was a $10 cover charge. It was a classy club," she laughed.

"I'll bet you were good. Ashton, was it just topless, or all the way?" I asked.

"Darling, it was topless and bottomless. Not every dance. The routine was the first rotation I was in a bikini. Then the next one we were topless. The third dance was all the way for the rest of the night. Do you want to hear more now?" she asked tentatively.

"Yes. Go ahead. I can just imagine you as a teenager. How did you get the job being only 16? And how long were you there?" I asked.

"I lied about my age. The owner didn't ask for any proof. But if cops visited, or someone he spotted as a possible undercover policeman, he would pull me off the stage. We got caught once and he was fined and warned. He blamed me, saying I had presented false age documents. We were more careful after that, and I turned seventeen. I stayed in that job almost two years, until I graduated from high school, with honors. The first year I met a guy who showed up at the club one night. He was Mexican. He seemed real nice, romantic and attentive. I needed someone. We got married a few months later. He wanted to move to Texas, but I insisted on staying until I graduated."

"Did you love him?" I asked, now becoming disturbed a little, finding out there had been someone else in her life. I reflected that she knew there had been someone else in my life, though. I asked her to continue. Her story was out of a book. I didn't know until she started talking again just how traumatic it would turn out.

"At first I thought so. I was young and had never had the kind of attention he gave me at first. I had never had sex except for the two rapes, either. But Dawson, he began to beat me." She began to cry again.

"Did you leave him?"

"No. A week after I graduated, he came to the club one night and told me to pack up. We were leaving for San Antonio. I was 19. We left. The beatings continued in San Antonio. One night I was battered and bleeding and a neighbor who had heard me screaming called 911. The police arrested him. When he got out of jail, he apologized and begged to come back. I took him back. At that point, getting beaten was the only form of attention I could relate to. The alternative was having no one. Then one night a swat team burst into our apartment and handcuffed him and hauled him to jail. I had not been aware that he had been involved in drug dealing. He spent all the money we had to hire a lawyer who got him off on a bail bond. He skipped town and forced me to go to Mexico with him. His family lived across the border in Juarez. We moved in with them."

"Down there it got worse," she continued. "The beatings continued. His family seemed to enjoy seeing him beat me. One night he tied me to a chair and cut my hair off in front of them. They just laughed. My hair had been long, almost to my waist. He cut it so short I looked like a boy."

"Love, why didn't you get out of that situation immediately?"

"I couldn't get out of the country. One day a cousin from the States came to visit. I formulated a plan. I played up to him. He was there two weeks. We had sex. He asked me to get a divorce and marry him. I got a quickie divorce and a quickie marriage. You can do anything in Mexico with a little money, and he had money. I left with him. That was the only way I could get out of the country legally and get back to the States."

"What happened then?" I asked incredulously.

"He was nice to me, but I didn't love him. I left him six months later. We were in Los Angeles and I had gotten a job in an upscale retail store in Hollywood. It broke his heart when I filed for divorce and left him."

"Question. Going back in time, did your mother not try to find you when you ran away to Atlanta?" I asked.

"Yes. Very hard. One day a teacher friend of hers checked my school records in Tennessee for her and found where I had asked for the records to be transferred to the school in Atlanta. Everyone in the community knew I was missing, but it was just bureaucratic bumbling that prevented that bit of information from getting the proper attention for more than a year. She came down to the Atlanta school and was waiting for me one afternoon after classes. We had a tearful reunion. I was already married at the time. I didn't tell her about the beatings or my job. She had found out what had happened and divorced my stepfather. He had acted guilty when I disappeared and her suspicions led her to force the truth from him. He was probably afraid I would get in touch with her and rat on him. He left quietly, probably thankful that she didn't press charges against him. His son stayed with Mom and she began her search for me. I told her that day I would come back to Tennessee if I could. We left for San Antonio two weeks later. My Mom eventually remarried and moved to Atlanta. My stepbrother works down there for Sun Trust. We stay in touch frequently now."

"Okay. Back to L.A. What happened next? How did you get from where you were to where you are?" I asked.

"After my divorce, as I mentioned, I got a job and was doing reasonably well financially, but living expenses were also outrageous in that area. I bought a car and got my license. The store promoted me to department manager. I decided to see if I could enroll at UCLA. When I presented my high school records and told them my situation, they offered me a hardship scholarship that covered about 80% of my costs. I was 21 at the time. The rest is history. I graduated with a degree in physics in 1996, went to graduate school at the University of Georgia, was offered a job by the Livermore Lab and assigned to their new project to help develop the super laser."

"Wow!!" was all I could say. She had certainly had a horrible time, going from a schoolgirl in what appeared to be a stable family situation one day to the kind of life she led for the next five or six years. Throughout, though, she had exhibited an immense amount of spunk and determination.

"Love, that's a summary of my life. I left out a few details of course. I want you to know that from my divorce in 1996 until I met you, there has been no one in my life. I dated a few times, but I was older than most of the college kids and met few single men at work. There has been no romantic relationship. I guess I was scared of a relationship, too. I pretty much devoted all my spare time to getting my degrees and to the work at Livermore. What we were doing was very important to me. I have felt that I needed to experience the kind of scientific success we had with the laser to give myself confidence and self respect after the life I had led in my late teens and early twenties. Now I need to ask you a question," she said, looking at me directly with her pretty hazel eyes.

"What's that?" I asked.

"Now that you know my story, can we still be together? Do you still love me? I did what I had to do to survive, but I am used. I have been raped twice, married briefly twice, abused and unknowingly associated with a felon. I can't blame you if you want to just forget "us". But I still want to be on the team and will do the best I can to help you , and..."

"And what?

"And I will still love you, no matter what. But I won't try to stop you from leaving if you don't want me now," she said, tears welling in her eyes, but still looking at me directly to find the answer in my eyes if not in my words.

I pulled her pretty face towards mine and kissed her. "You are even more beautiful and special to me now than before I knew your story. It took a lot of courage to tell me all this, and I know it was painful for you. I love you, Ashton, more now than before. We are still 'we'."

"I love you. And I feel comfortable with our little Laser Team family and I am so glad we met, Dawson. You are special to me. I love you, love you, love you!" She kissed me passionately.

We made love again before going to sleep. This time it was slow and less frantic—more love than sex. In our bliss, neither of us could foresee or even imagine that our little family would be brutally reduced from eight to seven in the near future.

CHAPTER TWELVE

The next three days we scoured Manhattan, spending most of our time in the Muslim sections, trying to find Mohammed and Saeb. It proved to be useless, just as we suspected. With only first names that were common in the community, and vague descriptions that were also undistinguished in the neighborhoods we visited, we didn't have a chance of picking up a lead on their whereabouts. The only thing we might have done with our questions was to alert the two people we were looking for. We also mentioned Abdul Mahmoud's name, thinking a connection between him and the other names might bring some information to light. No such luck. It was frustrating, because we really didn't have anything to go on, but hated to just twiddle our thumbs and not try to do something while awaiting any information that Mike may come up with to share with us.

7:00 AM January 8th, 2003, Mike called. Ashton was still tucked in bed asleep. We had planned the night before to all meet at eight, have breakfast together and hit the streets again for another futile effort to find our quarry. I had gotten up to shower and shave when I heard the phone. Ashton sleepily answered it, then called me to the phone when Mike identified himself. Now Mike knew we were sleeping together.

"Good morning. I'm glad to see you are still saving the taxpayer's money," Mike said when I came to the phone.

"Well, we are doubled up in rooms for security reasons, but Ashton and I have plans together for the future. Our being together won't effect the performance of the team, Mike. All the guys know about us and the team is solidly together," I said.

"I know. I have full confidence in you and all the team members. Larry told me when I called yesterday and the rest of you had already gone down to the lobby that Ashton was a superb marksman---or should I say markswoman. He said she was very beautiful and very smart, too. Take care of her, Dawson. It sounds like you are a lucky guy."

"Thanks, Mike. I think I am, too. Have you got anything for us? We've been beating our heads against the wall trying to develop leads with the sketchy information we have."

"Yes I do. The guard at Livermore was uncooperative. We are still holding him and got a warrant to search his apartment because we were convinced he is involved with Infama. A background check didn't jive with what we knew about him and he couldn't answer any questions related to the check as far as former employment, locations of residence, etc. We found that the name he was using, Stanley Morris, was a recently deceased police officer in San Francisco. Somehow he had gotten his social security number and all his other personal data and that was what the check was run on. A further search found that his real name is Faed Mustafi, a Saudi who entered the country on a student visa three years ago. He had signed up with the University of California, but there was no record that he ever attended class. He simply disappeared."

"Did you find anything in his apartment?" I asked.

"Yes. We found a lot. Willoughby did a good job retaining "Stanley" and getting the cops there quickly. Otherwise, I'm sure he would have been gone and destroyed the evidence in his apartment before disappearing. We found evidence that he, Mahmoud, Saeb and Mohammad are involved with Infama and we have those two last names. That should help you some, although don't expect that knowledge to necessarily open up any more doors for you. We also confirmed through evidence found there that the unit they are trying to develop and the people who are working on it are in Jakarta as the note fragment from Mahmoud's room suggested. We don't know where in Jakarta, though. It looks like that will be your next stop, after you try to locate Saeb and Mohammed in New York."

"Wow! It sounds like you found a gold mine!" I exclaimed.

"Yes, and we found some disturbing information also. It appears that Alziddi has taken a personal interest in eliminating you and your team. There were instructions from him to all four of those people to take you out. He cautioned that nothing should stand in the way of completing their mission. Although he realizes we could assign other people to hunt this thing down if something happened to you people, he is concerned about the makeup of your team. The combination of topnotch investigative people and scientific talent scares him. The instruction basically says that if anyone can screw up his plan, your group has the best shot at it. He wants you out of the way—all of you."

"Anything else, Mike?"

"Nothing except the coded appointment book has not revealed anything yet. The code has not been totally broken, but there are indications that "Cedric" might have been a contact of Mahmoud's who passed relevant information on to him. He was there, of course, but may have needed help to find everything he needed. We are checking out everyone, including Willoughby, to see if anything suspicious turns up. Our first background check was done on your team member, Ashton Smyth— the girl you have "plans" with. You can feel comforted that she came out completely clean. Her background for a few years in her late teens until about 21 is a little fuzzy. We haven't found much, but would not expect there to be any problem since nothing was found that would lead to any suspicion at all concerning her or her family, friends or associates before or after that void period."

I knew now why he could not find anything during that time of her life. Even her mother couldn't find her for much of that time. She had stayed incognito, with some of that time taking place during that horrible period in Mexico. I'm glad Mike didn't find that part of her life. She had told me that I was the only one she had ever told about the 17 to 21 period. That was a time she wanted to forget.

"Saeb's last name is Sedeqi, an Iranian. Mohammad Khartam is a Saudi by birth, but spent most of the last several years in Yemin before illegally entering the U.S. two years ago. There is apparently a girl, in her late 20's or early 30's, Reza Pahlavi, nationality unknown, who is here in the states and associated with them also. There was a picture of her and Mahmoud in 'Stanley's' apartment and a notation for Saeb and Mohammed to look her up, that Mahmoud would know where she was. She is very pretty. There may have been a romantic relationship between her and Mahmoud, but that is just speculation based on the pose of the two in the photograph. She is in Manhattan somewhere. Her picture will be arriving at the hotel early this afternoon. You probably will want to wait and get that before hitting the streets. She would be easy to spot."

"Okay. So far, Mike, you've been a big help. Anything else?" I asked.

"No. If we get anything more I will be in touch with you. Stay in New York a while longer to see if you can turn those folks up. We will talk later about Jakarta."

"Okay, Mike. Thanks. I will check the desk this afternoon for the photo and any other mail." We all had arranged to have our personal mail forwarded here too, for now. "I probably have some bills to pay."

"One last thing, Dawson---"

"What's that?" I asked.

"Be very careful. Alziddi has resources in this country and he will not hesitate to use everyone he has to destroy your team before it gets started. He probably knows we know about Jakarta now and knows you are on the trail of his people in New York. Just recognize that they are on your trail, too. I have a feeling you will find each other. Just be alert and try to find them before they strike you. They likely know exactly where you are and will be watching and waiting while you are looking for them."

"We will, Mike," I promised as we hung up.

The eight of us had breakfast and decided to hang around the hotel that morning and wait on the photograph that Mike was sending. I described our conversation to the rest of the team with special emphasis on Mike's warning to be alert and careful. After breakfast we went up to Larry and Ernest's room and played poker to wile the time away until the mail came. Ashton did better than I, but Ernest had the big payday. We were playing a quarter ante and three raise limit. He ended up with forty-two dollars in winnings.

"Well, Professor, I guess you can buy us all a beer tonight," Darby said.

"I will do that, Darby. You know, I'm glad I volunteered to help out on this thing. We haven't had a chance to do much yet as far as closing in on our mission, but being on this team has given me the opportunity to be with a great bunch of guys. I include you in that Ashton, even though you are hardly a guy. I feel like we are becoming a family. Our mission is important to our country and I couldn't be with a better or more talented group of people to help accomplish our goal. I will buy you all a drink tonight with my winnings," Ernest said sincerely.

It seemed to me, too, that we were all beginning to bond together in the days we had been with each other. I felt confident that we would be effective as individuals and as a team when the time came to act. And it had become obvious to all of us that we liked each other and considered ourselves friends.

"I'm going down to pick up the mail. It should be here by now. Be back in a minute," I said. It was about 1:30 PM.

The mail had arrived. The photograph that Mike had sent overnight was in a manila folder. I would wait and open it with the others when I got back to the room. Darby had a letter from his girlfriend. There were some bills for all of us, utility bills and the like from the apartments we leased in the DC area. Ashton had a letter that the return address indicated was from her stepbrother because the last name was Smyth and it was in a Sun Trust envelope. Ashton had told me that she had changed her name back to her maiden name after her divorce. And I had a letter. It was from my ex-wife. It read:

Dawson--
Dalton and I are getting married Sunday. Thought you should know. Hope all is well with you.
Linda

Okay. I guess that closes another chapter in my life. I decided not to send a wedding present. The letter went in the trash can. I returned to the room.

"Here's the mail, guys. Darby, I read yours and really think it should have been marked X rated. Ashton, here's one from your brother, I guess."

"Oh. Skipper." She opened the letter.

"Skipper?" I asked.

"Oh, that's what we all call him. He's being transferred to Baltimore," she said after opening the letter. "He's really doing good with Sun Trust. I'm proud of him."

"I think I will cancel my lease in DC. I plan on getting married after we finish this mission and will need a larger place than the one I have now. No sense in paying for it while we are gone," Ernest said.

"Congratulations!" we all said in unison.

"Okay, let's take a look at Ms. Reza Pahlavi," I said, ripping open the package from Mike.

"Wow! I would like to capture her alive!" Percy exclaimed. He was the only one of the group who did not have a steady girlfriend.

Pahlavi was indeed beautiful. She had long black hair, a beautifully structured face and full lips. She was relatively tall, standing at least two inches above Mahmoud in the photograph and had a slender but well proportioned figure. She looked as if she could be a model. Later, we would find, that was exactly what she was.

"Let's hit the streets. Everyone go back to your rooms, get ready and we will meet here in Larry's room in thirty minutes. Make sure your handguns are loaded and take some extra ammunition. Remember they are going to be looking for us, too. And they know where we are now, I'm sure. We are probably being watched. We just need to be sure we don't get lured into a situation we can't handle. Be alert and watch for an ambush. With this photo, we should make some progress today and if we get close, they will be waiting on us," I cautioned.

We met back at Larry's at 2:15 and decided to stay together in the same general vicinity, but split into two teams so we could cover more territory. We would start in the Soho district.

"I think we will be lucky today," Steve said as left the room to catch the subway down to Soho.

He would prove to be right as well as wrong. We would find them, but it would cost us significantly when we did. We got off the subway a little before 3:00 PM.

CHAPTER THIRTEEN

"Okay, let's split up. One group go down the side of this street, the other the other side. Don't get too far apart and keep your cell phones live. Talk to everyone you see in this neighborhood, mention the names and show Reza's picture. If you get information to follow up on, call. We'll regroup before we confront anyone," I instructed. We had made another copy of the picture of Reza and Mahmoud at the hotel.

Ashton and I, along with Thom and Steve were in one group with Larry, Darby, Ernest and Percy in the other group. We took the right side of the street. They took the left. It was a rundown neighborhood off the main Broadstreet thoroughfare. There were shops along the walkway interspersed with rows of tenement houses. The streets were relatively crowded with pedestrians. This is where we had run into quite a number of Middle Eastern people yesterday. Most of the shops were run by people from places like Pakistan, Afghanistan, Sudan, and Iran. There were a few people from Egypt, Saudi Arabia, Iraq and Indonesia. They had migrated to this country to share a piece of the American dream. They were a diverse group that shared the faith of Islam, a peaceful religion. There was a mosque in the center of the neighborhood. The vast majority were legal immigrants who were happy and proud to be American. Most were U.S. citizens. Hidden among the buildings and throngs of people though were the fanatical terrorists whose main goal was to destroy the United States. It was our job to find them.

We were a third of the way in canvassing our side of the street without any admitted recognition of the names or the photo. A call to the other team, who we could see occasionally on the other side of the street, indicated they had not been successful either. Then we came to a shop that sold leather goods. The proprietor looked to be about 70 years of age.

"Sir, I am with the FBI," Steve said as we approached him standing behind the counter. Steve showed the gentlemen his ID and introduced himself and the rest of us.

"Good day, gentlemen. What can I do for you?" he asked.

We showed him the names and the picture, explaining that they were wanted for questioning relative to a potential terrorist plot. He looked at the information thoughtfully.

"Tahmineh!! Take care of the front. I need to talk to these gentlemen in the back," he called to an elderly lady that we took to be his wife. She came to the front, smiled at us, and he motioned us to follow him through a door to a room in the back. The room was large with stocks of leather goods hanging on racks and it had a musty, leathery smell. He continued to a small office and led us through that to a room in the back with a large dining type table a number of comfortable looking chairs and a small table with a coffee pot on it. There was a small refrigerator in this room also. They must use this room for a break and conference room. He motioned us to be seated.

"Could I get you coffee? And Tahmineh makes wonderful cookies." He offered us a tray of sugar cookies and poured coffee for us after we graciously accepted his offerings.

"My name is Ibrahim Hassan. You met my wife Tahmineh. I came to this country thirty-seven years ago from Lebanon to get away from the constant strife going on in that part of the world. I was a young man of 32 at the time. Initially, I worked in a restaurant, then as a cab driver before starting this leather business with Tahmineh who I met and married when I was thirty-five. We had a child—our only child. She was a beautiful girl. You remind me of her," he smiled at Ashton.

"We are of the Muslim faith, as most of the people in this neighborhood are. So many of your people misunderstand our religion," he shook his head sorrowfully.

"Yes Sir. We know that most of the people of your faith are good, law abiding citizens and that your religion teaches peace, tolerance and hospitality," I said.

"Yes, it is the fanatics of all of our religions that taint the way we view each other. Do you know that the three monotheistic faiths of the world — Judaism, Christianity and Islam — are all descended from Abraham? We are all brothers. It has been determined through DNA analysis that male Jews and Middle Eastern Arabs---among them Syrians, Palestinians and Lebanese, for example, share a common set of ancestors. We all serve the same God. And yet we kill each other because we worship that God in a different manner and through different historical translations and perspective. The teachings that should be important to all of us are really very similar between our faiths. It would be interesting to know if our God is laughing or crying from our efforts to prove our way is the only way to Him," Ibrahim said, sadly shaking his head again.

"Well, Sir, you are obviously more versed in theology than we are, but I, for one, can't disagree with your thoughts," Larry said.

"Well, I'm sure you gentlemen are far to busy to listen to the ramblings of an old man. I am an American of Lebanese heritage. I may help. I have seen the men you seek in this neighborhood. They have been in this shop and made purchases. Saeb Sedeqi is an Iranian and I believe Mohammad Karhtam is a Saudi. I do not know the girl or the man in the photograph with her. She is very beautiful and also reminds me of my daughter," he said, lowering his head.

"Sir, earlier you said your daughter was beautiful. She must be close to the age of Ms. Reza Pahlavi. Perhaps they know of each other. Would we be able to talk to her?" I asked.

"No. She was killed in the World Trade Center bombing September 11, 2001. She was an accountant in a brokerage firm on the 98th floor of Tower 2. She was 32, a beautiful girl, in love, just starting her life," the old man whispered, tears coming to his eyes.

"I'm very sorry," I said. "Sir, thank you so much for helping us. One more question and we will let you get back to your business."

"If these people are the same kind who killed my daughter in the name of our God, I will help you if I can," Ibrahim said.

"Thank you. We sincerely appreciate that. Can you give us any idea where we might find these men?" I asked.

"Oh, yes. I know where they live, approximately," he said. His words stunned us.

"Where!?" we asked in unison.

"Well, as I said, they have been in here a few times. They never said much but, trying to be friendly, I asked them one day if they lived in the neighborhood. The one called Saeb responded that they lived in an apartment over Luganos restaurant. Mohammed looked at him sternly and Saeb looked like he had made a major blunder. They quickly paid for their purchase and left. I thought that was a little strange at the time. I was just trying to make conversation, not be nosey. I hadn't thought about that until you gentlemen came in asking about them."

"How far is Lugano's from here!?" Thom asked.

"Oh, about four blocks down on the left," Ibrahim responded.

We all had the same thought. The left side of the street was where our other team was working! We had been here at least fifteen minutes. Unless they had run into a situation where someone had information and was willing to share it, as we had, they would be there by now! If they were asking questions in that part of the neighborhood, it would be possible our two suspects would be tipped off. It was just as possible that Saeb and Mohammed already knew we were canvassing the neighborhood and would be setting up an ambush when we got around to finding their lair. In either case, our people could be in danger. We needed to be there!

"Thanks again, Mr. Hassan! We have a team down in that area right now. We better go join them!" I said as we rushed out.

"Try to call Larry on the cell phone!" I shouted to Thom as we raced down the street.

Larry answered. Before Thom could speak, Larry excitedly reported, "Hey guys!! We think we've found where they live! Come on down! We're going up now to their room so they can't get away in case someone has tipped them off! It's on the left over a restaurant called Lug — Holy shit!"

The phone apparently dropped and clattered to the floor. In the background we heard a sound that sounded like a thud and a half scream and half gurgle, immediately followed by two thundering shots. Then silence. We were running at breakneck speed now and were almost there. Lugano's was just across the street. We ran across and rushed up a set of wooden stairs beside the restaurant that appeared to lead to apartments overhead. Thom's cell phone crackled, but we didn't stop to answer. We had our firearms drawn and ready as we ran through the door and entered an enclosed hallway that led to another interior set of stairs leading up to the four apartments on the top floor. We heard another shot.

Suddenly, almost running into us was a swarthy man racing down the stairs. He fitted the description of one of the suspects and his shirt was covered with blood spatters and he had a pistol in his hand. We didn't stop to talk. Ashton was the first to react with a quick shot that struck right above his left eye. My shot followed to his chest before the sound of Ashton's shot had finished echoing through the hallway. He tumbled down the steps landing at our feet. He was dead before he ever hit the floor.

We cautiously moved up to the landing. Then we saw Ernest, crumpled on the floor beside an open utility room door at the entrance to the hallway from which the four room doors fronted. I felt Ashton shrink and shudder beside me. Out of the corner of my eye I saw Larry, Darby and Percy standing in front of the second room door, weapons in their hands, with a silent, stunned look of disbelief on their faces. My gaze came back to Ernest and was fixed on the horror at my feet.

Something had almost completely severed his head and it was lying at a grotesque angle to the rest of his body. What looked to be gallons of slippery blood pooled around where he lay and had begun to drip down the stairway like little red rivulets. There was a curved Arabic sword lying beside him, splotched with crimson. Looking up again, I could see the lower part of another body resting halfway in and half out of the doorway. One arm was at a distorted angle behind him and his glazed stare seemed to be looking up into distant nothing.

"What happened?" I half whispered, wanting to, but not being able to take my eyes off of the carnage at my feet. After a long moment, Darby responded.

"A lady next door recognized Saeb and Mohammed's names. She said she had cleaned for them and had heard them converse with each other and seen correspondence with their names. She was certain that was who it was and showed us how to get up to their apartment and told us which one it was. She didn't like them. She said they never paid her for the cleaning she did last week and were very unfriendly. She asked us to try to get her money if we saw them. She told us they were in and out frequently and sometimes were gone for days, but she had seen them arrive just minutes ago."

"That's when we called you," Larry picked up the story. "We were afraid they might have seen us talking to the woman and seen her pointing out directions to their place. Rather than take a chance on losing them, we thought it best to at least block the door until you arrived and, if necessary in case they had sighted us, take them into custody. We knew you couldn't be far away."

"What happened next?" I asked.

"We started up the stairs. At the head of the stairs when you reach the landing there was the utility closet behind you. The door was ajar and I noticed some mops and brooms but it was dark in the closet. Darby and I had taken the lead as we approached the landing and headed towards the apartment door in front of us. Expecting a potential problem, we wanted our better shooters up front. Percy was behind us and Ernest was in the rear. We had gotten almost to the apartment door when Ernest, bringing up the rear, passed the utility closet. All of a sudden, we heard the door bang open and looked back. This guy had sprung out of the closet with that sword and, before Ernest or any of us knew what was happening, he took a vicious swing at Ernest and----"

Larry continued, "Yeah. No sooner than he had jumped poor Ernie, the apartment door burst open and the other guy stood there with a gun. He took a shot at me and would have blown my head off, but I had turned to see what was happening down on the landing. Before he could get a second shot off, Percy blasted him. Damn! I'm glad Darby trained him well."

"That's about it, Dawson. While Percy and Darby were taking care of the apartment guy, I had started towards the steps to get the one who killed Ernest. He pulled a gun, fired a wild shot towards me and started running down the steps. That's when you came in. Sounds like you got him," Larry finished.

We called the police and an ambulance. I would later contact Mike and Ernest's girlfriend. She was devastated. As Ernest had said, they were planning to get married as soon as he completed this mission. We had found Mahmoud, Saeb and Mohammed and they were all dead now. Except for the bit of information we recovered in Mahmoud's room, we had not attained any leads to the laser other than the likelihood that it was being developed in Jakarta, Indonesia. We had only one more lead to follow here before heading to Jakarta. That was to try to find Reza Pahlavi.

In the meantime, we had lost Ernest, one of our eight team members and one who had become a close friend to all of us. We were sad. We were mad. We were now seven.

CHAPTER FOURTEEN

That night at dinner together there was a solemn mood. The loss of Ernest and the manner in which he had died cast an aura of gloom over all of us.

"What did Mike say when you told him about Ernest?" Larry asked.

"He was saddened and horrified, just as we all are," I said.

"Well, where do we go from here? I, for one, would like to avenge his death," Darby said.

"Mike thinks we have put a big dent into their operations in New York by taking out Mahmoud, Sedeqi and Khartam. For security reasons, Infama's cells are usually small, from four to eight people. Although there could be more than one cell in New York, they probably don't communicate with each other and may not even know the other cell or cells exist until such time as they might need to know in order to work together to accomplish a mission. Mike thinks it's possible that Pahlavi is the only remaining member of this particular cell. There has been no other information or names mentioned in association with these four that would indicate otherwise," I replied.

"Is he ready for us to go to Jakarta, or do we stay here and continue to hunt for Reza?" Steve asked.

"He thinks we should stay for a reasonable amount of time to continue the search for her. Obviously these four were connected to the anticipated attempt to use the laser. Their loss would tend to delay the implementation even if the weapon were ready for that," I said.

"I doubt that it is ready. There would be quite a lot of development and testing work to do to bring it to that stage," Ashton volunteered.

"Plus it would be unlikely the President would visit Indonesia. Jakarta must be seen as a safe place to finish the production of the weapon. It seems obvious to me that, once completed, it would be moved to a location that the President would more likely be exposed to. D.C., New York, L.A., Houston, Chicago, Atlanta or one of the Western capitol cities that he might be expected to be in over the next few months is probably where they would want to have it in place to use," Thom said.

"I think you are right, Thom. The best place to achieve their publicity desires as well as the place that would present the highest number of practical targets, would be right here at home. The next best place would probably be a European or Asian city where it would be an additional embarrassment to the host government if the President of the United States were assassinated on their soil. London, Moscow or Tokyo would be the most likely targets outside the U.S., I think," Percy joined in.

"Well, anyway, Mike thinks it would be worthwhile to find Reza Pahlavi before we go to Jakarta, on the chance we could attain information that would help us find the weapon when we got there," I said.

We had gotten a table in the back of the dimly lit little Italian restaurant where we had chosen to eat and made sure that we could see the door. All of us were edgy after what had happened today. But the remaining seven of us were drawing even closer together and becoming increasingly more confident of and secure with each other. Ashton had reaffirmed her marksmanship and value to our team by stopping Ernest's killer coming down the stairs with her instant reaction and a clean shot to the head. Percy had made a contribution by probably saving Larry and Darby's life with his quick reaction in disposing of the one in the doorway before he could get off another shot. We were a diverse group, but we meshed together as one. I was optimistic that we would be successful in our quest.

We spent the next two and a half weeks walking over most of Manhattan, talking to people, showing Reza's picture. No luck. She was such a strikingly beautiful girl, we thought finding her would be easy. Anyone who had seen her would likely remember her. We were wrong. Even if she had skipped town due to the demise of her friends and her possible knowledge that we knew about her and would come looking for her, we thought someone would remember her and lead us to where she lived so we could search the place. She must have led a very secluded life or gone out in public in some sort of disguise.

Mike had decided we should go on to Jakarta if we did not find her in the next few days. We had almost given up, but would find that our luck would change Saturday, January 25, 2003.

Ashton and I, over the two and a half weeks after Ernest's death, had grown even closer together and even more in love. We were with the team all day and into the night most days but later at night, when we were alone, it was nice. We talked, made love, snuggled together and whispered secrets and promises of the future into each other's ears before dropping off to sleep. When I would wake at night, it gave me a sense of warmth having her there beside me, sleeping contently. I would look at her in the dark and be thankful to be there with such a perfect girl. In the mornings she looked even more beautiful, with her rumpled hair and quirky little frown when I woke her up. She was not the easiest person to arouse in the morning.

Saturday morning I took a shower then gently shook Ashton who was still asleep on her side. She rolled over on her tummy. I shook her again.

"Love, leave me alone. I don't want to get up yet," she said sleepily.

"We don't have to meet the others until 8:00. You still have 45 minutes, so I'll let you sleep another ten minutes," I said, still standing over her.

"I don't want to sleep. I want you to make love to me," she smiled and turned on her back. The sheet slid away only covering a part of her. We slept naked and the sheet had slid off her top. One of her pretty legs was exposed with the rest of the sheet resting between her legs, hiding the love that laid between them. I was still naked coming out of the shower.

"Do we have time?" I asked, knowing that it didn't matter now. I couldn't resist the temptation. If we were late, the others would have to wait.

"You know I don't take long. I only need twenty minutes. Besides, you want me, too. I can tell," she said sexily, eyeing my dick which was beginning to stiffen.

I pulled the rest of the sheet aside and settled on my knees between her legs. She bent forward and placed her soft lips on my now rigid cock, running her tongue lightly around my shaft. Then she thrust her mouth around it and slowly took it within her. I felt like I could not have gotten harder while she began to move her mouth up and down and slightly sucked when she got to the tip. When I thought I was going to explode, she quickly disengaged, lay on her back and spread her legs. I was still on my knees looking down at the inviting opening between her legs. She took her hands and spread the lips of her pussy so I could see the moist pink little hole waiting for me.

When I began to enter her, she thrust upward sharply and grabbed my hips, continuing to thrust herself into me at a frantic pace. I couldn't wait any longer and exploded violently into her. She gasped and continued to move erratically, now coming to an orgasm herself.

"See, that didn't take long did it? I'm going to take my shower now. Be back in a minute! We won't be late," she said and hopped up, heading for the bathroom.

I just lay there spent and content. She had made sure it didn't take long. She was so good. I was still lying there when she got out of the shower.

"Okay, get up and get dressed! You were soooo good," she bent over and kissed me.

"I don't know if I can after that. You know you really had me turned on don't you?" I asked.

"Yes, but if you don't get ready I will go down by myself and tell them why you're late." She laughed and started brushing her damp hair.

We were down in the lobby at 7:55. Everyone had arrived by 8:05 and we walked down the street to a café for breakfast.

"I need to get a haircut today somewhere. Either that or a dog tag," Percy said.

"Yeah, we're all getting a little shaggy. Guys we've covered about all of the area between lower Manhattan and midtown. Let's concentrate in this area today, just on the chance Pahlavi might be recognized. After all, she obviously was very friendly with Mahmoud and he was staying here at the Salisbury. We're fast running out of options. If we don't find her in the next few days, I think we will be heading to Indonesia and it would be nice to talk to her before we go. I think there is a hair cut and styling shop down on Avenue of the Americas. We can stop there. It will be a little pricey, but your next cut may be in Jakarta," I said.

"Sounds good," Thom said. The others nodded agreement.

We hit the streets and spent the morning without any recognition from anyone relative to the photograph or names we showed to store clerks, passersby, taxi drivers, policemen, businessmen, secretaries, everyone we could get to stop and talk to us. We worked in teams of two, but stayed on the same block, close together. After lunch, we decided to go ahead and get the haircuts since we were close to the shop I had remembered from one of my previous visits.

"How do you want me to have my hair styled, Love?" Ashton asked me. The shop was not busy and could handle four of us at a time while the other three waited. Darby, Thom and Steve would wait for the second turn while the rest of us were getting cuts.

"Don't change a thing! I like your hair long, the length it is now. Just get the ends trimmed and shaped," I said.

"What about a butch cut?" she asked teasingly. The look in my eyes told her the answer.

The four of us were just about through with our cuts when Darby let out an exclamation and jumped up from his chair. They had been browsing through the magazines while we were being attended to. Most of the magazines were dull fashion and styling magazines, but that's all there was to read.

"Damn!!" Darby exclaimed and thrust one of the magazines in front of my face. The magazine was called W and he had turned to a page advertising Moschino Parfum. There, in a full length pose was a sexy looking beautiful model. It was a dead ringer for the girl in the photograph we had. There was no mistaking it. It was Reza Pahlavi!

"Let me see that!" Percy said. Darby handed it to him. His eyes glazed over. "Damn! She's beautiful. I know she's a bad guy, uh, girl, but let me question her and take her into custody. Please— You know, it would give me a thrill just to talk to a beautiful girl like this, even if I have to take her to jail afterwards," he pleaded.

"Okay, Percy," I laughed. "You can be the lead interrogator on this one. And when we cuff her, you can do that too," I said.

"Thanks Dawson," he grinned.

"First, we've got to find her, though. While you guys get your cuts, I'll call W's publishing office and find who the modeling agency is that handles Ms. Pahlavi. They likely know how to get in touch with her," I said.

I was in luck. A lady at the publishing office was familiar with Reza. Their advertisers had used her frequently. She told me where the agency was. We were only a few blocks away. After the others had finished getting their cuts, we headed to the agency for our ultimate meeting with Reza Pahlavi.

CHAPTER FIFTEEN

We arrived at the Manhattan Modeling, Inc. agency about 2:30 PM. Since it was Saturday, we didn't know whether it would be open or not and doubted any of the models would be there if they were. The building had a granite facade and looked to be quite large. This was expensive real estate, too. They must be doing quite well. We were somewhat surprised to find that the agency was, in fact, open.

"Good afternoon, Ma'am. Is your manager here?" I asked the receptionist upon entering the building.

The lady, who looked to be in her mid-fifties, raised her eyebrow and said somewhat haughtily, "We don't have a manager. The owner, Ms. Attenbaum, is in."

"May we see her, please? We are with the government and would like to ask her some brief questions concerning one of your models," I asked politely.

"I'm sorry. She is a very busy person. Perhaps if you would state more clearly your business, you could make an appointment to see her next month after she returns from Paris. She will be leaving Monday," the lady replied. It was clear she was done with us as she answered the phone and took her time about returning her attention to us. I motioned for Steve to intervene.

Before Steve could say anything, a tall beautiful blonde who looked to be in her early twenties came in the front door. She must have been one of the models from the agency.

"Hi Alice! Is Ms. A. in? I need to sign the contract for Ralph Lauren. My photo shoot starts next week," the blonde said.

"Yeah, Jeana. She's in her office. I don't think she has anyone with her right now," Alice, the receptionist said.

I would like to interview some of the models on the chance some of them could give us information on Reza Pahlavi in addition to what we may find out from Ms. Attenbaum. Steve produced his ID and went into action.

"Ma'am, I am with the FBI and my associates also work for government security agencies. We are part of a task force looking into threats to our national security. One of your models may have information that would be helpful to our investigation. We must see Ms. Attenbaum for a few moments right now —without delay," he said politely but firmly.

"Very well. I will let her know, but she is very busy," the receptionist responded in a huffy manner. She called and , presumably, spoke to Ms. Attenbaum.

"She will see you for a few moments, but I must tell you —" Alice spoke to us after hanging up.

"We know. She is very busy," Larry finished her sentence for her. We followed her directions through the lobby to an office on the end of a hallway with lettering proclaiming that Mary Attenbaum, Proprietor resided there. We went in the open door and saw a huge, well appointed office with life size photos of models on the walls. Ms. Attenbaum was seated behind a large solid cherry desk. She was a tall, angular faced lady with a stern expression, probably in her late fifties or early sixties.

"Yes, gentlemen, and lady. What can I do for you? I am really very busy," she asked.

We introduced ourselves and told her we would like to question her on one of her models, Reza Pahlavi. She seemed taken aback.

"Reza!? She couldn't possibly be involved in anything illegal! She is so quiet. And her features are beautiful. I see you have a copy of the thing she did for Moschino in "W" magazine. She is magnificent! I just arranged a contract for her with a major clothier here in Manhattan. Her career can do nothing but go up. I won't be a party to anything that might sidetrack her. You know how sponsors are. If there is a hint of anything wrong with anyone representing their product or company, they tend to shy away for fear of being embarrassed. Just why do you want to talk to her?" Ms. Attenbaum questioned.

"Well, we know she was an associate of people who have been involved with wrongful transfer of sensitive information and plots to assassinate the President of the United States, as well as other Western country leaders," Larry volunteered.

"Yes. Her involvement may well be innocent with these people. But circumstantial evidence indicates otherwise. At any rate, she may be able to shed some light on the people and organization that we are seeking. We need to talk to her," I said.

"Why did you come here to find her? Couldn't you have talked to her at home or elsewhere? I have my business to protect. We are one of the top three modeling agencies in Manhattan. I can't believe Reza has done wrong as you suggest or is in anyway involved in the things you speak of. I find that preposterous! But I don't especially want my agency or any of my clients to be connected with something like this," she said.

"We have been searching for her without success. Quite by accident we saw this layout in "W" and the publisher directed us to you," I responded.

"Can you tell us where we could find her? Does she list a home address with you?" Steve asked. About that time the blonde came in.

"Here's the contract, Ms. A. It's signed. I'll let you know how the shoot comes out. I've worked with that cameraman before. He gives me the creeps, but he's good. See you when you get back from Paris!" She dropped a folder on Ms. A's desk and started to the door.

"Thanks Jeana," Ms. A said as she exited.

"By the way, we would like to interview any of the other models who have had contact with Pahlavi. Anything they may be able to add to the information you may give us and what we might find from Reza herself might prove helpful," I said.

"Well, I can't help in that effort. I won't release any of my girl's addresses unless you have a warrant for that information. You understand why that information must be confidential. Many of these girls are quite famous in their profession and , if we loosely guarded their residence information, all kinds of weirdos could bother them. And I would prefer you not talk to them here at my place of business," Ms. Attenbaum responded tersely.

"Very well. If necessary to add to the information we need, we can attain warrants for that information. Now, back to Ms. Pahlavi. Can you tell us where to find her?" I persisted.

"She's here today. At the moment, she is interviewing a potential client in the conference room down the hall. This could be a great opportunity for her and I must not allow her to be disturbed. Also, I can not allow you to approach her on these premises. I am very busy in preparation for my trip. Now, I must ask you to leave." Ms. Attenbaum was drawing the line.

"Ma'am, we have authority to make an arrest of a suspect at any place and any time we find them. We will want to question you and others with the agency after we question Pahlavi to see if you can add to our knowledge about her and her associates. Right now, we are going to take her into custody since she is here," I said firmly and we all rose to proceed to the conference room. We were all shocked and elated to find her here on this day. In light of Ms. A's resistance, it was probably fortunate that she was here. Otherwise, she may have been tipped off and we might have never found her.

"I see. Alright. Go ahead. But I will be checking with the authorities on this. And I have some political connections. You had better be sure you are right," Ms. A said as we began to exit.

"One moment, Ms....Smyth, is it?" she continued before we got completely out of her office.

"Yes?" Ashton asked.

"You are not quite thin enough or tall enough, but are never the less very nicely built, and you have an intriguing face. It's not often that I chance upon someone in the public that has the beauty to do well in this business. Why don't you talk to me after this nasty little business you are involved in?" Ms. A inquired.

"No, thanks. I'm happy what I'm doing," Ashton laughed as we exited the office.

"That came across more as a business proposition than a compliment. Do you think I'm not skinny enough?" Ashton whispered as we walked down the hall towards the conference room.

"Well—," I teased.

"I guess you'll be sleeping by yourself tonight," she said, jabbing me in the ribs. We were just outside the conference room door now.

"Okay, what's our plan, Dawson? Should we burst in on her conference or wait until it's over?" Larry asked.

"Courtesy would say we wait. But remember that she very likely is a part of the same group that murdered Ernest and she very well could be armed and dangerous. I'm not convinced that Ms. A. hasn't already called the conference room and warned her. I think we should go on in and be very careful. We won't barge in with drawn guns, but have your hands near your weapons in case she has a gun in her purse. These people are fanatics. And remember, we promised Percy the takedown," I smiled.

I opened the door quickly. Larry and Steve squeezed in right beside me moving to the right and left. Percy was behind them. Darby, Thom and Ashton followed. Two men and a strikingly beautiful girl who we recognized as Reza Pahlavi looked up sharply as we entered their domain. One of the men was very effeminate looking in green slacks, a pink shirt and classy black loafers. The other I would take to be a lawyer with his big briefcase and natty dress.

"What is the meaning of this intrusion!?" Reza asked with a slight accent, rising from her chair. The two men just froze in their astonishment.

"Ms. Pahlavi?" I asked.

"That is correct," she responded.

"We are with a specially appointed task force on law enforcement. Mr. Whitt is with the FBI. We have an open warrant to pursue and detain people suspected of being involved in or having knowledge of certain activities that would be detrimental to our national security. We would like to question you relative to your association with certain individuals," I said. Steve displayed his credentials.

For a brief moment their was a flash of shock and anger on Reza's beautiful face. Then she quickly regained her composure.

"I'm sorry. I'm sure you have mistaken information and I am involved in a business discussion with these gentlemen. You will have to contact me at a later date. Ms. Attenbaum can set up an appointment for you. Now, please leave us alone so I can conclude my discussion. Perhaps on Monday if you wish to speak to me," she said very firmly.

Yes, I thought. By Monday you will have disappeared. "Ma'am, I'm afraid you will have to reschedule your appointment with these gentlemen. We must talk to you now, and I would ask that you gentlemen excuse us and leave so we can" I said just as firmly.

"Just a moment, Sir!" The one I had judged to be a lawyer finally came to life and jumped up from his chair, speaking in a confrontational tone.

"Ms. Pahlavi just informed you that you could speak to her at a more convenient time. My name is Robert Attison, attorney at law. Unless you have a warrant allowing you immediate detention for cause, I suggest you follow her advice. Just what charges are you prepared to present to Ms. Pahlavi? We are in a business discussion and my time and that of my client, Mr. Dudley, is very valuable, as is Ms. Pahlavi's. As a witness to your despicable action, I am prepared to file suit on Ms. Pahlavi's behalf for unlawful use of your authority if you can't present just cause for your action!" Attison continued, puffing up his chest and handing me his business card.

I had had enough of his theatrics. "In answer to your specific question, Mr. Attison, we can cite suspicion to accessory to the fact of capital murder, subversive activity, perhaps illegal entry to the U.S. and any number of lesser charges. Our authority to pursue this case is granted to us by the President of the United States through the offices of the FBI, Secret Service and CIA. If you have a problem with this, I suggest you follow it up in court at a later date. At this time, I must again ask you and Mr. Dudley to leave immediately. Otherwise I will have you escorted out by Mr. Peters," I nodded to Darby and he edged closer to Attison and Dudley who had remained seated and looked like he wanted to run out of the room.

Attison paused for a second, then apparently decided he didn't want to get into a confrontation with Darby.

"Very well! I can assure you that you will hear from me!" he exclaimed in a final burst of belligerence as he grabbed his briefcase and stormed out of the room with Dudley close behind. Reza had remained standing with an impassive look on her face.

"Okay, Percy. Ms. Pahlavi, this is Percy Thackett with the State Department He will lead off with some questions we want to ask you," I said. Percy approached her, obviously still stunned by her beauty, but fully prepared to do his job in a professional manner.

"Ms. Pahlavi," he started, "were you acquainted with Abdul Mahmoud, Saeb Sedeqi, or Mohammad Khartam and do you know of or are you acquainted with Walid Alziddi?"

"No." she replied impassively.

"Let me show you a photograph of you and Abdul Mahmoud," Percy said, producing the photograph. I noticed a slight change in her composure.

"Perhaps I did meet this gentleman at one time. In my business, I am photographed with a lot of people, many of them strangers," she replied.

"Yes ma'am. Well, if you did remember this gentleman, you would probably know that he is recently deceased," Percy pressed on. A noticeable change in her expression now took place.

"What do you mean!?" she asked.

"When we found him about three weeks ago he blew himself up, trying to take some of us with him," Percy responded.

You could now see genuine surprise and, I thought, anger and hurt on her face. Was it possible that she and the person who appeared to be her lover in the photograph had been used to long periods of not communicating, perhaps for security reasons, and she might not yet be aware of his demise? That was a real possibility. The news of his death obviously took her by surprise, causing her to completely drop the guard on her emotions.

"Darling, may I see that photograph again, please?" Reza smiled seductively, seeming to completely regain her composure.

I thought Percy was going to lose it then. He blushed and fumbled in his pocket for the photo, approached Reza, stood alongside of her and held the picture up so she could see it closely.

All of a sudden Reza turned sideways and viciously swung her leg up, connecting with Percy right in the groin.

"You bastards!!!" she screamed as Percy doubled over in pain and dropped to the floor. Darby and Thom immediately jumped into action and pinned her. She continued to struggle, kicking and scratching at them until they finally were able to subdue her. Percy moaned and began to throw up.

We waited until Percy was able to finally regain his footing and limp to a chair where he slumped, holding his hands between his legs.

"Oh God! I will never have babies now! I think I'm neutered. I'll talk like a girl for the rest of my life! Oh, shit. I feel sick," he finally managed to say before he started throwing up again.

After a long wait, we helped Percy out of the room and took Reza out handcuffed. Ms. A. was standing outside of her office when we came by on the way out. She just stared at our little parade with the handcuffed model and Darby supporting Percy down the hall.

"Ms. Attenbaum, you may want to have the janitor clean up the conference room. Mr. Thackett here had a little accident," I said as we walked by.

When we got back to the hotel with our prisoner we tried to interrogate Reza but she totally clammed up. Finally, after four hours, the federal marshals we had called after talking to Mike arrived to transport her to D.C.

Before they left I asked Percy, who had recovered somewhat by then from his encounter with Reza, if he wanted a last shot at interviewing her before they left.

"Fuck you!" was his response.

CHAPTER SIXTEEN

7:30 AM Sunday the phone rang. We had planned on sleeping in today. I reached to the night stand and picked up the receiver. It was Mike.

"Hey Mike! You're in to work early on a Sunday. What's up?" I asked sleepily.

"I've been up all night interviewing the pretty girl you sent to me last night. The marshals arrived with her last night about nine o'clock. I decided to keep her up most of the night to see if she would tell us anything. Sometimes if you interrogate them immediately after they are caught, before they have a chance to think or conjure up stories that would be misleading, is the best time to talk to them," he said.

"Did she tell you anything worthwhile?" I asked.

"At first nothing. Maybe she thought we couldn't hold her and was counting on getting sprung, or maybe she was just trying to be tough. At any rate, we were doing some checking on her and found that she was in the country illegally on an expired visa, so we had grounds to hold her. When we informed her of that, she didn't break immediately, but about 4:00 this morning she started answering some of the questions," Mike replied.

"What did you find out?" I asked.

"Well, she tried to claim innocence in being involved with Infama or the activities of her buddy, but she did finally admit that she had a romantic relationship with Mahmoud. We pressed on and she claimed to have met him at a mutual friend's one night and that things just progressed from there," he answered.

"Did you believe her?" I questioned.

"At first she was believable. But I had sensed that she had been very much in love with the guy and decided to push her button to see if she slipped up. She did," Mike answered.

"What did you say to her?" I was curious.

"I lied. I told her that before Mahmoud pushed the button to blow himself up he asked you guys to inform his wife who he told you still resided in Pakistan that he had sacrificed his life as a martyr to Allah."

"Wow!! What a lie! How did she react to that?"

"She exploded. She jumped up and said that was a lie, that she and Mahmoud and the others had trained together, been screened and came here together. She knew he wasn't married. She described me with some choice expletives for trying to make her believe that bullshit. I think that as soon as the angry words got out of her mouth she realized she had been tricked," Mike responded.

"Yeah. I'm surprised she let herself get duped like that," I said.

"Me too. But she did have strong emotions about the guy. I had already figured that out. And she was tired. Remember, it was four in the morning and she had been through a trying day. In the state she was in, she just let her emotions overrule her brain," Mike continued.

"Anything else?" I asked.

"No. After that admission I just smiled and told her we would call it a day and get back to further questions Monday. She knows now that we know she is involved and will be pressing her for specific information. We'll see how she reacts."

"Do you want us to go on to Jakarta now?" I asked.

"We need to get the team there soon, but plan on leaving about the first of the month. That will give you four or five more days to talk to some of the other models and Ms. Attenbaum. I am faxing you the specific warrants you need to force her to open her files on Reza. You need to find where she lived and search her apartment. You may find information that would prove valuable in Indonesia. Plus that gives me more time to work on Reza to see what else I can pull out of her," Mike said.

"Okay. We won't be able to start on our end until tomorrow. I may have to serve the warrant on Ms. A. at the airport. She may decide to postpone her visit to Paris. I'll tell her that if no one at her place knows where the personal information files are, we will have to ransack her office until we find what we want. I'll bet she will decide to stay. I'll try to call her today. I've already checked and she has an unlisted phone, but we can get around that with the phone company," I said.

"Okay. Oh, one last thing, Dawson---," Mike said before hanging up.

"What's that?"

"Before we broke off our conversation with Reza, her attitude was defiant. She realized that she was in deep shit due to her slip of the tongue. The last thing she said was that she was glad she kicked that prissy little State Department puke in the balls. She hoped that they were the size of grapefruits today. She sure is a pretty girl, but she has a mean temper."

"I'll tell Percy. He'll be happy to know she's thinking about him. Bye Mike," I laughed.

I was telling Ashton about the conversation when the phone rang again. It was for Ashton---a guy. I handed the phone to her.

"Skipper!! Where are you?" she exclaimed. There was a pause, then she said, "I don't know. I sure hope we can. Let me ask Dawson."

"Hon, it's Skipper. He's in New York on business with the bank. I had told him when I called him last week that we were staying at the Salisbury and he was hoping we were still here. He wants to know if we would be able to meet him for dinner tonight. He has to go back tomorrow afternoon," she explained.

"Sure. There's not anything we can do today anyway. I'd like to meet Skipper. Why don't we meet at Ruth's Chris about four blocks from here about 7:00 PM. We can walk down if it's not raining."

We spent the rest of the day sitting around with the rest of the team chatting and joking with each other. All of us but Percy got a big laugh out of Reza's last comment to Mike. I had to go to the phone company with Steve and talk to the weekend supervisor to get Ms. A.'s number. When I called her, she did decide to delay her trip rather than have us rummage through her office on our own. She was not a happy camper. It turned out to be a crisp but clear night and Ashton and I walked down to Ruth's Chris, arriving about ten before seven. I was alert during the walk. We thought we had eliminated the cell members that might have been gunning for us, but couldn't be sure.

"Ashton! Hi Sis!" A handsome young man rushed to us when we entered the waiting area and hugged Ashton. "You must be Dawson," he said, turning to me. We shook hands.

We had made reservations, so were seated immediately. We had a couple of drinks each, then ordered dinner. For me, they had agreed to sit in the smoking section, even though neither smoked. I had the opportunity to find out more about Ashton and her brother and liked what I saw. He appeared to be an intelligent, unassuming young man and seemed to have a great brotherly affection for his sister---or stepsister as it was. The conversation turned to their life at home before Ashton ran away.

"You know, Dawson, I didn't find out until much later about my father and what he did to Ashton. She told me that she had told you all about that. My mom finally told me. She's really Ashton's mother, my step mom, but I always felt like she was my mom. Even before I found out the truth about him, I had elected to stay with Mom after he left the house and they got a divorce. We were never close," Skipper related.

"Do you to ever talk to each other?" I asked.

"No. After the divorce he contacted me a couple of times. I talked to him, but he didn't show a lot of interest in me. He never asked me why I didn't go with him when he and Mom split. I didn't tell him that part of the reason was he never asked me to, and the other reason was that I probably wouldn't have gone if he had. Then I found out about him and Sis. The next time he called, I hung up on him."

"Has he tried to reach you since then?" I asked.

"No. He moved away somewhere. I don't even know where. He finished his twenty years in the army and took retirement. He had joined when he was eighteen, so he was only 38 at the time. He just disappeared after that. I don't care if I never see him again after what he did to Sis."

"I take it that you two were pretty close growing up," I stated.

"Yes. I was her younger brother. She took care of me when I was little. Mom and Dad weren't getting along much of that time and we had each other. Ashton was always getting scholastic awards, was captain of the cheerleading squad, voted as class Vice President, etc. I never got any recognition for anything except getting my Eagle Scout award. Ashton wanted to share her honors with me and got in the habit of using my name anytime she was eligible to get credit for any honor. She submitted an essay once in a contest the newspaper held and used my name. It won. I had a lot of compliments on that and felt guilty, but she made me take credit. She even did a lot of the Eagle Scout work and submitted it in my name."

"Now, that's not the whole truth Skipper! Sometimes I used your name to keep myself out of trouble!" Ashton laughed.

"Yeah. I do remember the time you signed my name on old Mrs. Brown's request for volunteers to clean out the dumpsters in the school parking lot. I got mad at that and you just claimed that you were so used to identifying yourself as me that you just put my name on the list without thinking. You were really just mad at me for telling Mom about me seeing you kissing Ralph in the car when he brought you home that night!" Skipper laughed.

"Seriously, we were close and still are. I'm proud of Skipper. He's done real well with the bank. It's really great to see you, brother," Ashton said.

We stayed and talked until about 11:00 PM, with Skipper and Ashton mostly recalling their childhood experiences, but including me in their conversations also. We told him we were part of a task force to investigate some missing documents from Livermore and would be leaving to go out of the country for a while soon, but didn't elaborate more than that. It was truly an enjoyable evening and it was nice to see Ashton enjoying herself so much with the opportunity to see her stepbrother. She was having a good time and she was prettier than ever, laughing and relaxing with the two of us.

The night broke up too soon and we had to say goodbye with promises to meet again the next time our paths crossed. I treasured a comment Ashton made as we parted.

"Skipper, you have to promise me that if Dawson ever asks me to marry him, you will be my best man. No matter where or when the wedding is, I want you there. Promise?" she said.

"I promise," Skipper replied.

"Is that a proposal, Love?" I asked.

"Well, you said you would never let me go. Do you want me to just live in sin with you forever?" she laughed.

"If you are going to propose, you have to get on your knee," I said.

"Please, please will you marry me?" Ashton said with mock gravity, dropping to her knees in front of me on the crowded New York street. Passersby stopped and stared at the pretty girl on her knees proposing to me. Skipper just grinned. He knew Ashton was capable of doing anything and didn't really care what other people thought.

"Hell, man! If you don't say yes, I'll take her!" one slightly inebriated man said as he walked by.

"Ashton Smyth," I said in a serious voice, "I accept your proposal for marriage. We will pick a date as soon as we finish this project we're on. And Skipper you definitely have to be there."

Ashton stood and I kissed her in the middle of the walk. We were oblivious to the crowds of people walking by who turned their heads to observe two people who were obviously very much in love.

"Do you really mean that?" Ashton asked, her eyes tearing.

"I promise. We will be "we" and I want you for my wife. Do you accept my serious proposal, my love?" I asked, wiping her tear and looking at her directly in the eye.

"I love you," was her answer. "Yes!!" We kissed again, holding each other for several minutes. Then we said our final goodbye to Skipper and returned to the hotel.

I knew that I was committed to my promise of love and marriage to this beautiful and exciting girl and was convinced she was also. I also knew that it might be difficult for us to fulfill that commitment we had made to each other. Only the future would let us find the answer to our love. At the time, I could only see the tip of the iceberg as far as just how demanding of our love for each other that fulfilling our desire would prove to be.

CHAPTER SEVENTEEN

Monday morning at 7:30 we met Ms. Attenbaum at her business. She had asked that we be there early, hoping we would be out of there before 9:00 AM when her models and the clients would start coming in. She was to be disappointed because we informed her we would like to talk to some of the other models after we finished going through the files on Reza. Actually, we would be done with the personnel file on Reza by 8:00. There was little relevant or truthful information in her file but there was a home address---1027 Barger Street, apartment 317---and that was what we really wanted anyway. There was also a phone number. We called and her sultry voice came on the answering machine after five rings, so it was a true address. It was important for models to be able to be contacted on short notice when a client indicated an interest in talking to them, so she could not have afforded to have given false phone and address info. We sat around in the conference room for an hour drinking coffee and waiting for the models that were scheduled in today to begin to arrive.

By 10:30 AM we had talked to four of the five models who were to be in that Monday. None could shed any light on Reza's private or personal life. They all indicated she was friendly, but aloof, and protected her private life emphatically. Any girl talk that led to discussions of boyfriends, places they liked to visit, personal thoughts on current events, etc. would cause Reza to leave the discussion or change the subject back to their professional activities. Answers to personal inquiries to her resulted in guarded or evasive non answers.

The last model that we would be able to interview came in at 11:00 AM. It was Jeana, the pretty blonde we had seen on Saturday.

"Ms. Brownlow, I'm Dawson Kohler with the Secret Service." I introduced the others and invited her to take a seat, telling her we had a few questions to ask her about Reza Pahlavi.

"You can call me Jeana," she smiled. "Ms. A. told me that you were investigating Reza and some of her associates who might have been involved in some security matters."

She was cute. A thought crossed my mind that, if I were charitable, I would have let Percy do the lead interview with this one. She was relaxed and not a suspect at all. His balls would most likely be safe. I smiled to myself and continued.

"Then you probably are aware that we would just like to know anything you might know about Reza's non-professional life —her acquaintances, habits, places she visited, anything that would allow us to know more about Reza outside of her career activities."

"Well, as I'm sure the other girls must have told you, Reza was a very private girl. She was good at what she did —the modeling part— beautiful and very photogenic. All the photographers liked to work with her. I don't think she had much of a personal life though," Jeana said thoughtfully.

"Why do you say that?" I asked.

"Well, I asked her to go to a party with me once. She did mention to me one time that her boyfriend was from Pakistan but they didn't see each other often. She told me his job kept him quite busy and, after work, she rarely left her apartment except to shop for groceries. I asked her trying to be nice because I felt that maybe they had not had the opportunity to meet people, considering they were both foreigners who had not been in this country too long," Jeana replied.

That probably explained why no one on the street recalled seeing her. "Did she say what his job was?" I asked.

"No, not specifically. When I asked her what he did, she just said he worked for an organization from somewhere overseas, I don't remember where, that had an interest in the States."

"Did she go to the party?"

"No. She said her boyfriend would be working and that he didn't like for her to go out without him," Jeana replied.

"Did you ever detect anything about her that you thought was strange or unusual?" I asked.

"Other than her being reclusive, only once. She had just started with the agency when the 911 thing happened at the World Trade Center and the Pentagon. Based on some comments she made, I gathered she had not been in the country too long. When that terrible event took place we were all shocked, angry, crying and glued to the TV. If you walked out to Broad Street, you could actually see the smoke coming from Lower Manhattan, even from here. Reza just seemed indifferent," she said.

"Did she comment on that event?" Larry asked.

"No, not really. We were so excited and horrified by what happened. She seemed to take it as pretty much a non-event. I just figured she might have come from a part of the world that these kind of things aren't all that unusual. There are a lot of places like that, you know —the Middle East, parts of Africa, Ireland."

We continued to question Jeana for another thirty minutes, not finding out anything of significance to our investigation. Finally we thanked her for her help and willingness to talk to us. I told her that if we thought of other questions, we would call. Otherwise we would not bother her again.

"Oh —one other thing," Jeana said just before she exited the conference room.

"What's that?" I asked.

"Well, I'm probably just being picky---but you said to tell you anything that I noticed unusual," she said hesitantly.

"Yes. Is there something else?" I pressed her.

"Well, I just thought a comment she made last month was strange. You remember when the President and First Lady lit the White House Christmas tree? Well, actually, they had a little kid press the button to turn the lights on."

"Yes, what about that?" I asked.

"Well, we were here in the conference room taking a break and they were showing the ceremony from the previous night on TV. The President made some comment about letting the light send a message to the world. Reza made a comment that just didn't make any sense. She usually didn't let her hair down, but she really laughed when she made the comment. It was almost like it was a private joke with her. The rest of us couldn't figure it out and thought it was strange at the time," Jeana said.

"What was the comment?" I asked.

"She said she was glad the President liked the light. It would most definitely send a message to the world. The way she laughed, we kept waiting for the punch line, but that was it. Anyway, I'll call if I remember anything else." Jeana said as she left.

We all exchanged knowing glances; I'm afraid we knew what the punch line was.

It was noon, so we said goodbye to Ms. Attenbaum and thanked her for her cooperation, then went to a café and got a quick lunch. Afterwards, we made our way to 1027 Barger Street and got the apartment manager to let us in apartment 317.

"Wow! She didn't spend her money on furnishings," Thom commented when we entered the apartment. It was neat but sparsely furnished. A quick walkthrough of the two bedroom apartment revealed only a bed and a dresser in the one bedroom where she must have slept. The other bedroom only had a desk, a filing cabinet and a waste can. The combined dining and living area had a couch, chair, small dining table and two chairs. There was a TV on a little stand in front of the couch. There were no decorations or pictures on the wall except one cheaply framed photograph of her and Mahmoud that must have been taken about the same time as the one we had. They were casually dressed with his arm around her shoulders.

An inspection of the kitchen found only four plates and bowls, a set of silverware, a few utensils, and a coffeepot . The cabinets and refrigerator were sparsely filled with foodstuffs, juice and some fruit. Ms. Attenbaum had told us that Reza's modeling fees were quite high. She certainly didn't use her funds to furnish her living quarters.

"It sure won't take us long to search this place," Steve commented.

"No, it won't. Let's go through the kitchen, her bedroom and living area first. That won't take long. Then we'll concentrate on the spare bedroom. If we find anything, it will probably be there where the desk and filing cabinet are," I said.

As expected, we finished searching all but the spare bedroom in about fifteen minutes. Then we went to the spare and each of us took a drawer out of the desk to go through. There were three drawers on either side and a center drawer. The filing cabinet was empty except for several modeling magazines.

"This is all modeling stuff, contracts and so forth," Percy said after starting through his drawer.

"My drawer's empty. What's taking you guys so long?" Darby laughed.

My drawer was full of newspaper clippings all the way back to the al-Qaida and Osama bin Laden activities to current terrorist reports, including reports on actions throughout the world attributed to Infama and Walid Alziddi. There were also a couple of brief articles on the NIF theft. Both articles were brief. There had been little publicity about that because only the agencies involved in U.S. security understood the potential significance of that theft. Interestingly, there were notes in the margin of both of those articles. One just had a single Arabic word that Larry said translated to something similar to "Bingo!" in our language. The other was in English. The notation was--- "Now my love will be coming to New York." We presumed she was referring to Mahmoud. After assisting with the theft at Livermore, it must have been planned for him to come to New York. The circumstantial evidence was building on Reza's knowledge of and involvement in the theft. She must know what the plans were after the theft was completed.

One of the other drawers was empty and the other two big drawers had apparently been used for storage of toiletries and other essentials. Reza certainly did exist in sparse surroundings. The only drawer from which we did not have a report on was the center drawer which Steve was exploring. After finishing our search and finding nothing that would help our investigation, we turned, somewhat dejected, to Steve.

"Well? What have you found?" I asked Steve.

"Oh, nothing much. Some pens and paper, a stapler, paper clips and — two sets of airline tickets," he said smugly with a smile on his face.

"Airline tickets! For who!? Where to!?" we all asked.

"For Mahmoud and Reza to Jakarta Indonesia. They were to leave next week as a matter of fact. The way I know they are for Abdul and Reza is because she had penciled their names on the top of the jackets. The tickets are actually in the names of Barry Segal and Atricia Lane and there are accompanying passports in Lane's and Segal's names in the drawer also," he replied.

"So they had fake passports and were going to leave the country after taking care of whatever business they had with Saeb and Mohammed," Thom said.

"Yes, and it looks like Jakarta is where the action is, at least for now, when they can finish developing a weapon that they can transport, possibly to New York. The President visits here often and is already scheduled to be present for a September 11th memorial for those who lost their lives at the World Trade Center in 2001. Plus he is going to visit the Pentagon for a similar ceremony that same day," I said.

"It might be that Saeb and Mohammed were part of a group to set up deployment of the weapon either here or in Washington. September is a long way off, but maybe they think it will take that long to make the weapon and get in in place," Ashton joined in.

"Well, the only other trip for which a timetable has been set is a trip to London in May. Of course the President will be doing a lot of traveling between those two dates," Percy said.

"You guys aren't letting me finish," Steve said, looking like a cat guarding a captured mouse.

"There's more?" Thom asked.

"Just one more thing. A note that was clipped to the airline tickets to meet Abu el Hassan at his Medeka Square place Tuesday morning, February 11th," he replied.

"What's that Arabic word for Bingo!?" Thom exclaimed.

We would celebrate that night. After talking to Mike, he decided we should come to Washington and help on the continuing interrogation of Reza Pahlavi, then plan on leaving for Jakarta around the 7th of February. That would give us a day or two to find what we could about el Hassan before the proposed meeting. It was likely that Hassan would know beforehand that Mahmoud and Pahlavi would be no-shows. Mike had a plan that might work though in convincing Hassan that they were still alive and well.

That night we toasted each other and expressed confidence that we would find our quarry and be able to recover the stolen information or, at least, eliminate the people who had it that could make sense of it and delay development or even disrupt the plan enough that it would never approach it's objective.

Later that night I had a sense of foreboding, but had no way of knowing just how costly to the team our trip to the dangerous, unstable, and inhospitable country of Indonesia would be.

CHAPTER EIGHTEEN

The six of us were back in D.C. Wednesday, January 29th. Mike had wanted to meet with us at 10:00 AM so we were gathered in the conference room down the hall from his office about 9:45. Mike walked in ten minutes later.

"Hey guys! Let's chat a few minutes, then have lunch. I've arranged for you to meet with Reza Pahlavi again about 1:00. We haven't gotten much more out of her, but maybe you can. Perhaps you, Percy, could spend some time alone with her before the others join you. I understand that you were able to establish a special relationship with her?" We had told Mike about the incident with Percy and Reza.

"Mike, if you put me alone in a room with that bitch, unless she's cuffed and chained to the wall, I will resign from the team," Percy responded. Everyone had a good laugh. I'm not sure Percy wasn't half serious though. He was still walking stiffly and was terrified of Reza.

"Well, she's so pretty. And you're the only unattached one in the group. Who knows? She may get out of jail in a few years unless we can find more direct evidence on her involvement in the theft. Maybe you could look her up and you two could become a pair," Mike persisted with a grin.

"Mike,—Sir— with all due respect, why don't you go to hell," Percy grinned back.

"Okay. Obviously the team needs to go to Indonesia. Really, it is urgent that you get there as soon as possible to start tracking down the Infama group who has the laser technology. Hassan appears to be the best connection to start with. I really don't think we will get much more out of Reza, but it's worth a try. Plus I need a little time to establish my ruse that might fool Hassan into thinking everything is alright with Mahmoud and Pahlavi," Mike got down to business.

"What is that?" I asked.

"Well, we kept the identities of Abdul, Saeb and Mohammed out of the paper when they expired. We don't normally give false information to the press, but this is so vital to our national security, if I have to buy some time,

I will do that," Mike replied.

"What information will you give them and why?" Percy asked.

"An "unidentified" official is going to tell them that the three guys were arrested for visa violations and suspected ties to terrorist groups. The report will say that they are being released from custody and expelled from the country next week. It won't make a big splash in the news, but the CIA has an operative in Jakarta that can see that the information gets on the front pages of the major newspaper there, with pictures and a story about how they were apprehended coincidently with a failed attempt to find information relative to a security threat to our nation," Mike answered.

"What about Reza?" Thom asked.

"On her we will release a picture and story on her relative to the upcoming ad campaign with the company she had just signed a contract with. I have already talked to the CEO of that company telling him Reza was in our custody and would either be going to jail or expelled. The company was just getting ready to release one photo and he was concerned about the adverse publicity. Their plans had been to start the shooting for additional ads next week. With the knowledge I gave him he already has started working with your friend, Ms. Attenbaum, to secure another model for the campaign. He was appreciative that I informed him prior to their printing and distributing the new ad," Mike responded.

"What will that do for us?" I asked.

"The same Jakarta newspaper will show her picture and the article about her upcoming ad campaign on the front page along with the other article. She had become somewhat of a celebrity in that part of the world anyway. The company CEO agreed to let us do that as long as it was restricted to being released to only that newspaper. He figured that, in Indonesia, the story might even help their sales which were minimal there anyway, even though it would have to be retracted when Reza's problems and the "real" news came out later," Mike concluded.

"Great!" Larry exclaimed. "So Hassan and others will think Saeb, Abdul and Mohammed will probably be coming there from their expulsion and Reza is free to go anywhere she wants."

"Right. I think this will work because the mess from the Abdul, Saeb and Mohammed things was kept very quiet and tidy. As I said, there were no names released and, unless there was an Infama witness to their demise, no one would know that they are not still going to be at the meeting next week. The fact that they supposedly have been in custody, and will be until sometime next week, will explain why they may have not been able to communicate. We have a tap on Reza's phone and are confiscating her mail. Her apartment is also under surveillance. Any attempts to communicate with her, we think, will be detected," Mike explained.

"Mike, I think the ruse will work, but how will that work to our advantage when we get to Jakarta?" I asked.

"It may not. But if Hassan felt there was a problem with the meeting scheduled with Mahmoud and Pahlavi in Jakarta, he might go into hiding and you wouldn't be able to find him, even if you left tonight for the almost two day trip to get there. Plus, you may be able to use your knowledge of the meeting as a way to get to Hassan even if he doesn't suspect anything. You might find him inaccessible unless you can somehow make him think you are representing them. It will be a short window of opportunity. Once he gets skittish, he will be gone most likely," Mike responded.

"Sounds like a good plan. We'll talk to Reza today and later if it looks worthwhile to do so and spend the rest of the time between now and the 7th to do some further research on Indonesia," I said.

"Right. I have the CIA reports I will share with you," Mike said. "Well that's it. I have lunch coming in a few minutes, then you guys can visit Reza," Mike concluded.

"Oh, by the way. I almost forgot one thing," Mike said as the sandwiches were brought in. "Bob Willoughby called a couple of days ago. He was anxious to learn if you had found Mahmoud or anyone else involved in the theft at NIF. Basically, he's just curious to know how the investigation was progressing and whether or not we had learned anything of value."

"What did you tell him?" I asked.

"Nothing but generalities. I didn't tell him about Mahmoud or the others. I just told him we had some promising leads that we intended to follow up on. His tone was of concern, but I couldn't tell if he was just curious or had some other reason to want to know what was going on. I think it is wise to keep everything under wraps on this, especially with your upcoming visit to Jakarta," Mike responded.

"I'm sure Bob was just anxious to find out if we had caught the perpetrators. He is so conscientious. I think he feels personally responsible for the information getting out of NIF, especially since he now knows how important it could be to our national security," Ashton said.

"Perhaps," Mike said. "But we don't need to take a chance on the progress of our investigation leaking to the wrong people intentionally or unintentionally ," Mike said.

We finished lunch then went to the D.C. jail where federal prisoners occupied a special section until they could be processed through the court system and be sentenced to spend time in a federal prison if they were found to be guilty. We got permission to use a small conference room for our interrogation. The jail had insisted that she be handcuffed though, if brought from her cell. When she came in the crowded room, her hands were cuffed in front of her. Percy made certain that he was furthest away from where she would be seated. Even in the orange jumpsuit, she was beautiful. She still looked seductive and the jumpsuit did nothing to hide her physical assets. It almost seemed a shame to see such a gorgeous creature confined like she was. My thoughts wandered to a vision of a beautiful parrot in a cage. It was sad.

"Well, we meet again, Reza," I said, reintroducing each of us to her again.

"Yes, I remember all of you. How are you feeling, Mr. Thackett? The last time I saw you, you were having some difficulty standing up," Reza said, feigning concern. She appeared to be very calm and in control, but we would be careful. We were well aware that she could fly off the handle without any warning.

"Fine, thank you. You know, that was not really a very nice thing you did to me," Percy answered.

"Yes, I know, sweetie. Come, why don't you sit on my lap and I will comfort you in your pain as a way to show my repentance," Reza said, smiling seductively and crossing her legs.

"Uh —no thanks. I can handle it," Percy said.

"Ms. Pahlavi, we know you have spent a lot of time with others who have had questions of you, but we would like to ask you some things if you care to answer," I said. She just smiled.

"Can you tell us who Abu el Hassan is, what his status is in the Infama organization, and how we might locate him?" Steve began.

Reza looked puzzled and a little startled for a moment but quickly recovered.

"I should have known you would be going through my apartment. You must know that my flight ticket is in the name of Atricia Lane, too. I have never met Hassan, but understand he is an extremely nice gentleman. You already know he is in Jakarta —or was. I would imagine that since you killed a friend of his, he has relocated somewhere where you can not find him. He would not be happy to see you. I don't know anything about Infama," she replied evasively.

"If the friend you refer to was Abdul Mahmoud, might I remind you that he killed himself while trying to kill us at the same time," I said. We would be careful not to give her any indication that, hopefully, Hassan would not know of Mahmoud's death or her incarceration.

"Ms. Pahlavi," Larry spoke up. "You will already be charged with association with known members of a terrorist organization and having knowledge of and being a part of the commission of a felony, among other things. You are young , pretty, have talent and have a potential future ahead of you. You will undoubtedly serve prison time. However, if you cooperate with us in apprehending the people and materials we are looking for, we will testify to that effect at your trial. Your term could very well be reduced substantially with cooperation."

"Oh, so you offer me a few less years of prison in exchange for helping you and incurring the righteous wrath of my friends. No thanks. I would rather stay alive and see you lose. You will, you know. You can get rid of me and Abdul and a lot of others. You still won't win. More will come. And you will lose, because Allah is with us," Reza responded passionately.

"Reza, I have a question," Ashton asked softly. "Why did you not use the platform of your rising popularity throughout the world as a top model to espouse your obviously anti-American views?"

"Oh, I wanted to. Very much. But I was afraid it would result in my being placed under surveillance which might endanger some of my associates. Besides, Abdul never really approved of my work. In some of my layouts I was scantily clad. He didn't like the whole idea of showcasing a woman's body, especially mine. I had promised him I would quit the modeling career after we left the country and I got paid for my last job," she readily responded.

"Well, you obviously didn't spend a lot of money on yourself. Why were you interested in making more money? Or did you enjoy what you were doing? You were very good, you know," Ashton continued.

"Yes, I enjoyed the modeling work. I was proud of the success and thought I was good---better than most of the money hungry models at the agency who just blew their money on frivolous things. But I was willing to sacrifice something that was rewarding to me for the cause. In the meantime I could do my part to help. I gave most of my money to helping our efforts throughout the world," Reza responded.

Ashton had been totally non-threatening in her tone and seemed to be just asking personal questions out of curiosity —from one woman to another.

None of us could tell where she was trying to go, if anywhere, with her questions.

"But if you left the country as you had planned to, how would you have gotten paid for that job? I know that most of the money comes after the client company decides whether or not to use the photos, where and in what quantity and kind of distribution and after the publication of the photographs. You get a shooting fee, but the potentially big money comes to the model and the agency after those decisions are made and implemented," Ashton pressed on.

Reza just looked blankly. She had an expression of being caught with her hand in the cookie jar. Moments before we figured out what had happened, Reza realized she had been trapped by Ashton. Then it hit us!

To get paid for her last job after leaving the country, someone had to know how to get her money to her! Most likely the payments would come to the agency and they would take their cut before forwarding the balance to the model. Ms. Attenbaum!! If Reza told her that she would be out of the country when the payment likely arrived, she must have given her instructions as to where to forward it! In Reza's case, the funds would likely be substantial.

We got nothing more from Reza after that. It looked like we would need to visit Ms. Attenbaum again.

CHAPTER NINETEEN

Later, Wednesday night, I was reclining in the easy chair watching TV and Ashton was in the shower. When she came out she was wrapped in one of the huge, soft hotel towels. She came over and sat in my lap, straddling me with one leg on either side. I could feel her softness and firmness between my legs.

"Love, remember I told you about my past?" she said, facing me with her arms around my neck.

"Yes. And I told you that your past didn't matter to me. We will look to the future together. Your past helped make you what you are today and I love what you are today," I replied.

"There are a lot of things though that I regret. One of the painful things about life is that you don't get to go back and change the things you wish you had not done," she said, looking at me while facing me in her sitting position on my lap.

"But the things you regret, at least the things you told me about, you were not in control of. And some of the things you did after those things happened were things you had to do in order to survive," I reassured her.

"Sometimes I did things to justify to myself that I was a worthwhile person and pushed myself to excel —for me— not anyone else. I wish I had met you when I was struggling to prove myself to myself. You would have given me confidence that I didn't need to be any more than what I was, Love. I'm so happy we are together," she said, leaning in towards me and giving me a quick kiss on the lips.

When she did that, she put more pressure on the now firm part between my legs that longed to be between her legs. Knowing that she had nothing on under the towel wrapped around her made it even more unbearable to remain calm, but she obviously wanted to talk right now.

"Tell me about you. Have you ever done anything you really regret, even if you thought you were doing it for the right reasons?" she asked.

"Sometimes. After my ex-wife and I met I felt like I loved her, but was never sure of her commitment to me. We had started living together and I felt like I should ask her to marry me, even with the doubts I had. She agreed to get married but, as it turned out, my initial reservations were well founded. Looking back, I think she had the hots for the TV anchor even after we starting dating and living together. We met him several times at parties and, if I had been more alert, I would have picked up the chemistry that was there between them. Even then, she would flirt with him. And there have been times when my loyalty to my job required me to do things that I knew were right, but still regretted," I responded.

"Like what?" Ashton asked.

"Well...for example, once I prevented a person that I didn't have a background on from attending a Presidential function. From his appearance and name he was obviously from the Middle East. Things were touchy then and I was guilty of racial profiling. He was very nice, but I could tell he was hurt by my action. I later learned that he was a prominent supporter of the President and his policies, that just happened to own a large publishing company on the West Coast. I still think I did the right thing under the circumstances of the security threats we were faced with at the time, but regretted that I had to do it and always wished that I could have apologized to him or made it up in some way. I never had the opportunity," I answered.

I was finding Ashton irresistible, but didn't want to interrupt her. She seemed anxious to find out more about me and how I felt about her. I could smell the freshness of her warm body pressed close to mine and feel the sweetness of her sex pushing against me erotically with steady pressure. She was so pretty, sensual and sexy it was hard for me to ignore my desire and I probably wasn't doing too good a job of doing that. I'm sure she could feel the opposing pressure from me now also.

"Dawson, I know we were sort of joking the other night with Skipper, but did you ask me to marry you just because we have been staying together and having sex," she asked seriously.

"Ashton, I was serious. You are so much different than Linda, my ex-wife. I can tell that you love me without reservation. And I love everything about you. I would never regret asking you to be my wife and I know it will happen, just as soon as we get off this project. If you still want me, we will be Mr. and Mrs. "We" forever just as soon as we can after that. We'll invite Skipper, you're Mom, Mike and the whole team. I promise," I kissed her parted lips and brushed her hair back from her beautiful face.

"What do you mean, if I still want you?" she leaned over again, pressed her body against mine and kissed me passionately. Momentarily she disengaged from her caress to murmur, "I want you now, more than ever. Can't you tell?"

I succumbed to the urge and slipped my hand under the towel wrapped tightly around her and found the softness between her legs. She was already moist and raised her hips slightly so that I could get my index finger gently touching the point of origin from which her fluids were beginning to flow. Simultaneously, she unzipped my trousers and brought forth the engorged member that now rested exposed between her legs.

"Love, just stay still. I want you like this," she said softly while raising her hips and sliding herself down so that I was inside her. I was still reclining in the easy chair with Ashton in my lap pressing deeply into me. She partially withdrew and I tried to surge upward into her, but she held my hips, pressing downward so that I couldn't move.

"You just relax. Let me do it," she said, looking at me while briefly running her tongue over my lips. Then she closed her eyes and, using her firm grip on my hips, leaned slightly forward and began to move upward slowly and back down again in a tantalizing motion that created an agonizing anticipation on my part. I felt as if I would explode into her but each time she sensed I was reaching that point, she would slow down even further or halt the movement of my shaft disappearing into her inviting orifice altogether. This went on for what seemed like an incredible, sensual eternity.

"Now! I want you to come with me," she gasped and began to pick up speed with her up and down plunges until she reached a crescendo, driving her pelvis into me with such force that I could no longer hold back. I grabbed her waist and thrust upward into her as my love was expelled with such force I know she could feel the rush of warm fluid forced into her. She grabbed me tightly around the waist and sunk my quivering member even deeper into her. I could feel her body shudder as she reached orgasm and felt the hot flow of her juices joining mine in a culminating ecstasy.

We lay there for several moments, exhausted, her head on my shoulder and her in my lap with me still inside her. I touched her damp brow and, with my fingers, brushed the strand of hair that lay across her face. She looked at me with her beautiful eyes, then we kissed, holding the kiss a long time and exploring each other with the passion of our lips and tongues as well as slow movement again down below. I hugged her to me and held her tight.

"You see now why I could never let you go? Never would I find anyone who could replace the lovemaking that we experience together. I love you, kitten. You are good," I whispered to her. Neither of us wanted to let go of this moment, but we finally disengaged.

Ashton crawled out of my lap. The towel had fallen from her and I for the thousandth time marveled at her exquisite body. Her hair was somewhat mussed from our violent lovemaking. She really did look like a nineteen year old---firm breasts, tight rounded little butt, tiny waist and her long hair flowing down her back and across her shoulders. Her skin was smooth as satin and her flat tummy descended down to the inviting dark thatch between her legs below. Her legs were shapely, reminding me of a pretty cheerleader I used to admire in her little short skirt when I played football in high school. And her face! Beautiful, sexy, pretty would be the combination of descriptions one would use. My musing was interrupted by the phone ringing. I answered. It was Bob Willoughby from NIF at Livermore.

"Dawson! This is Bob Willoughby. How are you?" Bob began.

"Fine, Bob. Mike told us you called a couple of days ago."

"Yes. I was interested to know if you guys had made progress in tracking down Abdul Mahmoud and had learned anything that would lead you to the stolen documents and the people who stole them or had them. He said you had made some progress," Bob stated.

"Yes, we've made some progress, but still have a long way to go I'm afraid to conclude our mission," I answered him evasively.

"Well, I'm glad you are making some progress and wish you luck in accomplishing your task. I feel so responsible for letting the info get out. Of course we really didn't know what we had and the potential implications of it until we had it. Then it was too late. Really, the reason I called, I've been trying to locate Ashton. The hotel operator gave me this number. Can you tell me how to reach her?" he asked.

"Yes, she's right here. I'll let her talk to you," I said, handing the phone to Ashton. She was still naked, so I could continue my musing while she talked.

"Hi Bob. How are things going at the lab?" Ashton asked.

There was a pause as I could not hear his part of the conversation.

"Good." Then another short pause. "What is that?" Then a long pause.

"Bob, you're kidding!? We thought it would take months to do that! How far along are you?" she asked. Another long pause.

"In any other scenario, that would be fantastic news. But under the circumstances, it's scary. Thanks for letting us know. How did you solve the beam consolidation problem in such a short distance?" she asked.

There was some technical conversation between them that I didn't understand, some small talk, then the conversation ended. I looked at Ashton quizzically after she hung up. She answered my question as to what that was all about before I asked.

"Bob said that since we left they had played around with the technology to reduce the requirement to deliver a lethal beam of having to have a massive structure like the one you saw. He said they had worked around the clock to try to duplicate what he thought the thieves would have to do to develop a reasonably mobile weapon that would work over short distances of maybe a couple of hundred meters or less."

"You're kidding! And they have been successful!?" I asked.

"Yes and no. What they have been able to do though is reduce the length required to deliver such a beam. They have a very rough prototype that can emit a laser with destructive ability over a short distance. And it is only twelve feet long. He thinks it could perhaps be shortened another two feet at most, but that would be the limit unless you wanted to restrict its effective power to less than fifty meters. To arrive at a reasonably mobile weapon with a 200 meter range, a lot of work would have to be done to design a triggering mechanism, accurate sighting capability and the design and structure of the weapon itself. And we know it would have to be set in a rigidly installed manner to be accurate and effective. But the major technology hurdle —the compression of the length required to produce a lethal beam at a relatively distant target —has been overcome through compacting hundreds of tiny mirrors and magnification glasses in a tube about as big around as a sewer pipe," Ashton explained.

"So how long would he or you guess it would take to complete such a weapon if they are able to solve this problem also?" I asked.

"The time frame, if they are able to duplicate what Bob has done, is probably shortened to about six months from that point, maybe a bit less. Then, of course, the time taken to transport and install it at the desired location could take another month. But it could be in place with the desired capability well inside of a year from now," she answered.

"Wow! We don't have a lot of time to go a long way, do we?" I said as much to myself as to her.

"No. We better leave for Jakarta as planned Friday. Well, Love, since I'm embarrassed standing here in front of you naked, I think I will go on to bed. First I will call Skipper and let him know I will be out of the country for a while. I won't tell him where. I just don't want him or Mom to worry if they can't get me. You can go ahead and take your shower if you want. I may be asleep when you get out," Ashton said.

"Okay. Let me call Ms. Attenbaum's home first to see if we can see her tomorrow," I said.

I called and her housekeeper said she would not be back from Paris until the weekend. We would have to wait until Monday, the 3rd of February to see her. I kissed my pretty Ashton on the back of her neck and left for the shower while she dialed Skipper's number.

CHAPTER TWENTY

Monday morning, February 3rd, 2003, the seven of us were waiting in the lobby of the model agency when Ms. Attenbaum arrived about 9:30. We had been there over thirty minutes. Thom, the only other smoker in the group, and I were standing on the sidewalk outside when her chauffeur dropped her off at the curb. Her housekeeper had obviously warned her that we might be there to see her today.

"Good morning, Ms. Attenbaum!" Thom greeted her cheerily when she stepped on the sidewalk.

"Hello, Mr. —Henson, isn't it, and Mr. Kohler. I assume your cohorts are inside?"

"Yes ma'am. We need a few more minutes of your time," I replied.

"Very well. You must be brief, however. I have a lot to do after being gone so long. I can't imagine what else you want of me. I thought we had covered everything in your previous visits," she said as she brushed past us into the building. We picked up the others and followed her back to her office. We had decided to let Ashton take care of the major part of this conversation.

"Ms. Attenbaum," she began, "we have talked to Reza again recently. She was telling us about her latest shoot. It must be slated to be a huge success —for her and your agency."

"Yes. As I told you, Reza is my highest earning model. She is very good and I hope she is back to work this week. We have another huge opportunity for her. I can't imagine what the problem was last week before I left, but I'm sure you have found by now that Reza, although high in temperament, could not be involved in anything illegal," Ms. Attenbaum said.

"Well, we are still investigating some of her relationships," Ashton responded without answering Ms. A's implied questions.

"You know, you asked me if I would consider a career in modeling. I am more or less a consultant at the moment, working with these gentlemen, but I expect this assignment to end soon. Were you serious in your query?" Ashton asked meekly.

Ms. Attenbaum arched her eyebrows and all of a sudden changed her detached demeanor. We were talking about her business now —something she was good at.

"Well, yes, darling. Really, you have all the physical attributes to do extremely well in this business. Several clients already come to mind that would be interested in what you might bring to the table. You have not only beauty, but a certain sexual quality that sells well in our business. And you appear to be tough enough. It is a tough business, you know? Of course we would have to run some test shoots. Looks alone won't make you a success in this business. You have to know how to handle yourself in front of the camera. And, if you are going to be truly a success, you have to be a good business person also," Ms. A. pattered on. She liked to talk about her business and was obviously very good at it. Her comments on Ashton's attributes came across less as a compliment than they did as a studied evaluation.

"I'm sorry, guys. I know we're here to talk about Reza. I was just curious. I really might like to take a shot at modeling if Ms. Attenbaum really thinks I might do okay. But its not realistic for me to think about that anyway. With the other things I'm involved in, my travel schedule, often out of the country, wouldn't permit me to do modeling. I could arrange the photography sessions around my schedule, but a friend of mine told me the big money, if you're good, comes after the shoot when decisions are made on publishing the photographs. I wouldn't be around to get paid. And I need the money. You guys know about my obligations, supporting my Mom and brother. I might not be able to wait until I got back in the country to get paid for work previously done," Ashton looked at me as if to dismiss the modeling idea and get on with our business of talking about Reza.

"Yes. Well it's an interesting thought for you, Ashton. But you're right. You may be in China when your check arrives and you do need a steady flow of cash. Now, Ms. Attenbaum, is there anything else you have thought of that you can tell us about Reza?" I asked, taking my cue from Ashton to get down to business.

"No —no. Nothing I haven't already told you. But let me get back to Ms. Smyth's comment," Ms. Attenbaum said, obviously not wanting to get distracted from the conversation that interested her.

"We can make arrangements to have a model's money sent to them if they are out of the country. We have had to do that on a few occasions. We can wire transfer or, as is the usual case where they may not have a banking relationship in the place they happen to be, we express mail and they have the funds in cashiers checks or any form they want it. Maximum three days. All we need to know is where you will be and where you want it sent."

" Oh, really. That could be a lot of money though —probably not for someone like me— but for someone like Reza, for example. Her fees must be enormous, she is so good," Ashton said reflectively.

"Yes, you are quite right. You very possibly could achieve that status if you are serious about the job and willing to learn. That's what we do. We take raw talent and train them, and we have the contacts to make it a great business venture for the model and ourselves. We are the most respected agency in Manhattan. You mentioned Reza. Her commission on this last job is going to be substantial. The number is confidential. But she is planning on being out of the country when the payment will likely arrive. For that sum of money, you don't want it just laying around waiting until you return. It can be invested or, as in your case, may need to be spent. I don't know what your obligations are, but they sound as if you wouldn't want to be too far away from your money," Ms. Attenbaum rattled on. She was really after Ashton and was enjoying talking about her business.

"Yes. I apologize for monopolizing our time with discussion on my personal situations, but just one more question, then we'll get back to Reza," Ashton was smooth. She said "get back to Reza" when, in fact, she had never left Reza. I could see where she was going now.

"Certainly. What is your question? I'm sure answering it is more important than whatever insignificant additional information I could tell these gentlemen about Ms. Pahlavi," Ms. A. said. Ashton had successfully established a 'them versus we' conversation, and it was obvious that Ms. A. was more interested in their discussion.

"Well, I have on and off again consulting assignments similar to the assignment I have now with these gentlemen. But there are times that I have no assignment and I desperately need an additional income source, at least until something else, perhaps modeling, turns into enough money that I can quit what I'm doing now. The problem is that my specialized knowledge relates to really out of the way places. I could be in places like Bangladesh, Tibet, Burma. It would seem to me that it would be very difficult to arrange for fund transfers to places like that, especially since I likely would have no banking relationship or contacts in those places," Ashton pressed on in a concerned tone.

"Honey, that can be worked out. For example, Reza is planning to be in a most out of the way and unstable place. In her case, she does have a contact that she trusts that will receive the funds for her and keep them in safekeeping for her use. But if you don't have contacts, my financial man is excellent. He can assist in finding a financial institution that is reliable in almost any area that we could wire funds to," Ms. Attenbaum responded to Ashton's concern.

Bingo!!! —or whatever the Arabic word was that denoted the same thing. I couldn't remember. Ashton had slickly pulled out of Ms. Attenbaum the knowledge that she knew where Reza's money was to be sent.

The rest of us could hardly contain our smiles. Now it was up to us to get the specific information out of Ms. Attenbaum without blowing Ashton's cover. Who knows? We may need to come back. Ms. Attenbaum was a sharp lady though, and it was likely she would figure out that she had been duped. If we got what we wanted though, it was improbable that Ms. Attenbaum could give us anything else we needed in the way of knowledge about Reza. Ashton had accomplished her objective. It was up to me now to take it from there.

"Well, uh, Ashton. Ms. Attenbaum is very busy and we must make our other appointment also. Let's get back to Reza. Ms. Attenbaum, the main reason we are here is to find the destination and contact that has been arranged for Reza's visit out of the country next week," I said.

"I'm afraid I don't know what you're talking about —" Ms. Attenbaum blurted out, before it struck her that she had just told Ashton about Reza's visit to an out of the way place and the contact who her financial man was to make arrangements to forward the funds to. As it hit her that she could not claim ignorance of the information we requested, she focused steely eyes on Ashton. Forget about trying to keep Ashton innocent in the ruse to attain this information.

"I'm afraid I can't divulge my client's financial arrangements. That information is strictly confidential," Ms. Attenbaum recovered slightly.

"Ms. Attenbaum," Steve interjected, " might I remind you that we have warrants which allow us to request and receive any information you have that might assist us in this investigation. This is a matter of national security. If you refuse to willingly give information to us, we can confiscate your records and that of your financial assistant, and hold you in contempt."

Ms. Attenbaum was visibly flustered now. "Well I just don't like to be responsible for releasing information like that! Why don't you just ask Reza? She should be in today."

"Ms. Attenbaum, Reza will not be in today. And she will not be making the trip. She will remain in custody. We know her original destination is

Jakarta, Indonesia and we know the name of the person she would have been contacting there. We did ask her for additional information and she would not cooperate. We want whatever information you might have that would add to the information we have concerning Reza's planned trip to Indonesia. Once again, I will ask you to share anything you have with us on this fund transfer right now," I said sternly.

Ms. Attenbaum looked defeated. We already knew about Jakarta and Abu el Hassan who likely was the contact. She didn't want her files confiscated and certainly didn't want a contempt charge filed.

"Very well. Jack, will you come in here please and bring Reza Pahlavi's compensation file including the arrangements for the Indonesian fund transfer?" she pressed an intercom button on her desk and spoke into it.

Jack came in, bringing the file, staring at us with a quizzical look. As we began to go through the file, we found Hassan was the contact and the correspondence from Jack to him was to Jakarta. The amount was $89,440. The surprise was that Hassan had arranged to have the money to be wired through a bank in Jakarta to the account of an obscure entity in Madura — a company called Yashid Buket. Larry thought Madura was an island off the coast of Java, but wasn't sure.

We had all the info Ms. A. could give us. We stopped and got an Atlas that had Indonesia in it and went back to the hotel to look at the map. I called Mike and asked him to fax the latest CIA report on Indonesia also, specifically anything they might have on Madura and Yashid Buket. Our next stop would be Indonesia. If we had the gift of prophesy, we would know that all of us that made the trip would not be returning. We were seven now, but seven would not survive.

CHAPTER TWENTY-ONE

It was pouring down rain when we landed in Jakarta, and the air was hot and humid. The climate in most of Indonesia changes every six months. Generally, the dry season is June to September and the rainy season December to March. It is a tropical climate and some of the tropical areas have rain throughout the year.

With the long trip going through several time zones being fraught with a flight cancellation and numerous delays, it took almost three days to get there from New York. The six of us were exhausted. We had no idea what day it was in Indonesia, but the pilot announced as we landed that it was 3:45 PM local time and we knew it was February 9th in New York.

Indonesia is the fourth most populated country in the world after China, India and the U.S.---over 225million. The terrain is predominantly mountainous with some 400 volcanoes. It is the largest archipelago in the world and consists of five major islands and about thirty smaller groups. There are a total of 17,508 islands. The largest islands are Sumatra, Java, Borneo, Sulawesi and the Western half of New Guinea.

There are 500 languages and dialects spoken in the archipelago corresponding to the 500 tribes. The national language is Bahasa Indonesia, originally the Malay language mainly spoken in the Riau islands. In its spread throughout the country, its vocabulary and idioms have been enriched by a great number of local languages as well as derived from foreign languages including Dutch, Chinese, Sanskrit, Arabic and Portuguese. Literacy rate is 84%.

Indonesia's religion is predominantly Muslim. In fact, with 88% Muslim, it has the largest Islamic population of any other country in the world. Much unrest and violence has occurred over the past several years in the region. Part of the killing has been motivated by attempts to gain independence in such places as East Timor in 1999, and part of it has occurred due to ethnic and religious disputes between the various tribes and the Muslims and minority Christian populations.

The most recent CIA report we had obtained indicated that it was one of the most dangerous and unstable places in the world due to the constant uprisings of the various militant groups. Indonesia's powerful armed forces are re-establishing themselves as an institution that can't be ignored. The Indonesian military, particularly the army, remains the most powerful force in the country. The report indicated that in the past year, since the attempted crackdown on terrorism by the U.S., the U.S. has thawed its previously cool relationship with the Indonesian military. U.S. counter-terrorism training of Indonesian forces has begun on a limited scale in an attempt to encourage military officials to crack down on radical Islamic groups such as the Java-based Laskar Jihad, as well as continue their action against violent separatists in trouble spots such as Aceh.

The collapse of Suharto's corrupt, crony-encrusted regime in 1998 made the way for the republic's first democratically elected government in over 40 years, and a chance to rebuild its badly corroded political and economic institutions. But the same surge of popular will that shoved Suharto aside also ended the steely controls he used to cap social unrest. Two presidents had somehow survived the turmoil and trauma that ensued, but the chance of the country fragmenting into smaller, independent segments still existed.

"Wow! Its muggy here," Thom said as we got off the plane and started through the security checkpoints. It had been prearranged that we would be approved to fly and enter the country with our side arms. Darby would have preferred that we would have been able to bring a couple of automatic rifles, but the relationship with the Indonesian government was still too tenuous to push our luck. We would be lightly armed. The security people took us to a special area to be properly cleared.

"Yeah. I'm glad I changed to some light clothing on that last leg," Ashton replied. She had a little tan skirt that stopped just above her knees and a white short sleeve blouse. Her brow was moist from the sudden humidity and straggles of damp hair hung down her forehead. As usual, she was cute and sexy looking. She couldn't help it. She just was.

"Okay, let's rent a car and find the hotel," I said as we left the terminal after getting through the security check. We had made reservations at the Banyuangi Sintera Hotel in central Jakarta.

We traveled the Cengkareng Toll road from the airport. We had rented a van and Larry was driving. Thom was acting as navigator in the front seat with Ashton and me and Steve, Percy and Darby in the two seats behind. We made two freeway exits before coming to the main thoroughfare that would take us into downtown Jakarta. The traffic had thickened to a crawl. We passed Merdeka Square, site of many of the government buildings and foreign embassies. High rise hotels and office buildings were visible to the South and East of Merdeka. The traffic and noise of downtown Jakarta was maddening, but we would get used to it.

Finally we exited Thamrin and somehow Larry and Thom were able to find our hotel. The desk clerk was very efficient and gracious. We would find that Indonesians were generally very polite and tolerant towards foreigners. Handshaking is customary for men and women alike when introduced. Usually a greeting is accompanied with a smile. But to give or receive with the left hand is unacceptable and the head is considered sacred and should be respected. Patting on the head, adults and children alike, is frowned upon. And pork is forbidden for Muslims but is available in the international restaurants.

By the time we got checked in and into our rooms it was 7:05 PM and we all felt like we had been dragged through hell backwards and slapped in the face with buzzard's guts. We decided to eat at the hotel restaurant and turn in early to get some rest before starting on our mission tomorrow morning. Thom and Steve were in the room adjacent to me and Ashton, and Larry and Darby were four doors down across the hall. Percy was by himself next to them. We had not been able to get all four rooms in a row. We agreed to meet in our room at 7:45 to go to dinner.

"I look sort of washed out, don't I Love?" Ashton asked me with a cute wry smile when we were alone. I didn't answer. Instead I embraced her, pulling her towards me firmly and kissing her kissy-looking lips. Holding her tightly with her body pressed against mine we held the kiss a long time as she closed her eyes and responded lovingly.

"Does that answer you?" I asked. "You are even prettier when you are like this. Besides, I love you."

"I love you, too," she said, giving me a quick kiss. "I'm not going to change, since we're coming back after dinner. But I think I will brush my hair and wash my face. I don't care what you say. You're just trying to seduce me. I know I look awful."

While she was in the bathroom, I mixed us a drink and sat down in the overstuffed chair to relax and smoke a cigarette. She wasn't long.

"Better?" she smiled when she emerged.

"Not really. Its hard to improve on perfection," I laughed, going into the bathroom to throw some water on my face.

"Dawson, where do we start tomorrow?" Ashton asked when I came out.

"I think our first stop should be with Abu el Hassan. We know where his office is supposed to be from the currency forwarding address attained from Ms. Attenbaum. From looking at the city map I picked up in the lobby, I think it is close to Merdeka Square," I responded.

Just then there was a knock on the door. It was only 7:35. I cautiously went to open it, revolver in hand. We had vowed to be on 100% alert at all times now that we felt we were getting closer to our quarry. It was Darby, Larry and Percy.

"How about a drink? The baggage crew broke my bottle. All my clothes smell like scotch now. I guess I'll be spending part of my night at the hotel laundry facility washing and drying my clothes," Larry said disgustingly.

"Sure. Come on in," I laughed. "Maybe you could be our street lookout tomorrow when we visit Hassan. You could just wear your clothes and pose as the town drunk."

Larry mixed a drink for himself. Thom and Steve came in a few minutes later and we all went down to the restaurant about 8:00. After a leisurely dinner at which we all selected the fresh seafood, we retired to our rooms.

Tomorrow we would try to find Mr. Hassan.

CHAPTER TWENTY-TWO

"Hon, wake up," I gently shook Ashton who was still curled up in bed after I had gotten up, shaved and showered.

"Dawson, I can't go with you guys today," she said, slowly rolling over. She looked like a doll with her auburn hair flowing over the pillow and her china doll face.

"Why not?" I asked.

"Love, I started my period last night and I have terrible cramps. Once in a while it hits me like this. If I went with you, I wouldn't be much help the way I feel," she said plaintively.

"Why don't you just go and stay in the background. If we even find Hassan, I doubt we will face any action today. That will start tomorrow after he knows we are here and passes the word we are looking for the people who have the stolen secrets," I said.

"Hon, I really don't feel like even getting out of bed this morning. Maybe I can join you this afternoon after you talk to Hassan, if you are able to locate him," Ashton responded. She did look to be in a lot of discomfort.

"Well, okay. We can handle what we need to do today I think, but I worry about you here alone. It's possible that the Infama people already know we are here and have us under surveillance. If they see us leave without you, they will know you are still in the hotel, alone," I said.

"I'll be alright. Check with me around noon. I'll probably be feeling better and able to rejoin you by then. In the meantime I'll be careful. I won't let anyone in the room and I'll keep my automatic close at hand. You go on now," she said.

"Just the same, we decided we wouldn't split up and leave anyone alone. I think I'll ask Darby and Percy to stay here with you. They can stay in the adjoining room in case there's any trouble," I countered.

"Love!! You aren't going to tell them and the others what my problem is are you!?"

"No. I'll just tell them you are feeling under the weather and may join us after we check out Hassan's office. They'll think you caught a travel bug. Darby won't mind. I just feel safer having him here and the other four of us can take care of ourselves," I insisted.

"Okay," she capitulated. " Call us around noon. And Love— ?"

"What?"

"Be careful," she said, sitting up to give me a kiss before I left.

Darby and Percy were okay with staying with Ashton. Thom, Larry, Steve and I left to walk the four blocks to the high rise where we thought Hassan's office was. The streets were crowded. We stayed alert with Larry and Thom walking in front, and Steve and I several paces back. After about 25 minutes we arrived at 1104 Merdeka Salatan across from Merdeka Square. It was about a twenty-five story building with a tinted glass facade. This was the address Ms. Attenbaum's financial guy had indicated Reza had given for Abu el Hassan, who arranged for the wire transfer from Jakarta to the company in Madura. Since today was February 10th, we had arrived a day before the planned meeting between Hassan, Reza and Abdul Mahmoud.

We had discussed a plan that was prefaced with the assumption that Hassan was not yet aware that Mahmoud was dead and Pahlavi was in our custody. Mike's ruse card had already been played in the local papers. If the misleading information had not worked, Hassan would probably be hard to find.

Steve and I would pose as being advance representatives of Pahlavi and Mahmoud and try to find out all we could about Yashid Buket, the company in Madura, the organization and perhaps the location of the prototype weapon we suspected they were trying to put together. He would be suspicious, but it was worth a try to find out anything we could before his caution caused him to clam up. When that happened, we would expose our true identities and try to extract the information from him in a more forceful manner. We had to be careful in that we could not make an arrest in Jakarta even if we had probable cause.

If everything went as anticipated and we ultimately ran into a stone wall as far as attaining additional information, we would be forced to violate our self-established rule of not splitting up. Three of us would most likely have to stay in Jakarta and place Hassan on 24 hour surveillance, while the rest of us would go to Madura. It was not the best scenario but, under the circumstances, would have to do.

The problem then became, if this plan began to be implemented, who would stay and who would go to Madura? Although we would all likely be marked people after our confrontation with Hassan, Ashton, our beautiful young girl, and Darby, our huge black man, would stand out in the populace of Jakarta or Madura. It was felt that the weapon being assembled, if it was still in the country, would likely be in the Madura location and Ashton would be the best person to recognize the significance of whatever was found with Thom being a distant second in that respect. Ernest would have been a closer second choice, but he was gone.

We had decided, if the plan developed in that direction, that Darby, Ashton, Thom and I would go to Madura with Larry, Steve and Percy staying behind to try to shadow Hassan.

We went into the huge marble lobby of 1104 Merdeka Salatan and viewed the tenant board located near a bank of four elevators. Abu el Hassan's name was listed as a counselor at law. His office was on the 14th floor. This was too easy, so far. We sent Larry up to the 14th floor to case the layout. After just a few minutes, he returned to the lobby.

"There is a small reception area on the 14th floor with a few chairs and a phone on a desk where the office or person you are visiting can be called when you arrive. It looks like there are about ten tenants on this floor. There is a diagram showing the location and office numbers of each occupant. Hassan's office is the last one on the left down the hall behind the reception desk," Larry reported.

"Is there a receptionist at the 14th floor lobby?" I asked.

"No, just the phone and the diagram," Larry answered.

"Okay. Larry, you and Thom come on up with us and you can just wait in the lobby up there like you have an appointment with someone while Steve and I go to Hassan's office," I instructed.

"Are you going to call first?" Thom asked.

"Yes. We don't want to immediately arouse his suspicion by just barging unannounced into his office. If he is there and already suspicious, there is no way out other than coming by us through the lobby by the elevator anyway," I said. We did call when we got there, but there was no answer.

"Okay, let's go," Steve said. Larry and Thom got on one elevator and pushed the 14th floor button. Steve and I would follow in a couple of minutes and, in case there was a surveillance camera in the 14th floor lobby, would not acknowledge Larry and Thom other than a curt nod of greeting like strangers might do, when we arrived in the lobby.

"What do you expect to find here?" Steve asked as we walked down the hall towards Hassan's office.

"If we find him here, I think we will find the money man of the organization, or at least one of them. I doubt a lawyer would be directly involved in field operations for Infama, but they need people to keep the money flowing from the multiple sources they draw from to the people that are involved in implementing their plans. If I'm right, this guy will be a pretty important person in their organization but may not be privy to specifics related to the operational activities," I answered.

We arrived at the end of the hall. The last door on the right indicated it was the office of Abu el Hassan, Counselor at Law. We paused a moment, instinctively touched our side arms to assure their readiness and slowly opened the door. We entered into a rather dark inner office which had a desk where a receptionist or secretary might normally be stationed. Through an open door exiting to the left rear of this little inner lobby, we could see a brightly lit office. Since it was on the corner of the building, we assumed some of the light came from the windows.

"Is that you Hafez?" a voice called in thickly accented English.

"Mr. Hassan?" I queried as Steve and I entered the man's office.

"Yes. Who are you?" he asked. Hassan had a fairly dark complexion, dark hair, a thick black mustache and a white shirt open at the neck. He was seated at his desk and his hands were both visible, so we didn't have to be immediately concerned about being shot. He most likely recognized us as Americans but seemed more curious at this point than alarmed. Perhaps Mike's ruse had worked.

"We didn't see anyone out front, so we just came on back. I am Dawson Kohler and this is Steve Whitt," I said. I decided that it would be best to use our real names since that knowledge would be revealed to him most likely before we left and certainly after we left. Since we were aware that some in the organization knew all the names of our team, I watched for a reaction. There was none. Probably the people involved in Infama field operations were the ones who knew of us and our mission and it was not necessary for him to know about us. In our search for the people who were involved in the laser information transfer and weapon development, it might not be expected we would be aware of or contacting the money man. So far so good.

"What can I do for you?" he asked rather brusquely, not offering to shake hands.

"We are acquaintances of Reza Pahlavi and Abdul Mahmoud in the States. We know of their scheduled visit with you tomorrow and Ms. Pahlavi's concern on the funds that were to be deposited for her. Since we arrived before she was to be here, we wanted to check for her to see if everything is in order for her visit," I said, none of that being false, just fuzzy.

Now we got a visible reaction. I watched closely to make sure he didn't go for a weapon, but his expression was one of disgust and anger.

"Females!! How do you Americans put up with all of this equality stuff?! Any time I deal with a woman from your country, I swear by Allah that it will be the last time! And Reza is one of us! I sent word to her that everything was taken care of, and now she sends you two to check on me. The funds are where I told her they would be and they will be used to assist in the project as she had instructed!" He shook his head.

"I understand. She was just anxious to be assured before she broke contact with the agency that everything had gone as planned. I think she wasn't real confident in the financial guy at the modeling agency and wanted to ensure that he had done his part properly," I replied, trying to sound apologetic.

Hassan calmed down some. "Well, we are appreciative of receiving the funds and I guess we do have to put up with some frustrations from the other gender, don't we? And, although I don't approve of her profession, she has been a loyal trooper and perhaps can continue to generate funds for us here in Indonesia. When my assistant arrives, I will show you the transfer documents."

About that time a man who appeared to be in his early twenties arrived.

"Hafez! You are late. Bring the wire transfer register to me. You Americans have female secretaries. My sympathy to you. As you can see, I employ males. It is far less stressful," he said with just a hint of a wry smile when Hafez left to do his bidding.

"Here. You can see that the transfer was made last week to Madura and placed in the account of Yashid Buket" He opened the register which had a copy of the document and a notation indicating the funds were for Project X-ray.

I tried to scan as much of the page which contained about five other transfer records. The one on top caught my eye. It was a transfer to the NIF at Lawrence Livermore in September, 2002. One of the notations was---Cedric Agreement. There were other notations, but I didn't have a chance to see them all before he closed the book. The NIF transfer was also noted for Project X-ray. This must be the money book for that project. We needed to get our hands on that book.

We wouldn't have an opportunity now though. We heard shouting in the hall. Moments later a man dressed in traditional Muslim attire burst into Hassan's office. He was carrying an automatic rifle. Our hands instinctively dropped to our weapons. The rifle was carried loosely, not pointed at us at the moment, but we were prepared if he indicated any threatening action. We saw Thom and Larry move in the outer office behind him. Hafez just stood behind his desk looking puzzled and alarmed.

"What are these people doing here!?" the man shouted at Hassan.

"They were sent by Pahlavi to check on her funds transfer prior to her visit tomorrow," Hassan said nervously. About that time the stranger noticed Larry and Tom behind him. It was clear that their hands were resting on weapons.

"You fool! These people are Americans. And those two back there are with them. I caught them out front and they couldn't explain why they were on this floor. Pahlavi is not coming. She is being held in the States by the police and these people are probably CIA!" the stranger shouted.

"I didn't know. Their story sounded true, knowing Pahlavi's tendency to be hyper about money matters," Hassan stammered.

The stranger probably realized that he was, at the moment, outgunned. Hassan had not made a movement to go for a gun if he had one. He looked scared.

"Leave. And I suggest you leave the country by tomorrow morning. We don't like U.S. law enforcement people in our country and it will not be healthy for you if you remain here past noon tomorrow," the stranger said quietly but intensely.

I thought we had gotten all we would get here at the moment and two more men came down the hall. Larry and Thom pulled their guns out in plain sight now and covered the two men. It was time to leave before the crowd grew larger. I still wanted the register but, just as I was going to grab it, Hassan threw it in a safe behind his desk and spun the combination lock knob. We didn't have time to extract the combination out of him. It was obvious that the stranger was just waiting for a distraction in order to level his rifle at us and it would be probable that the other two were armed too, even if Hassan might not be. And there were probably more of them in the building.

I presented my revolver and demanded that the stranger hand me his rifle slowly. He did, but defiantly. Larry frisked the other two while Thom covered him and produced two automatic pistols.

"Okay. The party's getting too large. Let's go guys. Thank you for inviting us in, Mr. Hassan. You gentlemen should stay here until we get on the elevator," I said as we slowly backed our way down the hall, carrying their guns with us. Steve and I got on one elevator and Larry and Thom the other.

"What are we going to do with these guns?" Steve asked when we were in the elevator going down.

"Well, we have two more handguns with a clip of ammo in each. Let's keep them. If we get in a firefight, we can use them first, then throw them away. It will conserve our ammo. As far as the automatic rifle, remember that Darby really wanted to bring a couple along but we couldn't. Now we have one with probably about thirty rounds of ammo in the clip. Darby will be pleased," I said, smiling. We arrived at the lobby level.

Larry quickly broke the automatic down into it's separate parts, handing each of us a piece which we concealed in our clothing as best we could before we left the building. We had punched all the floor buttons on the two elevators before leaving.

"Let's go back to the hotel to see how Ashton is and the seven of us will plan our next course of action," I said.

We hurried back to the hotel, mindful that it wouldn't take long for our friends to re-arm themselves, find out where we were if they didn't already know and get more friends to pay us a visit. Darby and Ashton cautiously let us in when we arrived. Percy was on the phone with Mike to see if there were updates on any info from Reza. There were none.

"All of you are okay! I was worried. I should have gone with you, or at least made you take Darby," Ashton said. She squeezed my hand.

"Are you feeling better, Hon?" I asked.

"Yes. I'm fine now. What happened?" she asked.

"Let's order room service. It may not be safe to go out right now. We'll tell you two about what happened, then decide what we do next," I said.

"Oh, we don't have anything to worry about now. He told us we could stay until noon tomorrow," Thom laughed.

Retrospect would tell us that, if we had taken the rifle toting stranger's advice, all seven of us would probably have returned from this trip.

CHAPTER TWENTY-THREE

Over sandwiches we had bought, we decided to stick with our previous plan. After lunch, Percy, Steve and Larry changed into some more casual clothes and called Hassan's office. Hafez answered.

"Hassan," Steve said tersely.

"May I say who is calling?" Hafez inquired.

"Mohammed," Steve replied. Steve thought that would be a safe name to use if Hafez didn't ask for a last name.

There was a slight hesitation. Hafez was probably debating whether or not to attain more information but, in Mr. Hassan's present mood, he decided to go ahead and put the call through.

"Yes!? This is Hassan!" Abu answered, obviously not in a good mood.

Steve clattered the phone rapidly then hung up. "Hassan will probably think it's a bad connection and wonder who the caller was. That happens frequently here."

"He's still there. Let's go Percy and Steve. Good luck to you guys. Be careful. We'll stay in touch by cell phone and see you in a couple of days hopefully," Larry said.

Larry, Steve and Percy left to shadow Hassan. Larry and Steve would definitely be the best on surveillance and Percy had come along well. We had decided to keep all the rooms and meet back there as soon as the other four of us returned from Madura, whenever that might be. If we found the weapon development site we would call the other three and keep it under surveillance until they got there. I wanted all of us on hand when we went in to destroy whatever we found. There would be sure to be plenty of armed people around that project.

Darby disassembled and packed in a suitcase the automatic rifle we had "borrowed". We left the hotel about 3:00 PM and rented a car. Dollar Rental Cars had a desk in the lobby. We selected a Jeep Cherokee for the trip to Madura, not having any idea what kind of roads we might find ourselves traveling on. A map and directions to the island were attained from the hotel clerk who seemed puzzled as to why people he assumed to be tourists or business people would want to go to Madura. There was no need to try to disguise our destination in the event Hassan's people checked with the hotel. Knowing who we were, there would be no doubt in their mind where we would be going. It was best to get there quickly before they had too much time to prepare for us or dispose of the material we seeked if it was there.

Darby drove, with Thom co-piloting. Ashton and I were in the seat behind them. As soon as we got out of the city, we assembled the automatic rifle and put it back in the luggage area. Although we looked on the way out of the city, we saw no commercial establishment that would likely have ammunition for it. At least we would have one thirty-round clip before the weapon would become useless. We decided that we might give the rifle to Darby and the automatic pistols to Thom and Ashton in case we got in a potential firefight situation. They would have two handguns until the clips ran out.

As we drove through the outskirts of the city into the countryside, the masses of people, shacks and filthy waterways crisscrossing the country side began to dwindle. Water supply and sewage disposal are inadequate throughout most of urban Indonesia and we all were fearful of coming down with a terrible bug. The other guys had assumed that this was what had affected Ashton earlier and were relieved to see that she seemed okay now.

Now we were driving along the coast. Thick vegetation was alongside of us with the mountains rising to our immediate right. It was beginning to get dark and we were just coming into the small town of Semarang, only about halfway from Jakarta to our destination, the island of Madura. We decided to push on to the town of Surabaya which would be the jumping off point to hire a boat to take us to Madura the next morning. We finally arrived on the outskirts of Surabaya. The moon was glistening on the Java Sea to our left with the ominous dark mountains continuing to loom on our right. We could see the lights of the town glowing in the distance. It was eerie and we were tired. Darby slowed down.

"Darby, let's stop here. Pull down that little road on your right leading towards the mountains," I instructed.

We traveled slowly down the little unpaved road for about a half mile. It was unbelievably dark with the luscious, thick overhanging jungle on both sides of the road. We had no idea where the road led to, but there was a little cleared out space on the right that was big enough to pull the car off the road.

"How about here?" Thom asked.

"Yeah. That's good enough. Darby, pull on by that clearing and back into it so we can make a quick exit when dawn breaks and we might get traffic on this little road. It may lead to a house or little village," I said.

"Are we staying here tonight?" Ashton asked somewhat fearfully as Darby backed into the clearing and doused the lights. All of a sudden the darkness was overwhelming. We could not even see each other in the car.

"Yes, I think so," I laughed. "We are real close to Surabaya and it's only about a mile across the channel to Madura. We'll try to hire a ferry to take us over in the Jeep in the morning, but we need not advertise our presence until we're almost there."

"I'll take the rifle over in the suitcase tomorrow, then assemble it after we arrive on Madura," Darby said. We still had the two automatic pistols that we would throw away after using them, too.

"Fine. That will be no problem. Larry checked with his office and they told him the Medurans often go armed so, from that standpoint anyway, we won't stand out. Otherwise, I would say that the minute we step foot on the island, the Infama people will know we are there. We'll have to move fast to find Yushid Buket and, hopefully, what we are looking for. I doubt we will be that lucky, but we're bound to be getting closer to our objective," I said.

"I'm going to get the snacks and bottled water we brought out of the back," Thom said.

"Can you find the back in this darkness, Thom," I asked him, only half joking.

"I'll follow the side of the Jeep until I get there," he laughed as he got out. The rest of us opened our doors. The dim interior lights gave welcome relief to the total darkness surrounding us.

I got out and lit a cigarette. The glow of the cigarette against the dark jungle backdrop accentuated our lonely feeling in this isolated place in this strange country. We were all apprehensive about tomorrow, but we felt very close to each other and just wished the other three were here with us. We had talked to Larry earlier on the cell phone. They were tailing Hassan somewhere and he could only talk briefly. He said he would call in the morning. Darby and Ashton got out and joined us when Thom came back around the car with the food and water. He laid out the snacks and drinks on the hood of the car and we ate standing up.

"So, since you're the maitre d' of this luxurious accommodation, tell us what our sleeping arrangements will be. I'm going to take care of a call of nature then get some rest. It's been a long day," Darby said to me.

"Ashton and I will sleep in the back end. One of you can sleep in the back seat and the other in the front. How does that sound?" I replied.

"I'll take the front seat. Thom, I guess you get the back," Darby said, disappearing into the jungle.

"Where is he going!?" Ashton whispered to me.

"To the bathroom. Do you need to go before we sack up for the night?" I replied.

"Well —yes, but I don't want to go in there by myself," she said.

"Darby's in there," I joked.

"Dawson!! Go with me. Please—" she pleaded. Just then Darby reappeared, seeming to just materialize from the undergrowth alongside us.

"Okay. Let's go. Thom you can be next for the toilet facility." I led Ashton into the thick vegetation.

"Love, stay close to me. I'm going to go behind this tree. Are there snakes here?" she asked hesitantly.

"Yes. But they wouldn't bite your beautiful butt. Go on. Take your time. I'll take care of my need while I'm waiting on you. Now if I get bitten, you may have to suck the poison out," I told her.

"Shut up! I'm serious. If I scream, come get me," she said as she disappeared into the blackness.

We went back to the car and waited until Thom returned and took our positions in the Jeep. Ashton and I snuggled up under one of the blankets we had brought from the hotel.

"Okay. Everybody settled in? I'm going to turn the lights out," Darby said, closing the car door when we all told him we were situated.

"Dawson, I love you. I have to. Otherwise I wouldn't be in this godforsaken place with you sleeping in the back of a Jeep in the middle of the jungle," Ashton whispered in my ear.

"I love you, too," I said, pulling her close to me.

The night was warm and humid, but we stayed snuggled together under the blanket. It gave us a sense of security and privacy. Darby and Thom had lowered their windows and we could hear the night sounds of frogs, crickets and night birds. Otherwise, it was quiet —so quiet.

We kissed and fell asleep in each other's arms, trying not to think about what lay ahead of us tomorrow. We had gone this far together and couldn't turn back now. I didn't want to take a chance of losing Ashton, yet knew I could be placing her in extreme danger in Madura. I yearned to make love to her tonight, but the awkward situation wouldn't allow that, so I just held her tightly, felt her warmth close to me and, as I dozed off, vowed to myself that I would do whatever I could to protect her and keep this precious little package alive and unhurt.

CHAPTER TWENTY-FOUR

The cacophony of sound from the jungle woke us up as morning light began to filter through the overhanging trees. There had been no traffic on this little path which was only wide enough for one car.

"Good morning Mr. Marriott! Would you have room service deliver my breakfast, Sir?" Darby said, awakening and rising to his massive full height outside the Jeep.

"Certainly!" I replied, tossing a Granola bar that had been left over from last night's meal at him. "I remind you that the customary tip is 15%."

"Sure. Here's your tip," Darby said, tossing three pennies in my direction. By this time everyone was stirring. Thom arose and stepped outside with Darby. Ashton raised up and looked at me with a wry grin. Her hair was bedraggled and her blouse was pulled up from her jeans on one side, exposing her flat little tummy. She looked even more like a pretty little teenager than ever when she was like this.

"I look so awful, don't I? Why don't you just leave me here in the jungle and you guys go on to Madura? Maybe a cute native will come by who won't mind how I look and he will take me into the jungle with him to swing through the trees with our pet monkeys?" Ashton said.

"Okay. I'm not cute, but I'll bet I could learn to swing with monkeys. I'll stay here with you and we'll let Darby and Thom find the bad guys. As awful as you look, who knows? I might find a cute monkey and let the native have you," I said just before she jumped on top of me and starting tickling me. She had found that this was the best tactic to get me back for something or subdue me. I surrendered and apologized.

"Okay, everybody. Let's freshen up and hit the road. We should be able to make it into Surabaya in about fifteen minutes from the time we get back to the main road," I said.

We hit the main road about 7:15 AM. Sure enough, we soon began to see a scattering of shacks. The highway shot thorough sunny patches of jungle along a river where small fat pigs ran for cover. There were women on the river banks washing clothes. We crossed a bridge over the river which led from the mountains into the sea and were immediately in the bustling city. Several shops, hotels and high rises lined the streets and crowds of people were hustling about, getting ready to start their day doing whatever they did. Most people gave us only a cursory glance as we proceeded cautiously through the city.

The main street led down to the waterfront where several small boats were docked. And there was a ferry pulled up alongside what must have been the public dock! We were in luck if it was running. We could see Madura in the distant early morning haze across the murky water. Maybe it was two or three miles away. It was hard to judge distance across the water.

"Hi! Can you speak English?" Thom asked a gentleman lounging beside the dock next to the ferry.

"Speak some," the man smiled through rotten teeth.

"Do you own this ferry?" Thom inquired.

"No own, but I run it," the man replied, still smiling broadly.

"Can you take us to Madura?" Thom asked.

"Sure! I take. But boat don't go until 9:00," the man answered.

"That's fine. Maybe we can get something to eat while we're waiting. How much do you charge?" Thom asked.

"$10 U.S. one way for you and car. $1 extra for each person," the old man replied.

"Okay. We'll go. We're going to get a bite to eat and will be back in about an hour." Thom said. The man smiled a toothless smile, nodding furiously. We suspected he normally just took people at a dollar a head and maybe some pigs or chickens to trade or sell. It was going to be a good day for him.

We found a food stand and all got a platter of rice and chicken with what looked like raw egg poured over it. Ashton was a little squeamish but we were all hungry and it was good. In a little general store, we stocked up again on water and various packaged foods that were available in case we had to camp out again. It was 8:45 AM when we got back to the dock. Probably 25 people along with some goats, pigs and caged chickens were already on board. When we arrived the man quickly shoved people aside so we could drive the Jeep on board. On the way over, we asked him if he knew where a company called Yashid Buket was located. He had heard of it, but didn't know exactly where it was. Few of the other people on board could speak English. The boat captain asked some of them, but none knew anything about the company. It was my impression that most of them just went to the Madura shore to barter their goods and returned on the ferry later in the day. After about forty minutes, we landed at Madura and drove off, thanking the captain and telling him we would be returning probably in a couple of days.

Thom took over the wheel when we drove off the ferry. I sat beside him and Ashton was in the back seat. Darby had gotten in the rear of the vehicle and was assembling the AR. He was happy to have it but wished we had more than 30 rounds for it. Still, that would be good for about 5 short bursts of lead if we needed it. And we all had our handguns with plenty of ammunition and Darby's knife. That would have to do.

As we wandered through the squalid shanties lining the road leading from the dock we noticed that many of the men in the teeming crowds had at their side a curok, a big curved knife. We would learn that Madurese Muslim custom allows men to carry the knife in public.

"Well, Darby, if any of these guys get mad at us, I hope you can hold them off with your 30 rounds long enough for the rest of us to get the hell out of the area," I turned and said to Darby in the back.

"I have a better idea, Dawson. I'll jump out of the car, make a quick conversion to Islam, grab one of those big knives myself and see if you can hold us off before me or one of the brothers relieves you of your head," Darby countered.

"Turn here, Thom," I said. I had seen what appeared to be a bank on one of the less cluttered streets ahead.

I went in the bank and straight to one of the teller windows. There was a young man behind the counter.

"Excuse me. Do you speak English?" I asked politely.

"Yes Sir. What can I do for you?" the young man asked in near flawless English.

"Would you know of a company called Yashid Buket and where we could locate it?" I asked.

"Yes Sir. I know of it. They have a very active account with our bank, mainly dealing with a branch closer to their location," he replied.

"And could you tell us where that location is and who are the principal owners?" I pressed.

"Why do you want to know?" he asked, looking directly at me.

We had been forewarned that the Madurese were renown for their straightforwardness and direct approach, which was particularly evident in their manner of speech. They are often considered rough and unrefined by outsiders. The generalization was that they were hot blooded and quick to excite, but also quick-witted, industrious, adaptable and could be charming.

If approached with politeness, they can be a loyal friend. If crossed, they could be a mortal enemy.

I had to be careful how I responded if I expected to get any information. Unless we got a hint, though, of where Yashid Buket was, it could take us several days to find it. Madura was a long island, 160 km east to west and 35 km north to south, covering 4,250 square kilometers. It had a harsh climate and landscape and over 3,000,000 people. There were four major cities. Sumenep was the largest at close to a million population with Bangkalan, Pamekasan and Sampang with populations each ranging from 625,000 to 725,000. We were now on the outskirts of Sampang.

Farming, fishing and small business provided the most activity, but technological progress had brought about increased living standards, improved roads, waterworks, electricity, good land and sea travel, and good communication systems. Oil and gas deposits being exploited in recent years had added to the improved standard of living. It was an ideal place to develop and hide the laser weapon. Most of the population were of the Islamic religion. Although mainly concerned with the internal political problems within Indonesia, they could be expected to be anti-western in their sentiments.

"We have a business relationship with Bushed, but have never visited them or met the people who run the business," I offered,

"Do you buy product from them?" he persisted.

"No," I smiled. "As a matter of fact, I don't even know what they make. My company was called into service to follow a wire transfer of money from a lady by the name of Pahlavi to Yashid Buket. It was a restricted contribution for a specific purpose and my group is trying to check that the purpose has been understood adequately and acted upon."

"How much money?" he asked.

"$89,440 sent the middle of January," I responded. He tapped information in his computer.

"Yashid Buket is located in the town of Lebac, just north of Sumenep. I won't reveal the names of the principals. You can introduce yourselves and ask your questions of them when you get there. I can confirm that Ms. Pahlavi's transfer to Buket in the amount you gave me was made at one of our branch offices in Sumenep on January 16th," the clerk finally announced.

"Thank you very much. We will do as you suggest," I said, starting to leave.

"By the way, Sir—" the clerk said after I had turned to go.

"Yes?"

"Buket makes farm equipment —tractors, mowers, that kind of thing," he smiled.

"Thank you," I smiled back.

I went back to the car and gleefully announced that we were closing in on our quarry.

"Looking at the map, it's about 75 miles away. We go through some rough country, so it probably will take at least two hours with the traffic and terrain," Thom said.

"Let's roll," I said.

It would take all of two hours to reach the outskirts of Sumenep. We were starved.

"Let's stop and find something to eat, darling. I'm hungry," Ashton said.

"Good idea!" Darby exclaimed.

We found a decently clean looking food establishment and ordered noodles and tea. Just as we starting eating, my cell phone rang. It was Larry.

"Dawson, where are you? Don't try to go into the vicinity of Yashid Buket until we get there! You may need help," he said.

I explained what we had found out and where we were, then asked him what they had been doing and asked the reason for the warning.

"We lost Hassan. He's disappeared. We went back to the hotel about an hour ago and found our rooms had been broken into and ransacked. When we reported the break-in to hotel security, they offered nothing but apologies and did only a perfunctory investigation," Larry explained.

"What did you do then?" I asked.

"We went to Hassan's office. We knew he wasn't there. Hafez wasn't there either, so we broke in the office, without leaving evidence that it was entered of course. Percy was a little worried about possibly getting caught as agents of the U.S. involved in a breaking and entering. I was pissed off though and wanted to see if we could find evidence of where he went to," Larry continued.

"Did you?" I asked.

"Yes. There was a note on Hafez's desk telling him to take some time off, that he would contact him later. Hassan's note said he was going to be at the Bandung location. We can follow up on that later. Right now, I think we should join you," Larry answered.

"Why?" I asked.

"Well, we went in Hassan's office then and he had an e-mail he had printed from somebody called Mustafa Muhammad Al-Wa'eli. That's a mouthful.

That could be the gun-toting guy we met in his office or it may be someone higher up in the organization. I called Mike and asked him to run a trace on the name to see if any of our agencies knew anything about him. Anyway, this guy had instructed Hassan to get out of town and stated that they knew the Americans were headed to Madura. They had alerted the people at Yashid Buket and he and his people were on their way. He told Hassan that he wanted him to be on vacation in Bandung when they disposed of us so no one could tie him to our disappearance. I think they will be waiting on you —in force. We better join you as soon as we can. From the tone of the e-mail, they must think we are all together on the way to Madura, not realizing the three of us stayed back to shadow Hassan," Larry explained.

"Okay. I agree. It sounds like we're on the right track. It will take you a day to get here though. We're going on to Lebac and locate Yashid Buket. We will keep it under surveillance until you get here to make certain they don't try to remove anything. By the time you get here, we'll have a plan to proceed," I said.

"Okay. We'll be on our way within the hour. Be careful and don't take any chances," Larry said.

"We won't. See you tomorrow. We'll stay in touch by cell phone to let you know how to find us when you get here," I said and hung up.

We wouldn't see Larry's group for four days and during that time a lot would happen to both parts of our little team.

CHAPTER TWENTY-FIVE

We finished lunch and got in the Jeep to leave. It was a little after 2:00 PM local time, February 11th, New York date. I had related Larry's conversation to the other three.

"Okay, from now on we go on maximum alert. Lebac is not far, but by the time we get through Sumenep and get to the town of Lebac, it will probably be close to 3:00 PM. We can expect that our friends will be on the lookout for any new arrivals in Lebac," I said. Thom and I were still in the front seat and Darby in the back end with Ashton in the back seat.

"What's our plan?" Darby asked.

"Oh, I thought we would just find the location of Yashid Buket when we got there, knock on their door and ask to see their laser model," I said.

"Yeah, right. Let me out then. I don't want to be there when you do that. Remember, Larry did say they planned to dispose of us and I doubt that meant they were going to send us on a luxury cruise," Darby rejoined.

"Seriously, our first objective will be to find the Buket location in Lebac before we get there. We'll stop when we get on the outskirts of Sumenep and ask a pedestrian or shopkeeper where it is. Lebac is not that big. If we know which side of town it's on and get some reference points or landmarks close to it, we can pinpoint it before we're right on top of it. We'll stop at that used car lot there on the right and buy a $500 junker. This new Jeep rental car is too obvious. We can park the Jeep in a bank parking lot and pick it up on the way back. Before we get out of Sumenep, we'll buy some local clothes, too. Darby, we better get you some makeup. You're a lot darker than the local populace. Along with your size, you will stand out like a sore thumb. Ashton, you can pull the veil around your face when we head out of town. You are about to become a fundamentalist Muslim," I said.

"Good plan. Maybe we will be able to get close to Yashid Buket without them recognizing who we are. What then, though?" Thom asked.

"After that we'll play it by ear. What I would like to do is keep the place under surveillance until Larry, Steve and Percy get here. Depending on the security, we would then determine if we could successfully break into the plant late at night and search it. That would only be possible if they are not working around the clock shift work. Plus, I'm sure, if the laser is there, that they will have round the clock security, especially since they expect us to be there. But we still might be able to figure a way to get in there under cover of darkness, even with the security. Maybe we create a diversion. That might depend on the size of the plant, how visible the access is to it and a number of other things. There's just too many unknowns right now. We'll try to come up with a workable plan after we have answers to some of the questions. Anybody got any other ideas?" I asked.

Nobody volunteered anything. We were able to buy an old 1994 Buick for $650. It looked like it had seen its best days. It had 140,00 miles on it, was rusted and had been wrecked. But Thom drove it around the block under the watchful eyes of the salesman and only after we had given him the money as a contingency of purchase. It ran surprisingly well. It would have to do. I suspect we paid too much for it from the smile on the salesman's face after we closed the deal and were driving off.

Next, we parked the Jeep in a crowded mall, locked it and got in the Buick. At least it was somewhat roomy, but not nearly as much so as the Jeep. We got the makeup and clothes and, after three inquiries of people who could speak English, we found a man who could pinpoint the location of Yashid Buket in Lebac. He said it would only take us about twenty minutes to get to Lebac and that the plant was on the west side adjacent to a water tower which was the tallest structure in town. His sister lived in Lebac and he told us it was a huge plant that had formerly been a salt processing plant prior to being converted to the farm equipment factory about ten years ago. It was one of the major employees of the town, employing about 450 people. He said it mostly just worked one shift in the daytime from 7:00 AM until 3:00 PM except during busy times when they sometimes worked a partial second shift from 3:00 PM to 11:00 PM. He didn't know whether or not they were working a reduced crew on second shift right now, but said they had never worked a third shift.

The man was very friendly and anxious to share any information he had with us. We had told him we were going to visit the plant and had a potential interest in investing in the operation. We wanted to ask him about the normal security on the night shift and some other questions such as visibility of approach on all sides, but did not want to arouse his suspicions. What he had told us already was invaluable. We thanked him and left. Soon we were out of Sumenep and driving through the harsh and arid terrain towards the town of Lebac. You could see the peak of one of Madura's two volcanoes looming in the distance.

"Are we ready, Sultan Peters?" I asked.

"Locked and loaded, Sheik Kohler," Darby answered.

"How about you, servant of your master and all males?" I asked, turning to Ashton in the back seat. She still looked pretty, even with her loose wrap over her jeans and blouse and the veil hiding all but her eyes.

"Yes, master. Your servant is behind you, as she should be. And her automatic under this cloak is aimed right at your butt," Ashton said with mock seriousness. Darby and Thom laughed. We had arrived at the outskirts of Lebac and the water tower was clearly visible in the distance on the left.

"The traffic is pretty dense. Let's drive around the perimeter of the plant and see what we can learn," I said.

"Good idea. In this traffic, I don't think anyone will notice another carload of people in an old beat up car even though there are people around here on the lookout for us, and I would like to case the place before we decide how to proceed," Darby concurred.

"You know, we need to find a place where we can observe the plant and perhaps easily enter the premises undetected if that option appears to be available to us. The road up ahead goes in front of the plant and there is a road coming out by the water tower on the side. Maybe it's the same road. I'm going to keep driving straight and see if I can make a left turn when we get past the plant," Thom said

"Look at the size of the plant! It's huge," Ashton exclaimed. We were driving right in front of it now.

"It looks to be between 750,000 and 1,000,000 square feet, all on one level," I said.

"Yeah, and there's only one entrance through the fence that looks like it encircles the plant. There's a guard shack by the entrance. Let's look as we go around to see if there is another gate on the back or sides," Darby said.

It was a busy thoroughfare. There was a fair amount of vehicular traffic on the road in front of the plant and, across the street, a number of commercial shops and small businesses of all types. Throngs of people were on the sidewalk in front of the lines of shops. We finally came to the end of the sprawling facility. There was a road that turned to the left going down the north side of the plant. Thom turned on this road.

"No gate on this side. There's a road turning left going down the back side," Thom said.

We turned back south. There was a truck dock with four bays on the back side, but there was no break in the fence. Anything leaving had to go around the perimeter road running around the plant inside the fence and exit out the front gate.

"Okay, take the road to the left by the water tower. That will complete our circle of the plant. Then turn right and we'll drive around a while and discuss our next step," I said.

The water tower was on the south side adjacent to the road we were on, situated towards the rear third of the plant. Just past the tower there was a trailer park with perhaps fifty trailers, several being for rent as deduced from the sign on a trailer at the entrance to the park that apparently served as the rental office. Between the park and the road we had originally come in on there were more shops and a couple of open air food markets. Vehicular traffic was sparse on this road, but pedestrian traffic was fairly heavy around the shops and markets. It looked like a working class neighborhood. Behind the trailer park and the commercial establishments along the road, row houses stretched back as far as you could see. Most likely, most of the people in this neighborhood worked at the plant.

"I have an idea!" Ashton was the first to offer a suggestion after we took the right turn away from the plant.

"What's that?" I asked.

"Let's let Thom rent one of those trailers. He is the least one of us that would stand out and we could think of some reason an English speaking guy would want to rent a trailer. They wouldn't have to know he might have three guests, and maybe three more after Larry and the others get here. We could give them a month's rent probably and we most likely won't be here more than a day or two. We'll either have the job done or find out we can't do it by then."

"Not a bad idea. We could pull shifts hanging around the market and observing the front gate until we can figure out a way to maybe get inside the plant at night," I said.

"That's a good idea! And I have a compliment to it that makes it even better," Darby said.

"What's that?" Thom asked.

"The water tower. It's right next to the trailer park. I know you could see the back side of the plant and the truck docks from the tower, and I'll bet that, from that vantage point, you can see the front gate, too," Darby explained.

"Hey! Good thinking. I noticed the tower has a ladder going up the side and a little walkway around the base of the tower. And I believe it had what looked like a little tool shed or something on the side of the walkway next to the plant. We could probably see the whole plant undetected at night and maybe even the daytime if we can break into the shed. I'll bet no one ever goes up there," I said.

We turned around and went back, letting Thom out right before we got to the trailer park office. We had decided to let him rent a double wide trailer with three bedrooms. With Larry, Percy and Steve coming tomorrow afternoon, we would have preferred to have rented two trailers but didn't want to raise suspicion on one English speaking guy renting two trailers. Thom would tell the rental agent he was there to provide technical assistance to rebuild a piece of U.S. made equipment at the plant and would be here about a month. He might have some other technicians join him later, so he needed the big trailer.

The explanation worked and did not seem to arouse any suspicions. Most likely the bad guys had not thought of alerting the trailer court to new English speaking tenants. Thom said the man was happy to rent as he had several vacancies and Thom only paid $50 U.S. plus a $50 deposit which we expected to lose.

Thom walked down the street and we picked him up then drove to our new temporary home with the rest of us crouching low so it would appear Thom was the only car occupant as we went by the office trailer. The trailer was a little rundown, but otherwise clean. It had electricity and running water.

"A shower!! See you guys. I'm going to take a nice, long, warm shower and get out of these cruddy clothes," Ashton said.

"I'd say all of us need that. Go ahead. Thom and I will go down to the food market while you do that. Then we'll all clean up, eat a good meal and go to work with our surveillance. It will be starting to get dark in a couple of hours. Unless we see something that looks like our target going out, we'll wait until the others get here tomorrow night to try to get inside the plant," I said.

We heard a scream. "There's no hot water!!" Ashton exclaimed over the sound of running water.

"Well, I guess your shower won't be quite as long as you anticipated," I laughed. "We're leaving to get some food. Be back in a few minutes."

Just then Larry called on the cell phone.

"Dawson. We ran into heavy traffic out of Jakarta, then I think we were being tailed. We took some back roads and lost the tail, at least for now. They are probably waiting down the road to pick us up again though. We're not quite to Surabaya yet. It may be late tomorrow afternoon or dusk before we get there certain that we won't bring our friends with us to where you are," Larry said.

"That's okay. We wouldn't try to get into the plant until tomorrow night anyway. We'll just watch it tonight and make sure they don't try to sneak the weapon out before you get here. One plus of your situation is that they may think we are all together and not realize that some of us are already here. That's why we need to be alert tonight that they don't run scared and try to remove it before they think we might get here." I described to Larry where we were and told him we would see him tomorrow night. Then Thom and I left for the market.

We wouldn't be here tomorrow night when Larry, Steve and Percy got here.

CHAPTER TWENTY-SIX

"That was a great dinner, Ashton!" Thom said.

We had gotten fresh fish, salad greens, rice, bread and spices. Everyone had their fill. It was a little after 7:00 PM. We had all been in the shower while Ashton prepared the meal and felt refreshed. I lit a cigarette. Darby and Thom lit cigars they had brought. Ashton disapproved, but tolerated our vice. She just opened the trailer windows to let the fresh air in.

"Well, it's time to hit the tower I think," Darby said.

"Yeah. The three of us can take shifts and let Ashton rest. One of us can take it until 11:00 PM, then someone else 11:00 to 3:00, then 3:00 until 7:00. If they try to sneak anything out, it will probably be during that time frame when their employees are out of the plant. I noticed when we were at the market that most of the cars that were left at the plant left at 6:00 PM. They must have worked about three hours of overtime after the first shift. There's still about eight or nine cars there though, in addition to the guard's at the gate," I said.

"They have two gate guards and two other guards patrolling the perimeter. They may have additional guards inside the plant. There are four cars parked next to the guard shack. I assume that is the parking place for the guards. The other cars could be night maintenance people or they could be the Infama people working on or planning to remove the prototype weapon," Thom surmised.

"You guys act like you were trained by Delta Force. You're pretty observant. And I thought you just went to get fish," Darby said.

"Thanks, Darby. But that compliment won't get you the first watch. We'll odd man out," I laughed.

We did that and I won the most desirable first shift, Darby the second and Thom the last shift. I left to walk to the tower. It was dark now. I had my Cobra, but didn't expect to run into anyone. The night was warm and sultry. It only took me a few minutes to get there from our trailer.

The tower loomed above me in the darkness and it was unbelievably quiet. I had an eerie feeling there alone in the darkness. The little fence surrounding the tower was scaled easily and I proceeded to climb the steps up to the catwalk around the tank about 65 feet above ground. The tank itself rose probably another 100 feet or more.

When I got to the catwalk, I walked around to the side facing the plant and tried the door on the little shed. It was not locked! Inside, there were a few rusted wrenches, other tools and a box of huge bolts. A dirty window looked down across the road onto the plant. I called the trailer on my cell phone. Darby answered.

"Hey. It's quiet up here, but the view is great! I can see the entire plant except for the North side. The truck docks on the back are clearly visible, even in the dim exterior plant lighting, and I have a clear view of the front gate also," I told him.

"Good. Well I'll relieve you at 11:00 then," Darby said.

"Okay. I'm in the little shack. It was open. There's nothing in here other than a few tools and there is a broad window looking out towards the plant. This is the best place to be because you are hidden from view at night, and would be even in the daytime. When you come though, bring a wet towel to clean the window. I can see okay, but it's pretty dirty. You could see better if it were clean," I said.

"Okay. See you after a while, buddy. I'm going to try to get a catnap now. Ashton and Thom are already getting ready to sack up —not together of course," Darby said as an afterthought.

"Go to hell, Darby. See you at 11:00," I laughed as we hung up.

There was a half moon and the stars were bright. I settled down for the boring watch, but fully alert to any observable activities at the plant. There was actually only one guard patrolling the perimeter and it took him about 45 minutes to walk around the plant slowly. The fourth guard must be used as a rotating relief guard. I noticed that most of the time there were three guards in the guard shack with one of them usually sitting on a bench behind the shack smoking.

Time went by slowly, but it was actually very peaceful up here. There was no activity observed outside the plant other than the patrolling guard. After what seemed like an eternity, I was startled to hear a noise down below. I quietly left the shack and, staying in the shadows, peered down in the direction from which the noise had come. It was Darby crossing the fence. I glanced at my watch. It was 10:55 PM. He climbed the ladder and was on the catwalk in about five minutes.

"Anything happening?" he asked.

"No, it's been quiet."

We went into the shack and smoked a cigarette. I filled Darby in on the guard rotation. He had brought a rag to clean the window and was amazed at how well you could view most of the plant from our perch. I left to return to the trailer about 11:15.

Ashton and Thom were already asleep, or so I thought. I quietly undressed and slipped in the bed beside Ashton, trying not to awaken her. I had no sooner gotten settled than her arms went around me and she was kissing me.

"I've been waiting for you. Do you realize we haven't had sex since we left Jakarta?" she whispered. We could hear Thom lightly snoring in the bedroom across the hall.

"I know. I've missed making love to you. You really do keep me shook up, you know —sometimes just looking at you is enough," I whispered back.

She had turned on her back and gently pulled me on top of her. I could feel the warmth of her body pressed against mine and hear her whispered words in my ear as our passion mounted. Simultaneously I reached down and spread her thighs slightly and she grasped me between the legs and began to guide me into her warm and wet vagina. We were trying to be quiet but, as my shaft sunk deeply into her we both exhaled and began to move in concert with each other. She was so warm and tight and I could smell the freshness of her hair and feel the sticky sweat of our bodies as we frantically sought release.

Finally, after several exotic minutes of alternating speeds of thrusting into her and her rising to meet me, we came together in a climatic end that left us both exhausted.

We were still cuddled in each others arms minutes later when the cell phone rang at the side of the bed. It was Darby.

"Guys, you better get up here quick! Something's moving at the plant!" he whispered loudly.

"We'll be right there," I said, jumping up and pulling my trousers on one handed while shouting for Thom and keeping the phone to my ear with the other hand.

"Bring the AR too and the ammo clips! We may need it. Get here as fast as you can!," Darby exclaimed before hanging up.

Thom and Ashton were almost dressed already. We checked our weapons, I grabbed the rifle and we rushed out the door towards the water tower. The phone rang again just as we exited the trailer. It was Darby again.

"I think they're moving the weapon! Are you on your way?!"

"We're on our way. We'll be at the tower in five minutes!" I assured him as we sprinted in the direction of the tower.

CHAPTER TWENTY-SEVEN

The three of us quickly climbed the ladder to the catwalk. Darby was in the shed peering intently towards the back of the plant where the truck docks were located. Without a word he motioned us to take a look.

There was a flatbed truck backed up to the dock nearest us. Carefully being loaded on the back with a fork truck was a cylinder that looked like one of the old WW II bazookas except it was larger and had several small cylinders running along the side of the barrel and a metal box attached to the rear that the small cylinders ran into. The main barrel extruded from this box and there were numerous cables and smaller attachments to the rear one third of the main barrel. From this distance we could not make out the minute details, but the dim lighting in addition to a portable spotlight that was trained on the activity illuminated the scene pretty well.

It was obvious they were very tedious in their efforts to get the equipment loaded without damage. The work was moving slowly and two people were on the back of the truck supervising the operation. Standing around the truck were six men, all armed with automatic weapons. The plant security guards were not around. It looked like they were all in the guard shack and had been told to stay off their rounds until this activity was completed.

"Ashton, what do you think? Does that thing look like it could be a mini laser that could have short range capabilities comparable to the one developed at NIF?" I asked.

She studied the shape carefully before responding.

"Yes —yes it could be. I've never seen anything like this, but the return tubes could very well be the beam recycling mechanisms. From the information they would have had from the Livermore theft, I would guess they would have installed several small powerful mirrors in the big barrel with even smaller mirrors in the smaller tubes. The structure in the back would be the original beam generation equipment, probably along with a sighting and firing mechanism."

"That thing is probably made with lightweight alloy, but it must still weigh close to a ton. And it's about 12 feet long," Thom mused.

"I don't want to get too technical, but several amplifiers, filters and a frequency converter would have to be contained in that cylinder to make it work for their purpose. The box in the back would have a small fiber ring oscillator that would generate a weak, single-frequency laser pulse on the order of a nanojoule. That pulse would be launched into an optical fiber system that amplifies and splits it until there are, as is the case at NIF, 192 10-joule pulses. The pulses enter the main laser system where each light pulse makes four passes in a beam path of mirrors, lenses, amplifiers and spatial filters. The multipass concept was one of the design breakthroughs at NIF. Next, the beams would have to be condensed and switched into a radial, three dimensional configuration and converted from infrared to ultraviolet light," Ashton explained.

"Wow! I'm glad you didn't get technical," Darby said.

"Sorry. I know all that doesn't make much sense," she apologized.

"All that being said, do you think that thing could duplicate on a small scale what you had at Livermore? I can't conceive of something that small doing what that huge facility was able to do," I said.

"They wouldn't have to duplicate what we did to make an effective short range weapon. They aren't trying to achieve nuclear fusion with this thing. A lot of our effort and precision as far as vibration, caliper and temperature control had to do with focusing the magnified beam on a target to achieve fusion. They wouldn't have to do that. All they want is a powerful destructive beam to kill with at a distance of probably no more than a hundred yards. Nuclear fusion may be a future objective with the information they have, but probably not their priority at this time," Ashton answered.

"Okay. So it could be a laser weapon. Certainly they are guarding it with care and trying to sneak it out of here in the dead of night, not wanting to risk that we would find it and disclose this location. Thom, what about delivery? Is this thing capable of being portable enough for their purposes?" I asked.

"Well, it's obvious it's not a one or two man carry weapon, and it would be difficult to conceal on the streets of New York, for example. My guess is they have elected to sneak it to a fixed location, perhaps a vacant building along a potential presidential route, install and calibrate it, and just sit and wait for the opportunity to use it. Advance knowledge of a presidential visit in time for them to get it in and set up would be helpful to them," Thom replied.

The workmen were now crating the "gun". It was probably on a solid skid and they looked to be installing sides, ends and a top for the container.

Once that was done, they would probably be leaving.

"Wouldn't you think the technical information and technicians would be going with the gun?" I asked.

"Definitely. The information of course could be copied, but it has to be with the gun to properly set it up and trouble shoot it. We don't know what stage of design, construction and experimentation this device is in. My guess is that they have a lot of work to do in that respect to get it ready to operate. Modifications will likely be required. The technicians have to be with it from start to finish, and on through the implementation phase. It's their baby," Ashton stated firmly.

"Okay. I think we have enough to make a strong assumption that this device is what we came after and the people and information will likely be with it. We can't wait on Larry, Percy and Steve, as much as I would like to. We have to move now. I'll call Larry and tell him," I said.

"Larry, where are you guys?" I asked when I got him on the line.

"Dawson, we're still in Surabaya. The guys tailing us were waiting when we approached the only road into Surabaya. I sighted them just before we got to the bridge. Obviously we can't take the ferry, so we ditched the car close to the docks and lost the tail on foot in the city. I found an old guy that will take us across to Sumenep early in the morning on a motorboat. We will leave about a half mile from the dock area. We'll buy or rent some transportation when we get there. If all goes well, we can be in Lebac by noon tomorrow," he explained.

I explained to him our situation and told him we would likely not be at the trailer when he got here. We had to follow the truck with the weapon and await an opportunity to overpower the well armed guards that would surely accompany it. We had no idea where that would take us.

"Dawson, don't try to take them on until we get there! You will need our firepower!" Larry cautioned.

"We may have no choice, Larry. We've got Darby and the AR with a few shells, and Thom and Ashton can take care of themselves. I will try to wait on you guys. You're right. We could use you now that we think we've found our objective, but we have to stay with it or lose it. And if the opportunity presents itself, we'll have to make our move," I said.

"We'll catch up to you as fast as we can. Be careful. These guys mean business. I'm convinced that the people following us were just waiting for us to get to Madura before trying to take us out. Now that they've lost us, they will probably converge on Lebac and join up with the bunch that you've run into. If you can stall before taking them on, do that. You could use me and Steve especially and Percy can hold his own, too," Larry persisted.

"I will, Larry. We've got to move now. I think they will be moving this thing soon. We'll just have to stay in touch by cell phone. Get here as soon as you can." We hung up.

"Thom, you and Ashton run to the trailer and grab all of our stuff and throw it in the trunk of the car. Then get back here as quickly as you can and pick us up. We've got to follow that truck when they pull out. Darby and I will stay here and watch it until you get here. Hurry! They're beginning to tarp it!" I said.

Thom and Ashton ran down the catwalk and scrambled quickly down the ladder before disappearing at a sprint towards the trailer in the darkness.

They would return just in the nick of time.

CHAPTER TWENTY-EIGHT

Thom and Ashton pulled up to the tower in the old Buick about the time the men finished tarping the truck. One armed man had climbed in the cab with the driver. Four of the other men, all armed with automatic rifles got in one of the cars and pulled in front of the truck as it pulled slowly out of the dock. Three armed men got in a second car that followed the little convoy when it started around the building towards the main gate. By that time, Darby and I had come down from the tower to join Ashton and Thom in the Buick. Darby swapped places with Ashton, taking the passenger side of the front seat with his AR and Ashton and I got in the back seat.

"Okay, Thom. When the truck leaves the gate, let's follow it at a distance. Try to stay back, but don't lose them. It's big enough and slow enough that we should be able to keep it in view without getting too close," I instructed.

"Yeah. They will be on the alert for sure. I will drive without my headlights some of the time so they will not think it is the same car lights behind them at a distance," Thom said.

"We've got to assume the driver is armed too, at least with a sidearm. So there are nine heavily armed men in the convoy. We need to be alert that they aren't joined by others when they get outside the gate. If not, the odds aren't too bad," Darby said, checking the bolt action on his AR and inserting the clip.

"Just like a Delta guy! Nine men armed with automatic rifles, side arms and who knows what else—probably rat poison— and you think three guys and a girl with side arms, two extra automatic pistols with one clip each, one automatic rifle with only thirty rounds and a knife is sort of equal odds!" I laughed.

"It's the people that make a force tough, not their hardware. And that's only a little over two apiece," Darby grinned, glancing back at me.

"That's right Dawson! And remember, I'm a tough girl. I make up for the lack of numbers," Ashton joined in.

"Yeah. Well, you take care of the driver if we confront them. The three of us will divide the rest of them up between us," I said, jabbing her in the ribs.

The truck didn't even pause at the guard shack. The guard just waved it on and it pulled out of the gate and turned left. We drove to the intersection and waited until the truck was well down the road before turning left and pulling out behind it.

We didn't have to wait too long to find what their destination was. About three miles down the road they turned right on a secondary road.

"They're going away from any heavily populated area I think. Does anyone know what's in this direction?" I asked.

Darby consulted the map. "The ocean. If they stay on this course, we couldn't be more than ten miles away," he said.

The truck went about four miles then took a fork onto a dirt road, still leading in a northerly direction. We felt comfortable that they had not spotted us yet. This road was dusty and Thom had turned the car lights off when we turned onto it. The cloud of dust raised by the truck would obscure any visibility that would show the Buick following at a distance. Thom carefully followed the road in the moonlight, keeping the truck lights showing through the cloud of dust in sight.

"He's got his brake lights on. We must be stopping. My estimate is that he has no choice. We must be right at the ocean," Darby said.

We slowed down and pulled into a little bare path on the right, plowing down small trees and undergrowth as we did so until the car was well hidden in the dense foliage. Thom cut the motor. The truck had obviously stopped about 100 yards ahead of us. We got out of the car, giving our weapons a last minute double check.

"Why would they stop here? Do you think they are just trying to hide the weapon in an out of the way place until we go away or they kill us?" Ashton asked in a whisper.

"I don't know. Let's ease closer quietly to try to see what's going on," I said.

We started stealthily down the road towards the truck with Ashton and Darby staying on one side and Thom and I on the other, making sure to travel close to the shrubs and small trees clinging to the side of the little road. They possibly could spot us in the dim light from the moon and stars if we walked down the middle of the road. When we got about halfway there we could hear the truck motor still running.

"Let's stop here a minute and see if we can hear or see anything," Darby whispered. By now we were only forty yards away. Beyond the truck we could hear the soft lap of waves and sense the vast, dark gloom of the ocean beyond.

"Look!" Ashton whispered excitedly. "There's a big boat of some sort right offshore!"

She was right. As our eyes adjusted to the light better, we could see a huge dark shape of a flat topped boat probably only about another forty or fifty yards offshore. Edging a little closer we saw that it was a barge. There was a long wooden, but sturdy looking boat dock leading out to within 20 feet of where the barge was docked. Closer examination revealed that the barge was equipped with a crane. They must be planning on loading the weapon on the barge!

"I'll bet this was a former loading area for processed salt. It was probably shipped out on barges. You can tell this must, at one time, have been a pretty active area. See, there's a couple of big run down shacks on the left that were probably shipping offices," Thom said.

"Yeah. It looks abandoned now except for a few motor boats and fishing skiffs tied to the side of the dock," I observed.

About that time the truck began to ease slowly onto the dock. The men were all standing around outside their vehicles except for the driver and his passenger. We eased just a bit closer.

The noise of the truck motor and the big crane beginning to swing into position over the dock, along with the excited conversation of the men that had accompanied the truck, covered the sound of our whispers to each other now. We were now just a stone's throw away from the men and the dock. We had to make a decision as to what to do next and act quickly before the loading was complete and the barge got underway with its cargo. There was still no indication at all that the men suspected that they were being watched, but they all had their weapons still cradled in their arms.

"Guys, we've got no choice now but to make our play. I can't even risk trying to call Larry to tell him where we are and what's going on for fear they will hear me talking. We've got to move now to take out these people, destroy the weapon and try to get out of here before reinforcements come. There's probably people on the barge, too, who will join the fray," I said. We had all gathered together behind a clump of shrubs.

"I can take out a few of the men at the dock with my one and only burst of fire from the AR," Darby said quietly.

"Okay. They will be caught by surprise. As soon as Darby starts firing, Thom and I need to rush the remaining people. Don't forget the two in the truck. Darby can fall in behind us as soon as the clip is expired. Ashton, you stay to the side in the rear. With your accuracy, you can pick targets from a distance without exposing yourself with us in the main attack force," I said.

The crane was now positioned over the skid with the weapon and two of the men began to hook the cables to the skid so that it could be lifted onto the barge.

"Are we ready?" I asked.

"Locked and loaded," Thom replied.

"Say when," Darby said.

"Okay Thom, let's you and I move to the other side of the road. We can rush to the left of Darby's fire. With thirty rounds, he's not going to be firing long before coming at them from the other side. We've got to get close with our handguns and rely on the element of surprise so that we can take most of them down before they're able to get AR fire on us. If any of us get close enough to pick up an AR from one of them that has taken a hit, do it. Darby, when we get in position, you start the party. When you fire, we're on our way. Coming out of the dark, we may have a chance if you take out three or four of the nine with the AR," I said.

"You can count on it," Darby said as Thom and I scooted across the road.

We were in position. Darby raised the AR to his shoulder. Before he could fire, all of a sudden lights flashed down the road behind us and we could hear the roaring of at least two vehicles fast approaching towards the dock area! We just had time to dive into the underbrush, Darby and Ashton on the right side and Thom and I on the left side of the road, when a pickup truck and a car loaded with armed men came tearing around the bend at breakneck speed past us, dust billowing behind them.

The two vehicles screeched to a halt at the dock and most of the men immediately fanned out in a perimeter of defenses while a couple of the men approached the men already on the dock. We could hear shouts and rapid conversation .

The crane lifted the skid, swinging it over the barge then setting it down gently on the deck. The barge engine had already started up with a deep rumble. We watched in frustration as the barge started slowly moving off in an easterly direction. By that time Thom and I, under cover of the lingering cloud of dust, had rejoined Darby and Ashton on the other side of the road.

"Shit!!" was all I could say.

"Dawson! Look! The men are coming back toward us!" Ashton exclaimed.

Sure enough, they had all climbed in the vehicles and were headed back down the road in our direction. We dove deeper into the underbrush.

The pickup led the procession with the cars behind. There were five heavily armed men in the back of the pickup. They were scanning the sides of the road with a spotlight! One of the men in the car behind had a handheld megaphone.

"Walid Alziddi says fuck you Americans!! You will all die with your Jew-loving leaders!!" the man with the megaphone kept shouting in English as they slowly scanned the edges of the road on both sides with their spotlight.

They passed us without seeing us. We were hunkered down flat behind thick underbrush. The light beamed right over us without detecting any of us. We all breathed a sigh of relief, but our anxiety returned quickly. Just down the road, they sighted our car hidden in the bushes off the road!

After a lot of excited chatter, we could see the headlights of the vehicles backing into the thick foliage on the side of the road and turning around. In the dim reflection of light from the headlights and the moon, we could see forms of men sixty yards down the road from us fanning out on either side of the road starting back in our direction. We were just moments away from being discovered and would be no match for the heavily armed group of about twenty men now heading our way!

CHAPTER TWENTY-NINE

"Let's get out of here!! Move towards the dock area! If they see us, at least they'll have to come across an open area to get to us and we can find some cover in the shack! They may not think to look there since they just left that area," I whispered.

The men were spread out through the brush along the side of the road, flashing lights. The closest group was only about forty yards away now but there was a slight bend in the road that might hide us if we made our dash now. We didn't have to be too concerned about noise. They were making plenty and the truck was driving slowly behind the rear elements shining the spotlight on both sides of the road.

We ran from our cover toward the dock, trying to stay on the right side of the open area away from the bend in the road. Miraculously, we made it to the dock without being sighted. They were concentrating their attention on the sides of the road. There was a mound of earth from which the dock began before sloping toward the water about 30 feet away. Just as we scrambled under the dock, the truck reached the end of the road where the vegetation on either side existed and its lights illuminated the open area around the dock.

"We would be better off staying here behind this dirt bank. I don't think those thin planks on the shacks would stop a bullet from the rifles," Darby whispered.

The truck had stopped. The men began to emerge from the undergrowth along the side of the road. They gathered around the truck and looked to be discussing their next action. They knew we were in the area somewhere. About that time we heard a large explosion and saw a bright orange glow coming from the direction where our car was. They had blown it up and knew they had us trapped, if they could just find us.

"Do you think they will come back this way?" Thom asked.

"If they do and they sight us, we can hold out a while but it won't take long for their numbers and firepower to overtake us. I sure wish Steve, Percy and Larry were here. The odds would be a little better. At least you've still got the thirty rounds for the AR, Darby," I said.

I squeezed Ashton's hand. She was huddled between me and Thom. Darby was a little higher up the embankment trying to find a depression from which he could fire without exposing himself too much.

"Hon, I wish you weren't here. I want you to stay down if they locate us. If we don't make it, try to surrender. Maybe they will take you prisoner without harming you. If you are able to explain to them who you are, they will consider you too valuable to get rid of. I don't want you to get shot. I love you —very much," I whispered in her ear, squeezing her hand again.

"I know. And I love you, too. More than anything in the world. I'm going to help. I don't want to be their prisoner, even if they don't hurt me, if anything happens to you. I'm terrified, but I will pull my weight if we have to fight, Love," she whispered back.

"Uh oh! Here comes a couple of them in our direction!" Darby said.

The two men were ambling towards the dock area, not seeming to be particularly alert. Apparently they had been sent down to check it out, even though they had just left that area less than ten minutes ago. They were walking right toward the dock that we were hidden underneath!

"Dawson! Look!" Ashton whispered excitedly.

"What!?" I asked, not taking my eyes off the two men who were now within 25 yards of us. They were both armed with automatic rifles which they carried casually. One paused to light a cigarette. I noticed most of the other men were fanning back out deeper in the underbrush, retracing their route back down the road. About four of them remained around the pickup truck.

"One of those motorboats tied to the dock out there on the left! Could we take one and try to get out of here!?" she asked excitedly.

I glanced over my shoulder and nudged Thom beside me, pointing towards the boats. There were three small boats with what looked to be about thirty horsepower motors on the rear. Without a word he slid silently towards the water, staying hidden under the dock. I saw him in the dim light slip into the water, still staying under the dock. He came up between two of the boats. In the meantime the two men were almost at the dock. It looked like they were going to walk right out on the dock, probably intending to check out the two shacks that abutted the dock on the left side between the dock entrance and the waterline.

I looked up in the other direction just as the first man stepped foot on the dock above us. Darby was gone!! He was not in the little depression he had found to the left side of the underside of the dock. And he was not down with us! He had disappeared! The second man was now on the dock. They kicked in the door of the first shack, pointing their rifles in as they did so. One of the men shined a flashlight inside. They were satisfied no one was there and began to move on to the second shack.

Suddenly I saw this huge figure emerge silently from the shadows at the rear of the first shack. It was Darby! He quietly fell in behind the last man and I saw the glimmer off the blade of his knife just as it descended into the shoulder blades of the man's back. From where I was below, I could hear a crunching sound and a gasp as the air expelled from the man's lungs.

As the stricken man slumped down without a sound, the other man jerked around sharply, only to be met with a crushing blow across his neck. There was a sharp crack and a gurgling sound. A follow up blow to his midsection produced a sound like the whoosh of air let out of a balloon. He doubled over, tried to emit a muffled scream from his fractured Adam's Apple and received a sharp blow to the back of his neck that drove him to the ground. He didn't move or emit a sound after that.

"Guys!! Come over here! Bring your knife, Darby! We can take this boat. It's just tied to the dock with a rope and it has a full can of gas!" Thom reappeared in the water beside one of the boats.

I glanced back at the men around the truck while Darby ran over to cut the rope mooring the boat. They were lounging around the truck smoking and had not yet been able to detect the fates of their two associates. They would be curious about them soon. We didn't have much time.

"Take the gas can from that other boat and throw it in," I whispered to Darby. Thom had already climbed in the boat and was seated in the rear beside the motor. Ashton and I slid in the boat from the water. The waterline would not be visible from where the truck was. Darby was standing in the water and shoved the boat away from the dock. Before climbing in he proudly handed me the two additional automatic rifles he had confiscated along with the one he had. We now had three rifles, each with a thirty round clip!

"Adid!!" A shout came from the truck area. Adid must be one of the recently deceased gentlemen on the dock. Of course there was no answer. The only noise was the soft lapping of the waves against the shore.

"Okay, Thom. Try it. Let's hope this thing starts. If it does, gun it as soon as the motor sounds okay. As soon as it starts up we're going to get some company rushing this way and some automatic rifle fire in our direction. Darby, use one of the rifles to throw some rounds in their direction. That might cause them to pause long enough for us to get out of range," I said.

Thom poised to pull the starter rope. "What if it doesn't start?" he said.
"We're screwed," I replied, nodding for him to give it a jerk.

"Adid!!" the man shouted again, then four of them started walking towards the dock. They were already well within accurate automatic rifle range and would be right upon us in about five minutes.

Thom jerked hard on the starter rope. There was a muffled chugging sound but the motor didn't start. The four men paused, puzzled, as if to comprehend what the noise they had faintly heard was. Darby leveled the rifle, but held his fire. We all held our breath. Thom jerked the rope again. This time the motor started, first with a soft chugging noise, then a loud clatter!

It suddenly dawned on the men approaching us what was taking place. There were shouts as they began to run in our direction. Two of them began firing shots from their rifles in our general direction. They still could not see us in the boat against the dark water background, but they could tell our general location from the now purring sound of the motor as Thom began easing away from the dock.

"Okay, Darby, put some fire on them! Thom, as soon as Darby fires, gun it and let's get some distance between us as quickly as we can in the moments it takes for them to recover from the hostile fire!" I shouted. There was no need for quiet now.

"Bam!! Bam!! Bam!!" Darby's rifle barked in a series of short bursts. Thom opened up the throttle and the little boat's front end rose as we roared out to the open sea in an easterly direction, leaving a wide white wake behind us. Darby emptied the clip on that rifle and tossed it overboard.

By now we were receiving fire from all four of the men who were now at the edge of the dock. Although the boat was still difficult to make out in the dark waters, the white wake in the moonlight clearly illuminated our position. We were not quite out of range yet.

Suddenly I saw Darby, who was in the front of the boat, jerk and slump forward slightly.

"Darby!! Are you alright?!" I shouted over the noise of the boat still going full throttle.

CHAPTER THIRTY

After what seemed like minutes, but was only a few seconds, Darby straightened up and clasped his right hand over his left shoulder. He turned back slightly toward me.

"I've been hit. I don't think it's bad. Just a nick. We're out of range now, I think," he said calmly.

Thom cut back on the throttle a little and the little boat settled down in the water. We were about a mile out to sea now, still going in an easterly direction. Ashton , who had been sitting beside me in the center seat, crawled up front to Darby to inspect his wound. With the throttle down, we could now talk and hear each other.

"Darby, you're lucky. It's a clean shot and exit wound in your upper arm. I don't think it hit a bone. I'm going to tear off a piece of your shirt and wrap around it to stop the blood flow. How do you feel?" Ashton asked.

"I feel fine. This is the most minor wound I have ever had. I'll be alright, just a little sore for a while. When we get to where I can put some antiseptic on it, I'll do that. I had a bottle of whisky in the car that would have done fine, but its gone now. Don't worry about me. Let's figure out where we're going now," he reassured her.

"Look!" Thom shouted. He was at the rear at the motor facing the front of the boat. "I believe that's the barge about a mile ahead of us!"

We all strained to see in the direction he pointed. You could not see the outline of a boat, but could see the unmistakable orange lights that were on the perimeter of the big, slow barge. They had left in an easterly direction also and our faster boat had almost caught up with them even though they had about a fifteen minute head start on us.

"You're right! I'm going to try to reach Larry to find what's been going on with them and bring him up to date with our situation. The barge is headed in the direction of Jakarta, but it will take the rest of the night and most of tomorrow for them to get there if that is their destination. Let's just stay on their tail without getting much closer than we are now," I said.

"Hey Dawson! Where are you guys?! We've been trying to reach you," Steve answered when the call went through.

"I've had my phone turned off. We couldn't take a chance on the noise that the ring would make," I said, briefly explaining what we had been up to.

"So you guys are in the middle of the ocean in a little motorboat chasing a barge with the weapon on it?!" Steve exclaimed. "Are you sure Darby's okay?"

"Yeah, I think so. Where are you three and what's been happening in your life?" I asked.

"We're finally in Lebac, just driving around in the vicinity of the plant, not knowing where to go from here. We ran into the bad guys, too, just outside of Sumenep. Percy had his baptism of fire too, and he has a little bullet crease on his forearm to prove it. After a short firefight, we got the hell away from them and took a circuitous route on into Lebac. We drove continuously and fast to try to get here tonight instead of tomorrow. We've been here about ten minutes. The only significant outcome of our little short gun battle, I think, was that they discovered there were just three of us," Steve explained.

"Yeah. That's probably why they rushed to Lebac to move the weapon. They figured out that the other four of us were probably already there," I said.

"It's funny, Dawson. When we saw that we were probably going to have to try to fight our way out of the little box we found ourselves in, Percy was worried about killing foreign nationals on their own home ground. But when he got hit, he became a little tiger. When the bullets starting coming our way, he forgot about possible political repercussions. He dropped two of them before we escaped," Steve laughed.

"Good! Remind him that these "foreign nationals" will have no compunctions about killing our president, and anyone else who gets in their way on our soil, if they are able to perfect the weapon and implement their plan," I said.

"What should we do now?" Steve asked.

"We need to join forces again as soon as possible. If we can stay on the tail of this barge, we will be heading for another showdown soon and we need your firepower. Let's assume the barge is heading for Jakarta. The best thing for you guys to do right now is to get off Madura and head East back to Jakarta. We'll stay in touch and let you know if they change course," I said.

"Okay. We'll go back the way we came, hopefully without running into trouble again. We'll cross over at a different location. It sounds like you will spend your night and most of tomorrow on the water. Do you have food and drink?" Steve asked.

"No. But the first settlement we come to on shore we will speed up, rush in and buy minimal supplies and get back out before we lose sight of the barge. We can close our distance on them prior to doing that. They are so slow, we should be able to catch up again quickly," I replied.

"Okay. Have fun. We'll stay in touch and join you as soon as we can. Since it is going to take you so long to get to Jakarta, we may stop and have a nice juicy steak on the way back," Steve said before hanging up. He didn't hear my go to hell comment before he hung up.

About twenty minutes later we saw lights up ahead to the left on the shore. It must be Tuban, a small town on the north coast of Java east of Madura. We speeded up and closed the gap to less than half a mile from the barge before turning in to shore. We pulled quickly up to the dock. Fortunately there was a little convenience type store right there at the dock.

"Okay, everybody take a quick potty break. I'll go in the store and get bottled water and plenty of snacks. Let's try to be back on the boat in fifteen minutes max," I said.

I was able to get bread, lunch meats, potato chips and plenty of candy bars, crackers and other assorted items along with the water and two six packs of beer and a carton of cigarettes. It was going to be a long night. We were back on the boat in twelve minutes and quickly caught up with the barge, shutting our running lights off and dropping back to our one mile distance as soon as we confirmed it was our ship.

By this time we only had about an hour until dawn would break. We were exhausted but enjoyed the camaraderie there in the stillness of the night. The moon cast its silvery, wavy light across the dark, seemingly endless expanse of water. The only sound was the lapping of the water against the sides of the boat as we cruised at little more than idle speed. Occasionally we could hear the distant soft chugging sound of the barge ahead of us.

We lounged back in the boat looking at the stars, drinking our beer and smoking the cigarettes I had bought. You could see the glow of the cigarette tips in the otherwise blackness where only the forms of our bodies were visible to each other. Thom, who normally didn't smoke, was smoking and Ashton even took a couple of puffs before gagging and throwing it overboard into the water.

Thom pulled into another village before dawn for another bathroom break and to replenish our supplies and refill our gas can. We also bought a tarp that we could rig up to shade ourselves to some degree from the blazing sun that would be up soon. I had figured we would be on the water at least all day. Judging from the landmarks we could recognize, it could be well into the night before we got to Jakarta if, in fact, that was the barges destination. We were back on the water a few minutes before dawn. It was the morning of February 13th, New York time. It was hard to believe we had only been in Indonesia barely four days. It seemed like a lifetime.

"How does your arm feel?" I asked Darby. We had gotten some alcohol and peroxide on the first stop.

"Feels fine. You know, when I was a kid —probably about eight years old— my older brother stuck a pitchfork through my arm," he said.

"A pitchfork! How did that happen?" Thom asked.

"My family was poor. My dad was a sharecropper on this little farm in Alabama. My brother was pitching hay over the fence to the four cows we owned. I was trying to help and got in the way," he said.

"I bet that hurt," Ashton said.

"Yeah. We never told my parents what happened. They would have beat hell out of my brother. We told them I fell out of the loft and landed on a board with a nail in it."

"Did they believe that?" Ashton asked.

"Yeah. I got hell beat out of me for being careless," Darby said.

"When did you decide to go into the military?" I asked.

"When I figured out that I couldn't make a living doing what my parents did. I always managed to make good grades in school. My mother saw to it that I studied. But there were no real opportunities in the little town I grew up in for a young black boy. I went into the Army thinking I would be able to further my education and do something important when I got out. I was good at the Army thing and came to believe that what I was doing was important. After several promotions and experience in the covert activities where you really get to see the real threats to our country that most people never know about, I decided to stay and make a career out of this job," Darby responded thoughtfully.

"Yeah, I'm sure the general public will never know about the threat we are chasing unless we fail in our mission. If we do, the whole world will know," I said.

The sun was beginning to pop up in the horizon. It was beautiful as the orange rays of light began to spread out over the glistening water.

"We'll be here all day. We need to close distance a little. It will be a little more difficult to track them in the daytime without the orange lights guiding us. Let's go in shifts piloting the boat while three try to get some sleep," I suggested.

"Okay. I'll continue at the wheel and take the first shift. I'm not sleepy. We should dash in to the shore occasionally and come back out so no one on the barge will notice a small boat continuously shadowing them," Thom said.

"Good thinking, Thom. Okay, I'll take the next shift, then if you feel like it Darby, you can relieve me," I said.

"I'll take my turn, too. Let me go before Darby. We can take about 2 and ½ hour turns," Ashton said.

"Okay, girl. Well let's try to get some sleep. We may have some action tonight and it's going to be a long uncomfortable day riding these waves. Fortunately, there is no wind and the water is relatively calm," I replied.

We rigged the tarp up as best we could and Ashton and I settled down together in the middle section of the boat. I scrunched down on the bottom of the boat and Ashton curled up alongside me with her head in my lap. I used one of the boat cushions as a substitute pillow. Darby got himself situated in the front of the boat and dozed off immediately.

"Dawson Kohler, how did I ever get mixed up with you? In the last three nights I've slept in the jungle, in a little trailer without hot water, been shot at and now bouncing around in a little boat in the middle of the ocean. I must love you," Ashton said before falling into a fitful sleep.

I remained awake a while longer thinking about our last three days too. And even in these uncomfortable circumstances, I couldn't help but be aroused by the pretty little girl who loved me, resting her head in my lap. She didn't even notice. She was asleep.

The day wore on with each of us taking our turns. The heat reflecting off the water would have been unbearable without the tarp to shade us. The sun began to set. I had talked to Larry and Steve a couple of times. Percy got on the phone once to tell me how much he missed the cushy State Department work and how he dreamed about Reza while sleeping in the back seat of the car on their way back to Jakarta. He also told me how delicious the steak they had last night was. They were back in Jakarta now and were just waiting close to the dock area for further word from us. It would be nice to have the three of them back with us when we next faced our enemies.

I had no way of knowing at the time that it would be another twenty-four hours before that would be possible, and it would be too late by then. We would not be able to reunite with Larry, Steve and Percy tonight and tragedy would befall us before tomorrow night.

CHAPTER THIRTY-ONE

It was dusk now and we were still heading East along the North shore of Java, somewhere between the town of Indramayu and Jakarta. We probably had a couple more hours if the destination proved to be Jakarta. We were all tired and anxious to get back on land. Along the way we had all jumped overboard for a few minutes to take a cooling swim and, I suspect for all of us, to add some salt water to the ocean. Our beer had been long gone but we still had a few crackers and plenty of water. We vowed to make our three missing partners buy us a steak and lobster dinner with fine wine the first opportunity that presented itself. In anticipation of action ahead, our adrenalin was keeping us hyper, but a nice bed to sleep in would be wonderful when the time came.

"I know now why I chose the Air Force instead of the Navy. I am making a promise to myself that I will never, ever get in a boat again the rest of my life," Thom commented.

"And I promise myself that the next time I meet a stranger in Atlanta, I will run for my life!" Ashton said, looking at me.

"Aw, hon. I thought we might go on a cruise for our honeymoon," I said. She just glared at me. She sure was pretty when she was angry, even when she was faking it.

"Look, there's Jakarta in the distance, probably a couple of miles away," Darby said. You could see the glow of lights coming from the large city. The barge was a mile away. We would know soon if they were stopping in Jakarta. It was now about 8:00 PM.

"Larry, if you guys are close to the dock area, you will see a big barge with orange running lights coming into view soon. That's the one we are chasing. The weapon is in a crate with a tarp over it on the front deck of the barge. We're about a mile behind, but can close the gap fast if we need to," I told Larry when he answered my call on the cell phone.

"Right. We'll look for it and see what happens. Stay in touch," Larry responded.

We could tell that the barge was slowing now because we were closing the distance between us without changing our own speed. It did not seem to be turning into the docks lining the waterfront though. Thom eased back on the throttle. We were running without lights, but didn't want to get too close yet. It now appeared to be stopped about a half mile offshore. We got close enough to see the outline of the ship and put the motor on idle.

"We see it now. It's stopped offshore," Larry reported.

"You won't be able to see us in the darkness, but we're about a half mile from it on idle. Let's hold in place to see if they anchor or move on," I said.

"We've got quite a crowd on the dock now. Six cars full of armed men. I recognize one of the cars from the bunch that attacked us. They're just parked at the dock across the water from the barge, but I don't detect any other activity. There has not been a boat launched towards the barge yet. They appear to be just lounging around waiting for something," Larry observed before hanging up.

"Dawson, look!!" Thom exclaimed.

There was a big helicopter flying from shore straight towards the barge. Someone on the barge was flashing signal lights to guide it in over the front of the ship.

"Gun it!! Let's get closer quick!" I shouted.

The copter was already descending and hovering over the barge. Cables could be seen rapidly descending from the helicopter in the glare of spotlights now trained on the crate. We raced to within 100 feet of the barge, but the crate was rapidly being hoisted upward and by the time we got alongside, the helicopter was already moving towards shore.

"Larry!!" I frantically called on the cell phone, "try to follow the destination of that copter on land if you can! We're coming into shore. Stay in touch on the phone. If you lose it, we'll meet you at the hotel."

I was dejected. We had the weapon in our grasp and it had slipped away. The people who had built it could be tracked down later and the information with them found and destroyed. But Ashton had told me earlier that the window of time that the technical information could have been passed to unfriendly people would have been between sometime before the funding freeze on the project and the time it became classified and the security restrictions were put in place. That would place it at least six months ago and possibly up to nine months. If the weapon was ready now, it had taken them at least six months to build it and it likely was not fully developed and tested yet. They took it out when they discovered we were on its tail. To find and destroy it now would set them back six months. And if we also found the people and technical information, their project could die. But now it had slipped from our grasp.

"Let's go into shore and dock over by that freighter. We'll try to get a cab and go to the closest place to rent a car," I told Thom.

We hastily tied the boat to the dock and scrambled ashore. All of us were stiff from the hours we had spent cramped together on the water in the little boat.

We had not taken ten steps though before half a dozen armed men appeared out of the darkness. They formed a half circle around us with our backs to the water. Darby had the AR in his hand and we all were armed with our handguns, but we had no chance to react. They had the drop on us.

"Drop the rifle. Now, or you will die! The rest of you keep your hands in front of you!" one of the men shouted. Darby reluctantly complied and laid the rifle on the sand in front of him.

"We've been waiting for you, gentlemen —and lady. Since you escaped from Lebac, we have been tracking you down the coast. We had people call us when you made your first stop for supplies. Once it was evident you had caught up with the barge and were following it, all we had to do was wait here for you," one of the men said with a sardonic sneer.

"Hassan! Come here! See if you can identify these people," another of the men shouted over his shoulder. I could feel Ashton shrink beside me. We were all scared because we knew they would likely kill us here and throw our bodies in the dark, murky water.

"Well, well, aren't we lucky?" Hassan emerged from the darkness. "Walid is at my vacation home in Bandung. He will be pleased at this surprise catch," he said, looking directly at Ashton.

"Are these the people?" the man who had summoned him asked.

"Only two of them. I recognize those two. They were at my office," he said, pointing to me and Thom. Larry was of course not with us and I remembered that Percy and Darby had stayed back at the hotel with Ashton when the other four of us visited Hassan.

"I don't recognize the black guy, but he was with them in Lebac, you say. The other two who were at my office must still be in the city. We'll round them up soon, I'm sure," Hassan continued.

"Okay, let's get rid of them," the man who seemed to be the leader said.

"Wait. The girl I will take to Walid. She will be of value to us. Get rid of the others," Hassan stepped forward and grabbed Ashton by the arm. As he did so, he ripped her blouse half off, exposing the little pistol which she had stuck in her shorts. He tossed it in the water and stood leering at her as her torn blouse dangled at her side, revealing one of her well formed breasts.

I lunged towards Hassan and was immediately tackled and wrestled to the ground by three of the thugs with him. They ordered me to stand, holding my arms behind my back as I did so.

A couple of the other men roughly patted us down, finding our handguns and Darby's knife and throwing them, along with the rifle, in the water. They tossed the cell phone down on the sand. Then they herded us to the edge of the water towards a metal trash dumpster that was partially out in the water.

"Get in!" the leader shouted.

We hesitated. One of the men slammed his rifle butt into Thom's head. Thom immediately dropped to the ground, blood pouring from a gash in his head.

"Get up! We can put you in here dead or alive!" the man shouted, kicking at Thom.

Thom slowly wobbled to his feet. Darby and I crawled over the rim of the container and helped Thom in. The top was open and we stood there looking out toward the men who had gathered around. Hassan was still holding onto Ashton. One of the men began to close the hinged metal top of the container.

"Before you close the top, let me show them how we treat a treacherous female who dares to threaten and humiliate us," Hassan halted them.

With us watching, Hassan turned and gave Ashton a vicious slap across the face. She fell to the ground, a trickle of blood showing on her cheek. He then jerked her up, ripping the rest of her blouse off.

"Now, take your shorts off, bitch!" Hassan instructed.

She didn't move and he slapped her again. Hassan motioned for one of the men to hold her while he unbuttoned her shorts, letting them slide to the ground. She was standing there naked except for her panties.

"I should turn her over to the men here to have their way with her for your final show before you die. But I want to take her untouched to Walid. Don't worry. Walid will have his fun with her, but we won't kill her, at least until she helps us complete our project. Who knows? If Walid likes her, she may be compelled to join his harem. He has three wives, but none as beautiful as this one," Hassan addressed us with a maniacal laugh before motioning the man to go ahead and close the lid. After closing it, a padlock was placed on it.

We noticed that holes had been drilled in the sides of the container. Water had already seeped in, covering our feet. We could raise the lid about two inches and look out. The crowd was still on the shore. Suddenly we heard a sound and saw a fork truck with wide tires approaching. It closed on the container, placing the forks on the front, and began to shove us further out in the water.

Water poured into the holes as we were pushed, until it was chin high. Then the tractor stopped and retreated back to shore. We raised the lid and saw the men leave, getting into vehicles that drove out on the sand. Hassan pushed Ashton in the back seat of one of the cars, waving at us before they all left. We were standing there in the darkness, shivering in the water when they drove off. My last view was Ashton looking out the car window, a big thug beside her. I couldn't really see in the darkness, but didn't have to see to know that tears were flowing down her cheeks.

"At least they left us alive. Even though this stretch of the beach looks to be deserted at night, if we can survive the night, maybe someone will come by in the morning and we can make enough noise that they will hear us and get us out," Thom said wearily.

"Guys, there's something you haven't noticed," Darby said.

"What's that?" I asked.

"We're at low tide. The high tide will be coming in later tonight," he said somberly.

CHAPTER THIRTY-TWO

"Fellows, we've got to try to get out of here. I have something I have to do —soon," I said, a determined look on my face.

"I hope it's not go to the bathroom," Thom said. Then he noticed the serious expression on my face.

"No. I have to rescue Ashton. And kill Hassan and his boss Walid Alziddi. If, somehow, we can get out of here, that will be my mission. And, if that can happen, I want the pleasure of accomplishing those two things all by myself. When we find them, save Hassan for me. I will cut his balls off and stuff them in his fucking mouth!" I said.

"I'll help you if you let me. I just can't believe we're going to die here tonight in this damn trash container! Let's try to make some noise," Thom said. He started beating on the top of the container.

"Stop!! What's that noise?" I exclaimed. There was a ringing sound from the beach.

We lifted the lid so we could see out. The ringing continued.

"It's the cell phone! They tossed our weapons in the water, but just threw the phone down on the sand. The other guys must be trying to reach us," Darby said.

The phone was at least twenty yards away though and there was no way to reach it, even if we could get our arms out of the container. Maybe it was our imagination, but the water seemed to have risen slightly.

"I can't believe we are stuck here while Ashton is probably on her way to being tortured, raped, maybe killed. We've got to figure out something quick. I think the water's rising," I said. A tear of frustration and anger slid down my cheek. As hopeless as our situation was, fear had not gripped me yet. I pushed up on the top of the container, but it wouldn't budge beyond the two inch crack.

"You know, I would like to see Hassan swallow his balls. Maybe Houdini Peters can get us out of here," Darby calmly mused.

"Darby, it's no time to joke. The water is rising. Let's start shouting. Maybe someone will hear us," Thom said.

"I'm not joking," Darby said.

"What do you mean?" I asked.

"Well, you remember the 9 mm pistols we got along with the AR at Hassan's office? You gave me one of the 9mms and the AR?" Darby asked.

"Yes, what about it? The AR and our handguns are in the water out there," I said.

"Yes, they are. Except for the 9mm that I had stuck in my boot when we got off the boat. When they frisked us, they didn't find that one," Darby said, producing it above the water where we could see it.

"Darby!! I love you!!" I said, putting my arms around his neck.

"Hold on. We're in too close quarters for you to start exhibiting your kinky sexual tendencies," Darby laughed.

"Will it still work after being under water?" Thom asked.

"I think so. To clean our rifles when I was in basic training, we used to put them in boiling water, then put a thin coat of oil on the moving parts. The sergeants would have killed us if they had found out, but it was sure a better way to get the grime and grit off than cleaning with an oily rag. The oil just made the dirt stick to the metal," Darby replied.

"Okay, you guys raise the lid as high as you can. I'll see if I can get a shot at the lock on the lid," Darby continued.

Thom and I raised the lid as high as we could. The padlock holding it down was slightly exposed. By now the water was almost to our mouths and Darby had to reach his arm above the water with his head tilted back to place the pistol in position to shoot the lock. Finally, he was able to place the tip of the barrel against the lock housing

"It may ricochet. Turn your heads. Ready?" Darby asked.

We held our breath. If this didn't work, we surely would drown within the next 15 to 30 minutes.

Blamm!!! The noise reverberated loudly through the 5" of steel remaining in the air space left in the container. The lock exploded from the force of the bullet at such close range! Thom and I pushed upward on the lid. The remaining hasp held for a second before breaking loose and sinking into the surrounding ocean, then the lid raised back on its hinges. We were free!!

We quickly climbed out of the container and scrambled through neck high water to the beach. Able to look at my waterproof watch now, I saw that the time was 9:20 PM. Hassan and his group had only left about fifteen minutes ago. Maybe we still had time to catch them before Ashton was harmed!

"Get the cell phone! The water is almost to it!" I shouted.

"I'm going to see if I can retrieve our guns. All we have now is this one 9mm with only eight bullets left," Darby said, then dove into the water in the vicinity of where the weapons were thrown in. I got on the cell phone and dialed Larry's number. He answered immediately.

"Larry!! They have Ashton!" I shouted into the phone. "We have to find her quick! They will harm her! Alziddi is here!" I blurted into the phone.

"Hold on. Slow down. What the hell are you talking about Dawson? I've been trying to call you and you wouldn't answer," Larry said.

I explained what happened to Ashton and why we had not been able to answer his call. In retrospect, looking at us dripping wet and having survived the ordeal, it would have been laughable if not for the abduction of Ashton.

"Wow! Did you say they were going to Bandung?" Larry asked.

"Yes. Hassan let that slip. I'm sure it didn't matter to him since he never expected we would get out of the locked container alive. Apparently Walid Alziddi is staying with him right now and that is where they are taking Ashton," I answered.

"Well, we lost the copter. We couldn't keep up with it in the air, but it may have been headed to the airport. We are close to the airport now. Just a minute—" Larry got off the phone a few moments and I could hear conversation with Percy talking in the background.

"Dawson," Larry got back on the phone, "Percy had done quite a lot of research on Indonesia when he found we were coming here. He says Bandung is over an hour's drive from here. It is the third largest city in Indonesia with a population of about 1.5 million and is considered to be the Paris of Indonesia. It is in the mountains and the best way to get there quickly is by train. It goes through a rambling verdant countryside that climbs to cooler elevations and is surrounded by forests. It is famous for its gardens and puppet shows in several places nightly. Unlike Jakarta, with its noise, crowds and constant traffic, Bandung is rather sedate and he says it is the center of Sudanese culture, more friendly and extraverted than the refined Javenese of Jakarta. I tell you, Dawson, Percy's a walking encyclopedia. Do you want us to come pick you up?"

"No. Don't waste the time. Go on to Bandung and spend the rest of the night there. It will be late when you get there. I would like to get a car and drive there now myself, but by the time we would get there it would be well after midnight. I can't stand the thought of Ashton being there alone tonight, but it will be fairly late tonight when they get there too. Maybe she will be safe tonight. Common sense tells me we should go to the Sentera and get a little rest. It's doubtful we could find any hints as to Hassan's location tonight. We'll take the early morning train out to Bandung tomorrow and meet you there," I said.

I was exhausted physically from the long boat trip and our ordeal and exhausted mentally from the frustration of Ashton's situation and not being able to do anything about it immediately. I was sure Darby and Thom were in the same shape. We needed to be in better shape when we confronted Alziddi's people or we could blow our chances of saving Ashton from whatever fate awaited her.

"Okay. Hold on again," Larry said.

"Percy says a good central place to stay would be the Hotel Panghejar. We'll meet you there in the morning," Larry said when he returned to the phone.

"Fine. Darby's trying to fish our weapons out of the water. Then we'll be going. But Larry, one thing—" I said.

"What's that?" he asked.

"When you get there tonight, make an effort to find where Hassan's place is before you turn in. If you luck out and find it, don't wait for us. Get the local police if you have to, but go in and try to get Ashton."

"We will, Dawson. The local police will be no help in this matter I don't think. In fact, Hassan could just get tipped off if we approach them. But we will handle it. I feel good with Steve and Percy. If we find where Ashton is tonight, we'll go in and get her," Larry reassured me.

"Thanks, Larry. One more thing," I said. "Don't take unnecessary chances, but if you do find them and can capture Hassan and his boss unhurt, hold them somewhere for me. I have a score that I intend to settle with them," I continued. I hardly recognized the cold determination of my own voice.

"I promise. But only if you let me help you settle that score. We're on our way," Larry said before hanging up.

Ashton wouldn't be found tonight. And tomorrow night would be too late.

CHAPTER THIRTY-THREE

"How are you doing with the recovery, Darby?" I asked after hanging up with Larry and seeing Darby emerge from the ocean dripping wet.

"I found all of the handguns, but not the AR, dammit! They didn't throw the handguns too far in the water and I watched where they went. But the guy that tossed the AR really slung it. I've been back in three times and can't find it. The tide coming in has probably covered it up with sand out there in the shoals. I give up," he replied.

"Well, at least we have our fully loaded handguns, but we are really lightly armed. I have six extra shells for my revolver in my pocket that they didn't find. Did either of you get by with any extra clips?" I asked.

"Yeah, I have one clip in my other boot that they didn't find," Darby said.

"They found the two clips for my automatic that I had and tossed them, so all I have is the full clip in the gun," Thom said.

"And look what else I lucked out and found. I actually stepped on it when I waded out to find the handguns," Darby said smiling and holding up his hunting knife.

"Okay," I laughed, "we have three guns, two extra clips and Darby's knife. That's enough, because when I find Hassan, I'm not even going to use a gun or your knife. I'm going to bite his balls off!"

"Uh oh. I guess you don't expect a kiss from Ashton when we find her, then," Thom said.

"Yeah—I just hope we find her in time. I can imagine just what she's going through—what's going through her mind even if they do get in too late to do anything with her tonight. Larry said he thought the first train left for Bandung at 6:00 AM. I want to be on it. Let's walk up on the road and try to find a taxi. We'll go to the hotel and get something to eat and a few hours rest and be ready to go early in the morning. Maybe Larry, Steve and Percy will have found information on their whereabouts before we get there about 7:15," I said.

"We better be alert when we come off the beach, too. Some of the bad guys may still be hanging around this area and there's no way I will let them get the drop on me again. We know what they will do to us, so if we go down, we may as well take as many of them with us as we can," Darby said.

We found a cab and got to the hotel without incident. The lobby was nearly deserted at this hour, but a little deli was open next door. We got a bite to eat, then turned in for a few fitful hours of sleep. I couldn't keep my mind off of Ashton and was anxious to do something to find her before they harmed her. Finally I dosed off from exhaustion for about three hours. At 5:00 AM I was up and dressed. Darby and Thom were ready too, and we walked down to the train station and were the first ones to board the train to Bandung. It left on time and we were wary of any of the other passengers, but did not observe anyone who acted suspicious.

We arrived at the station in Bandung at 7:20 AM. I had talked to Larry again the night before and told him to meet us at 7:15. At that time, they had arrived in Bandung and were getting ready to scout around to see if they could make any progress on locating Hassan's place. I didn't call him this morning, knowing they would need rest, too, and assuming he would have called me if they had located our quarry. But Larry was not there to meet us.

I tried to call Larry. The phone was not activated.

"That's strange. Maybe they did find Hassan last night. But surely they would have been able to call by now. Now I'm worried about them. I guess the only thing we can do is go on to Hotel Panghejar. Maybe they'll show up or will have left a message," I mused.

"Maybe they just got slowed in traffic," Darby said.

"No, they would have called. I agree with you Dawson. It's not good that they're not here and we haven't heard from them. Something's happened to them or they are in a position like we were a couple of times where they didn't want the phone to ring. Either way, it's not good," Thom said.

We got a cab and arrived at the Paghejar about 8:15 AM. We checked in and I asked the clerk if there were messages for any of us. He said no. He did confirm that two rooms had been reserved in Steve Whitt's name and that they were still in use. He would not divulge their room number but did call the rooms for us. There was no answer in either room.

The three of us got adjoining rooms with Darby and Thom taking one and me the other. It was the first decent place we had been in in several nights except for the fitful stopover for a few hours last night. I missed Ashton terribly and was worried about the other three.

"What should we do now —wait here for them to hopefully contact us, or go try to find them or Hassan?" Thom asked after we had gotten settled in our rooms.

"Let's start our own search. Under the circumstances, if we find Hassan, we may find the others there or in that vicinity. I don't want to sit idly by while Ashton is being held and if Steve, Larry and Percy might be in trouble too. Besides, we have the cell phone. If they can call us, they will," I said.

"Before we leave, let's do the simple thing —check for Abu el Hassan's address in the phone book," Darby said.

We did that. No luck. He probably had an unlisted number. We asked the clerk and the hotel manager if they knew Hassan. They said they did not. Next we walked out on the street, impatient, but not really knowing how to start in our search.

We didn't risk splitting up, even in the crowded city, but by noon the three of us had talked to probably 100 people we found who could speak English. No one knew Hassan. We stopped for a quick lunch. Still no call.

Just as we were ready to leave and begin again what had, so far, been a fruitless search, the phone rang. I grabbed it quickly and we all sat back down.

"Dawson?" It was Steve and I could barely hear him. He was whispering.

"Yeah. Where are you guys? We were worried when you didn't meet us and we didn't hear from you. What's going on?" I asked.

"Can't talk much now. Just wanted you to know we are okay right now, but in the midst of unfriendlies. We may have found what we are looking for. Will have to call you later when we can talk. Hang loose. I'll get back in touch as soon as I can," Steve whispered and quickly hung up.

"Damn!! They may be with the people we are looking for and we don't even know where they are! Steve couldn't talk. He said he would call back as soon as he could," I explained to Darby and Thom.

"What do we do now?" Thom asked.

"Keep scouting for clues to Hassan's whereabouts and wait on Steve's call is all we can do," I said dejectedly.

"I sure wish we knew where they were. We need to find Ashton soon and I'm anxious to meet up with Abu Asshole and his rectal boss," Darby said impatiently.

"Yeah. We'll find them, Darby. But Asshole is mine. Remember. Let's go guys," I said determinedly.

We spent most of the rest of the afternoon with only one respondent indicating he knew of Hassan. He had heard of a man by that name who was an associate of a cleric in Bandung named Kahlid Bassyir. He told us where

Bassyir's mosque was but warned that the fundamentalist Islamic cleric was a dangerous man who associated with, and some said led, a militant organization renowned for their harsh treatment of westerners. Rumors placed the blame on Bassyir for the murder of a number of moderate Indonesian officials and visiting foreigners just last year. We thanked the man who seemed genuinely concerned for our safety, but was careful to not linger with us after our brief conversation.

"Okay! We finally have a lead. Let's go. Damn! I wish Steve would call!" I said.

As if on cue, the phone rang. "Dawson, it's Larry." He was talking at a normal volume.

"Larry! Where are you. What's happened?" I asked.

"Wow! We finally are by ourselves and could call you. It's been an interesting day, but I think fate has intervened. By the luck of the draw and a miracle of coincidence, I think we know where Hassan and Alziddi are and Ashton has to be with them or close by," Larry said.

"Don't worry about finding Ashton. Just find Hassan for me," I said.

"Huh?" Larry was perplexed.

"Look. If I get my hands on Hassan, I'll guarantee you he will tell me where Ashton is —that is if he can talk with his balls in his mouth. We'll just tell Percy to turn his head so he won't have to observe an atrocity by a representative of the American government on a foreign national," I answered.

"Okay. I see," Larry laughed. "Well, let me tell you our story, then we need to hook up with you guys. It's not going to be an easy operation to get to them."

"Shoot," I said.

"Well, we left the hotel this morning in our rental car early—about 6:30— to meet you. Traffic was light. We were driving along when all of a sudden Steve saw two guys on the sidewalk he thought he recognized from our encounter on Madura and we decided to check it out. We knew we couldn't get out of the car. They would recognize us if Steve was right. So we parked down the street, and got out and fell in well behind them when they passed us," Larry began.

"They turned right on the next block and we found ourselves in front of a big mosque in a crowd of probably a thousand people. No sooner had we arrived than there was this huge roar from the crowd as they focused their attention on a cleric who came out the front door of the mosque. He was a short, pudgy, studious looking guy with a beard, mustache and a turban.

From his enthusiastic reception from the crowd of people, he obviously was a person of importance," Larry continued.

"Probably Kahlid Bassyr," I commented.

"Why, yes. That's who we found out later he was! How did you know?" he asked.

"Just a guess. Go on," I said.

"Well, we folded into the crowd. Larry can pick up some of the language, you know. This guy had a hand held megaphone and evidently was lambasting the U.S., the U.K. and the whole western world and they were cheering and screaming after every sentence. Then he turned and motioned over his shoulder and another guy dressed similarly to him but much taller and leaner came out of the mosque. Talk about going wild, the crowd went ballistic when this guy came out. He was obviously some kind of hero to them," Larry said.

"Walid Alziddi?" I asked.

"Right! We recognized him from the photos we had been given. He addressed the crowd and they got really worked up. We were nervous, but nobody was paying any attention to us and we looked like most of the guys in the crowd. We even screamed and cheered and pumped our fists in the air when they did. The Sheik came back then and they both talked. By this time the crowd was in a fervor. The speeches lasted a couple of hours. There was no way we could get on the cell phone and try to call you in the middle of that charged up crowd," Larry said.

"I understand. What happened then?" I asked.

"Alziddi and Bassyr, after their harangue, walked together around the side to the back of the mosque. They were heavily protected by armed guards. Someone else took over the megaphone, but a lot of the crowd followed them around to the back of the mosque. We followed. There were four fairly large cottages back there. When they got to the second one, who do you think comes out to greet them?" Larry asked.

"Our friend, Hassan?" I asked.

"Right again. We had everyone in sight that we were looking for except Ashton. I'll bet she is in one of those four cottages; but we couldn't do anything. We were still protected in our anonymity by the crowd, but they had a dozen armed guards surrounding them. There was a little garage on the right side facing the cottages and it had dirty windows on the back side. The door was cracked open. We decided to sneak in there one at a time when we could do so without being observed. We were able to get on the fringe of the crowd by the garage and, one at a time, drift over and slip in when the crowd was preoccupied with Alziddi's impromptu comments from the porch of Hassan's cottage. It took twenty minutes for all of us to get in unobserved. We hid behind a big pile of lumber and watched from one of the dirty windows. By this time it was late morning," Larry continued.

"Why didn't you call then?" I asked.

"Well, we had only been there five minutes when it became obvious that Bassyr, Alziddi and Hassan were going in the second cottage. They waved at the crowd who cheered them again, then went inside as the crowd began to disperse. The guards dispersed to take up posts surrounding the cottage complex. And wouldn't you know it. One of the guards chose our little garage to camp outside of. We've been here all afternoon without being able to make a sound until he stepped off behind a tree to take a leak and we were able to give you the whispered call. They changed guards about twenty minutes ago and we were able to sneak out while the two guards chatted and smoked next to the cottages before the new guard took his post," Larry concluded.

"Okay. Where are you now. We're on our way," I asked.

"We are at a little café about four blocks away from the mosque. We're in the back in a dark corner sipping beer. It's 5:15 PM now. You can get here in thirty minutes," Larry said and gave me directions.

"We're on our way!" I said.

"Good. One other thing, Dawson," he said.

"What's that?" I asked.

"We didn't see Ashton, but suspect she is in one of the cottages. Before we left —I think it was about 3:00 PM— Alziddi and the cleric left the cottage Hassan was in. The cleric went into the cottage on the far left and Alziddi went to the one on the far right. Unless she is in the cottage next to the cleric, she has been with either Hassan, Alziddi or Bassyr since then. I don't think she is in the one next to the cleric because there have been other people including some of the guards going in and out of that one. My guess is that she is either still with Hassan or with Alziddi. Alziddi, being the probable ranking one of the group, may have her," he said quietly.

CHAPTER THIRTY-FOUR

We found the café about 6:00 PM. Larry, Steve and Percy were in a dark corner in the back as they said they would be. In fact, it was so dusky in the place, we didn't even see them at first. It was a perfect place to meet and discuss our next move. We could see anyone who came in, but they couldn't see us very well.

It was great to finally see them! We were once again reunited with the rest of our team. Except there were only six of us. The seventh member was being held by those fiends and none of us wanted to think about the trauma she was enduring. She thought the three of us were dead in the container on the beach and had no idea that the other three of our team knew what had happened or knew that she was missing. She had to be completely desolate and I would not let myself think of the horror she might be going through at the hands of Hassan, Alziddi and their buddies.

We shook hands warmly and briefly brought each other up to date on the details of what had gone on with each part of the team the past few days. We decided to order something to eat while we decided on the most effective action to rescue Ashton, try to take out Hassan, Alziddi and their cleric friend, and get back on track of finding where the weapon went.

"Okay, the first order of business is to get Ashton back. I don't think they would have killed her yet because she probably is too valuable to them in forcing her to help them get the weapon functional to the highest degree. Hopefully, she is still here and has not yet been moved to wherever the laser is," I said. In saying that, another part of me hoped that she had already been removed from Hassan and Alziddi. She might be safer away from them.

"In doing that, if we can eliminate the money man, Hassan, and capture or kill the real prize, Alziddi, that would be fantastic. In the process, if we can learn where the laser went, our little foray into their den would be a resounding success. The problem, of course, is how six lightly armed guys can do all that and get away alive. Any ideas?" I continued.

"Well, we have seen the layout. Apparently, there is not a lot of fear on Infama's part in exposing themselves in this country. Otherwise, Alziddi would not have been here and made his public appearance. Their only concern might be the knowledge that we are here and they think three of you are dead and they have another one of us. They know there are three more of us, and are probably looking for us, but they probably realize we are lightly armed. They don't appear to be overly concerned about security. We only saw about a dozen guards around the compound. They are all heavily armed, but the place is not covered up with security," Steve advised.

"Yes, Indonesia is considered a relatively safe haven for Alziddi and his people. The government is wary of his group's presence and is certainly concerned with the outbreaks of violence instigated by Bassyr here, but a strong minority of the populace is attracted to his teachings and admire how Alziddi has stood up to the western world, who they consider infidels. Most of the populace can be considered moderates relative to violent confrontation with the West but, on the other hand, most of the populace is Muslim," Percy said.

"Does that mean the government and the majority of the populace back Alziddi and his terrorist activities?" Thom asked.

"I wouldn't say back them. In fact the government is probably nervous about his being here. They fear his influence will increase the radical fundamentalism that is a danger to the more moderate political structure. But they will turn their heads to his presence for fear that to confront him would increase the sympathy for his cause and that his organization will then turn on them. And there is a lot of sentiment for, and some pride in, Alziddi and Infama due to their couching their terrorism in terms of Islamic teachings of Jihad. Even though most don't condone his methods and radicalism, he is not seen as the villain that he is to the West," Percy answered.

"So, if we go in and create a visible confrontation, we will have no truly safe haven as an escape route?" Darby asked.

"That's right," Percy said.

"What do you think, Larry?" I asked.

"Well, the three of us were talking about it and there may be a way to pull this thing off. The risk will still be great, but the operation is possible if everything goes right," Larry said.

"Let's hear your plan," I said.

"Okay. There are actually, I think, fifteen guards assigned to the security of the compound around the mosque. They are using the cottage next to Bassyr for their sleeping quarters. It looks like they are pulling three, eight hour around the clock shifts, with five guards each shift. We happened to be there when one of the shifts changed at 3:00 PM. They probably go 3:00 PM to 11;00 PM, 11:00 PM to 7:00 AM and 7:00 AM to 3:00 PM.," Larry said.

"So we only have to worry about five guards and being quiet to get into the cottages?" I asked.

"Essentially, yes. But I would emphasize the quiet, because the other ten are probably on high alert. Any warning from the five on duty and they would come out like ants out of an anthill. Also, you can be sure that Hassan, Alziddi and probably Bassyr are armed. And there may be personal guards that were not visible to us, staying with them in the cottages," Larry responded.

"Darby, what's your take?" I asked.

"We can't risk a shot. If there is some cover to get close to them, I could take them out silently with my knife or could break their necks. But the five would have to be taken down almost simultaneously I think. I'm sure they are visible to each other most of the time. If one of them disappears, the others will investigate or sound the alarm. Five of us would each have to take one guard and have a way to get close before attacking them. And the method of attack would have to be very quiet," Darby said.

"What does the layout look like?" I asked.

"In back, there is a big stone wall with notches at the top, like a castle. Facing the complex from the street, it ties into the left rear of the mosque. The wall extends across the back behind the four cottages, then turns and comes all the way to the street. On the right between the mosque and the wall, there is an open courtyard that runs across the front of the mosque on back to the left side all the way to the rear wall. The entire front is open to the street. There is nothing but the little shed we told you about, and several big trees and some sidewalks in the courtyard running from the front all the way back to the cottages in the rear," Steve said.

"How high is the wall?" I asked.

"Probably about 20 feet," Steve answered.

"Where are the five on-duty guards posted?" Darby asked.

"There is one each on the far left side and the far right side of the cottages. They roam back and forth a little so they can observe most of the rear where the wall is and the front sides of the cottages. There are two more stationed in front of the two middle cottages and the other one is further to the front by the little shed where we hid. The shed is about fifty yards in front of the cottages," Larry said.

"And your best guess is that Bassyr is in the left cottage closest to the mosque, the guards are using the one next to that, then Hassan next with

Alziddi in the far right cottage?" I asked.

"Right," Percy said.

"Do you think we could scale the wall behind the cottages?" I asked.

"With a rope with a metal bar of some sort we could toss it between the slots on top of the wall and climb up to the top, then attach a rope and rappel down," Darby said.

"Wouldn't the bar make a noise and alert the guards on the rear side when tossed over the wall?" Thom asked.

"Not if you wrapped the bar in cloth —a T shirt or something," Darby answered. "It would make a dull thud that might not be noticed."

"What if we scaled the wall on the side that runs into the mosque?" I asked.

"Hey! That's the best place to get on the complex grounds without being seen," Larry said.

"Okay. See what you think about this plan. We'll wait until after the 11:00 PM shift change. It will be good and dark then. One of us can try to get to the shed by approaching from the front keeping the shed between us and the guard so he won't see us. Right at the shift change would be a good time for this person to get into position, while they are chatting. It will be that person's job to take out the shed guard, then signal the rest of us by lighting a cigarette when that is done. Once the action starts, that person can rush to join the rest of us around the cottages.," I began.

"Where will the other five of us be?" Percy asked.

"Well, I still think three of us will have to come over the back wall between the second and third cottages, in spite of the noise risk. Two of us can sneak between those cottages and, after the cigarette signal, kill the two guards out front. The third will go around the back side to Alziddi's cottage and get the guard on the right side," I continued.

"What about the other two?" Thom asked.

"Those two would come over the wall on the mosque side and get as close as they can in the darkness without being seen. They would kill the guard on the left side, then rush Basyr's cottage, killing him and anyone with him," I said.

"So you think we will be shooting immediately," Darby questioned.

"The shed guard hopefully can be disposed of quietly before giving the signal for the shooting war to start. By that time that person should be moving to position himself to cover Hassan's cottage. When the signal is given though, I don't think we can avoid fireworks. There's no way we can reach all the guards quietly. The two coming between the cottages would, thirty seconds after the signal, shoot the two front guards simultaneously with the two entering from the mosque side killing that guard and rushing Bassyr's cottage. The other one coming around the back on the right side would shoot the guard on the right and cover Alziddi's cottage," I went on.

"Okay, let me get this straight. If everything goes as planned, the five on duty guards are taken care of, Bassyr, who is probably alone, is disposed of, and Hassan's and Alziddi's cottages are covered to make sure no one comes out. What about the ten off duty guards?" Larry asked.

"To pull this off, and take care of Alziddi, Hassan and Bassyr along with the on duty guards and anyone else in the cottages and free Ashton, it's too much to expect we can do all that quietly without the ten off duty guards getting involved. The two coming through the middle from the rear will have to take them on, helped as quickly as possible by the two coming from the mosque side who will be taking care of that guard and Bassyr. That's four against ten, but I'm counting on surprise and, hopefully, being able to pick up automatic rifles from the fallen guards. The other two will be guarding Hassan's and Alziddi's cottages, taking on any one coming out the front door. If everything works, the four taking on the guards can kick the door in and spray the inside and then back off and pick off anyone trying to come out the door," I responded.

"It's a risky plan, but I can't think of a better one," Larry said.

"Anybody else got ideas that would improve on this plan?" I asked. They all, after thoughtful hesitation, nodded that they didn't.

"It sounds like a good plan to me. I have just one question though. What if the cottages have a back door?" Darby asked.

"Good thought. I guess if we find, after scaling the wall, that the cottages do have back doors, one of the four attackers of the guards should station himself in back to pick off anyone who tries to exit from the rear of any of the four cottages," I said.

"The key to success will be the surprise factor and the quickness of carrying out our assault once the action starts. I guess, after the other jobs are done, we all converge on Hassan's and Alziddi's cottages and hope to kill them and free Ashton, since she is likely to be with one of them," Darby said.

"Right. And to avoid a potential hostage situation, the two responsible for those two cottages should rush them as soon as the firing starts, I think on second thought, rather than waiting for someone to come out the front door," I said.

We worked out more details and made assignments. I wanted to come over the center rear wall and be the one to take out the guard on the side where Alziddi's cottage was. I felt that Ashton was probably with him and wanted to be the one to barge in and free her. Darby and Steve would come over the wall with me. Thom and Percy would enter from the mosque side. Larry would be the shed guy. It was 9:00 PM. We left the café to find rope and the other items we needed.

10:40 PM we were assembled ready to go. Larry would leave in about 15 minutes to start working his way towards the shed at shift change. The rest of us left to take our positions behind the side and the back walls. Our planned attack was going to be bold and risky. We were all high on adrenalin, because we knew that everything had to go like clockwork to pull off our mission of rescuing Ashton and capturing or killing Alziddi and his henchmen, Hassan and Bassyr. We also knew we would have to accomplish the mission quickly and get out before the disturbance woke the surrounding populace. They very well could join the Infama people in sympathy with their cause and might even perceive our action as an attack on their mosque. We all expected that some or all of us might not survive this excursion, but we had no choice but to act now.

"Good luck, Larry," we said, shaking hands with him as we departed.

I was well aware of the magnitude of the challenge ahead of us. What I wasn't prepared for was what I would find upon entering Alziddi's cottage.

CHAPTER THIRTY-FIVE

It was 10:55 PM. Darby, Steve and I had made our way around behind the back of the wall behind the cottages. We assumed that Thom and Percy were in position also behind the left wall which tied into the mosque. Larry should by now be closing in on the shed while the guards were in the process of changing posts. The plan was for Larry to take care of the shed guard at precisely 11:10 after the previous guard had returned to their cottage. He would then start the action by lighting a cigarette and making a signal with the lighter which all of us would be watching for. The other five of us should be over the wall behind and to the side of the cottages at that time. If everything went as planned, the fireworks would start about 11:15. We needed to get over the wall. This was a critical juncture to see if we could do this without being heard or detected. If we were, the fireworks would start prematurely and our chances of success would be diminished.

"Are we ready?" Darby whispered.

"Go ahead," I said softly.

Darby took the rope we had purchased and attached a metal bar wrapped in cloth. He swung it high over the 20 foot wall and we held our breaths as it made a soft thud when it hit the wall on the other side. It had landed nicely between the turrets. We paused a few seconds to listen for any reaction to the slight noise we had made. There was none and I emitted a sigh of relief. Darby slowly took up the slack on the rope until it was nestled tightly between two of the projections on the top of the wall. When it was taut, Darby silently began to scale the wall to the top. I was next, then Steve. The three of us were perched in the darkness on the top of the wall. Darby silently pulled the rope up and reversed it whereby it was attached behind two of the notches and hanging down towards the cottage side of the wall.

Next, I rappelled down and got to the ground behind the second and third cottages. Steve followed, then Darby. So far, so good. We took a deep breath, silently shook hands and went to our positions. Darby slipped in between the first and second cottages and Steve between the second and third. The guards they were to take out were in front of those two cottages. We could hear them conversing. By the tone of their voices, they had not heard us and didn't suspect anything yet. I slipped around the back behind the fourth cottage which my guard was in front of. I backed up in the darkness against the wall where I could see Larry's signal. There were no back doors to any of the cottages!

It was 11:05 PM. We hoped Thom and Percy were in place. Obviously they had not been detected or we would have heard from the guards. I removed my revolver from my belt holster. The quietness of the night was eerie and just added to the tenseness. In five minutes there would be no turning back. We waited.

There was the signal! We saw a lighter flicker and wave by the shed! Larry had done his job and should now be moving towards Hassan's cottage while we counted down thirty seconds to begin our action. I began to move from the wall. The guard I was to take out was now clearly visible about twenty yards away, lounging against the side of the fourth cottage. Lights were still on in all the cottages except for Bassyr's, but the windows were shuttered and we could not see inside. Steve and Darby would start the attack by shooting the two guards in front. The rest of us would take that as our cue to take out our assignments. The toughest job would be handling the ten retiring guards. I would learn later that Darby would kill his guard in front of the cottage with his knife to conserve his ammunition. Then he would take his AR.

Blam!!! The silence of the night was sharply interrupted by the sound of Steve's pistol. I immediately went into action. My guard jumped to his feet and started to the front of the cottages where the firing had begun. By now there were sharp reports coming from the left side where Thom and Percy were. Out of the corner of my eye I saw Larry converging on the front towards the cottage next to me. I was now only four steps behind the guard who was racing in front of Alziddi's cabin. I took careful aim and blew the back of his head off. He had never been aware that I was behind him.

All of a sudden all hell broke loose. Thom and Percy must have taken care of the guard on the left side then stormed Bassyr's cottage. They probably caught him sleeping and quickly joined Darby and Steve who were taking on the ten off duty guards. I could see in the dim light Darby standing in the doorway directing bursts of fire from the automatic rifle he had confiscated into the front room of the cottage. There were screams of fear, pain and death blending with the automatic rifle fire and the single reports from the hand guns as the other three picked off some who tried to escape out the front where Darby was and out the side windows. Larry was now beside me.

"Sounds like everything is going well for now. All of our guys are still standing and there couldn't be many of the guards left alive. We need to get out of here quick though, before reinforcements might show up!" Larry shouted.

"Right! You try to get in Hassan's cabin, but be careful. I'm going into this one. Ashton has to be in one of these two cottages," I shouted back.

Larry was already moving towards the door of Hassan's cottage. "Save him for me if you can, but don't take any chances!" I shouted as an afterthought and turned my attention to the last cabin.

I kicked in the flimsy door, then quickly ducked to the side on the little porch fronting the cottage. The lights were still on and I peeked in the window through the wooden slats. There was no sign of anyone in the front room which ran all the way across the front of the cottage. It was filled with chairs, a couch and a few small tables. I could see two doors leading into what must be a bedroom and perhaps a small kitchen area. Both doors were cracked open.

I heard a sharp report from a pistol next door. There were two quick shots. I prayed that they were Larry's shots, not Hassan's. Then I rushed into the front door of Alziddi's cottage, ran across the small living room area and slammed my body against the wall between the two internal doors. There was no sound coming from either room.

"Alziddi!!! I know you are in here! Get flat on the floor and extend your arms through the doorway!!" I demanded.

"Dawson?!!" I heard a feeble voice filled with fear. It was Ashton!! But I couldn't tell from which room it came from. The sound of gunfire outside was sporadic now but made it difficult to hear.

I foolishly dashed into the room to the left with my revolver cocked and ready extended in front of me. A quick survey indicated that it was a small kitchen and there was no one there. Ashton and Alziddi had to be in the other room!

Cautiously now, trying to subdue my impatience, I eased my way out of the kitchen back to the section of wall between the two doors.

"Ashton! I'm here. You're going to be okay! Alziddi, come on out with your hands up or I'm coming in! There are six of us. Your friends are dead. You may as well give up! If we have to come in to get you, we will shoot to kill. You can't get all of us. Give up. Now!!" I shouted.

"Dawson. He's gone! He went out the window when the shooting started.

Please don't come in though...please... I don't want you to see me. Just leave me here—" she sobbed.

I rushed in the bedroom, still alert and poised to fire in case her words were a ruse that he was forcing her to say. Damn!! He must have jumped out the side window about the same time I rounded the corner to the front to kill the guard! The window shutters were open. There was no one there in the small bedroom —except Ashton!

She was lying on the bed —naked. She had tried to pull the sheet over part of her body but it did not hide the astonishing sight of her cowering on the bed, sobbing uncontrollably, her face turned away from me.

Her face was bruised and a trickle of blood ran down the corner of her mouth. There was blood running down her leg from between her legs. Each of her legs was tied with small rope to opposite corner posts on the bed. She was on her back and her legs were spread apart. It was plain to see what Alziddi had been doing with her.

Even in the grotesque shape she was in, she was beautiful. I was overcome by pity for her and by the overpowering love I felt for her, along with relief that I had found her at last. And I could feel the quiet, burning hatred I had for this man that had done this to her. I was furious and longed for revenge, but had more important things to do now. My rage would have to wait.

I quickly cut her bindings with my pocket knife, bundled her in the sheet and picked her up. She clung to me tightly, still sobbing so hard her body was shaking. The shooting outside had nearly subsided except for an occasional small arms report.

"Dawson, Dawson —he raped me and made me do awful things with him. He was brutal. I feel so dirty. I know you hate me. I feel like I did with my stepfather, except worse. He was so evil— " she couldn't go on and just clung more tightly to me, shivering now, in spite of the hot, humid weather.

Still holding her tight, I made her look at me. "Ashton, don't talk about it. It's over now. We are together again. What happened is not your fault. I love you very much. I will never let you leave me again. I'm just sorry I could not get here in time." I kissed her lightly. She closed her eyes and laid her head on my shoulder.

"I thought you were dead," she whispered, tears rolling down her cheeks. "I didn't care if I lived or not. I fought him. Then he tied me up. When I heard the shooting, I didn't know what to think. I wished they were coming to kill me. Then, he...he...jumped out the window. I can't even say his evil name. I hate him! Please catch him and kill him for me!"

Larry came charging in, closely followed by Darby and Thom. They took in the scene quickly, then went back into the living room.

"Dawson, what happened to Alziddi?" Larry asked.

"He got away —jumped out of the window before I came in. What about Hassan?" I asked.

"He's next door, still alive. We got the rest. They're all dead, but we need to get out of here. We may have company soon," Larry said.

"I know. You two stay here. Hon get dressed," I said to Ashton, setting her down gently on the bed. I had seen her shorts, panties and blouse on the floor. "Darby and Larry will be with you in the living room. I need to go next door a couple of minutes, then we have to get out of here."

"I'll get the others and we'll meet you back here in a couple of minutes. According to Darby, everybody got through this thing unhurt except poor Percy. He caught a bullet in the forearm, but it was a clean shot. That son of a gun is going to have more purple hearts than his chest is big enough to carry," Larry said.

"Okay. I'll be back in a minute," I said.

"You'll find him on the floor in the front room. He's alive but whining. He's disarmed. I shot both his kneecaps out. Just for you, Buddy," Larry said as I left.

"Dawson, wait," Darby said.

"What?" I turned around and asked.

"Here's my knife. Wipe it clean before you bring it back. We'll take care of Ashton. Hurry back. We need to go," he said handing me his razor sharp hunting knife.

CHAPTER THIRTY-SIX

I rushed over to the next cottage. Just as Larry had said, there was Abu el Hassan sprawled on the floor, writhing with pain. He was holding his knees which were bloody and shattered. When he saw me enter his look was a mixture of pain, surprise that I was alive, fear and pleading.

In any other circumstances with another human being I would have felt sorry for him. But I remembered his disdain for females in our discussion in his office. I saw the look on his face when he had us locked in the trash container, expecting the incoming tide to slowly drown us. My thoughts flashed to the known instances where Infama had mercilessly killed and maimed innocent people in their terrorist activities. And this was the man who had arranged for and handled the financing for those activities. I thought of our present mission relative to this man who was a key player in the plot to kill our President.

But mainly I saw the smirk on his face when he thought we were just minutes away from death in the container and he slapped Ashton and threw her into the car savagely as a last living thought for us to have before the tide rose. And I saw Ashton in my mind as she was just a few moments ago after this man had turned her over to his monster boss, Alziddi, knowing full well how he would treat her. I kneeled down beside him so he could plainly see my face. My rage was controlled, but I'm sure my face reflected my feelings towards this despicable person.

"Hassan, Ashton is okay. We have her now. All your people are dead except your boss. We will track him across the face of the earth and make certain he joins you in hell as soon as possible. Now I want you to watch as I repay you for what you have done. I have to leave in a minute. Otherwise I would like to stay here with you and watch you die a painful death," I said.

I unbuckled his belt and took the knife and ripped his pants off. His look of fear was almost comical, but he had no idea what I was doing until I exposed his private parts and lowered the knife between his legs. He let out a sound that was a combination of a moan and a rasping gurgle of fear. He had forgotten about the pain in his legs at this point.

Making sure I had his attention, I thrust the knife under his balls and with a slow back and forth motion severed them from his body. He let out a bloodcurdling scream that I'm sure the guys in the next cottage could hear. I waited a moment until his cries had subsided somewhat. I slapped him hard in the face and momentarily had his attention again. Then I shoved his severed and bloody privates into his mouth until he began to choke on them. Blood was now flowing profusely from between his legs. His eyes widened until I thought they would pop out of his head as he gasped for breath.

"Goodbye, Mr. Hassan. I have to leave now. It's been a pleasure making your acquaintance. By the way —you lose," I said.

I then thrust Darby's knife deep into his lower gut and slowly twisted it. His body convulsed and rose abruptly as the pain overcame him. He then relaxed as he passed out from the excruciating pain. That I regretted. Maybe I shouldn't have done that. But he would come to again before he died a lingering and terrible death. I went to the sink in the kitchen and washed my hands and the knife thoroughly, then left without even looking at him on the way back.

"Did you clean my knife?" Darby asked. Everyone was gathered on the porch of the cottage. Thom had his arm around Ashton. She had gotten dressed and was just standing there, still looking stunned and fragile.

"It's clean," I handed it to him. "Thanks. Let's go."

"Wait, Dawson---the papers," Ashton finally spoke.

"What papers?" I asked.

"That monster," she still couldn't say his name, "he had all the plans for the weapon with him. I'm not sure, but I think it's the only copy. He seemed to covet the fact that he had the only available information that his technicians could use for their destructive purposes. He tried to get me to look at them and comment on a few minor difficulties they still had. I refused and that's when he started beating me. But my impression was that the weapon is being sent somewhere and they still have some development and testing work to be done, but plans are to continue work on it and implement it some time this year. He made a comment that our pig of a President wouldn't live to see another year."

"Where are they?!"

"In there on the coffee table," she pointed in the cottage. Steve immediately ran in and gathered up all of the papers in the room. A quick glance indicated that they were, in fact, drawings and technical descriptions of a laser. And they were the originals. They still had the NIF stamp on them in indelible blue ink.

I took Ashton's hand and led her off the porch. Our two cars were parked around the corner. We walked cautiously but quickly toward them past a gathering crowd of locals who had been aroused from their sleep to come out in the night to see what the commotion was. They were puzzled and didn't know what had happened or who we were. Darby had picked up another assault rifle and, in their sleepy and uncertain state, didn't seem to want to delay or mess with us. We got in the cars and drove quickly off, all of us letting out a sigh of relief as we sped away from the neighborhood.

We drove back to the Panghejar hotel on the other side of the city and attained rooms for an indefinite stay. We were on maximum alert and got adjoining rooms. But, before leaving Indonesia, we needed to try to find where the laser went.

When Ashton and I checked into our room, she fell exhausted on the bed. I sat down beside her.

"Love, why don't you just crawl in bed and try to get some sleep," I said tenderly.

"I will. But first I want to take a long hot shower with plenty of soap. I feel so dirty. Dawson, you know what happened to me?" she said, looking at me with a guilty look.

"Ashton. I know. But you couldn't help it for God's sake. Look at you. He beat you, tied you up, tortured you. You can't blame yourself. I won't let you. I told you it's over. After all you have gone through, we are still we. We are back together again and I'm going to hold on to you. I love you now more than ever. Just remember that. I love you very, very, very much. Now get this bad experience behind you. It's gone and you have me. And I'm so proud to have you. You're a brave little girl," I kissed her lightly on the cheek.

"I love you so much— I was so scared and felt so alone and devastated when I thought they had killed you. I really didn't want to live without you. I kept praying that he would just kill me." She hugged me tightly and left to go take her shower.

We had decided to just get room service that night. All of us were physically at the end of our ropes and needed to just relax and get some rest that night. Ashton slept and didn't even wake up to eat. I tried to awaken her, but she just mumbled that she wasn't hungry, she just wanted to sleep.

Darby and Steve were on one side of us with Percy and Larry on the other side. Thom was by himself next to their room. Leaving the door open, I went into the adjoining door to Steve and Darby's room to call Mike. We needed to bring him up to date on our activities. After several rings and his secretary tracking him down, he came to the phone. It took a while to fill him in on everything that had happened. He was pleased with our success in sighting the laser, attaining the technical papers and eliminating some of the people who were high on the U.S. most wanted list. He was disappointed, as we were, that we weren't able to get the kingpin, Alziddi. I told him what happened to Ashton, but asked him to never mention it to her.

"I agree with you, Dawson, that you need to stay there long enough to try to find where they sent the laser to. But there is some information I need to pass on to you," Mike said when we were about to conclude our conversation.

"What's that?" I asked.

"Our CIA agents on the ground over there tell us that you guys have made quite a rumble among the questionable characters," Mike said.

"Yeah, I imagine so. Is that a problem?" I asked.

"Not for us. They don't want a lot of noise about their activities because, if the full scope of their activities were known, it would cause a further crackdown on them by their government and invite external intervention. The problem will be yours and you need to be alert to it," Mike replied.

"What do you mean, Mike?" I asked, puzzled now.

"Well, your presence risks exposure to them of their purposes which include the assassination of the President of the United States. They can't do anything about that, such as going to the authorities to stop you. Their only recourse is to deal with you in the same way that you are dealing with them —in a covert manner. In other words, they would like for you to just disappear—quietly, as if you had never been there. Dawson, they will try to eliminate you. Their best scenario would be for the seven of you to cease to exist. That would serve a twofold purpose for them. It would stop your hounding on the laser project and force a delay for us to get another team in the field. And they may not need much of a delay. Secondly, it would eliminate any possibility that your interaction with them while you are there will break out into the open and embarrass them or make their lives tougher. Understand?" Mike explained.

"I think so. What you are telling me is that they would like to kill us, quietly without a lot of fanfare or any ties to their organization.. Something like dumping us into a trash hopper and letting the tide come in?" I said.

"Exactly. So be careful. Stay a while to see if you can dig up anything on the whereabouts of the laser, but stay out of their way unless you have to get in their face, and watch your backs," Mike said.

"We will, Mike. I think they know now that we can take care of ourselves. But we'll be alert. Anything else?" I asked.

"No. Dawson, I'm sorry about what happened to Ashton. She's something else. And Percy does seem to have nine lives. You're a good group. Be careful and stay in touch," Mike concluded.

That night Ashton and I slept snuggled together. I finally got her to eat a bite. We talked for a while but mostly made up for the several nights of little sleep. I wanted to make love to her, but felt that, after her experience with Alziddi, she needed time to feel comfortable having sex with anyone. She appreciated my understanding and hugged me tightly before we both fell asleep in each other's arms.

Tomorrow we would relax and go out that night to have a leisurely meal at a nice place. Most of us had not had anything to eat but crackers and quick sandwiches for the past few days. It seemed like an eternity just since we got off the boat. Four of us were going to make good on our vow to make Percy, Larry and Steve buy us a great meal and expensive bottle of wine. They reluctantly agreed to treat us. The next day we would start seeing if we could pick up the trail of the laser.

The next day dawned bright and sunny. It was February 14th, Valentine's Day. I promised Ashton we would make it a special day, since it was our first together. We all expected to wrap up our business in Indonesia, quickly find the destination of the laser, which we suspected had been sent out of the country, and be out of Indonesia in a couple of days. The trail had to start here though, and it would be over four months, late June, before we would be back in the States.

CHAPTER THIRTY-SEVEN

We had all decided to sleep late the 14th and meet in our room about 10:00 AM. I woke up about 7:00 and shortly after that Ashton stirred. Even though the hotel was air conditioned, we had opened the window the night before after the heat of the day had subsided. The curtains were fluttering lazily in the slight breeze and sunlight was beginning to filter through the windows.

"Dawson, I love you. Did you know that?" Ashton asked when she realized I was awake.

"Guess what?" I asked, turning on my side so I could see her. Even with the bruises still visible on her face, she was so cute. Her dark hair was tousled around her pretty face and I could feel her soft, firm body as she snuggled up close to me.

"What?" she asked , gazing at me sleepily with her beautiful blue-green eyes.

"I love you, too," I said. I placed my arm around her tiny waist and kissed her. At first we just pecked at each other's lips, then held our kiss for a while. She darted her tongue around my lips and we began to explore inside each other with our tongues while firmly holding our lips pressed together. My hand slid from her waist along her silky smooth skin around the firm contour of her little butt. It was as if we had melted together. With little pressure on my part, she pressed her body tightly against mine and we became as one. I could feel the soft hair between her legs against my now stiff member between my own legs.

"Dawson, my love," she whispered when we finally broke our passionate kiss, "I love to have sex with you because you are in love with me and you are so good and make me feel so good. It's strange how the same act with someone you want to be with and someone you respect and love so much can be so nice but so brutal and unpleasant when forced on you by someone you detest."

"Hush," I said, placing my finger over her lips. "Sex with you is so nice because we do love each other and want to be together. You are the prettiest, most exciting girl I could ever hope to have love me and I want to keep you and love you forever."

"Forever?" she gave me a cute little questioning smile. "Why don't you try that then, because I want you now and I don't want you to ever stop once you are inside me."

"I'm not sure I can fulfill the promise of that statement," I grinned. "But I'll try."

Ashton spread her legs and, rolling on her back, gently pulled me on top of her. I was already so hard I was afraid I would burst and, when she reached down and placed her hand around the protruding shaft between my legs, I got even harder. Then she slid her fingers lightly up and down around the part she had grasped. At that moment I was wondering whether my "forever" was going to last more than an instant.

She must have realized that she had already brought me close to the limits of my capability to control myself because she then gently placed what she had been caressing in her inviting orifice and slowly raised her hips until it had sunk as far into her as it could go. She held me in that position, keeping herself pressed tightly against her so that I could not withdraw. I could feel her warmth and wetness surrounding me in that part of me that had entered her.

"Love, just rest and relax. Let's stay like this a little while. It feels so good, you being inside me, I don't want it to end too soon," she whispered in my ear.

I did as she asked and we remained meshed against each other tightly and just held on until I regained a degree of control that would allow me to slowly, partially withdraw from her vagina. We then began to move together in synchronization —slowly, to prolong the ecstasy we both were experiencing.

"Ashton, you are great. Each time we make love, I long for you more," I spoke softly into her ear, then kissed her lightly on the neck. She shuddered slightly and I could feel her tighten around me.

"Dawson, take me! Take me now!" she said. Her eyes were closed and lips parted in anticipation. She clung to me more tightly, with her arms around my waist now, pulling me toward her as if she could plunge me deeper inside of her.

Our "forever" was beginning to end. We both wanted to climax. Our bodies were transported into an aura of sensation that could only be described as unimaginable bliss.

I withdrew quickly then thrust deeply into her. She sobbed and tears of sensual happiness welled from the corners of her eyes as we moved to achieve the fulfillment of our desires. My movements in and out of her tight sheath of love elicited a guttural sound from her that begged to be delivered into utopian physical satisfaction.

Increasing the speed and force of my thrusts deeply into her, I was coming close to experiencing the ultimate exhilaration of sexual intercourse. She was approaching the same threshold and her hips began to thrust upward, meeting my thrusts. Suddenly she let out a little cry and her whole body seemed to stiffen with a final sharp thrust of her pelvis to meet my downward push into her. Not able to wait any longer, I forcefully expelled my love into her quivering pussy, which was already wet with the juices of her love that had flowed out from her in our final moment of ecstasy.

We fell into each other's arms, relaxing in contentment, not saying anything—just reveling in the satisfaction we had experienced between ourselves. I would make similar love to Ashton many times in the future, but would never exceed the ultimate satisfaction that I felt, and believe she also felt, at that moment.

We continued to lie there, snuggling and kissing until the sun had risen well into the sky. I marveled at how beautiful and sexy she looked, now fully exposed on the bed in the sunlight. We were both very much in love and had forgotten, at least for the moment, the trauma that we had gone through in recent days.

"It's 9:15! They will be here before long!" Ashton said, jumping up from the bed.

"You go ahead and get your shower, Doll. I'll jump in later," I said.

"Okay! By the way. Your "forever" didn't last forever, but mine didn't either. It was nice. That's why I love you—for your body!" she gave me one of her flashing, seductive smiles before disappearing into the bathroom.

I had just finished my shower and gotten dressed in slacks and a knit shirt when there was a knock on the door. Ashton went to the door. She looked striking and fetchingly sexy in a short little skirt and loose fitting blouse.

"Hey! You guys look fresh and awake. I just got up thirty minutes ago. I could have slept forever. By the way Ashton, you look great!" Steve said approvingly as he entered our room. "The other guys will be here in a minute. Darby has been doctoring Percy."

Darby and Percy arrived next. Percy's left arm was in a sling made from a pillow cover. When we inquired about his wound, he explained that the bullet had not fractured the bone in his forearm, just gone through the flesh.

His arm was sore, but functional.

"You know what this Delta guy did to me!? He poured whisky on my wound!! It burned like hell!" Percy exclaimed.

"Wait until you get my bill," Darby said. "You'll really be complaining then."

"What's our agenda today?" Larry asked.

"Well, today we will take it easy and just do some telephone and address research. We need to find out the firms who can provide industrial helicopter service in this area. That would be a start if we can find where they took the package they picked up off the barge. Tomorrow we will hit the field again and try to trace down any leads we can get but, after our little exercise last night, it will probably be best to lay low here in the hotel today to see if we have any immediate repercussions. As Mike said, we need to be especially alert and not expose ourselves unnecessarily. If we stay together the odds of them taking us on will be diminished for the reasons Mike mentioned. They won't be inclined to attempt a major assault on the group of us. It would cause too much notoriety. I'm sure they would prefer to pick us off one or two at a time," I said.

"Sounds good. Can I make a suggestion, Dawson?" Percy asked.

"Sure."

"Well, I'm sure you guys aren't going to forget the meal we agreed to treat you to. So, since this is our take-it-easy day before we go back to work, I can recommend a fantastic place to have dinner tonight. I haven't been there, but did some research on the internet and talked to a couple of our guys who have spent some time here," Percy said.

"Sounds good. What is the name of the place and where is it?" I asked.

"It's in the suburbs of Bandung, near the Sheraton Hotel. The name of the place is Dago, and it is a traditional tea house on a hill that provides a great view of the city. There is a little waterfall right behind the restaurant and the food is supposed to be excellent," Percy said.

"Okay. We'll plan on going there then. One thing we'll do today is go down and trade our two cars in for a van so we can go together from now on. I'll have to pay for the one that was blown up at Lebac. I'll bet the Service's insurance won't pay for that either," I said.

We spent the rest of the day finding directions to the place we wanted to visit tomorrow and traded the cars in for a van. It was a relaxing day after the excitement we had experienced the past several days. One thing I noticed is that the seven of us had bonded together into a close knit team. We all liked each other and respected each of our abilities to do our job and protect the team. There was a lot of good natured banter, but I knew I could depend on all of them. We missed Ernest, but had not gotten to know him that well. What the remaining seven of our original eight person team had gone through together had erased everyone's doubts that they may have originally had about each other being able to make an equal and important contribution to the team.

And I was pleased that all of them had fully accepted Ashton in our team and they all had gone out of their way to welcome her back without embarrassing her over the trauma she had experienced. Alziddi had brutalized one of our team members, and I had the definite feeling that what he did would be remembered by all of us if we were to ever meet up with him again. If anything, we would have to fight each other for the opportunity to make him sorry for what he did to one of us.

Tonight would be a special night. If we had been able to look beyond tonight, it would have been frightening, but we were determined to make this Valentine night a night for us.

CHAPTER THIRTY-EIGHT

On the way to the place called Dago, we spotted a gun shop and were able to replenish our depleted ammunition for our handguns and bought several clips of ammo for the AR Darby had taken from the mosque area. We would keep it in the van.

We parked at the Sheraton and walked to Dago. It was beautiful and romantic. Percy's information had lived up to it's billing. Before going into the restaurant, we walked around looking at the waterfall and the view of the city from the mountainside. It was about 8:00 PM and the sun was setting over mountain. Lights illuminated the waterfall and the surrounding gardens giving the surroundings an enchanted aura.

We had all dressed up since this was our special night of being reunited and, for mine and Ashton's sake, because of it being Valentine's Day. Ashton had worn a simple black, straight line dress that complimented her figure nicely. As usual, everyone stared at her when we entered the restaurant. She was so striking and pretty, I'm sure many of the patrons thought she was a visiting movie star. The rest of us had abstained from wearing ties, but we wore slacks, open shirts and sport jackets. The waiter seated us by a window where we could enjoy the vista that was before us.

"Okay, here is the wine list, Dawson. Don't get Dom Perignon though. Our budgets can't stand it," Larry said.

"Cheapskate," I said.

"Come on! Just because we had that delicious steak on Madura while you were eating crackers in the boat. If you hadn't gone dashing off on your little joy ride on the water, you could have been with us!" Larry rejoined.

We ordered two bottles of medium priced wine and told the waiter to give us some time before we ordered. We just wanted to savor this time together, relax and enjoy ourselves. Some of us lit up cigarettes and Ashton didn't even register her usual complaint.

"You know, I just don't understand what drives Alziddi and the Infama people. Why do they hate the U.S. so much?" Thom asked after the wine was served.

"I think a lot of it is envy, but the root of the animosity is in religion. The radical Islamic mindset has a historical hatred for Jews and they see the mostly Christian western world as infidels who support their traditional enemies," Larry said.

"Yes, if you read the Bible, the Koran, the Talmud or any of the books of the major world religions, they are full of conflict, war and atrocities. And even sub-sects and different denominations within the various religions seem to disagree, often violently, with the other group's interpretations of God and the way to achieve some form of blessed and eternal life. It's sort of ridiculous when you think about it. All major religions believe in only one God. I guess they each think it's just their God. Kind of arrogant, and a little stupid, don't you think?" I commented.

"Well I have my own theory of God and where He is found," Percy said.

"What's that, Percy?" Ashton asked.

"I think God is within all of us—all peoples of the world. He built Himself into our genes, our DNA. He and His complex plan of life are a part of all living things and the regeneration of those things. His plan extends to the inanimate things and activities around us, such as the seasons, the tides, the solar system, etc. The difference with us humans is that he instilled the ability to reason in us. And we are the ones who have tried to use our logic to interpret Him and His plan. We are the ones who have screwed it up by trying to devise reasons and religions and philosophies and organizations whose purpose is to claim Him for our own, exclusively," Percy replied.

"So you think God's presence is within all peoples of the world, including the Infama people?" Darby asked.

"Yes, I do. I think he is a universal God, not just a God for a special few. Infama has taken a radical viewpoint, but they are probably sincere in their religious beliefs. The instinctive knowledge that a God exists is within them. But they have distorted that knowledge to the point that they feel they are acting out God's will when they try to destroy anyone whose cultural or philosophical teachings are different from their own. They are different only in degree from the adamant, fundamentalist proponents of other religions. And history has proven that all the religions can be pretty brutal and narrow minded in their disdain for those who do not believe in their book or their own interpretation of their book," Percy continued.

"Yeah, and if you read any of the books in which the authors claim to be passing on the word of God through them, it stretches your imagination to give any credence to any of them. I think it has been a historical and cultural thing that has resulted in people believing what they have been brought up to believe when, if the same book were written today, it would be ridiculed as being derived from a sect of lunatics who claim to have had personal conversations with God. The shame is that an awful lot of the believers have never even read their book from cover to cover. If they had, there would be a lot of the content that would be seriously open to question from any intelligent mind. And that is probably more true of Christians than of Muslims," I said thoughtfully.

"I've thought the same thing," Larry said. "It's nice to just have the knowledge to quote some truly great thoughts and verses from a religion's sacred book of authority. But when you read the whole book, with the fantasies, the miracles, the visions, the claims of conversations with God, their own interpretations of events, etc. it comes across as mostly poorly written and documented fiction," Larry said.

"And if you look at the Christian, Jewish and Islamic beliefs and books, they are all based on the same genealogical and historical accounts. All three of those religions take from the same general information that had been passed on through the ages. Abraham spawned the proponents of all three religions. The Jews believe in the Old Testament of the Bible, but not the New. The Christians believe in the Old and the New Testaments of the same book and that Jesus, born of a virgin and risen from the dead, is the son of God, and Islam has many of the same characters and events that are in the Bbible, but with a little different interpretation. Just look at the historical conflicts between Catholics and Protestants, and the differences of interpretation between Baptists and Methodists to break the ego thing down even further," Percy continued.

"If we agree that radical fundamentalism focused on a narrow man-interpreted definition of God derived from their particular culture and reliance on whatever book they were brought up to believe in is what terrorism is born of, how do we use that knowledge to combat terrorists?" Darby asked.

"We don't, I think. We simply recognize that they think they are following God's will and are willing to kill and willing to die for this conviction. We have to believe that God's will does not call for indiscriminate murder in his name. With this knowledge and belief, we need to be very careful that we don't become victims of their fanaticism ourselves and we have to go after them and stop them with deadly force wherever we find them," I said.

"Does that mean we become like them? Historically, will our actions go down as just continuing the ethnic and religious slaughter?" Thom asked.

"No. It means we try to stop the killing. We defend ourselves against a foe whose only deterrent is death without fear. We survive by making known our disdain for their twisted beliefs. We stand up in support of our vision of a peaceful world under one God who we believe looks on their actions in his name with combined amusement and sorrow. If our vision is wrong and theirs is right, then the credibility of any of the books we are taught by, the image we all have of God and the whole instinct of right and wrong that Percy believes is instilled in all humans is lost," I replied

"Well, now that we have solved the theological mysteries of life and determined that we must stop these lunatics, let's order our meal and enjoy this beautiful place! After we eat, I want to take all of you on a walking tour of this unique neighborhood," Percy said.

"I agree! Enough about Infama and their motivations. Let's push them out of our minds and enjoy the night. We'll go after them tomorrow," I concurred.

We had a delicious meal capped with another bottle of wine. Most got the fresh seafood, but I had a steak just to pay myself back for the one I missed. Afterwards we all went on a leisurely stroll through the neighborhood, keeping a watchful eye out for anyone who seemed overly interested in our presence. The streets in this section of town were much like the streets of Paris, very quaint and pretty, with baskets of flowers hanging from the balconies.

Returning to the hotel about 11:00 PM, the seven of us went to our separate rooms. It had been a night of good fun and companionship. Tomorrow, we would start to work again. About midnight, Ashton and I made love again, then fell asleep in each other's arms.

Although watchful, none of us had noticed the two strangers who had followed us into the restaurant, seemed like tourists following the same route we did on our stroll through the area around the tea house and followed at a safe distance on our drive back to the hotel. We would meet them again later —much later.

CHAPTER THIRTY-NINE

February 15th we started what would prove to be a long, arduous and frustrating detective endeavor. We would follow leads and false leads before we got on the right track. Leaving the pretty city of Bandung and driving back to Jakarta, we first checked back into the Banyuangi Sintera Hotel.

"Let's start with the industrial helicopter service. It's out on Thamrin road, close to the airport," I said after we got settled in our rooms. "We'll grab a bite to eat first, then get on our way."

"You know they will be watching us every step we take, just waiting for the opportunity to pick one or more of us off," Steve said.

"Yeah. And we won't be too hard to spot either —a big black guy, a pretty girl and the rest of you guys that don't stand out except you don't look like natives," Darby said.

"Yeah, you're right, Darby. Why don't you go on a diet so no one will notice us?" Thom said.

"I could do that, but you need my strength, little man. Besides, I can't change my color and you can't do much to Ashton. She would still be pretty if you put a sack over her head," Darby rejoined.

"Oh Darby! I don't look that great. I could get ugly somehow," Ashton grinned.

"Yeah. About as easy as I could get white," he countered.

After eating a quick sandwich at the hotel restaurant, we loaded up in the van and headed for Hambali Air Transport Company located about a half mile from the airport. So as not to overwhelm the people we talked to, we decided that Steve and I would ask the questions while the rest stayed around the van and observed anything that might be of assistance in our investigation.

The office was an old rusted metal structure. In a grass field behind the office was a concrete pad and, resting on the pad was a huge helicopter which we presumed was the one we saw pick up the laser off the barge.

"Good afternoon, Sir," Steve said when we entered the office and encountered a stocky gentleman in his fifties, dressed in khaki pants and a stained tee shirt. "Are you the owner?"

"Yes. I am Juwono Hambali. What can I do for you?" he asked impassively.

"We would like to ask you some questions about a job you were on three nights ago," I said.

"Who are you?" he asked, not changing his expression.

"I am Steve Whitt and this is Dawson Kohler. We are from the U.S. and our company is interested in locating a crate you picked up off a barge in the harbor that night. It is destined for the United States and we would like to inspect it before it leaves the country," Steve replied with half truths.

"Why don't you ask the owners?" the man asked, still with no expression.

"We can do that, but haven't been able to locate the owners. The equipment was made in Lebac and our company would like to purchase it, but we want to make certain it meets our specifications before committing to a deal. We thought if you could tell us where you took it, the owners would be found there and we could discuss taking it in our possession with them," I answered.

"How do you know what was in the crate and that you have an interest in it?" the owner persisted.

"Good question," Steve said. "We had expressed an interest in it in Lebac earlier this week, but had not yet met the owners before the piece of equipment was shipped out. By the time we found it was headed to Jakarta on a barge, we got here just in time to see it lifted off the barge by your copter. It is a finely made searchlight that our company can perhaps create an interest in on the part of our government. But the Lebac people would not reveal who the owners were and indicated we would have to contact them in Jakarta."

"If you're interested in it, then I guess you should do just that," Hambali said.

"Well, yes. That is what we would like to do if you can tell us where or who you took it to so we can locate them and talk to them," I said.

"You've come to the wrong place if you are looking for that information. I don't give out information on my customers unless they approve me doing so and are specific as to who I should give information to and what. Now, gentlemen, I'm very busy. You will have to excuse me," Hambali said and turned his back on us, going into an inner office.

Steve and I just looked at each other, then slowly walked out. We were disappointed. This should have been our best resource of information in trying to locate the laser. The others were waiting expectantly outside the van when we came out. Larry was over by the helicopter talking to a mechanic who appeared to be working on the engine. Hambali came out of a side door and shouted at the man to come see him just as we got outside though, and Larry walked back to the van and joined us. We all got in and drove off.

"Well? What did you guys find out?" Darby asked as we drove off of the property.

"Nothing. Absolutely nothing. He wouldn't tell us a thing," I said.

"I would love to get in his filing cabinet. He probably has a copy of the invoice for his work and the delivery destination," Steve said.

"Maybe we'll come back later. Did you find out anything talking to the mechanic, Larry?" I asked.

"Not much, except that Hambali did all the flying and this guy goes with him and handles the cables and wenches when they pick up a load. He also does most of the mechanic work. I was just trying to show interest in his work while you were inside. I mentioned that you guys were inquiring about the package they picked up on the barge the other night —that we were trying to locate the owners so that we might purchase what was in the container," Larry answered.

"Did you ask him where they took it?" I asked.

"Yes. I got around to that just before you guys came out. His answer wasn't much help to us. He said they brought it back here and the next day when he came in to work, it was gone. He said Mr. Hambali took care of all the customer contacts, so he didn't know who the people were that contracted for removing it from the barge. The only other thing he said was that it was a light container, not nearly as heavy as most of the work they did. He assumed someone came in and picked it up with a truck," Larry replied.

"So, where do we go now that our best lead is shut down?" Darby asked.

"I'll bet the weapon is still here around Jakarta. It came inland from the barge and didn't go directly to the airport," Thom volunteered.

"You're probably right, but I don't want to make any assumptions at this point. We need to investigate both possibilities —that it is still here or that it has left, or is leaving, the country," I said.

"I agree," Steve said. "We should check out the commercial airlines, boat freight companies and any other means of getting it out of the country as well as continue to investigate the possibility that it is still here."

"The problem is that we have no authority to demand this kind of information from the officials associated with these transportation alternatives. If we were in the U.S., we could have access to airline records as well as private companies. But we can't even tell the authorities why we are here. Like Mike has told us, we have to keep our mission under wraps for political reasons, at least until we might discover that their objective is in imminent danger of being carried out," Percy said.

"Yeah, I know. We'll just have to request the information we are seeking, using some legitimate sounding ruse. And it's unlikely they will volunteer it and we have no authority to force them to give it to us," I agreed.

"That sure puts us in a bind and lengthens the time it will probably take to get back on the trail of the weapon," Larry said, shaking his head.

"Well, we'll just have to do some gumshoe detective work---talk to a lot of people, ask a lot of questions. We'll check Hambali's place out tonight to see if we can get in there. If it is still in Jakarta, it will be difficult to find because it is small enough that it can be carried into a house. Let's get started. We'll try the commercial airlines this afternoon, then hit the ocean and air freight companies over the next few days. Trying to find if it left the country has to be the top priority. If it's still here, we have time to try to find it before it does get out of the country," I reasoned.

"Boy, I sure hope we find it left the country and where it went to. The thought of staying here much longer isn't too delightful. I feel like a punching bag. I've been kicked in the balls, doctored by a sadistic Delta guy with whiskey and a pillow case, shot at and hit twice, and I get the feeling they are just waiting for the opportunity to try again," Percy laughed.

We all agreed with Percy that we would be glad to get out of Indonesia. Unfortunately, after tedious and frustrating hours and long days of investigating all angles that might lead to the whereabouts of the laser, both here and outside the country, led to nothing substantive. Hambali had placed a 24 hour guard around his place and, as we had expected, the various agencies and businesses we checked with either had no helpful knowledge or would not divulge what they knew, if anything, that would help us. Mike though, felt our time would best be spent in Jakarta trying to find clues that would lead to our objective. In the meantime, he would have some people checking ports of entry in the states where information was easier to come by. If he found anything, he would summon us immediately. In the meantime, we continued to look in Jakarta.

It would be almost three and a half months, May 28th, before a break would allow a change in venue. The break that allowed us to pick up the trail of the laser again and leave Indonesia was welcome until we discovered it would be accompanied by heartbreak.

CHAPTER FORTY

As the days, weeks and months rolled on, our search covered all of the potential transport companies in Jakarta that could conceivably get a crate out of the country. We were constantly shadowed and had, by now, identified the two men who were following us, at least by appearance. We chose to call them "Sam" and "Charlie". Sam was short and ominous looking. Our guess was that Charlie was the leader of their little team. Charlie was much taller and bigger and, out of the corner of our eye when we had spotted them following us, he seemed to be giving directions to Sam to cross the street or other instructions when they wanted to get a better vantage point from which to observe us. When we drove somewhere, they would be seen following us from a distance in an old, white Bronco.

Sam and Charlie weren't too good at their surveillance trade, especially judged so by me, Larry, and Steve, who were experienced in undercover work. Still, we were careful. Although they had not made a move to confront us, we never really gave them a chance. When we went outside the hotel, we were always together and on the alert. Sam and Charlie became sort of a joke between us.

During this period, the camaraderie between the seven of us increased even beyond where it had previously evolved. We were a team and had become like brothers —and sister.

Ashton and I fell even deeper in love with each other, if that were possible. Making love to her was the most satisfying physical experience I had ever encountered. Our desires and bodies seemed to mesh together as one when we were together in bed —or on the balcony late at night and the many other places we made love—out of view, but never too far from the watchful protection of the rest of our team. We opened our minds as well as our hearts to each other and had many late night conversations about our future together. One night we were having one of those conversations.

"Dawson, when we get married, I want everyone in our wedding—the rest of the team," Ashton said.

"Okay. I'm sure they will want to be there and be a part of it. We'll invite

Mike Reilly and Bob Willoughby, too," I said.

"And Skipper," she said.

"Absolutely. He promised. We couldn't have the wedding without him and your Mom," I agreed.

"You probably have noticed how close we have all come to each other. I feel like our team are a family—the family I never had," Ashton said.

"Yeah. Darby told me the other day that, at first, he thought Percy was a prissy little bureaucrat. He said he has found out how tough, and smart, he is. He respects him now and really likes him. He told me he was going to try to keep him from getting hurt again, but he might have to put a leash on the little shithead to keep him out of danger. He told me how courageous Percy was in our firefight at the mosque. He said Percy charged in the room where the guards were ahead of him," I said.

"And Larry. I know he wasn't real happy when I came on the team. Now he's the most protective one of me—except you, of course," she gave me a little peck on the cheek.

"Well, that's just because I love you. I've found that you can take care of yourself pretty good, though" I said, brushing her hair back from her eyes.

"And Thom and Steve get along with everybody. We are good together, don't you think?" she asked.

"If you mean you and me—yes," I teased her.

"That's not what I mean you sex-crazed animal!" she said, hitting me with her pillow.

"Oh. You mean we're not good?" I pressed.

"Yes, we are good together too, Love," she answered, snuggling up to me.

We made love. Every time seemed better than the last. I don't think I would ever tire of loving her. In all my dreams I never imagined that I would be with such a pretty, loving, smart and fun girl as Ashton. She seemed just as happy as I.

One morning, after working for eight straight days, we decided to take a break and the seven of us went down to the beach and rented a couple of catamarans. Larry, Steve, Ashton and I got in one and Percy, Thom and Darby the other. We were going to go around part of the island.

"Hey! Sam and Charlie may want to go, too!" Thom said as we shoved off. Our two bird-dogs had pulled their old Bronco around the side of the building where we rented the catamarans.

"Yeah. They look a little frustrated that they can't follow us on the water.

Maybe Charlie can't swim," Larry said.

"They'll be waiting when we come back. We better check the car out real good this time. They will have plenty of time to rig it before we come back," Steve said as we sailed around the dock headed further out to sea, leaving Sam and Charlie standing close to the dock just watching us.

We had been thoroughly checking the van for tampering each day and night before heading out. Our concern was that they might plant a car bomb to try to get all of us together.

We had a great day of fun and laughter. It was nice to briefly get our minds off the mission and the frustration of not yet having found a clue to the whereabouts of the laser. We had carried a picnic lunch and found a remote part of the shoreline to pull in and enjoy our picnic. It was beginning to get dark when we finally returned. A cautious check of the car did not indicate that anything was amiss. We then drove to a good seafood place we had found and had a couple of drinks and a great meal before returning to the hotel. Sam and Charlie had reappeared. We debated whether or not we should buy them a drink and decided not to.

The next morning we started our exhausting search again. It was May 28. Mike had told us that, if we had not discovered a lead by the end of the month, we may as well come back and help the search in the U.S. that his limited resources had begun on ports of entry—boat and air.

We had decided to widen our search a little the past few days. We all felt we had exhausted all avenues of inquiry in Jakarta and decided to expand our radius to two miles around the city limits. That morning we were on the outer edge of our new limits of search when we arrived at a private commercial transport company on the far outskirts of Jakarta. It was a small company that we would later find had a single DC10 which would transport items to Australia, Malaysia, Singapore and other nearby places. A hand painted sign indicated the name of the company was simply SP Air Transport.

Convinced we were on another fruitless visit, Steve and I got out of the van and knocked on the front door of the small shack that apparently served as an office. There was no answer. We knocked again and waited patiently for someone to come to the door. Steve tried the door. It was locked.

"Well, they must not be in. Let's go on down to the next stop. This is probably a wild goose chase anyway. This operation doesn't look like an outfit that Infama would trust their precious little package with," I said.

Just as we turned to leave a man rounded the corner from the back where we could see the fuselage of an old plane.

"Sir! We were starting to leave. Are you the owner of SP Air Transport?" I asked.

"Yes," he answered in halting English. "I am Salem Pangestu, owner, pilot, mechanic, salesman and accountant of SP. What can I do for you?" he asked.

"We wanted to inquire about a package that was picked up in Jakarta over three months ago," I said, introducing myself and Steve.

"Sorry. I do a lot of small business. I'm the cheapest hauler around. Some days I will make two trips if it's not too far. In the last three months I've probably made over a hundred trips. My memory doesn't go back that far and I don't keep records. I get at least half the cost up front and the rest when I return from the delivery unless the people I take something to pay me the other half on arrival. Those are my terms. I don't often get stuck on a bill. But if your concern is something that happened over three months ago, I probably won't remember it," the man said dismissively. He was pleasant enough, not rude and evasive like Hambali, but just didn't seem interested in wasting his time talking about something that happened that long ago.

"Well, this took place back the middle of February," Steve said.

"Too long ago. Sorry, guys," Mr. Pangestu said, turning to go into his office.

"Well, thanks for your time. When it was picked off the barge that night, all we know is that it came inland," I said turning to leave.

"Barge!!!" Pangestu exclaimed, immediately turning back. "Did you say barge?!"

"Yes Sir. We saw it come off the barge but don't know where it was taken," I answered.

"Are you with the company who contracted with me?" Salem asked.

"No. We are trying to locate the owners. Do you remember handling that job?" Steve asked.

"Only because I never got paid the last half payment! I didn't do the barge pickup. All I've got is a DC 10. A guy called Hambali who has a copter called me. I rented a truck and picked it up at his place. He paid me with a check signed by a man named Hassan and told me how to contact this Hassan for the second payment after the crate was delivered. I remember Hambali telling me it had come off a barge earlier that night. That's unusual. It would have been about mid-February," Salem told us.

"So you never got paid the other half?" I asked.

"No! He had told me this Hassan would bring it to me when the job was done. He never showed up and Hambali says he doesn't know how to reach him and that he hasn't heard from him either since that night," Salem said, plainly agitated now.

We knew why—especially me. I had a brief picture run through my mind of Hassan laying on the floor of the cottage at the mosque with his balls in his mouth.

"Do you know where this Hassan is!? That's the first time in over three years I've been stuck for a bill! I told you. I'm the cheapest. I have a small profit margin. That trip cost me a lot of money because I didn't get paid the rest of the bill," Salem asked.

"No Sir," I lied. "But if we find him, we will certainly let you know. Can you remember where you took this crate?"

"Yes. It was an expensive trip. I took it to Kuala Lumpur, Malaysia. A truck picked it up right at the end of the runway at the airport. It had no markings or I would have been trying to find this deadbeat through them. If you find them you let me know!" Salem Pangestu told us.

I promised again that we would. We thanked him and got back in the van.

"Well?" Larry asked when we got under way.

"Bingo!!!—or whatever. Guys, we're headed to Malaysia tomorrow!"

"Fantastic!! I get away from this Godforsaken place!" Percy exclaimed.

CHAPTER FORTY-ONE

It was May 29, 2003 and the day had dawned with a bright sun against a deep blue sky. It was a beautiful day and our spirits were high. After months of futile searching, we were now back on the trail of the laser. We knew we would be hitting a cold trail and would require a lot of luck to pick it up again. But at least we knew where it had gone from here and we were finally getting to leave Jakarta. None of us had fallen in love with the crowded, bustling city and, with the trauma we had already gone through coupled with the constant, lurking presence of Sam and Charlie, we felt fortunate in being able for all of us to get out of Indonesia alive.

In our anxiety, we arrived at the airport at 9:00 AM for an 11:15 flight to Kuala Lumpur. We turned in the rental car, purchased tickets and decided to wait in a coffee shop in the terminal until closer to time to board.

"Where do we start in Kuala Lumpur?" Thom asked.

"We'll start at the airport. The Malaysians have, in the past couple of years, become a little more cooperative in the anti-terrorism effort. Although the country is predominantly Muslim, they are afraid of the backlash abroad and further problems on the home front from the radical element if they harbor and protect terrorists. We will identify ourselves and try to get their assistance in checking the logs to find who picked up the laser and where it may have been taken," I said.

"And if they don't cooperate?" Darby asked.

"We do what we did here. We will have to consider that it may have stayed in Malaysia, but I have a hunch Kuala Lumpur was used as a jumping off point to send it somewhere else, possibly the U.S. That's why time is of the essence now," I answered.

"You are probably right. With the crackdown on terrorists at least being partially effective there, that would not be the likely place to harbor it for long," Larry said.

"Yes, and from the information I gathered from that animal at the mosque, I don't think it's ready to use yet. They will need to take it somewhere to work out the problems and fine tune it. But they will probably try to get it closer to the place they intend to use it to complete the development," Ashton said. She still could not use Alziddi's name.

"If we have any problems with the Malaysians, I will contact the State Department and get them to exert a little pressure on them to cooperate with us," Percy said.

"Your buddies at State won't even listen to you now, Percy," Darby said.

"Why not?"

"Because you are now a twice wounded, or thrice if you count the ball kicking Reza gave you, combat soldier and State never pays attention to the people on the ground," Percy answered.

"Oh you Delta guys never are able to see the big picture!" Percy rejoined.

"Hey! You're talking to your Doctor here. I should have let gangrene set up so you would have to have had your arm amputated. I wasted good whisky on you!" Darby shot back good naturedly.

"Look!!" Steve whispered. "There's Sam and Charlie. They saw us sitting in here and walked on by trying to make out like they weren't looking for us."

"Well, we'll be rid of them soon. They must have followed us in from the parking lot, but I'm sure they weren't around when I went over and bought the tickets. They must have tailed the rest of you when you came down to the café," Larry said.

"Yeah. They don't know where we're going. We'll wait until the last minute to board, then wave at them when we get on the plane," Steve said.

"Speaking of getting on the plane, it's about time to move in that direction," I said.

"I'm going to get a magazine to read at the newsstand over there before we leave," Steve said.

"And I'm going to the restroom. Be back in a second," Percy said.

"I think I'll go to," Ashton said.

"Okay. You guys hurry back. We board in about ten minutes," I said.

Steve got his magazine and returned. Ashton returned from the restroom a few minutes later. Percy had not come back yet.

"Where's Percy!? We've got to go!" I was getting impatient. We should be boarding in five minutes.

Just as I rose to go to the restroom to see what was keeping Percy, Darby, who had been watching the restroom door about 50 yards away, stiffened.

"There's Charlie coming out of the restroom!" he exclaimed.

As a group we jumped to our feet and began to run towards the restroom. Reaching it in 15 seconds, we all rushed in the men's restroom, including

Ashton. Percy was not to be seen in there. The room was empty. Then we saw the last stall before the exit door slightly ajar. Darby ran to the stall, looked in and ran out the exit door. The rest of us reached the stall door a step behind Darby.

What we saw turned our stomachs. There was Percy, slumped over the toilet with his head down between his knees, a puddle of blood spreading across the floor underneath him!

"Oh my God!!" Steve was the first to react verbally. We had all been too stunned to say anything immediately.

Larry walked over to Percy and gently raised his head. The sight before us was gruesome. Ashton turned her head and walked away. I felt like doing the same thing. Percy's throat had been cut from ear to ear. Blood from the recent attack continued to gush from his neck, pouring down over his shirt and soaking his lap. When Larry let go, his head just wobbled to one side and he slid to the floor. He was obviously dead.

"Those bastards!" Thom said. "Those chicken shit bastards!"

"Where's Darby!?" I asked.

"I don't know. He looked in and saw Percy and left on the run," Steve said.

We all had stepped back out into the terminal aisle. About that time a man who had apparently entered after us came running out behind us. He must have seen the blood which was now seeping out in front of the stall and gone to investigate.

"Help!!! A man's been murdered!!" he screamed, running down the terminal aisle.

Soon there were several armed Indonesian airport policemen swarming into the restroom. We went back in to identify Percy and explain what we knew about his murderers. When we identified ourselves as U.S. citizens with the U.S. government, they summoned the city police detectives and, I'm sure, higher ups in the vast Indonesian bureaucracy. In ten minutes we had to explain again that we were in the country on a security matter and give them contacts to speak with at State Department, making sure to have them route all of their requests for information though Mike. In the meantime, ambulance attendants came and removed Percy's body and we told them we would contact them and make arrangements to have his remains shipped back to the States. There were endless questions to be answered and people were dispatched to search the terminal and surrounding areas for the suspects, who were probably long gone by now. Some time during this process, Darby returned and joined us silently. Finally, when the authorities were satisfied that we had told them all we were going to tell them, they released us.

We were all shaken. We had lost another valued team member and one who had touched all of us deeply with his friendship, intelligence and bravery. Darby seemed especially shaken. Due to the tragedy, we had missed our plane and none of us wanted to continue on our trip right now anyway. Plus we had to call Mike and relate the news to him.

"Larry, you and Thom go and change our tickets to tomorrow's 11:15 flight. I'll call Mike while you are doing that, then we'll get out of here. We'll go back to the hotel tonight and leave tomorrow. We need to stop on the way back to the hotel and make sure Percy is taken care of and his body shipped back to the States," I instructed.

When I called Mike, he was shaken with the news. He gave me instructions on where to have Percy sent and said he would contact the State Department immediately to make sure everything was properly taken care of by our embassy here. Larry and Thom returned with the new tickets, minus one, just as I hung up and we went to baggage claim to rent a van.

As we pulled out of the rental car area and drove through the parking lot towards the airport exit, we noticed a commotion in the distance on our left. Between the rows of parked cars there were several police vehicles with lights flashing, an ambulance and a small throng of people gawking. We were only one row over and would drive right by whatever was going on.

"Slow down, Thom," I instructed to Thom who was driving. "That looks like the white Bronco that Sam and Charlie drove. Over there where all the cops and people are gathered.

Thom slowed. We were right alongside the disturbance now and could clearly see what was going on. Lying on the ground just outside the Bronco were two men. There were no cars behind us. Thom stopped so we could plainly see the men outside the Bronco. They were lying in a pool of blood, obviously dead. Unmistakably, it was Sam and Charlie! Their bodies were covered with blood, not just in one place like a bullet wound would tend to look like. They looked like they had been slashed repeatedly with a knife.

I looked over at Darby. He wasn't even looking at them—just staring ahead stony-faced. At that moment it dawned on me where he had run off to immediately after seeing Percy.

"Drive on, Thom. We don't want the police to see us," I said softly.

We drove to the hotel silently, all of us still grieving and in shock. Now there were six of us.

CHAPTER FORTY-TWO

That night we had a somber dinner together. Everyone just picked at their food and there was very little conversation —no banter as had generally been the case when our team was together. And in the back of all of our minds was the thought that we had started out as eight. Now there were six, and all of the rest of us had narrowly escaped death at the hands of these fiends. They were obviously determined to stop us. Who would be next?

"Poor Percy was so anxious to leave Indonesia. He will be leaving now I guess. We should have knocked off Sam and Charlie as soon as we had suspicion that they were following us," Larry said.

"Yeah, I agree. If we ever sight anyone trailing us again, we'll shoot first and ask questions later," Thom said.

"I don't disagree," I said. "If we are being tailed on this mission, we know that the people behind it are ruthless and will strike at us at the first good opportunity they find. I take responsibility though for what happened to Percy. We were so close to losing Sam and Charlie that we just had a security lapse. We should not have let him or Ashton, or you, Thom, when you went next door to get the magazine, go alone."

"I should have gone with Percy," Darby said.

"Don't blame yourself, Darby. We all were lax. There will be more of them as long as we are on this mission. It happened in New York with Ernest and in Indonesia with Percy. It could happen anywhere. We just let our guard down." Steve said.

"Please, guys. Let's look out for each other extra carefully now. I don't want to lose any more of you. You are all my best friends—the best friends I have ever had. I know you know what happened to me at the mosque, and it didn't change the way you treated me at all. I feel special around you. And I love you all. I remember the way I felt when I thought the three of you had been killed in the container that night. I just didn't care if I lived—" Ashton said softly, tears glistening in the corners of her eyes.

"You are special—to all of us—and very special to me, Ashton. I think we all feel the way you do. If they come after us again, they will be sorry. I promise that," I said.

"They will. And I won't hesitate to kill them for what they did to Percy, to Ernest, to me and to the rest of you and for what they plan to do with the laser. They are evil, dangerous and disgusting. They aren't even civilized and yet they talk about doing the things they do for God. I want them all to meet their God before they hurt anymore!!" Ashton said emotionally, but with fire in her eyes now.

We all vowed that we would show no mercy in defending ourselves in the future and would act even on suspicion of a threat. Late that night we turned in. We had insisted on adjoining rooms with Darby and Thom in one, Steve and Larry and me and Ashton in the other rooms.

The next morning we contacted our embassy to assure that there were no hitches in getting Percy back to the U.S. We were told we had to go to the morgue to positively identify him before we left. We all went down but I went in to make the identification myself, not wanting to put that burden on any of the others . We were running late when we got to the airport and were stopped by the authorities when we arrived at the gate. They wanted to question us about the deaths of the suspects.

Sam was identified as Fawaz Al-Shrari and Charlie as Issam Wirayuda. They actually seemed more interested in finding their killer than in finding Percy's murderer. We were all angered by the Indonesian authorities' seeming indifference to Percy's fate while showing great concern for the guilty party involved in the two thugs death's.

We got through the questions okay but missed our plane once again by the time they allowed us to leave. They were not able to relate with any evidence Darby's brief absence during the investigation of Percy's death to the deaths of the Infama people, but the road they were trying to take was obvious. Darby told them he got sick when he saw Percy and had to run to another restroom on the other end of the terminal. They couldn't prove otherwise and I could sense Darby's anger towards their concern over the wasting of those two.

"All of these Islamic idiots can get fucked!!" Darby said when we were in private later. "A good man is dead and they are worried about the two scum that killed him! I'm just glad you didn't issue your "all go together" rule until after I had a chance to "go to the restroom" after I saw Percy."

"You killed them didn't you, Darby?" I asked.

"I did them a favor, Dawson. I introduced those idiot sons of bitches to Allah. And that's all I'm ever going to say about that," he said stoically.

I smiled. "How thoughtful of you."

"Percy was my friend," Darby simply said. We never talked about it again.

As it turned out, we had to stay to assist the State Department in making proper arrangements for Percy and be interviewed several more times by the Indonesian authorities relative to Percy's death and the deaths of Sam and Charlie before they would release us to leave the country. It was Monday, June 2nd before we were finally able to leave for Kuala Lumpur.

The night before we left, Ashton and I made love for the first time since Percy's death. She was still upset over losing Percy. She told me again that he had become like a member of her family and the loss really hurt. Other than Skipper and her Mom, she told me that her other relations with people had been kept at arm's length emotionally because everyone she had been involved in tried to hurt her. From that point on, I could sense an extra protectiveness from her when we got into dangerous situations. She didn't seem concerned for her own safety, but worried about me and stayed right at my side when we were confronted with lethal force.

After a weather delay at Jakarta, we finally arrived in a heavy rain in Kuala Lumpur at 2:30 PM. We rented a van and drove to the Park Plaza International hotel where we got rooms. Ashton and I were on one end with Darby and Larry and Steve and Thom in connecting rooms next to us. It was already 4:30 PM when we got checked in, so we decided to have dinner about 7:00 PM at a restaurant the hotel people recommended. It was right off the Kapung Baru stop on the world's second-longest, fully automated monorail. After dinner we would return to the hotel and be prepared to start out on our continuing search the next morning.

At dinner most of us tried some of the local Malaysian and Thai dishes. I got Pad Thai and it was delicious, but hot. The dish consisted of shrimp on a bed of noodles mixed with peanut and pepper sauce. Darby and Thom decided to stay with the more traditional fare.

"I'm having the water buffalo. They look a little like cows. You guys can eat that Asian stuff if you like. I'm strictly a meat and potatoes man," Darby said.

"I agree with you," Thom said. "but I think I will have the fresh fish. We'll ride back together in the front seat, Darby. That way, if the rest of you barf all over the place, you won't get it on us and we'll lower the windows in the back so we can't smell you."

"Dawson! Let's dance!" Ashton exclaimed. There was a small combo playing western type music at the lounge adjoining the restaurant section.

Several couples were dancing. Although a fairly strict Muslim country, western dress and social activities were fast encroaching on the traditional values in the big cities throughout Malaysia.

"Hon, I'm not that good," I protested. It didn't help. She grabbed me by the hand and drug me on the dance floor.

Fortunately, I didn't have to do much other than stand there and move around a little, pretending to know what I was doing. Ashton was very good, and all eyes were on her anyway. She had a short skirt and knit top on that were very sexy looking and her long hair, pretty face combined with her perfect body that moved suggestively to the beat of the music kept the band going extra long on their song selection.

She was having fun, but I convinced her to let me rest after the second song which had a little faster beat than the first. I think the band was sadistic. They probably could see that I was struggling, but they didn't care. They, and most others in the room were watching and admiring Ashton.

"Hey! You guys are good!" Larry said when we returned to our table.

"Thanks, Larry," I said.

"Oh, I didn't mean you, Dawson. I meant Ashton and the band," Larry laughed.

He shouldn't have mouthed off. The next thing he knew, Ashton had grabbed him by the hand and half pushed, half pulled him on the dance floor. The band immediately struck up a new song with a faster beat. It was hard not to notice Ashton. She was definitely the most desirable looking girl in a room full of pretty Asian girls and some foreigners. But the rest of us were enjoying watching Larry as he tried to keep his body moving to the beat of the music. We laughed until we cried at his futile effort to keep up with Ashton.

We had a lot of fun that night. The next morning we would start to work again, but this night we were just six good friends enjoying each other's company. We were down to six now, but we were six tough and capable operators. We had a top CIA agent, an outstanding FBI agent, a lead agent in the Secret Service, an experienced Delta Force guy, a former combat pilot and aeronautics engineer and Ashton , a smart, pretty scientist who could handle herself well in tough situations and who we all loved —especially me.

CHAPTER FORTY-THREE

Tuesday, June 3rd we hit the streets and the highways. Since Mr. Pangestu had told us he delivered the crate to the airport, we decided to start there. It took us a while, but we finally found an administrator who apparently could make a decision as to whether or not they assisted us. His name was Ishmael Ahmad.

"Gentlemen, it would be highly unusual for a package to be picked up at the end of the runway as your Mr. Pangestu has told you," Mr. Ahmad told us. "It has happened on special request on occasion. If we grant the request, there has to be a good reason and we route them to the East runway during a slow traffic period. They are required to not be on the ground longer than thirty minutes during which time they must refuel if necessary , turn the plane around at the turn way and take off on that same runway. All of the movement is controlled by our tower."

"Could this have happened on that night?" I asked.

"What night was this, did you say?" Mr. Ahmad asked.

"Mr. Pangestu said it would have been the night of February 17th, about 9:00 PM, when he landed," I answered.

Mr. Ahmad shook his head. "That is a long time ago. Do you realize how much traffic we have had through here since then?"

"Yes Sir. But you say this kind of pickup is rare and needs to be approved for a good reason. Who would approve something like this? Might that person remember something that would be helpful?" I asked.

"Perhaps. It has been a long time, but you are correct. The supervisor who handled the request would possibly remember. Normally those requests are made in advance, however. So you would have to talk to each of the shift supervisors. There are four of them that rotate plus a relief person so we can cover 24 hours on a seven day basis. You would have to talk to all five of them to be sure that you would talk to the person who approved the request as well as the supervisor who was on duty the night of the delivery," Mr. Ahmad told us.

"May we do that?" Larry asked.

"Yes. I will arrange that. But you will have to question them in my presence, which will take at least a week to listen to all of them. And one of the four is on vacation and won't be back until next week," he responded.

And that is how the next two weeks went. We did find while talking to the third supervisor that he did recall a request about that time for a flight coming from Jakarta that claimed to have radioactive material that they needed to load on a special lead insulated truck so as not to potentially expose people at the terminal or the general populace to dangerous levels of radiation. He approved the request.

None of the others we talked to that week recalled being on duty when this crate was delivered. Finally, the next week, when we talked to the supervisor who had been on vacation we found that he had been on duty when the crate arrived. But he didn't remember anything unusual except the truck that picked the crate up did not seem any different from any truck. The ultimate delivery destination is not required for approval for this kind of pickup. He did not remember that the truck had any markings on it.

It would be futile to check all the trucking firms in Kuala Lumpur. The truck could have been a privately owned truck also. It was Friday, the 13th of June by this time.

The next week was spent in checking with the various airlines, but we had nothing specific to tell them about the crate we were seeking, except that it originated in Lebac, Indonesia, and arrived here on a private airplane from Jakarta. We were hoping some of the markings on the crate or the documentation that might have come with it would ring a bell with someone. Although generally cooperative, the event had been a long time ago and the only record that would have been helpful to our search would have been the destination of the crate. We had no clue on that. That was the information that we really wanted to know.

By the end of June, our search for clues had turned to taking the limited information we had to ocean freight companies. Our investigation continued well into July with no promising information uncovered that would lead us to where the laser was. We visited all of the boat companies, industrial and commercial, that shipped to anywhere in North America. Some of the company officials were reluctant to talk to us while others opened up their records to us. An exhaustive search of shipping records made available to us did not result in any suspect information. By now we were grasping at straws, trying to find if any single crate items were shipped to any organizations that were on the FBI watch list. Shipments to what looked like legitimate companies were passed over, considering the immense volume of material we had to sort through.

"Sweetheart, I feel like we're not getting anywhere—just spinning our wheels," Ashton said to me late one afternoon after we had spent an exhausting, but fruitless day.

We were lounging on the bed with the windows open and the curtains fluttering in the breeze. It had been hot and muggy most of the time we had been here, but today a tremendous storm had blown in late in the day, cooling the air a little. We had opened the window to capture the smell of fresh rain and feel the cooler air that was still humid, but no longer muggy. Due to the torrential rain, we had quit a little earlier than normal today. The others were in their rooms just relaxing for a change, as we were.

Ashton had put on her tan shorts and a navy blue blouse after taking a shower. I had pulled on some old blue jeans and a T-shirt, mixed myself a drink and was propped on a couple of pillows on the bed smoking a cigarette. Ashton had long since given up on harassing me about my addiction.

Her tanned legs and shapely body along with her long dark brown hair and hazel eyes made her so pretty and sexy looking that I, for the thousandth time, marveled at my luck to have met this beautiful, loving girl. She was cuddled beside me, resting her head on my shoulder.

"Yes. I feel the same way. And I'm impatient. I have this dread feeling that, while we are wasting time getting nowhere, Infama is getting closer and closer to being able to carry out their murderous plan," I finally answered her.

"Do you think Mike will call us back to the States soon?" she asked.

"Yes, I do. We aren't getting anywhere here. We probably would be better off trying to locate the laser where we think it will be used. Of course it could be planned to be used in some other country to catch the President on one of his State visits. It's frustrating. We came so close and confirmed the weapon's existence and the plan to use it. Now we've run into a brick wall," I said.

"I know you worry about it, baby," she said, putting her arms around me and pressing herself closer to me.

"Ashton—?"

"Huh?" she mumbled, kissing me on the neck.

"I like you," I teased.

"You better love me," she said, taking a nibble out of my neck.

"I know. And I do. And I will, if you let me," I said, lifting her chin and kissing her moist lips.

"I want you to," she said, turning on her back. "Take my shorts off..."

I leaned over her, and unbuttoned her shorts. She raised her hips while I slid them down her legs and off her ankles. While I was doing that, she unbuttoned my jeans and helped me take them off. Her white panties made a sexy contrast with her tanned legs and flat tummy exposed partially as her blouse had ridden upward when we were disrobing. Below the waist, I had only my boxer shorts on and she just her panties. We kissed with me still resting on my elbows and knees above her. She was passionate with her kiss and reached upward, grasping my shorts and sliding them down so she could see what was awaiting her. I finished sliding them off, letting them fall to the floor.

"Oh baby, don't make me wait. Take me now..." she whispered, lightly running her fingers around the now throbbing part she wanted inside her.

I hooked my fingers in the sides of her panties and, while she raised her hips once again, slid them down over her ankles. She never let go of me while I was doing this and, when I had finished and tossed her panties beside my shorts on the floor, she spread her legs slightly and guided me in her. I could feel the wetness and warmness of the place she was causing me to enter.

"I love you, little girl," I said tenderly, lowering myself until I was deeply into her.

"I love you, too. Will you always be here for me—no matter what?" she asked, looking straight into my eyes, before closing her eyes and giving up to our desires.

"Yes—I promise..." I whispered in her ear, slowly withdrawing partially from within her.

We didn't talk for a long while after that. She held me tightly around the waist, pushing me upward while she began to thrust her tummy towards mine, sinking me sharply back into her. Then she, just as quickly withdrew. I caught my breath as she repeated this thrusting motion until I was brought on the brink of taking charge again and finishing immediately what we had started.

"Okay, Love, you do it to me. Rock me—hard. I'm ready. I want all of you—now!!" she made one final thrust upward before I followed her request and held off as long as I could with several forceful downward plunges into her before we both finished simultaneously.

"You are nice," I said after we had exhausted ourselves and were once again cuddling beside each other.

"I know. That's because I love you," she smiled, pecking me on the cheek. "Feel how wet you made me."

She placed my hand down between her legs where the moistness and liquids of our lovemaking was still evident in the warm, fuzzy place where she had exuded and received the juices of love.

We were suddenly interrupted by the loud ring of the phone beside our bed.

"Hello," I answered.

"Dawson, Mike. You guys can come on back tomorrow. We've attained information here that will put you back on track to find the laser. It arrived yesterday in Long Beach, California on an ocean freighter chartered by a company from China."

"China? You mean Taiwan?" I asked.

"No. Mainland China. Communist China. We get a lot of imports from there, you know," Mike answered.

"Where is it being delivered to?" I asked.

"There's a strange answer to that. It's being trucked to a little town in Tennessee. We're looking into possible connections between the company it is being delivered to and Infama. And we have no idea at this time how the Chinese may fit into this puzzle," Mike said.

"It sounds like we should leave here as soon as we can get out and head for this little town in Tennessee," I said.

"Yes, you need to come on back to the U.S., but why don't you come here first. We're just now trying to put together information on what we know so far and fill in the blank spaces. It will take them at least four days to truck it across the country. We don't want to tip them off yet until we are able to find the identities of the people involved. We will keep the truck under surveillance the whole way to make sure they don't offload it along the way. By the time you get here, we hope to have a lot more information for you to work with," Mike said.

"Okay. We'll be on our way first thing in the morning, Mike," I said.

"Good. One other thing, Dawson," Mike said before hanging up.

"What's that?"

"When you get here, after our briefing, you may be racing against time. The comment Ashton passed on to us from Alziddi about our President not seeing the New Year appears to have some validity. Of course we have half the year left, but the end of the year is not a magic number. We have intelligence that indicates Infama's plans are to use this laser to assassinate the President in the fall, which could be as early as August. The information is a little fuzzy at this time, but it is unmistakably from a credible source. I'll fill you in when you get here," Mike concluded.

I passed Mike's comments on to the rest of the team. They were sobering to all of us. We booked an early morning flight which would take us around the world to our ultimate destination, Washington, D.C. The consequences to our country and the entire free world of our failing to stop this plot in time were unthinkable. We would leave Malaysia tomorrow with a renewed sense of urgency.

CHAPTER FORTY-FOUR

It was Thursday, July 3, 2003 when we finally arrived in D.C. about 6:30 PM, after only one flight delay during the whole trip. Due to the critical importance and urgency of the situation, Mike had scheduled an unprecedented meeting in his office July 4th. Representatives of all of our agencies would be there.

After a fitful night's sleep trying to let our bodies sort through the jet lag and going through two nighttimes to get here, the six of us arrived at Mike's office a little before 9:00 AM. The others were already there when we walked in.

"Happy holiday guys!" Mike greeted us when we arrived. "Of course the six of you have spent the last few months basking in the tropical paradise of the South Pacific, so you can just count this as an extension of your vacation."

"Mike, since you're Dawson's boss, he can't say to you what I can. Why don't you get made love to?" Ashton rejoined with a perky smile.

Mike roared with laughter. "Well, Miss pretty girl. I guess that's a nice way to tell me to get fucked. Alright. Let me introduce you guys."

"This is Harry Simmons, deputy FBI Director. You know Harry, Steve. And this is James Cothern, Intelligence Coordinator with the CIA. James told me you two had met, Larry," Mike began the introductions.

"Okay," he continued. "Let's get down to business because the six of you need to get out of here and head to Tennessee tonight or early in the morning. Harry, why don't you lead off with the information you have."

"Alright. Knowing that you guys had found the laser in Indonesia and discovered it was sent to Malaysia, Mike asked me if I could spare a couple of agents to check out likely ports of entry on the West coast. We started in L.A. but hit the jackpot in Long Beach, probably the largest arrival port for shipments from Asia and the Pacific region. With the security on airlines now, we felt this item would likely be shipped by ocean freight," Harry began.

Actually," he continued, "our guys lucked out. They were mainly checking on shipments from Southeast Asia, with Malaysian originated traffic being the top priority. Then they learned that shipments from Southeast Asia sometimes are routed through China—a lot of the cheap items sold in U.S. stores are manufactured in China or one of the SE Asia countries, but are brokered through Chinese companies. As a fill-in while waiting on manifests from Malaysian shipments, they started looking at some of the shipments from China."

"How did they come across the laser crate in that mountain of paperwork?" Steve asked.

"Well, China requires a separate listing for anything originating from anywhere other than China, so their quantity of listings was greatly reduced. And they were looking for something originating from Malaysia that would fit the description you gave us, as well as any indication that the original country of origin was Indonesia. June 29th, they found such a listing. The ship was just being unloaded. Before going to the staging area for ground shipment, they found the crate. It still had the Lebac markings," Harry answered.

"I'm curious, Harry. Since the laser was located, why didn't they just confiscate it right on the spot?" I asked.

"Good question," James joined in. "Mike, Harry and I talked about that. It was tempting to take it and destroy it. But the strange thing was that the ultimate delivery address was a company called Munson, Inc. in a little town in Lawrenceburg, Tennessee. We were curious about their connection. Harry felt like his guys could keep it under surveillance, so we decided to let it go to its' destination to see how the whole thing played out and maybe be able to catch more of the people involved in this thing."

"So did we find out anything about this company?" Larry asked.

"Yes, but let me finish the story at the dock," Harry said.

"Sure. I'm thrilled that we now have the weapon essentially in our control," Larry said.

"We all are," Harry agreed. "Okay. We didn't want to tip anyone off. Once the crate was moved to the ground staging area to be signed out by various trucking firms who were contracted to pick up the cargo, we just kept our eye on it. A Roadway moving truck accepted the shipment. It was combined with a number of other items, machinery parts and such, that were also destined for Munson. They have been tailing the truck continuously since then. The driver is taking his time. He got to Memphis last night, so is still about a six hour drive away from Lawrenceburg and he hasn't left Memphis yet. Our guys report that he met a girl in Memphis and they spent the big part of the night doing the bar scenes. An hour ago, they were still shacked up together in a motel. The truck's in the motel parking lot. They'll call us when it moves."

"Okay, I'll pick up the story now," James said. "In conjunction with our office and the FBI, we found that Munson has a strange, rare, but not illegal, corporate structure. It is owned by an offshore investment group that is in turn owned by a group of mainland China investors from the industrial city of Guangzhou. Munson manufactures appliances and is the largest employer in that area, currently employing about 1,500 people. The company was originally an American company making a similar product line, but has changed ownership twice since its start in the 1960's."

"That's scary—that there may be a connection between communist China and the terrorists who plan to assassinate the President," Ashton said.

"Well, the more we look into it, the less likely we think there is a connection. Historically, there has been much mutual suspicion between China and Indonesia, dating all the way back from when Jakarta accused Beijing of backing a communist coup attempt in 1965. Many Chinese companies eager to invest abroad have felt unsafe in Indonesia. But in the last three years, there has been an acceleration of interest from both to expand their business cooperation. China makes no secret of its global ambitions and is attracted to the vast natural resources in Indonesia—oil, gas, timber and coal. China's inroads into Indonesia, the world's fourth most populous nation and Southeast Asia's biggest economy, mark its arrival as an economic power in the region and herald the end of an era when Japan and the U.S. were the only growth engines that mattered," James told us.

"What we suspect," James continued, "is that someone in Jakarta connected to Infama—probably Hassan—requested that the laser be sent with the balance of the shipment destined for Munson, so it could be picked up by their people once it got to Tennessee. The Chinese-owned company was more than happy to oblige by doing a favor for a prominent Indonesian who approached them to ship a "tractor component" from their Lebac plant. We have done extensive background checks on all the top management people at the Lawrenceburg plant and find nothing even slightly questionable. Likewise, the Chinese investors who own the Tennessee plant would not appear to have anything to do with the Infama movement."

"So why is it being shipped there?" Thom asked.

"If it stays there, our theory of non-conspiracy with the Chinese company will be proven wrong. Our best guess is that, once it reaches the plant, the crate will be picked up by Infama operatives and taken to wherever they plan to take it to complete their work on it and get it in readiness to use sometime in the next few months. Lawrenceburg is an ideal, out of the way place to complete the development or to ship to the major East Coast cities of D.C., New York, Philadelphia. It would be about a 12 hour drive to deliver it to one of those places."

"And if you are wrong?" I asked.

"If someone at Munson takes delivery of the crate, we will close in on them, take the laser and do a full scale investigation of Munson," Harry said.

"Yes. And if we are right and the laser is merely offloaded at Munson and picked up later by someone else, then we want to know who those people are and where they are going. Staying with the laser before tipping our hand could lead us to the major Infama operatives working in the U.S. This has to be their most important project. Taking the weapon is the important thing immediately, but shutting down the people is a high priority future security objective," Mike concluded.

We spent the rest of the morning going over the details of information that the FBI and CIA had gathered for us to be aware of now that our object of interest was on U.S. soil. We then had lunch catered and finished about 3:00 PM. Harry got a call from his agents in Memphis who were tailing the truck about that time.

"They say the driver is apparently taking the 4th off. Most drivers don't like to drive on the weekends either, unless contracted to do so. He may not leave to complete his trip until Monday morning the 8th. They will call us if the truck moves tomorrow, at which time he will be only about six hours drive away from his destination. We will stay in touch with the team to let you know," Harry reported.

"Good. Well Dawson, I think you and your group need to take off for Lawrenceburg early tomorrow morning. Your best bet is to fly into Nashville, rent a van and drive to Lawrenceburg. It's about 75 miles south of Nashville, only 20 miles from Alabama. Once the truck arrives in Lawrenceburg, we'll release the two agents who have been tailing it and your team can take over from there.

That night in the hotel before separating to go to our respective rooms for the night, we gathered in our room a few minutes. We were elated that the laser had been located and would be turned over to us to take any time we wanted to. In the meantime, we might be able to get our hands on some of the high level Infama people operating in the states. Who knows? Alziddi himself might show up for the anticipated action if he could get in the country and there were numerous ways he could slip in, in spite of heightened security. And, if everything went as planned, our project would be done.

The one negative of all that was that we all expressed remorse that it looked like we would soon be splitting up to go our separate ways. The six of us had truly become a close team, bonded by mutual respect and liking for each other. As hard as it had been along the way, none of us looked forward to our work being completed in one sense, because it would mean we would lose a once in a lifetime experience of being "us" and all the good times we had shared with each other.

We would find that we had a while to go yet before we finished our task and that the President would be put in peril with tragic results. Along the way, the six would become five also, and there would be only four of us left at the finish line.

CHAPTER FORTY-FIVE

We were able to book space on an American Airline flight leaving D.C. 6:30 AM Saturday, July 5, 2003. After arriving, we rented a van and were on our way to Lawrenceburg, about a two hour drive from the Nashville airport. We were in no hurry. I called Mike from the Nashville airport before leaving. He told me that the FBI agents assigned to the truck had reported that the truck was still in Memphis. Apparently the driver was not going to hit the road until Monday morning.

That was good for us. Even if he left early Monday morning, he could not arrive in Lawrenceburg before noon. That would give us some time to case the town and check out the Munson plant before taking over from the agents and going to work. We all could use a little time off from the constant tension of this chase, also.

We booked ourselves into the Richland Inn, a motel on the main 'drag'. Later we would find that it was less than a mile from Munson. Of course, nothing was too far from anywhere in Lawrenceburg. Exploring the town Saturday afternoon, we found that it was a quiet little rural town of about 12,000 population. Other than Munson and a few smaller companies in an industrial park there, the primary activity appeared to be in small, family-owned farming.

There were the usual service stations and numerous used car lots. I sometimes felt that a lot of people in small Southern towns must make a living trading cars among themselves. I never could figure out the economic equation in that. It puts me to mind of the story about the two farmers who bought and sold the same mule back and forth to each other for years until the mule died. One of the farmers lamented that now they would go broke since both of them had made a living off of that old mule for the last ten years.

Additionally, there was a 'strip' where our motel, the Wal-Mart, food stores, a few restaurants, fast food places, small retail outlets and other commercial activity took place and a downtown square that was almost deserted of commercial establishments except for antique stores, a couple of specialty retail shops and a family-owned clothing store that had been a fixture in the town for many years.

On the square was a life-size statue of Davy Crockett. We learned later that it was the only such statue in the world of Crockett. He had a gristmill there and had helped lay the town out just prior to moving to West Tennessee and then on to the Alamo. On the opposite end of the square was a monument commemorating the county Spanish American war dead. It looked very much like a miniature Washington monument. The old courthouse which used to sit in the center of the square had been demolished years ago and been replaced by a modern building several blocks away.

A ride through the countryside took us to various little farming communities surrounding the town in every direction. We had driven about ten or fifteen miles in each direction on the main highways intersecting the town. North of town, between the little communities of Ethridge and Summertown, we ran into what appeared to be an Amish community with the black horses and buggies and the men, women and children dressed in black. The men all had flowing beards and wore brimmed hats. The local people we stopped and chatted with told us they were locally called Mennonites and were of the old order that did not believe in using electricity or any mechanical devices. They were reputed to be honest, peaceful and hardworking, but kept to themselves. They spoke with a strong German accent. Most were farmers and they self taught their children. Before leaving the Lawrenceburg area, they would unknowingly and unfortunately become embroiled in our dangerous game.

By Saturday evening we had gotten a good feel of the town and surrounding area, including the sprawling Munson complex located inside the city limits. There was a little steak house down the street from the motel called the Show Ring. We decided to stop in there and eat about dusk, before going back to the motel.

"Well, what do you think of this little town? It seems a strange place for Infama to be readying their weapon for activation," I asked the group after we had eaten and ordered beer.

"I grew up in a little town like this," Thom said. "Really, you learn to have fun even though there's not a lot of attractions like there are in the bigger cities."

"Where was that?" Larry asked.

"Dothan, Alabama."

"I grew up in the Bronx. I can't imagine what you would do as a kid or teenager in a town like this. It seems to me it would be boring as hell," Larry said.

"What did you do with your friends in the Bronx?" Thom asked.

"We hung out together, roamed the streets, got in trouble sometimes and I played baseball in high school," Larry replied.

"Did you go to the Broadway shows or any of the professional ball games? Or did you eat at any of the fine restaurants around the New York area or take advantage of the ease of getting out of the airports there to take a trip somewhere?" Thom asked.

"Hell no! I couldn't afford to do those things. My friends and I just found ways to do the things we could do and had fun at it," Larry responded.

"Well, it sounds like you and I had about the same kind of childhood," Thom grinned. "Except we had hills and valleys as well as streets to roam. And I played football and was able to date the prettiest cheerleader at our school. She only lived two doors away and her dad and mine worked together at the same place. You had all those exciting things to do that probably didn't even interest you that much at that time and you weren't able to take advantage of them if they did. So you did what my friends and I did. The big difference was probably that you were just a tiny grain of sand in that beach of humanity and I was, for a while, big man on campus—or in Dothan, I should say."

"Okay, okay. I still think you are deprived in a place like this. What about you, Dawson?" Larry half-conceded.

"I grew up in a town in Tennessee about three times this big, but nothing like the Bronx. I was like Thom and you —just made do with the environment that was available to me. I didn't know anything about other places anyway, except what I read and saw in the movies. That knowledge allowed me to dream and think about the things I wanted to do and places I wanted to go in the future."

"I think everyone likes the place where they grew up, but no one ever wants to go back once they leave. Right?" Steve asked.

"You're right about that, I think. I know I don't want to go back to the Bronx and I doubt any of you want to go back to the places you came from. Where are you from, Steve?" Larry asked.

"Canton, Ohio. A fair-sized city, not like the Bronx, but not like the places the rest of you are from. We had a lot of school rivalry between Canton, Massillon, Youngtown and some of the other cities in Ohio and Pennsylvania. I attended Canton McKinley High School. I played football, wide receiver on the state championship team. A lot of my activities revolved around sports and the school. Otherwise, I did the same things you guys did," Steve replied.

"So, we have two Alabamians, me and Thom, a Tennessean, a New Yorker and a Midwesterner. What about you, Ashton? You've never talked about your childhood?" Darby asked.

Ashton blushed and seemed momentarily flustered. She glanced quickly at me as if asking me to help her answer that question. Then she seemed to quickly recover. No one but me probably noticed her initial hesitation.

"Oh, I'm from Tennessee, like Dawson. Maybe that is one of the things that attracted us to each other. I'm from a little town in West Tennessee, between Memphis and Nashville. I had the normal activities and relationships in high school that all of you probably had, but I left before finishing high school due to some family problems and had to finish school in Atlanta and, in a round-a-bout way and after a few years, got a scholarship to attend UCLA where I got a degree in physics. After that I did graduate work at University of Georgia. I had only been at Livermore a year when I joined you guys, but was fortunate to immediately get thrown into their foremost experimental project —the super laser work," she answered.

"Well, back to this little town —why here for Infama?" I asked, quickly changing the subject before someone might ask another question that might embarrass Ashton.

"I think," Steve said, "that it just happened through coincidence that this town served a number of their purposes. The shipment through China to a company that just happened to be located here certainly allowed them to get the laser into the country easier. They would be aware that our agencies might be on the lookout for the laser coming through suspect channels and a shipment, along with other equipment parts, to a legitimate company would be easily overlooked. The new relationship between Indonesia and the Chinese made this an easy deal to accomplish."

"I agree," Larry said. "And the fact that the laser is being shipped to an out of the way place like this definitely is a plus, also. This would be an unlikely place for us to suspect as a destination."

"Of course all of this assumes that Munson is not involved in this thing other than being an unsuspecting conduit," I said.

"Right! That is a proper assumption, I think, but we'll find out real soon if it is a correct assumption. If the crate is picked up by someone not associated with the company and transported off-sight, we can assume that, as far as Munson was concerned, arrangements were made by someone else to just ship this item along with their goods, perhaps to save on freight costs. The

FBI and our agency will continue to check, of course, to see if there could be a connection," Larry said.

We continued to talk for a while then retired back to the motel. It was about 10:00 PM when we got back to our rooms.

"Thanks for getting me off the hook, Love," Ashton said when we got in our room. "If I were asked to fill in too many holes in my background, I would either have to lie or be embarrassed. You know, you are the only person outside of Mom and Skipper that knows my whole story. By the way, I need to call Skipper tonight and let him know where I am. I haven't talked to him since we left the country and he's probably worried about me."

"Okay. Let me say hi to him when you get him on the line. First, though, we better check our messages," I said, noticing that the phone message light was blinking.

The first message was from Mike, telling me the truck was still in Memphis and that the two agents tailing it would call me on my cell phone when it moved, but they assumed the driver would not leave until Monday. He said they had the truck under 24 hour surveillance and nothing had been removed from it. The seal was still on the rear door. He also said that the agents would follow the truck closely enough to ensure nothing was off-loaded on the way here. The message continued, to tell me that the take over from the agents to us would be at the point they arrived in Lawrenceburg.

The second call was from Bob Willoughby.

"Hey Dawson and Ashton! This is Bob Willoughby. I talked to Mike a few minutes ago and he told me you were back in the country. My security clearance and his kindness allowed him to give me the number where I could reach you. Ashton, I have been worried about you. Mike didn't tell me where you have been or why you are there—just that you are still on the search for the laser. He did tell me that you lost another team member, Percy, so I know you have all been in some dangerous situations. I shared with Mike the limited information we have gathered that might help in the investigation but nothing I have will help in the accomplishment of your mission. We miss you, Ashton and the project would be progressing much faster if you were here, but what you are doing is far more important. I just wish it were safer for you. I know you are doing everything you can to prevent irreparable damage resulting from the loss of the laser information from our facility and I appreciate that and will help you any way I can if the opportunity arises. Best wishes to all of you and take care."

Ashton smiled. "Bob feels like he is a father to me. I never told him much about my past —none of the things I told you. But I have indicated to him that I had a troubled youth and had been on my own since I was sixteen. He worries about me, I think."

"Can he be trusted?" I asked.

"Oh yes. He's definitely not connected to Infama and would not share information even on our whereabouts with anyone for fear it could get in the wrong hands and hurt us. Bob would do anything to protect me. Before you and the team, he was the closest I had to family and he feels responsible for me. He has top security clearance and is a man of great integrity. He will always do the right thing, even if it hurts. He's the one who blew the whistle on ourselves when he discovered some of the information had gotten out of the facility."

"I like him. I judge people as to whether or not I would want to go into combat with them. My impression is that he is one that I would," I said.

"Yes, he is not a middle-of-the-roader. He is a lot like you. He is passionate about anything he does. He is responsible for pushing us to expedite the laser project within our funding capability and look for potential alternate uses for it. He has great vision, sense of urgency and ability to focus on the things that are important. His philosophy is that if you drive in the middle lane you don't have to worry about oncoming cars in the left lane or cliffs off the side of the road in the right lane and it is easy to change lanes from right to left. But he has no use for those people who stick to the middle of the road. He thinks you should choose your course and go for it and take on the cars and the cliffs as they come at you. He is also compassionate, but doesn't shrink from doing the difficult thing if he feels it is the right thing to do," Ashton commented.

"I think I would like him," I laughed. "You better try to call Skipper. It's getting late, Doll."

"Hey, Skipper! Did you think I had disappeared?" Ashton asked when she rang and Skipper answered.

They talked for a while, Ashton explaining that we had been overseas and were now back in the states. They promised to get together again as soon as they could.

"Skipper wants to say hi to you before we ring off," Ashton said, handing the phone to me.

"Hi Skipper. Your sister is hard to keep up with. I've had to chase her all over the world and she keeps getting me in trouble."

"Yeah. I know how she is. She told me she was still in love with you though, so just imagine how she would be if she didn't love you," Skipper laughed.

"Yeah. That's a scary thought," I said.

"Well, I know you two are tired, so I'll let you go. I just wanted to say hi. I told Ashton we need to get together again as soon as we can. I don't want us to wait until I have to come to your wedding. I might forget what you look like and don't want her to marry a stranger," he joked.

"I hope that won't be too long. I love her, too, Skipper, and that will be the first thing I want to do when we get done with this project and the aftereffects of it—that is, if she will have me," I promised.

We said goodbye and Ashton and I took a shower and finally got to bed about midnight. We made love. It was nice. We had one more day of relaxation before we would be under the gun again. As I dropped off to sleep afterward, I thought about Ashton being my wife. That would be nice, too—if she would have me. First we had to finish the trip we had started.

CHAPTER FORTY-SIX

Sunday, July 6th, we received a call about 9:00 AM from agent Rodriquiz Pancheros. He was one of the FBI agents in Memphis. His partner was observing the truck. He identified his partner as Bobby Smith. Mike had already given us their names.

"You can call us Pancho and Lefty. Bobby's left-handed," Pancho told me. "Your guy went for breakfast with his girlfriend, then came back to the motel. As we suspected, he's probably not going to move the truck until tomorrow. I don't get the impression he has any idea what he's carrying. He seems very laid back and not nervous or furtive at all. They went nightclubbing again last night. I've had about all the smoke filled rooms and loud country music I can take for a while. Bobby likes it, though. He even danced a couple of times. Damned redneck!"

"Will you give me a call when he moves out?" I asked, laughing at his description of their night.

"Sure. And we'll keep you posted periodically on his progress. You have the truck description and license number. We'll be close behind in a 2001 Blue Taurus. We changed cars yesterday. We'll call you when we get about thirty minutes out, too," he informed me.

"Good. How do you want to make the switch?" I asked.

"Well, we'll stay the night in Lawrenceburg before heading back—maybe have dinner with some of you guys before we leave the next morning, if you aren't already chasing the cargo by then. Why don't you fall in behind us when we reach the city limits and he's all yours when he pulls in the plant gate—if that's where he goes. We'll do a drive by. You will be behind us and can take over from there," Pancho suggested.

"Sounds good. Thanks for helping us out on this one," I said.

"No problem. If you run into something you need help on tomorrow afternoon or night, let me know," Pancho offered before hanging up.

"Okay, guys," I said to the others who were all in our room at the time. "We have another day off. Everybody can do what they please today. Just keep your cell phones live in case Pancho calls and says they are on the move. I think Ashton and I will rent a car and drive to that Davy Crockett Park we drove by yesterday and maybe explore some of those interesting little country roads. Why don't we all plan to meet back here by 7:00 PM and we'll find a place to eat."

"I know where I want to go," Darby said. "I want to go to that place the service station guy told us had good catfish. I think he said it was in that little community called Leoma that we drove through about ten miles south of town."

"Yuk!! How can you eat something that feeds off the bottom of the river?" Larry asked.

"Hey! I like Darby's idea. Good catfish is fantastic. We'll call ahead and make sure they have something that your tender stomach can abide," Thom said.

There was no rental car agency in town but we found a used car lot that would rent us a car, so the other guys dropped me and Ashton off there and we proceeded to the park.

It was a small but pretty park. We parked the car close to a reconstructed covered bridge over a creek and sparkling waterfall below. Ashton and I got out and walked, holding hands, across the bridge then turned onto a little trail leading through the woods. We saw several deer along the way.

When we got out of sight of the hand-full of other people visiting the park, we sat on a large rock beside the little bubbling creek. Ashton and I both had on blue jeans and polo shirts. As usual, she looked great in her faded jeans and powder blue shirt. We took off our shoes and dangled our feet in the water. It was really nice being alone with her here and, at least for today, not having to worry about Infama or the laser. I'm sure the other guys were having fun relaxing and exploring, too.

"Did I ever tell you how beautiful you are and how much I love you?" I asked.

"No, you never have," she lied, giving me her quirky little grin.

"Oh? Maybe you're right. It must have been some other girl I've said that to so often lately," I teased her.

At that she suddenly gave me a little shove and I slid right off the rock into the water, coming up soaking wet from my waist down. Ashton just stood on the rock laughing.

"And just who is this girl you love so much, Dawson Kohler? I'll bet she wouldn't do that to you," she said, giving me that grin again as I pulled myself out of the ice cold water.

"Okay, you little witch. I guess it was you after all that I love. Give me a hand to get back on that slick rock," I said, meekly reaching my hand out to her.

She kneeled down and took my hand to help me up and I quickly gave it a jerk and brought her down into the creek with me. She landed face first, soaking herself from head to toe.

"You liar!" she screamed at me and grabbed me around the neck, bringing me sprawling down on my back into the water with her. Now we were both soaked through and through.

We playfully wrestled each other until we both surrendered in a wet embrace. Ashton was cute with her hair hanging down in her face dripping wet. Her jeans and shirt clung to her, outlining her shapely body. I kissed her and drew her close to me with us standing together, knee deep in the water. We had gotten over the shock of the cold water and clung lovingly to the warmth of each other.

"I have an idea," I said.

"What's that, Love?" she asked, looking straight into my eyes with her pretty hazel eyes. She still had her arms around my neck and we were standing with our bodies pressed closely together.

"Why don't we climb back up on the rock, get these wet clothes off so they can dry some in the sun and make love on the rock?" I asked, smiling at her expression.

"Dawson!! We can't do that! There are people here—kids!" Then she saw I was joking and pushed me back into the water, crawling up on the rock herself.

"Well, I just thought it was a good idea," I said, joining her back on the rock.

"It does sound nice, but not here. You know what, Babe? I would like to make love to you under the open sky, but not where anyone could walk up on us," she said, looking at me seriously and seductively.

After drying off a bit, we left the park and drove down several of the gravel country roads on the outskirts of town. Before the day was over, we did find such a place down a little trail at the end of an isolated farm road we found. We went several hundred yards down the tree shaded trail until we came to a small clearing under a huge oak tree. There we did make love, with the deep blue sky and soft white clouds floating above us, and birds and squirrels flying and playing around us.

We made love with abandon and with the thought that there was something elicit about what we were doing there out in the open. Ashton had two orgasms and I longed for more stamina myself. Afterwards we lay there on our backs together, naked, looking into the depths of the sky and talking about ourselves, our dreams and our love for each other until the sun began to set low in the sky, casting shadows under the canopy of leaves above us. We, regretfully, had to leave. We would already be late meeting the rest of the team and I'm sure Darby was starving for his catfish.

It was 7:20 PM when we drove up to the motel. All the guys were lounging on the balcony when we got out of the car, rumpled, Ashton's hair stringing down in her face and our clothes still damp in places. We were the butt of several jokes and speculations about what we had been doing. We laughed it off, amused at knowing that we were guilty of most of the things they were accusing of us. That was our little secret. And it was a secret that I would remember forever—a time when Ashton and I were truly free with ourselves, a time of closeness, excitement, satisfaction, contentment and love.

After having a drink together at the motel and Ashton taking time to get straightened up a little, we drove to Leoma and got Darby and Thom's catfish. Ashton and I loved it too, but didn't let on to that fact so we wouldn't have to share the barbs, jokes and insults that Larry and Steve directed in their direction. Larry and Steve ordered steaks. They weren't that good. We tried to tell them that you didn't come to a fish place and order beef.

We had a lot of fun and drove around some more after dinner so they could show me and Ashton some of the places they had discovered that day. We didn't dare reveal to them where we had been, other than the park.

The next day, around noon, we would all be back in the saddle again— the six of us—all focused on the objective of our Laser Team.

CHAPTER FORTY-SEVEN

We were waiting at a country store close to the golf course about two miles west of the Davy Crockett Park. It was almost 1:30 PM. Pancho had called us earlier and said they were coming in on Highway 64 from Memphis. He had called again about ten minutes ago to tell us they were leaving Waynesboro and should be coming into Lawrenceburg about 2:00 PM. He said the driver was taking his time. The girl was still with him and Pancho was convinced that the driver was totally unaware that he was carrying the laser and was being tailed.

"Here comes another truck!" Thom said. It was about 2:10 PM.

As it got closer, we saw that it was a Roadway and a blue Taurus was about a quarter of a mile behind it. We started the engine and pulled out right behind the Taurus. Pancho and Lefty waved at us and we signaled our response. The truck was headed in the direction of the Munson plant with our two vehicles close behind.

When we got to the front gate, we pulled over and let Steve out. We had called the shipping supervisor for Munson this morning and told him that a representative from Roadway would be visiting today for a quality check on their service and that he wanted to observe the unloading, make sure that everything on the Bill of Lading was there and undamaged and interview the supervisor and truck driver relative to timeliness of delivery, courtesy of driver, etc. The supervisor said that would be fine as long as he didn't create any inefficiency at the plant and mentioned that he could not spend a great deal of time with him. It would be okay to interview the driver and observe the unloading. The supervisor would arrange for his entry into the warehousing-shipping-receiving area and would be expecting him. Mike had overnight expressed fake credentials to the motel and even sent a Roadway shirt tag which Steve had hand sewn on his shirt the night before.

This was further indication that the Munson people, at least at the plant, were not involved in the laser shipment. It would have been far more difficult to get in if there were something to hide that they were aware of. Our backup plan was to just enter the building, present Steve's FBI credentials to the

Plant Manager, and be there when the shipment arrived. But, if there were something amiss, it would perhaps give someone the opportunity to tip off the people who were to receive the crate. So far, so good.

The truck turned its signal lights on, turning into the side gate where a sign indicated receiving gate. After a brief check at the gate, he proceeded to a waiting area alongside two loading docks, each of which had a truck in them.

Pancho and Lefty waved and drove on by while we pulled into the parking lot of a little barbeque place that provided plain view of the receiving docks. We had two pairs of binoculars which Darby and I were using so that we could watch the truck from our vantage point. Steve would communicate with us by cell phone from the dock area.

"There's Steve now," Darby said after we had been waiting about ten minutes.

We could see Steve walk out to the truck, introduce himself to the driver and stand there and chat with him. The girl did not get out of the cab. After a few minutes a man in short sleeve white dress shirt, slacks and no tie came out and said something to Steve and the driver. This was presumably the supervisor. Steve walked back to the dock and the driver got back in his truck. The truck at the dock closest to us began backing out and our Roadway began backing his truck into the dock as soon as it was clear to do so.

From that point on, we would have to rely on Steve to surreptitiously convey to us what was going on. After a few minutes, the phone rang.

"Okay, guys. They are starting to unload the truck with a fork truck. Pancho and Lefty had told us that the crate was placed in the nose of the truck, but on the pretense of checking the Bill of Lading against the shipment, I am looking closely at everything coming off. I notice that there is one item here that is only described as unidentified tractor part. I'll bet that is our baby. I'll get back in touch with you as soon as I can," Steve relayed.

We waited another twenty minutes before hearing again from Steve. Darby had gone in to get us a sandwich at the barbeque place.

"Man!" Larry exclaimed when Darby brought the sandwiches back. "Is this more of your Southern eating?! Next thing I know you'll be bringing grits and turnip greens."

"Now, Larry. Just think of poor Steve. He's not getting anything to eat," Darby said.

"He's the fortunate one," Larry grumbled. Just then the phone rang again.

"The truck's unloaded. Our crate is here and still has the Indonesia and

Lebac markings. They just set it aside right by the dock. I asked the supervisor about it. I have no reason to stay longer. I'll tell you what he told me when I get back. Where are you guys?"

"We're at the barbeque place across from the dock. We have a sandwich for you. We'll pick you up at the front gate," I said.

"Barbeque? Is that what's made out of pig's feet? Give me ten minutes to get back to the front gate. Pick me up in the parking lot," Steve said and hung up.

We waited ten minutes then picked Steve up on the edge of the parking lot. He at first declined the sandwich, but his hunger plus Larry's comment that it wasn't too bad allowed him to accept it.

"Here's the deal," Steve began after wolfing down his sandwich. "The supervisor said the entire shipment was for them except the one crate from Indonesia. He had a note from their corporate office indicating that the Lebac crate was added on to their shipment as a favor to a gentlemen in Jakarta who had a facility in this same location. They were to just set it aside and a man named Soled would pick it up within a day or two of arrival and pay for the pro-rated share of the freight bill. He would pay in cash since they did not yet have a business account established here. The corporate office had given the Jakarta person an expected date of arrival of today, so the supervisor expected it to be picked up today or tomorrow. He hoped it would, because it was taking up space on his dock."

"Did he have a further description of the contents other than what was on the packing list?" Larry asked.

"No. I got the impression that it was nothing more than a minor nuisance to him. I didn't want to press him too much because I was posing as a Roadway representative who was just spot checking to ensure that they received this shipment in good order. He was not really concerned with our crate other than the fact he had been told to expect it."

"How can we tell when this Soled comes to pick it up?" I asked.

"Easy. He said the instructions told him they would pick it up in a small flatbed truck and his crew would be expected to load it. He indicated that would be no problem. They rarely shipped anything out on flatbeds, but his fork truck could run it on the truck in five minutes. Plus, I'll bet with your binoculars, you can see the back edge of the crate on the left side of the loading dock. We will have to keep the dock under 24 hour surveillance. They have around the clock crews except on Sunday," Steve answered.

"Okay. So we begin surveillance now and look for a flatbed entering the dock area and keep our eye on the crate. Be prepared to follow it when it's picked up," I said.

"Then we need to set up a schedule and the ones not on duty need to be ready to roll at a moments notice. Right?" Thom asked.

"Right. We still have the car Ashton and I rented. Darby, why don't you and Steve walk back to the hotel and get it. It's less than a mile away. Bring it back here. We'll use it as the surveillance vehicle with a couple of people here at all times while the rest are at the motel. Ashton and I will take the first shift. It will be 4:00 PM by the time you get back. We'll work four hour shifts in pairs. The rest of you can go on back to the motel when Darby gets back," I said.

"Who will be next on duty?" Larry asked.

"Let's let Darby and Steve take the next shift and you and Thom pick it up at midnight. Ashton and I will relieve you at 4:00 AM," I said.

"Where should we keep the car parked?" Thom asked.

"I think we will be alright to keep it across the street in that grassy spot where those old junkers are parked. We will blend in and be well hidden, but still have a good view of the dock and the gate. If the cops or anyone sights us and gets suspicious, Ashton and I will just cuddle up and make out like two lovers parking. We may have to move down the road, but I don't think anyone will even notice," I said.

"Fine for you and Ashton. But what about me and Thom?" Larry asked.

"That's up to you," I grinned.

After about 20 minutes Darby and Steve returned with the car. Then they, along with Thom and Larry, left in the van to go back to the motel. I told them to tell Pancho and Lefty that Ashton and I would have dinner with them tonight if they didn't mind waiting until a little after eight.

"Dawson Kohler, just exactly what did you mean when you said we would "make out like" we were two lovers?" Ashton asked when we had moved the car and were alone.

"Well, what I really meant was we would make out," I grinned with my lame answer.

"Oh, I see. I can just see the headlines now—'Weapon designed to assassinate President slips out of grasp of leading Secret Service agent while he is making out with young scientist that helped design weapon.'"

"Oh well. The President would understand, especially if he met you," I said as we settled down to watch the dock across the street.

CHAPTER FORTY-EIGHT

Ashton and I had an uneventful shift. There was plenty of traffic at that time of day, but no flatbed and the crate had not moved. Darby and Steve relieved us at 8:00 PM. We went back to the hotel and had an enjoyable late dinner with Pancho and Lefty. They offered to pull a shift before they left, but I knew they were driving to Nashville the next morning to fly back to D.C., so I thanked them but told them we could handle it. Ashton and I then went to our room to get some rest. We would be back on duty 4:00 AM, relieving Larry and Thom. I talked to Darby on the cell phone before turning in. He said the traffic had diminished considerably. There had been only two trucks going in so far, and no flatbed. The crate was still there.

3:30 AM came sooner than I was ready for it to. It had only seemed a few minutes since Ashton and I had gone to bed about 10:00 PM. We had kissed and snuggled together but both of us had dropped off to sleep by 10:30. The alarm jolted us out of bed. At first I thought it was the phone and that Larry was calling to tell us the truck was there. Then I realized it was the alarm.

"Okay, Honey. Time to go to work," I said, gently shaking Ashton. She was a sound sleeper.

"Oh, Dawson—" she yawned and turned over sleepy-eyed and with rumpled hair. She always looked especially cute and innocent when she awoke. I wondered that she had maintained this quality after everything she had been through in her teen and younger years and, more recently, at the hands of Alziddi.

"I know. You were having a nice dream and aren't ready to get up yet," I said, pulling on my trousers.

"Yes. I was dreaming about you," she smiled dreamily, finally beginning to awaken. "I would go back to sleep and let you go alone, except I would worry about you."

"Oh, so you want to protect me?" I asked.

"Yes! Remember, I can shoot. You may need me!" she said, jumping out of bed and pulling on her jeans.

"I do need you," I said, giving her a little hug. "I'm going to run in the bathroom a minute, then I'll be ready to go."

"I'll be ready five minutes after you. You can go on and pull the car up," she called after me, fully dressed by now.

It was 3:58 AM when we pulled alongside Larry and Thom waiting in the rental car.

"Must have been a quiet shift," I said, getting out in the darkness amid the clutter of old cars scattered around.

"Yeah. Only one truck. The crate is still on the dock," Larry said.

"Okay. You guys take the van and go get some rest. Ashton and I will take over," I said.

"Alright. We'll see you —Wait!!" Larry exclaimed. "Look coming down the road!"

Sure enough, there was a small flatbed truck approaching. It had to be our pickup!

"Thom, rush back to the motel and get Darby and Steve! I'll call them on the cell so they can be getting ready! Hopefully you guys can get back before they get loaded and pull out. Larry, you stay with us. If the three of us have to follow them before you get back, we'll stay in touch as to where we are on the cell phone, Thom," I said. Thom left immediately and I called and awoke Darby.

The truck pulled into the gate and, after a brief check-in, moved to the loading dock area. There were no trucks in the dock. The driver got out and went into the dock office. In about five minutes he came out and began to back the truck into the dock. He had someone else in the truck with him and that person got out to help guide him into the dock.

"It's been about ten minutes since Thom left. It won't take long for them to load that one crate," Larry said. He had crawled in the back seat of our car.

"Darby and Steve won't take long getting ready. I figure they will be here in about ten minutes. Hopefully, the truck won't be out by then. If it is, we'll follow it and direct them to catch up and pull in behind us at a distance. I think we will tail them with both vehicles anyway. That way we can switch off just in case they are watching. The same vehicle won't be behind them the whole way," I said.

The tenseness increased as the truck was loaded with the crate. The driver lingered, signing a receipt, then got in the cab and started backing out. Just then the phone rang.

"Dawson, it's Steve. We're just leaving the motel. We're five minutes away. What's happening?" Steve asked.

"It's our target. They got the crate and are on their way to the exit gate now. We'll pull out behind them with our lights off, then follow them from a distance when we get on a main road. You guys just stay there. Keep your motor running. I'll call and tell you which way they are going and you can pull in behind us. We'll switch off some until we get to their destination," I instructed.

The truck turned to the right, driving right past where we were well hidden among the other cars. Then it took the road towards highway 43 which went North towards Nashville through the little communities of Ethridge and Summertown and South towards Leoma, Loretta and on to Alabama. They turned left in the North direction. I called Steve.

"Steve, they're going North on 43 and will be coming right by you in about three minutes. I'm going to turn North too, but I'll drop back. Why don't you pull out behind them when they get past you. The truck should be pretty easy to follow. It's got a horizontal row of tail lights running across the rear and one of the lights on the right side is out," I told him.

"Roger. I see him coming," Steve said.

Our little convoy continued on for several miles. Twice, one of us would turn off and let the other take the lead behind the truck, then pull right back on the road behind the lead car. The people in the truck did not seem to suspect anything, however. They were taking no evasive action and didn't seem to be in any hurry. We passed through the Ethridge community. Steve was in the lead again.

"He's got his direction signals on, Dawson. He's turning left," Steve relayed to us.

"Okay. You just drive on straight, then turn around and come back to the road he's turning on. I'll take the lead and follow him on into the turnoff road at a distance. We have to be careful now to not get too close and spook him. This time of night it would be unusual to have much traffic on these little side roads. I may turn in and try to drive without my lights on the rest of the way," I said as I saw the truck up ahead making the turn onto the dusty little gravel farm road. Steve's van continued on 43.

The rising cloud of dust from the truck ahead of me made it difficult to see the road with my lights off. Fortunately, the moon was near full and I could barely make out the gravel path we were following and still see the running lights of the truck about 100 yards in front of us.

"Look! Those old farmhouses off the road. There are buggies parked beside most of them," Ashton said. "We must be in a community of those Mennonites we saw earlier."

She was right. We passed several farm houses on the right and the left. Most, but not all of them, appeared to be the big white, two story Mennonite homes set off the road. Buggies were parked in the yards of some and there were no lights or signs of electric lines leading to those houses coming off the poles alongside the road. After a couple of miles, the truck ahead of us began to slow. We slowed to match his speed.

"He's turning," Larry said.

The truck had turned left and appeared to be stopped. We stopped and pulled over on the side of the road. After about three minutes, the truck proceeded in the direction it had turned, then stopped. A few minutes later it appeared to be backing in a 90 degree direction from the place it had stopped. We waited. After several minutes the truck's lights were extinguished.

"What do we do now?" Steve asked.

"Let's pull our two vehicles off the road down this little gravel farm path. Keep the lights off. Darby and I will sneak on down in that direction on foot and see what's going on," I said.

"Be careful, Dawson," Ashton said after we had hidden the vehicles. Darby and I left to reconnoiter the situation.

It took us about 15 minutes to get to the place where the truck had pulled in. We hid in the undergrowth on the side of the road across from the drive where it had entered. In the moonlight we could see a gated gravel drive leading to a small house on the left about fifty yards off the road. On the right, behind the house was a sturdy looking barn. The truck was backed into the barn door and we could see lights and activity in that area. It looked like the crate was being unloaded off the truck with a winch. We could hear the muffled conversation of several men. It was hard to tell just how many men there were, but Darby and I agreed there must have been at least eight people around the truck and the barn entrance.

"Okay, Darby. Let's go back. We've seen what we need to see. Did you notice the old two story farmhouse we passed just before we got to this one?" I whispered.

"Yeah. It had a For Sale sign out front," Darby answered as we began to stealthily move back down the road toward the others.

"Right. We're going to buy it tomorrow," I said.

We rejoined the others and I told them of my plan. We knew where the laser was, at least for now. Ashton and I, posing as a farmer and his wife would buy the property tomorrow, and sneak the rest in as soon as we took possession. Right now, someone would have to stay hidden in the woods across from the barn to watch the barn, just to make sure the laser wasn't moved before we moved in across the road. It would be unlikely that it would be moved that quickly since it just got here. I was certain we could observe the entire property across the road from the second floor of the farmhouse we would be occupying.

Larry, Thom, Ashton and I went back to the motel. Dawn was approaching. Darby and Steve stayed with the car, would find a better place to park it, and set up surveillance while the rest of the group got a little rest. About 10:00 AM Ashton and I would visit the realtor.

The six of us were about to become a little farm family for a while. I would remember this brief period of time that we would actually be living together as a "family" fondly. But that memory would cause the pain of our family being shattered to be more enduring also.

Sometimes our most precious memories are those that bring the most painful reminders of how it was when—that fleeting time in the past when everything nice seemed so real and permanent. But that same place in time—somewhen—can also exist in the future along with our hopes and dreams.

CHAPTER FORTY-NINE

"Sir, my name is Dawson Kohler and this is my wife, Ashton," I introduced ourselves to Mr. Pridemore, the real estate agent whose name was on the sign at the farmhouse. "We would like to talk to you about the small farm property you have out on Gimlet Road.

"It's nice to meet you, Dawson, and Mrs. Kohler," Mr. Pridemore smiled and grabbed my hand, shaking it vigorously. "You can call me Bob. You're talking about the property on the other side of Ethridge. A nice piece of property. It's only been on the market a little over a month. Would you like to see it? We can drive out there if you want to."

"No. No thanks. We're new in town. Ashton and I have always wanted a little farm in the country to settle down on, raise kids. I was raised on a farm. No better way to bring up kids, I've always said. Actually we've been driving around and saw the property yesterday. We've already walked around it. Hope you don't mind. It's about twenty acres, right? I think it exactly fits what we want if the price is right," I said. Out of the corner of my eye I could see Ashton blushing at my comments. She would jab me sharply in the ribs when we left.

"Oh? Where're you from? No problem walking around. I'm glad you did that. I've got a good price on it, too," Bob chattered on, going back to his desk and shuffling papers.

"We're both from Memphis. Just tired of the city life. I had a good job managing a K-Mart there, but started worrying about the company and we decided this was a good time to make a change in our lifestyle. I've saved a little money—enough to make a down payment on a small farm and maybe buy some used equipment to get started. She sells baskets for Longaberger and makes a little, too," I said, motioning towards Ashton.

"Good, good. I can introduce you to a good bank here who can do your loan and take a mortgage on the property. They will want 20% down and will do a 20 year loan at a good rate of interest. My brother-in-law is a Vice President there. How much were you looking to pay for this little jewel, Mr. Kohler?" Bob asked. I detected that, now that we were getting down to business, I was Mr. Kohler again.

"Well—how much is the owner asking? There's a little creek running across the back, but not a lot of pasture. It will need some clearing to grow anything or raise any cattle," I replied.

"Dawson, you don't know this because you're not from here. But that little farm is right in the middle of the Mennonite area. Good people. And they're the hardest working son-of-a-guns I ever saw. I bet you could hire some of them to clear the land for almost nothing. And they'd do it all by hand. Trust me. Wouldn't cost you much at all. And this little farm is a steal. Owner getting too old to farm it. Hadn't done anything with it in years. Had to move into a retirement home—wife passed away last year. He's 80 something years old. Just wants to get rid of it to pay his bills," Bob rattled on.

"How much?" I asked.

"Well—he wants $60,000. Includes the little house of course. And all the rooms are still furnished if you want to keep some of the furniture. Or you can sell the furniture at a flea market down the road and make a little cash."

"Too much. More than I can handle. Guess we'll just have to keep looking. I appreciate your time, Mr. Pridemore," I said, rising from my chair as if I were preparing to leave.

"Wait, wait. I've got other properties. Let me show them to you," Bob said, standing and moving around his desk as if to keep me there.

"I'm sure you have, but we—Ashton and I—have been looking around and we just had our mind set on this property. The little creek and all. It would be nice for the kids," I said, still moving in the direction of the door.

"How much you willing to pay?" Pridemore asked, still walking with me towards the door.

"Oh, I know that farm might be worth it, but I really didn't want to spend more than $40,000," I said, pausing at the door.

"How about 50?" Pridemore asked. We both had stopped now.

"Maybe I could see 45," I said hesitantly.

"47 and you can have it," Pridemore said with an air of finality.

"It's a deal," I said, turning back into his office.

We signed the papers. I wrote him a check on a bank in Memphis that Mike had set up an account for us with. I paid for the whole $47,000, explaining to him that I would rather use my credit to buy the equipment I needed. He gave me the title, having his secretary notarize it, and said he would file it for me at the courthouse. My negotiations had saved the CIA, and the taxpayers, a little money and perhaps they could sell it and even make a little profit when we were done. More importantly, we needed that property badly to conduct our surveillance operation from, and to not have negotiated some would have possibly raised some suspicions in this small town.

"You are awful!" Ashton admonished me when we were in the car. "You took advantage of that poor man."

I laughed. "The truth is, he probably took advantage of me. That was still almost $2,400 an acre and the house is probably not worth $10,000. I'll suggest to Mike that the agency hire Pridemore to sell it for them when we are done with it. At least we've got a home now. Let's pick up some groceries, linens, towels, etc., get the others and move in."

"Yeah. It will be nice really, all of us being together like a family. And I don't think they can really see us from their house or the barn too well," Ashton said.

"No, I think you're right. Just in case though, when we move the others in, we'll have them stay down—just in case someone drives by when we turn in. I noticed the little house has a big back porch. They can't see that at all from their place or the road. That's where we'll probably hang out a lot. Of course we'll always have to have someone on watch duty with the binoculars at the front window on the second story."

We picked up Larry and Thom, did our shopping, then called Darby and Steve. I told them we were on our way and that I had the keys to the house. I asked them to meet us at the house and told them to park the car in the rear. We would leave the van parked out in front of the house.

The little farm house was really quite neat and clean when we arrived and entered it. It had a living room, kitchen, bedroom, bathroom and dining area downstairs. There was also a fairly large den on the side that looked like a garage that had been remodeled at some time and made into living space. Upstairs were two small bedrooms in the front, a large bedroom in the rear and a bathroom. Ideal for our purposes, there was also a little alcove in the center of the upstairs with a window. We could set a chair up there and that would be a great place for the person on surveillance duty to be without disturbing anyone in the bedrooms.

I helped Ashton make the beds and put up the groceries we had bought. We decided that Ashton and I would take the downstairs bedroom with Darby in the right front upstairs bedroom, Larry in the left front and Steve and Thom sharing the big upstairs bedroom in the back that had two beds.

Ashton and I had to run back downtown to pick up some shades to put on the front windows and a few other odds and ends that we had not thought of. By 5:00 PM, we were settled pretty well. Someone had been continuously watching our neighbors since we had arrived. The view was perfect! We had an excellent view to our right front of not only the farmhouse across the road, but the barn as well.

"Let's cook some steaks tonight! They have a grill out back and Dawson and I found a little store that had really good meat," Ashton said when we were all done and had relaxed with a drink. Thom was up top at the moment, observing our neighbors. So far, nothing eventful going on over there.

"Sounds good! I'll cook them," Darby said.

"Okay. I'll put the potatoes in. They will take about an hour. I love this place!" Ashton said. "Come on, Dawson! After I put the potatoes in, let's take a walk down to the creek!"

We did that, holding hands and tossing rocks in the creek. It was shaded by beautiful large white oak trees and there was a little path running alongside the creek. We wandered aimlessly down the path running towards the rear of our new property.

"Did you mean that—about the Mr. And Mrs. thing with Mr. Pridemore? And the kids and everything?" Ashton asked me. "Or were you just acting?"

"I wasn't acting. I want you to be my Mrs., Ashton. If you will have me, that is the first thing I want to do when we get done with what we are doing."

"I want to be your Mrs., Dawson. I love you. Don't run away from me if I ever disappoint you. I know I could never leave you, no matter what, if you wanted me. But I won't ever try to stay if you don't. It would break my hear if we had to part, but I love you too much to ever hurt you."

I stopped and held her close to me. I brushed her hair from the side of her face and kissed her tenderly. We melted together out there in the woods alongside the little trail following the creek. I had never felt so close to anyone, or as much in love. At that moment, it seemed that we were the only two people in the world—and that we would always be like this—together and in love.

"No matter what. I will always love you and you could never disappoint me—no matter what. I love you too, Ashton. And I won't ever leave you— no matter what. We are not you and me. We are we. Understand?" I kissed her again. She had a tear rolling down her cheek.

In her typical effervescing way though, she quickly recovered.

"I'm so happy!" she smiled, grabbing my hand. "Let's go wading!"

She pulled me down the bank and we spent the next 15 minutes wading down the creek, catching periwinkles, little crawfish and laughing together when one of us would slip on the slick rocks on the creek bank and take a fall into the water.

"We better go back, Love. My potatoes should be done. You know, being together like this—all of us—is nice. We all get along so good. It's hard to think about what a serious task we have ahead of us—and the danger. I worry about all of you," Ashton said seriously as we started back to the farmhouse.

"What about you? I worry about you. We're dealing with ruthless and dangerous fanatics, you know. Will you promise me you will stick close to us and not take any chances, little girl?" I asked.

"Maybe. I will go where you go though. I only worry about me when something happens that might take us away from each other. Hey!! There they all are, waiting for us on the back porch! If they've been drinking all this time, they're probably drunk! Poor Dawson. You've been stuck with me while they're having fun together," Ashton laughed and started running towards the house still holding my hand and me in tow behind her.

We had a great time that night together, laughing, joking and enjoying a delicious meal. We switched off watching our neighbors. Later, before going to bed, we played poker for nickels, dimes and quarters and Ashton won the big pot, showing no mercy on me or the others.

Later, when we went to bed, she apologized, telling me she didn't mean to take all my money. I told her it was okay. She would have to love me extra special to pay me back.

She did.

CHAPTER FIFTY

The next morning, Thursday, July 10th, 2003, we set up a continuous watch schedule with one person watching at all times and at least four at the house at all times. Occasionally, two of us would drive into town to replenish our supplies. The watch schedule wasn't too burdensome. With the six of us, we each had to pull only four hours out of each 24 hours. Ashton and I were the only ones who showed ourselves outside in the front of the house, in case one of our neighbors drove by. It could create suspicion if someone saw six people appearing to live in the house—especially five guys and one girl.

The flatbed truck had remained parked outside the barn and had not moved since the crate had been unloaded. Two other cars were there and one would go out once in a while, usually with two or three people, but would return later in the day. We surmised that they were doing the same as us—having to go out for provisions occasionally. One thing our surveillance confirmed was that there were actually nine men living at the house. Two of them, always the same two, were in the barn quite a lot, sometimes joined briefly by one or more of the others. Ashton felt like the two who spent most of their time in the barn were probably the technicians working on the laser and the others were probably guards. We decided she was right. We did notice with our binoculars that all nine were armed with side arms and, on at least one occasion, we sighted one of them carrying an automatic rifle.

Mennonite buggies traveled up and down the road frequently. Otherwise there was little automobile traffic on this little gravel road. The Mennonites appeared to ride to and from their farms which were along the road before and after where we were located. We gathered that they often pooled their labor to work on one of the clan's farms, then would move to another farm. Also, their routine was for some of the elders to go into Lawrenceburg every Saturday to stock up on bulk provisions—sacks of flour and other staples— and perhaps conduct business.

Otherwise, our days and nights were uneventful. The nights were quiet and the days went by in a lazy, relaxed way that sometimes made us almost forget why we were here. Our neighbors across the road had a more feverish schedule than we did. The "technicians" were up early and generally worked until almost dark. There were several nights when lights in the barn were visible, indicating they often worked at night.

It would be August 23rd before we would be rudely shocked back into the reality of our mission and its murderous overtones. In the meantime, we relaxed, enjoyed ourselves and enjoyed being with each other. The six of us, in these close quarters bonded even closer together as a "family". It was almost as if we were on vacation together, with the full and certain knowledge that we would have to go back to work at some point in time.

One day, after Darby and I had finished watching a ballgame, I stepped out on the porch. Thom and Steve had gone hiking in the woods in the back of our property and Larry was on watch duty. I didn't see Ashton. She had gone out on the back porch when Darby and I had started watching the game. I called for her and she didn't answer. Concerned, I walked around to the front of the house.

There she was, kneeling, in her shorts and Tee shirt, planting flowers in the front of the house. She didn't see me at first. I watched her as she dug a little hole for each flower with her trowel, placed the flower in, covered it with dirt, then watered it from a bucket she had found in the shed back of the house. It was hot. She was sweaty and dirty and she looked like a beautiful little girl playing in a sandbox. Finally, I spoke.

"Hon, what are you doing?" I asked.

She was startled and jumped when I spoke. When she saw me, she smiled and looked at me with an air of pride and satisfaction.

"Do you like them?" she asked cheerily.

"Yes. They're pretty. But you know we won't be staying here," I said.

Her face clouded briefly before her cheery smile returned. "I know, Love. But I found these pretty daisies and tiger lilies growing wild back of the house and thought how pretty some of them would be planted along the front side of the house. Do you really like them?" she said, rising and giving me a hug.

"Yes. And I like the pretty little person planting them, too—even if she does look like a little pig right now," I laughingly slapped her on the butt.

"Ouch! Dawson, some day I'm going to kick you where it hurts! I know we won't be here forever. But Hon, it seems like a home here with you and the others. I sometimes forget about why we are here and just think about how nice it is being here. I just couldn't resist planting these flowers and trying to make it look more like a home. I'll do this for our home some day.

And maybe you'll help me," she said, giving me her little questioning, cute smile.

"Maybe. If I can keep my mind on the flowers. That will be hard to do around you. And can you imagine what the neighbors would think if they saw us making love in our flower bed. Just think how it would be. Plant a flower, make love, plant a flower, make love—" I teased her.

"Well, we'll just have to find a place that has no close neighbors," she grinned.

I kissed her and hugged her close to me.

"Larry likes my flowers," Ashton said.

I glanced up over my head. Larry was up there above us on watch from the alcove. He had the window open to get some air on the muggy day. I blushed slightly, knowing that he had heard my comments.

"Yeah! The flowers are real pretty, Dawson," Larry spoke above us. "And I agree with the problem anyone would have staying on task trying to help Ashton plant. She's doing a good job. I've been helping her place them. From my vantage point, I can see along the whole front."

"Oh. So this is a joint beautification project?" I laughed, looking up at Larry above us.

"Something like that. Right Ashton? She's invited me to help her at your house later. I guess I'll be there while you're—what was it you were saying— plant a flower, make love, plant a flower..." Larry broke out laughing.

"No way!" I tossed a rotten apple from the tree in the front yard through the window at him.

Then there was the night in mid-August when Steve and Larry approached us sheepishly.

"We have a suggestion to make, Steve and I," Larry began.

"What's that?" I asked.

"Well —maybe we could send you guys to town and, uh, get us some of that—you know—that fish —catfish. It's not that Steve and I really like it. Right Steve?" Larry looked to Steve for support.

"Right! It's just that, well, we know Darby and the rest of you guys like it and, uh, we want you to be happy, you know," Steve lamely added.

"Oh ho!! You like it!! You want it! Right?!" Thom exclaimed.

"No. No—it's just like we said. We want you guys to be happy. I mean it's not that bad. Larry and I could make a sacrifice for the rest of you," Steve said.

"Oh, we could do without it, seeing as how much you two detest eating that—what did you call it—bottom feeding fish?" Darby laughed uproariously.

"Okay, dammit! It's okay. I mean it's pretty good. And we're getting tired of pork and beef. Steve and I will eat it. Yeah! We want some catfish. It's probably due to our being stuck here in this little southern farmhouse so long. Maybe it's some kind of hillbilly disease. Go ahead and laugh! Just go get the fish!" Larry said.

We had a delicious catfish dinner that night and everyone enjoyed it thoroughly, especially Larry and Steve, in spite of our ribbing.

Later that night I called Mike from the downstairs den. I had been keeping him up to date on the non-event of our present watch. Once again I asked him if we should just move in and take the laser and take out the nine men with it.

"No. Mine and Sam's bosses briefed the President. They told him all about the laser and the fact that our best intelligence indicated that Infama was going to try to use it against him before the year was out. The President was adamant in his position. He said, as long as we had it under surveillance and under control, he wanted to use it to lead to others that were behind this plot. He fully recognizes the danger and risk that it could get away from us as it did before, but it's very important to him to net as many of these people as we can before the show is over. He thinks that if we don't get all the people we can that are involved in this plot, we will just have to deal with them later. To take them out now will eliminate or slow down other plans that these people and their cohorts may have for the future," Mike relayed to me.

After the phone call, I went up to our bedroom. Ashton was propped up in bed reading.

"What are you reading, Hon?" I asked as I got ready to go to bed myself.

"I'm reading a book called "Somewhen". It's really good. A few nights ago I finished the previous book by this author, titled "The Part". You need to read them. The main characters remind me a lot of us, Love. With one difference."

"What's that?" I asked.

"The girl in both books doesn't love her man as much as I love you. The endings are not happy. That won't happen to us. I promise..." Ashton said thoughtfully.

"I know. I love you, too Baby. Remember what we said to each other. We are we —forever. Well, let's turn the light off and get ready for another boring day tomorrow. Actually this little interlude has been nice—being with you without having to worry about being shot at every minute. I guess I'm just ready for a little action."

"You men. Always looking for danger and challenge. Come on to bed darling. I'll give you some action if that's what you want. I want you Babe—"

As I fell into her loving arms and melted with her in our passion, I decided that this was the only action I, or any other man, would ever need—to be loved by Ashton. I would find out before the week was out that the other kind of action, the deadly kind, would erupt into our lives with brutal consequences that would send us on the last leg of our journey together with the laser team.

CHAPTER FIFTY-ONE

It was about 7:15 AM Saturday, August 23rd. We were all up early. Ashton was on watch duty and the rest of us were finishing breakfast. In our inactivity and boredom, we had set up an elaborate croquet course in the back of the house and bought a croquet set last week. We had split up into two teams with me, Thom, Darby on one team and Ashton, Larry and Steve on the other. We had played four lengthy games the previous four days and were tied two to two. Today would be the tie breaker and final round of our little tournament. The competitiveness had reached monumental proportions. We had decided to get up early and finish this thing off in the cool of the morning. Whoever was on watch duty would be relieved when it was their time to play.

It was a hot, sultry morning though and storm clouds were gathering in the distance. It looked as if we might be getting one of those rare summer morning thunderstorms. Usually they occurred in the late afternoon. Our game might be delayed.

"Larry, don't eat too much and get sluggish on me! I'm depending on you to support me and Steve!" Ashton hollered down from the alcove. Larry had been the weak sister on their team. But then we had Darby who hit the ball 20 yards from any position, usually in the wrong direction.

"We'll swap Darby for Larry for this final round if you want to!" I hollered back.

"Hey! Who was it that saved your ass on the last leg of yesterday's game?!" Darby retorted.

"Lucky shot, slugger. Just a lucky shot. We wouldn't have needed our ass saved if you hadn't hit so many dumb shots earlier," Thom countered.

The banter was going back and forth when all of the sudden Ashton shouted at us. There was a serious tone to her voice.

"Guys!! Come here! Quick!!"

We all rushed up the steps to see what she was talking about.

"Look! They're moving the laser out! And it's uncovered! All nine of the men are out there in the yard. Something's happening!" Ashton said as we gathered around the alcove window.

Sure enough, the laser gun was out in the front yard of the house across the road. They had rolled it out on a dolly table with caster wheels and were positioning it in front of the barn, pointing down the road in the direction away from us. This was the first time we had seen the laser close up and uncovered. It looked sinister—longer but more slender than we had imagined. The short stainless steel barrel protruded from an aluminum casing that had several gadgets and compartments jutting out from both sides and underneath it. There was a small cylindrical object extending across the top that probably was a sighting mechanism. The closest thing that came to mind in describing it was one of the old water cooled 30 caliber machine guns used in WWII, except this piece of equipment was bigger, more the size of a 106mm recoilless rifle.

Under closer examination with the binoculars, one thing was apparent. It was a classy looking piece of equipment and looked to be sturdy, finely machined, and technically attractive. There was nothing thrown together looking about it. The technicians who had spent so many hours working on it had done their job well—at least from the external appearance of it.

We were all crowded around the window now. The men across the way to the right were crowded around the machine, too. They seemed to be positioning it for some purpose. Then the two technicians kneeled behind and to the side of the gun and the others stepped back, gazing down the road.

"Do you think they're getting ready to load it on the truck?" Thom asked.

"Maybe. We better be ready to move fast. But it looks more like they are trying to aim it for a target," I said. "Let's wait and see what they do next. There's nothing out there that I see that they would shoot it at."

The dark, gray clouds were almost on us now and we could distinctly hear rolling thunder in the distance. Over the top of the long ridge that descended into our little valley you could see jagged flashes of lightning.

"Look!! Down the road!" Larry exclaimed.

Around the long bend in the road, a black Mennonite buggy appeared about a half mile away. It was coming in our direction. The thought struck us all that it was, in fact, Saturday morning and the Mennonite elders would be making their weekly trek to town about this time.

Suddenly, the men across the street seemed to tense up and gather in a tighter circle around the gun, peering intently down the road.

"No. You don't think—" Larry uttered the thought we all had first.

"Surely not. They're not going to test that thing on those poor Mennonites!"

I said, still gazing intently at the action unfolding below us.

"Christ!! I think they are, Dawson!! We've got to warn them!" Thom half shouted.

"How!? They can't hear us! And if we run for the car and try to reach them, we will probably become the target!" Steve said.

"What do you think the gun's range is, Ashton?" I asked. The horse and buggy was now only about 300 yards away. We could now see that there were two bearded men in the buggy in their wide brimmed hats and dark clothes.

"200 yards I would think. Maybe a little more or a little less—" Ashton responded.

If Ashton had anything else to say, she didn't get an opportunity. Lightning was striking close by now, accompanied by loud cracks of thunder. The buggy was probably a little over 200 yards away now, running at a pretty fast clip with the horse trotting in front of the light buggy. Our thoughts and eyes were focused intently on it. It was as if we were frozen in time, hoping that it would pass on by and that our thoughts of what was taking place were in error. Hurry, hurry—

Suddenly, there was a blinding flash, different from the lightning that was crashing in around us now!! This beam of light was traveling at the speed of light on a horizontal track right towards the Mennonite buggy. Actually, we could not really see the beam traveling to and crashing into the buggy. It looked like a connecting beam of light that suddenly appeared between the gun and the buggy. It was all over in a split second. The horse, buggy and its occupants had simply disappeared in a brief puff of smoke. All that remained after the instant of the light beam was a dark smoldering smudge in the middle of the road where the buggy had been. One wheel had been all that remained as it lazily rolled off to the side of the road on impact with the beam.

We were all frozen in a stunned silence. It was at least 30 seconds before anyone could even open their mouth.

"Shit!!!" Darby emitted the first comment.

Glancing back in the direction of the barn, we saw the men quickly place a tarp over the laser to protect it from the big drops of rain that had now begun to fall, and roll it back in the barn. A quick look through the binoculars showed the elation that was evident on their faces as they all followed the laser back into the barn and closed the door.

We now knew the deadly potential and accuracy of the thing we had been chasing and observing for seven months. There would be no more croquet. We would never know who would have won the championship game. From this point forward until the end of our quest, which would not be in the too distant future, we would be deadly serious in our intention and desire to stop these people before any more people were killed.

Larry had the most succinct comment. "Laser Team, we're going to get these bastards along with all their sadistic, fanatic, cowardly, asshole friends. As far as I'm concerned, they will meet our justice which will be quick, deadly, and final. To hell with trying to bring them in alive just to have the taxpayers finance a high-powered asshole lawyer to defend their rights. They lost their rights when they came into our country to kill our citizens and our President. The only right they have left is the right to die!"

We all wanted these people across the road, their associates, Alziddi, the fucking Iman, and anybody else that would be sympathetic to their demented philosophies, so bad we could taste it. We were ready to roll.

All of a sudden the rain stopped and the sun began to creep out from behind the retreating clouds. There was an eerie calm in the air. We were all still standing by the window, transfixed by what we had just seen. Ashton and I looked at each other with the same thought, I think. The calm before the storm.

We would roll. And they would pay a price. But we would hit a few bumps in the road on the way. Deadly bumps. The Laser Team would pay a price, too.

CHAPTER FIFTY-TWO

We still stood by the single alcove window, each of us straining intently through a small section of the window glass. The Infama group across the road exited the barn, closed the door and all proceeded to the house, obviously in a jovial state of mind after the successful experiment. I went downstairs to call Mike. Steve and Larry accompanied me while the rest stayed at the window, just in case the men re-emerged. After three rings I got his secretary and she transferred the call immediately to him.

"Mike, we have a situation here that you need to know about," I began. I, as briefly as possible, went through the whole scenario about what had just happened. He asked a couple of questions. When I was through, there was a thoughtful pause before he spoke.

"Dawson, I know what I think we should do. I would be in favor of trying to take them out immediately and destroy the weapon before any other innocent people get hurt, or before they somehow are able to get the weapon to its destination in spite of your being on top of them. They are excellent planners and there's no telling what they may have up their sleeves to get the laser out of there. Remember how the copter picked it up right in front of you in Jakarta? And they most likely have a contingency plan similar to that in case they feel like they have been discovered," Mike finally said.

"Sounds good to me. Is that what you want us to do Mike? We can be on their ass in fifteen minutes," I said.

"No— We need to run this by the President's people first, since he has been involved in the decision making on this thing. You know I told you that his desire would be to stay on them discreetly until they got to the end of their road and try to put the finger on as many people involved in this at the end as we can. I share that desire, but now there have been U.S. civilians murdered. And it could happen again. Who knows? They may want to run another test. Plus, I just have a queasy feeling about not taking them out now. It appears we have the situation in control, but these guys are smart. I can't believe they haven't got something more elaborate than simply loading it on a truck and taking it to D.C., New York or wherever they plan to use it.

Obviously it won't be used in Lawrenceburg," Mike continued.

"Yeah. Every time we think we have them in the palm of our hand, something happens that allows them to slip by us just like it did that night on the boat and just like Alziddi was able to sneak out of our grasp at the mosque," I replied.

"Well, I just need to be sure the whole story of where we are is run by the President and that he is aware that innocent people have been killed. That may take a day or two. He's in South America now. We can get through to him, but I may not be able to get back to you right away. One important question, Dawson?" Mike asked.

"What's that?" I asked.

"Do you think they know you are there observing them?" Mike queried.

"No, I don't. We have been careful for no one other than me or Ashton to be seen in the front of the house and they don't appear to be at all jumpy about doing whatever they do," I said.

"No, it doesn't seem so. Otherwise, you wouldn't think they would pull the laser out in plain view and test it in the manner they did," Mike agreed.

"Right. I think they were just waiting for one of those frequent summer lightning storms to conduct their test. They probably are thinking that everyone will think the Mennonites were just struck by a lightning bolt. The test looked to be so successful, though. I doubt they will test it again. They might. But it wouldn't surprise me to see them try to take the laser out soon and get it on its way to whatever destination they have planned," I stated.

"Okay. Do this. For now, continue watching them. If they start out with it, follow them until you hear from me. If it appears that innocent civilians are in danger again, or if something happens that creates a risk of losing them, take them out immediately. I will get back to you as soon as I can, no later than two days from now. In the meantime, keep me posted as to what is happening down there," Mike concluded.

We had no sooner concluded our conversation than Thom softly called us from the top of the stairs.

"We have visitors!"

The doorbell rang. I looked up at Thom with an alarmed and questioning look.

"Ashton says it's our real estate agent," Thom whispered. The doorbell rang again.

"Get out the back door," I whispered loudly.

"We can't! He has a lady with him. She's gone to the back," Thom said.

I turned around just in time to see a lady waving cheerfully at me through the back screen door which was open. Larry and Steve were standing there with me and she could see Thom at the top of the stairs. I went to the door and opened it for her. The front doorbell rang again.

"Hi!" I smiled, trying to act casual. "Come on in. Excuse me. Let me get the front door."

"Oh, that's just Bob! I'm Joann, his wife. Go on. Let him in. He'll wear your doorbell out if you don't," she laughingly said as she came into the kitchen. I went to let Bob in.

"Hello, Mr. Pridemore! Sorry it took so long to get to the door. We just met your wife at the back door," I said, trying to not show my frustration and impatience at the unexpected interruption.

"Mr. Kohler!" Bob said jovially, grasping my hand and pumping it. "Where is your beautiful wife?"

"Oh, she's upstairs. We had some friends from out of town drop in to see us in our new home. Here she is now," I responded. Ashton had come down the steps along with Thom. Darby had remained by the window. We dare not leave our neighbors unobserved now! Mr. Pridemore could see him standing at the top of the steps though.

"Hi, big fellow!" he waved up at him. Darby waved back awkwardly, still keeping his post.

"Well, Dawson, I see you have a house full, so we won't stay. Joann and I just like to visit our clients after they have a chance to get settled in their new homes that we have helped them find. That's one of the many special, personal touches that set Pridemore Realty apart from our competitors! We care. Don't we Joann?" he continued. He must have forgotten that we found this location, not him.

"Yes, darling. And I wanted to meet the beautiful girl Bob was babbling about the day he closed the deal with you. Now I'm jealous, Bob," she giggled. "I'll bet you are responsible for the beautiful flowers out front. We didn't think you were home when you didn't answer the ring right away, and I just had to come around the back to see what you've done around here."

"Well, uh— I've not gotten around to doing the back yet," Ashton lamely replied.

Mr. Pridemore and his wife babbled on for about ten minutes. She managed to wander in every room during their stay. It was obvious, I'm sure, that the six of us had been here together for a while. Finally, after we let the conversation stall, they took the hint and started to leave.

"Well, I know you two want to spend time with your guests, so Joann and I will leave you alone now. It's been nice meeting all of you." He waved again at Darby who was still at the top of the steps keeping a watchful eye across the road. We had explained to him that Darby was a deaf mute who had worked for us for years and our friends had brought him along with them to see us.

"Just remember, Dawson—and Mrs. Kohler—Pridemore Reality prides itself in our continuing service to our clients. More Pride, that's what we're all about!" he laughed heartily at his play on words. "If you or any of your friends ever have a need for our services again, we are at your beck and call! We consider our clients a part of our family and we'll check on you again to see if there's anything we can do to help you get settled in our little community!"

"And darling, when you get ready to replace those shades on the front windows with curtains, just give me a call. My aunt is the best seamstress in town! I'll make sure she gives you a good deal!" Mrs. Pridemore called back to Ashton as they left. We had followed them to the door.

"We're going across the street to see our new tenants over there. They are renting that house. It's one of our listings. We do a lot of business in this community. When someone wants to do a real estate deal, they think of Bob Pridemore!" Mr. Pridemore said, opening the door of their car. Then, leaving the door open, he glanced over his shoulder and came back to the front porch.

"You know, there are nine men staying there. They signed a six month lease. They wanted three months, but six is our minimum," he said in a conspiratorial tone. "Most of them are foreigners. They didn't say much and I don't know why they're here. The neighbors tell me that, as far as they can tell, they don't do anything. They're not farming or anything, and they must not plan on being here long. Something about them I didn't really like, but they're like all my customers. I'll drop by and let them know that Bob Pridemore is here for them if they need me."

"But you folks, you've bought a home and plan on being here a long time—raising kids and all. If you have any trouble with these people while they're here, you just call me. My first cousin is the sheriff in this county and he'll set them straight if they cause you folks problems," Pridemore patted me on the shoulder, then returned to his car. He pulled down the road to the right and turned left into our neighbor's drive.

No, they've not caused any trouble—just wiped out two of our other neighbors down the road, I thought, as I went back into the house. Everyone was waiting for me inside except Darby, who was still up on the landing.

"Well, I think we can assume our cover is being blown," I said. "Our loquacious realtor friend will surely tell them about their neighbors just as he told us about them. They will be suspicious about five guys and a girl across the road from them and, if he describes us, they surely know of us from our exploits in Indonesia. I can just hear him now—a beautiful young girl, a big black guy, etc."

The others nodded their heads glumly. We had to be prepared now for them to either attack us or try to get out of here with the laser. And Mike was probably right. They most likely had options that we had no knowledge of.

"Do you agree, Darby?" I asked, looking at him on the landing.

"Can't hear you. Remember, I'm just your poor, dumb, deaf mute farm hand. I'm surprised that I've finally found my voice, after years of not being able to say a word," Darby said with a straight face.

We all had a good laugh. That would be the last time in a while that we would be able to laugh together. Right now, we had to check our weapons, pack our bags and be ready for whatever was to come. The lull was over. It was time for the storm.

As if on cue, the sky darkened and approaching clouds backed by thunder and lightning descended from an ominous looking sky. A few minutes later, we saw Mr. Pridemore pull out from our neighbor's drive and head back towards town.

As he passed by, he stopped briefly to set back up a sign that had fallen in the ditch in front of the house across the road. It read----For Sale or Lease---Pridemore Realty---931-615-4322.

282

CHAPTER FIFTY-THREE

Nothing unusual happened across the street the next day. In fact, our neighbors did not even come out of the house that day unless, like we had done, they were staying in the back. If they did come out the back door, they could get access into the back of the barn without being seen by us. We had gone to a schedule of two people on watch at a time, fully armed and ready to go with the rest not too far removed from that state of readiness. We had the uneasy feeling that they were now watching us watch them. The next day, Monday, August 25th, that feeling would be substantiated as being accurate.

Early Monday morning, just after daybreak, several of the men emerged from the house. Ashton and I happened to be on watch together at that time. We would not rouse the others unless it looked like they were getting ready to move.

"Look, Hon!" Ashton whispered. "Two of them are coming to the edge of the road. Should I wake the rest of the team?"

"No, not yet. Let's see what they are doing. Right now, they are just standing there facing this way," I answered. We had pulled back from the window so they could not easily see us through the glass.

The two men were not really looking in our direction, but would frequently send a furtive glance in our direction. We had never noticed this kind of nervousness in them before. Ashton and I both felt certain that they knew we were here and probably were wondering just when we might try to move in on them. They must have known that we saw their little experiment a couple of days ago. Then, moments later, we saw why they were on the edge of the road.

Coming from the direction of highway 43, there was a custom long bed white van. As it got closer, Ashton and I saw two men in the front, a driver and passenger. It turned into the drive where the two men were standing. The men in the van chatted a few moments with the two standing in front of the house, then the van pulled around to the back of the barn. Before doing so, two other men opened the rear door of the van and got out, walking around to the back of the barn with the others.

"You better rouse the others, Hon. It looks like they may be planning to move the laser. And now there are 13 of them and only six of us," I said.

Ashton went downstairs. In just a few minutes, our team was gathered on the landing where the observation window was. Nothing had visibly taken place since Ashton left.

"What do you think, Dawson?" Steve asked.

"It looks like they may move the laser in that van. The van looks to have about a 14 foot area behind the cab and the laser is only about 12 feet. The van is plenty wide enough for it. How much do you think it weighs, Ashton?" I asked.

"It's not that heavy. They took it off the boat with the helicopter wench and handled it at the Munson plant and here with a fork truck, but my guess is that it wouldn't weigh more than about 500 pounds maximum. A lot of the guts are just mirrors, electronics and computer relays. Four strong men could carry it, even with the casters they have welded to the bottom frame. It would be important not to bump it into anything too hard or to drop it. Now that they have it calibrated, they wouldn't want to jar it too hard," Ashton replied.

"Well, you guys keep watch. I'm going to call Mike. I think we should contact the Tennessee Highway Patrol and have them block both directions on the road and be prepared to give us backup. The odds are not good now. I think we should go ahead and take them and the weapon now. We can't afford to let it slip away from us now," I said.

"One other thing, Ashton—" I said as an afterthought.

"What?" she asked.

"If Mike agrees with my assessment, and agrees we should enlist the THP, I want you to let them take you out of danger if we can get you to them," I said.

"No! I'm staying with the team until we finish this thing," she said firmly with fire in her eyes.

I didn't have time to argue with her right then, but I did not want her involved in this thing. It was shaping up to be a dangerous situation. I put in the call to Mike.

"Mike, we've got some activity going on. I think things are going to start popping here soon," I said when I got through to him. I told him the whole story, including the untimely visit from Pridemore.

"Dawson, I was just getting ready to contact you. I was finally able to get through to the President's people. I gave them the information we had at the time and they brought the President up to date. Of course the situation has changed quite a bit since then."

"What did they say?" I asked.

"Well, the instructions are the same as they were, with minor modification. Of course, the President was told that you would have the element of surprise, and the odds weren't as bad as they are now. Both those advantages have since deteriorated based on what you just told me. But he does not want to get local or state law enforcement involved unless it is absolutely necessary. That would blow the secrecy of our operation and damage our chances of bringing as many of those people into our net as we can. If you had a shootout involving the local or state police, it would hit the papers and questions would have to be answered. Keeping the action within our secret federal team would better protect the confidential scope of our operation."

"They want you to continue to try to tail them to their destination if they start moving the laser. The only thing that would change that instruction would be if any other U.S. citizens were in eminent danger. Then you would be authorized to use necessary force to try to stop them, even if that destroyed the chances to make this a broader scale sweep of these militants," Mike continued.

"So we just wait for them to move, then try to keep up with them," I said.

"Yes. Again, if civilians are in danger, you move in immediately with whatever force you can muster, including calling in the cops. I will try to get back to the White House with this latest info as soon as we hang up, and if there are further instructions, I will let you know. That will probably be tomorrow, though. And it sounds like they might be getting ready to move out today or tonight," Mike replied.

"And, since we think they know we are here now, what if they try to stop us from following them?" I asked.

"You will have to fight them. You can not let the laser get away from you now that it has been tested and is probably going to end up soon in some place where God only knows what may happen with it," Mike answered.

"Okay. Anything else, Mike?" I asked.

"No. I will try to get Pancheros and Smith back down to help you, but they are in D.C. now on assignment. It would be some time tomorrow before they could get there and it sounds like that might be too late. And Dawson?"

"Yes?"

"I realize we are giving you an impossible assignment, but a lot is riding on us stopping them before they are able to implement whatever plan they have with this thing. As I said, I don't feel good about your situation, especially now that you have lost the element of surprise and the odds have increased to the point that they now have more than twice as many guns as you have. But the President doesn't know about these latest developments, and I concur with his desire to round up as many of these fanatics on the other end as we can."

"And, one last thing. If the situation deteriorates further, you always have the right to call the shots in the field with your best judgment. No one will blame you or second guess you if this thing doesn't go down exactly according to our optimum desires. Be careful, Dawson. You've already lost two of your team members and I don't want to lose any more of you. I especially regret putting Ashton in harms way. Is there any way you could get her out of there before this thing breaks loose?"

"There probably is, Mike. But when I saw what happened today, I've already approached her on getting her to safety. I want her out of here, too. I'll continue to try, but she won't hear of it. She wants to stay with the team. She's pretty, but she can be very stubborn, too. I don't think I could force her to get out of here unless I tied her up and forcefully took her out," I said ruefully.

"Well, maybe you should try that," Mike laughed. "She's some girl. Good luck, Dawson. I'll get back to you as soon as I can."

I told the rest of our group of the conversation with Mike. They accepted the decision soberly, but with resolve. We all knew how important this assignment was to our national security. The life of the President literally hung upon our ability to stop these people and their ugly weapon.

I also tried once again to convince Ashton to get out of here. I took her in the bedroom and backed her against the wall, threatening to do just what I told Mike I would have to do. She didn't budge. When I got angry with her, she concluded the argument by just smiling sweetly and saying, "I love you. And I'm staying."

As we rejoined the rest of the group, in the back of my mind, I was hoping that at least Pancho and Lefty would get here before we went to war with these people. I was certain that when they pulled out with the weapon, they would try to stop us from following them. And they surely had plans up their sleeves that we could only speculate on. We had to stay with the weapon or attempt to destroy it. And I knew that all of that would be difficult to do without further loss of life from our team.

Before the sun set, I would be proven wrong on one count and right on the other. Pancho and Lefty would not make it in time. And the team's ranks would be reduced once again.

CHAPTER FIFTY-FOUR

It was a sweltering hot, humid day. We were constantly on full alert and the anticipation was exhausting. Nothing happened until late afternoon. Ashton and Darby prepared sandwiches for us about 5:45 PM. We had finished eating and were discussing how we would man the watch through the night. Steve was watching at the window. The time was now 6:33 PM and the blazing red sun was low on the horizon. In another hour it would be dusk.

I was sitting in one of the easy chairs in the den and Ashton was curled up on my lap. After several more attempts to talk her into getting out, I finally had given up. But I resolved in my mind to do my best to keep her as far removed from the imminent danger that the situation presented.

"Love, I'm glad you finally quit harassing me about leaving. I belong here with you and the rest of the team. Aren't you glad I'm here, now?" She snuggled in close to me and buried her head on my shoulder, nibbling at my neck.

"I want you with me. You know that. But these will be real bullets coming our way when we stir up this hornet's nest. And I don't want you with me when that's happening," I told her.

"I know—and I worry about you in that situation, too—and the rest of the guys. Dawson, I'm scared—scared for me, for you, for us—for all of us. But that's why I want to be there. I can help. I know I can. You know I can handle a gun. And you need all the help you can get."

"Get ready to roll!" Steve shouted from the stairs. We all jumped up as if we had been electrocuted. We had brought three assault rifles and had decided that Darby definitely should have one since he was the most proficient with that weapon. Ashton had declined, saying she was more effective using aimed shots from her handgun than with bursts of fire scattered with an AR. The other four of us drew lots and I got one. Larry got the other.

We had rushed up the stairs. The white van had pulled around to the side of the barn and stopped. We had to assume that the laser was on it, but would have to check the barn somehow. It could be a decoy. If it was on board, we assumed the two technicians were in the back of the van with the laser. There were two men in the cab of the truck and we could see that the man in the passenger side had a rifle sticking up beside him.

They had two other vehicles that had been there, other than the truck which they apparently were going to abandon, because the other nine climbed into the two other vehicles. Four got in a Buick LeSabre and the other five climbed into a Honda Passport. They were all heavily armed.

We grabbed our weapons and rushed out the back door. Ashton, Larry and I jumped in the car and Darby, Steve and Thom got in the van. Since we had accounted for all thirteen men, our quickly formulated plan was to let the van pull out behind their caravan of three vehicles while we quickly checked the barn. If the laser was gone, then we knew their exit was not a decoy and we would quickly catch up with the rest. I was driving the car with Ashton and Larry in the back seat. Thom was driving the van with Darby alongside him and Steve in the rear. Their instructions were to, in no event, lose sight of the white van.

We had already packed all of our meager belongings in the vehicles and locked the house. We didn't expect to be back and would have the agency sell the house later. In a sense, all the actors in this little play were playing a stupid game. We, of course, knew they were there, and we had every reason to believe that they now knew we were here. Still, when they pulled out, Thom would follow them at a distance, on the surface maintaining our 'discreet' surveillance. And we would follow soon after checking out the barn, unless the laser was still there for some unknown reason. We would then probably switch off like we had done before, even though that ruse would not now be effective since they knew they would be followed.

To do otherwise and confront them now, though, would ignite an immediate firefight. And we had our instructions to not do that unless there was no other alternative, because that would blow the chance to find the people at the destination. We were ready to play the game, with some reluctance and trepidation.

Then, something totally unexpected happened! The van began to pull out, but the other cars stayed behind. Did that mean the laser was still in the barn?! Or did it simply mean they were ready for a showdown with us while the van and the laser got away?!

We couldn't take a chance either way. I waved Thom on and he, Darby and Steve pulled out and began following the van at a distance. We were now split up and the three of us were facing nine of them. We decided to wait a few minutes to see what the group staying behind did next. It didn't take long to find out. Two of them got out of the passport and got into the flatbed truck. The crate was still on the back of the truck, but to our knowledge, was still empty. None of us on watch had seen the laser loaded back into the empty crate. But had it been done at night and we somehow missed it? We couldn't be sure.

The truck motor cranked up and began to pull slowly out from the barn. The direction it was beginning to turn indicated it was going to go out in the opposite direction of the way the white van went!

Now we had a real dilemma! The laser could be in the white van with four guards and our van with three of our people were following it. Or it could still be in the barn with seven men staying back. Or it could be on the flatbed with two men getting ready to pull out in the opposite direction. We could not split the three of us remaining any further. If one followed the truck in the car, then the other two would face seven of them alone in order to check out the barn. Once again, I had to admire Infama's cunning.

It was time to make a decision. I quickly called Darby on the cell phone to explain our predicament while pulling the car out from behind our house. I told Darby for them to stay with the van. We had to stop the truck and take on all nine of the remaining bad guys. At least we had two of the ARs with us.

To heck with the perfect world and the desire to shadow the laser to it's destination undetected, or at least unopposed! This decision had to be made in the field. We were going to war, I thought as I wheeled the car across their drive, blocking the truck's exit!

The nine men immediately piled out of their vehicles. Larry and Ashton dove out of the car into the ditch on the right side of the driveway and I took the ditch on the left side. Within seconds, blistering volleys of small arms and automatic weapon fire was zinging all around us!

I heard Larry's AR giving them answering fire and saw one of the men drop in the dust by the truck. I could hear the pop! pop! of Ashton's pistol and saw another man drop, squealing in agony. Ashton and Larry were about 30 feet to my right.

"Keep down Ashton!!!" I screamed, then trained my AR on a couple of the other men who were scurrying for cover. I think I wounded one of them.

By now they had all three of us pinned down. To poke our head up from the cover of the ditch we were lying in would have been sure death. There were still seven of them, most with automatic rifles and they were all now behind cover. The noise was deafening and bits of grass and dirt were showering down on top of me as the bullets grazed over my head, in front of and behind me. None of the three of us could safely return fire against that onslaught.

"Dawson!! Cover for me if you can! I'm going to try to make it to that big oak tree on my right and flank them!" Larry shouted to me during a lull in the firing.

I rolled to my left where there was a stack of cinder blocks about three feet high in front of the ditch. The blocks had apparently been left there after some abandoned construction project, but they offered much better cover than the ditch alone. I could at least raise my head and be out of the line of fire of about half the attackers.

Immediately, I started firing at the car and the trees that some of the men had hidden behind. Out of the corner of my eye, I saw Larry dash for the oak tree only about fifteen feet to his right front. In spite of my covering fire, he started taking fire before he got to the cover of the tree. I thought I detected a jerk in his body before he finally reached the tree. He was about forty feet away from me now. Ashton was still in the ditch, but had managed to move down to the right a few feet where she could better support Larry's dash.. She had managed to get in position where the abandoned truck cab was actually hiding her from view of most of the shooters.

"Larry!! Are you okay?!" I hollered. The firing had actually stopped momentarily from both directions.

"Yeah! I took a bullet in the leg! But I'm okay! I just can't run very fast now!" he shouted back.

I still had the AR but had stuck my revolver in my belt, getting ready for close in fighting that was sure to come as each side was trying to maneuver closer to each other. I could see Ashton reloading on my right.

"Look out, Ashton!!! To your left!!" I shouted, seeing one of the goons sneaking around the cab of the truck. I took careful aim with my revolver and shot him in the back just as he was taking aim at Ashton who was still reloading her handgun.

Three down for the count and one wounded on their side. Six to go. Odds were getting better, but still two to one in their favor. And one of our three was wounded.

Larry was at the oak tree about twenty feet to Ashton's right front. I was still in the ditch behind the cinder blocks on the left side of the drive now about forty-five feet to Ashton's left. The remaining Infama people were scattered across our front, with two behind cover in front of the barn, right behind the rear of the truck trailer. Two more were behind a stack of lumber almost directly in front of Ashton's position and to the front side of where Larry now was behind the big tree. The other two had taken cover behind trees in front of my position.

There was another short lull in the firing. Then, suddenly, the two behind the trailer rushed Larry's position, ARs blazing. They were forcing him to move slightly to his left behind the tree, exposing him partially to fire from the two behind the lumber. In the meantime, the other two directed heavy fire on mine and Ashton's position.

Ashton, with only the ditch to protect her had to flatten herself and could not safely return fire. I had a better position to fire from, but now the two coming around the trailer were hidden from my view. I directed my fire towards the two behind the lumber pile that were threatening Larry and squeezed off a few bursts towards the two to my front who had Ashton pinned down.

I saw one of the two men rushing towards Larry from the trailer, gun blazing, only about 20 feet in front of his position. Larry stepped to his left and stitched a bloody pattern across his chest with the AR, causing him to drop instantly. In doing so, though, he briefly exposed himself to the two behind the lumber. They both let loose with a sustained volley directed at his position.

I immediately placed fire on their position, ignoring the two to my front. But it was too late. I saw Larry jerk convulsively, then fall forward face down. About that time, the second man coming from the trailer rounded the corner and shot Larry lying on the ground. I dropped him immediately.

I was too stunned and anguished by what I had witnessed to even notice that the remaining four terrorists were now moving from cover to cover converging on my position. They were now spread out in front of my position and Ashton's so that we could only engage one of them at a time, thus exposing ourselves from fire from the rest.

"Dawson!!! To your left!!" Ashton screamed.

I jerked to my left just in time to see one of them flanking me. I jerked my rifle around. Then two of the remaining three still to the front of my position began charging in my direction, while the other one kept Ashton busy. All of a sudden the one on my left charged. I knew in a split second that I could take him, but not the two closing in on me from the front. As if in a dream world, I squeezed a shot at the one approaching at my left, dropping him immediately, but knowing the next, and last, thing I would feel would be bullets tearing into my body from the two who were almost on top of me now.

In that long second when I began to swing my rifle towards my front, it almost seemed as if my movements were in slow motion. My last thought was for Ashton, valiantly taking on her guy , who had an AR, with her pistol. I knew I would be dead in the next second. I felt a bullet graze my arm with searing pain and knew the next one would be more accurate and tear through my chest before I could train my fire on the two attackers.

Then, suddenly, I heard a loud chatter of an AR right behind me. My first thought as I jerked around was that somehow I had miscounted and one of them had gotten behind me, not that it mattered now. Before I could fully turn, though, both of my attackers dropped suddenly in their tracks, one of them falling forward dead, almost on top of me.

Then I saw Darby behind me and Steve and Thom on his left, diving for cover. I had not even heard them drive up, with all the noise.

"How many left?!!" Darby shouted, sliding down with me behind the cinder blocks.

"Only one!" I replied. "Behind the lumber pile."

About that time, we saw him dash for the barn. Steve and Thom both shot at the same time, dropping him in his tracks before he got half way to the door.

There was a deathly silence as the acrid smell of gun smoke began to waft across the battlefield. There were bodies lying everywhere, including one of our own. After checking to insure the Infama people were all dead, we all walked silently over to where Larry lay, crumpled beside the tree and bleeding from numerous rifle wounds.

"He's dead," Darby said softly after checking his pulse.

Tears were rolling down Ashton's cheeks and a tear slid down mine also. None of us could say anything. Our team numbers continued to dwindle and we still did not have the laser in our possession.

"Where is the white van?" I finally asked.

"We lost it," Steve said. "Just before we got to 43, they raised the back and took a shot at us with the laser. We saw the door go up and Thom swerved just in time."

"Where's our van?" I asked. I had just noticed it wasn't around. That's why I didn't hear them drive up.

"It's useless. Thom's evasive action saved our lives, but the laser crashed into the engine block, destroying it. Hearing the shots, we ran down here on foot and got here as fast as we could," Steve said.

We checked the barn and the crate on the back of the truck. They were both empty. The laser had slipped from our grasp once again. Trying to keep up with it had cost us another precious life.

We called the THP. This would require some explaining. Still numb from the loss, we made arrangements for Larry to be taken care of and for his body to be returned to his hometown, where a brother would make the local arrangements. It was almost midnight when we finally went back to our house across the street, unlocked it and fell exhausted into bed. Tomorrow I would call Mike and we would decide what to do now.

None of us could talk much. We had, once again, lost a member of our "family". Ashton and I had gone to bed and we could hear Darby , still down in the kitchen alone, slowly sipping coffee. He had the radio turned down low. Before dropping off into a fitful sleep, I heard the strains of the old Eagles song coming up from the kitchen "There's going to be a heartache tonight—"

There were eight. Now there were five. In my mind there was a silent roll call of those of us left: Dawson Kohler—Ashton Smyth—Darby Peters— Thom Henson—Steve Whitt. And those who were gone: Dr. Ernest Brown —Percy Thackett —Lawrence Childress. "There's going to be a heartache tonight, I know..."

CHAPTER FIFTY-FIVE

The next morning we were up early and had a solemn breakfast. It just didn't seem right not having Larry there to kid about eating catfish and barbeque. He also was a solid asset to our team. We would miss him terribly, as a very special friend as well as a proficient team member.

After breakfast, I decided to call Mike. I dreaded the phone call, having to give him the tragic news about Larry and the loss of the laser. His secretary put him through to me immediately. He listened quietly while I related the whole story.

"Dawson—I'm so sorry about Larry— We'll make sure everything is taken care of for the family on this end," I think Mike was choking up. In typical fashion though, he did not cry over spilled milk when told about the laser getting away from us. He got right down to business, discussing what we should do now.

"You know, I think we should have followed your advice to go ahead and move on the laser before something like this could happen. Unfortunately, our hesitancy cost a life, and we still don't have our hands on the laser. Actually, I just got a call from the President's office and was going to call you. He had gotten personally involved and told his people he didn't want any more lives lost. He instructed us to take them on now, destroy the laser and we would get all of our departments together to try to smoke out the other people who might be involved. You did the right thing, Dawson. And, under the circumstances, your team can't be blamed at all for the fact the laser is still on the loose. All of you were very brave and you did the very best you could."

"Thanks, Mike. We all appreciate your support and understanding. But, especially now, we want to get this thing and these people. Any suggestions?" I asked.

"Well, we'll put out an APB on the white van description and license number, but I'll bet they've already ditched it and switched to another vehicle," Mike replied. Within the hour, he would be proved correct. The van would be found less than 20 miles down the road on Highway 43—without the laser.

"Check out the house and barn over there for any clues that would identify the people or the destination. Then you guys might as well come on back to D.C. I'll see you in my office about 2:00 PM, tomorrow, Wednesday, August 27th. That will give us all a little time to decide what the next course of action should be. I am concerned that now, a working weapon is on its way somewhere to be used in the near future most likely. I will check the President's schedule over the next few weeks and alert his security people," Mike continued.

"Okay, Mike. We'll see you tomorrow afternoon," I said and we hung up.

The five of us spent the rest of the day combing through the abandoned farmhouse and barn across the road. By 5:00 PM we had thoroughly searched both buildings without finding anything useful. The only thing we all noticed was that they were horrible housekeepers. Trash was all over the house. We went through every shred of paper and trash though, and there was absolutely nothing found of even remote value.

In the barn, we didn't find a lot of trash. Obviously, the technicians had taken whatever prints they had on the laser with them. It appeared to us, from the brief observation of the laser when it had been in the open, that they had mostly adjusted the guts of the weapon to fine tune it before their test. There was some welding spatter on the floor of the barn, but we suspected this was from the undercarriage with the casters they had built for it to rest on.

We were getting ready to leave when Ashton noticed a small crumpled piece of dirty paper that was lodged over against one of the posts supporting the barn rafters. It was paper from a computer printer that had Arabic writing on the back. On the front it just had a web page address for a company called Freightliner LLC. We would take that with us to Mike's to see if the Arabic writing had any significance, and to let his people check on this Freightliner company in case that would give any clue that would be helpful.

That night, the five of us had a quiet last meal together in our Lawrence County farmhouse. Our kitchen table had six chairs. With just me, Ashton, Darby, Thom and Steve, it seemed like someone was missing. Of course, there was someone missing.

"Never, ever, if we find the Laser and those fanatical bastards again, should we hesitate to wipe them out and destroy their fucking light machine!" Darby said.

"I agree! Unless we have specific restrictive orders, the decision in the field will be to shoot on sight," I said.

"You know, we lost three really decent, tough and brave friends," Steve interjected. "The five of us ought to vow that we will exact revenge for their deaths."

"We will. That's a promise to Larry, Percy and Ernest. And to the President and anyone else these maniacs plan to kill. I don't know about you guys, but if we find them, I'm going to aim below the belt if I have time. But I won't leave them alive to have some jerk-ass lawyer spend our money to defend them and then let the taxpayers keep them up for the rest of their lives," Thom said with resolve.

"You know, I miss Larry and Percy and Ernest so much," Ashton said softly. "I don't understand these people's thinking. Why do they hate us so much?"

"A big part of it is their religious fanaticism," I said. "But a big factor too, I think, is envy. Except for those lucky assholes that have found themselves sitting on top of oil, their fundamentalism has not left them with much in life to be proud of. Socially, economically, militarily, educationally or by any other measurement, their fundamentalism and misguided thinking has left them at the bottom of the world's heap. For the most part they are concentrated in poor third world areas that have given them none of the comforts of life that more progressive, democratic nations enjoy. And they can only blame their religious fundamentalism for their plight. Their way of thinking is egotistical, backward and stupid, just like any fundamentalism of any of the religions tends to breed."

"They are angry, jealous and trying to grasp the fruits of life by attacking those who have been successful. And, since their poverty does not allow them to have a decent military option to express their aggressiveness, they find something in "their" book that tells them they can kill at will to try to enforce their beliefs and share in the good things in life," I continued. "And they have even, in their lunacy, convinced themselves that "their" book condones cowards who would attack women, children, people like the innocent Mennonites, unarmed representatives of the free world like the President, or anyone else who may not have the ability to confront them in their cowardly actions," I continued.

"Yeah. And not only will they not confront anyone face-on that could whip their ass, they convince themselves that, if they die in their actions, that is 'God's will' and he will reward them in some kind of heaven! Some even claim to believe God will give them 72 virgins in heaven if they blow up a busload of school kids!" Thom agreed.

"They're sick, demented, ruthless, ungodly people!" Ashton said.

"They're fucking idiots!" Darby said. "And they will pay, just like they have historically paid through the ages. Can you imagine if they were successful in whatever they were trying to achieve?! The world would be set back 1,000 years. And Ashton, you would have to cover your face and not talk directly to a man other than your husband. What the hell have they ever accomplished that they can be proud of?! I get angry just listening to them pop off on TV. It's laughable! You'd think they've found the answers to life. And, except for those stupid looking cowboys in gowns that have inherited so much oil dollars they don't know how to spend it, most of these "brilliant" terrorists are starving to death. I will actually enjoy blowing these vermin's heads off if I get the chance. Let them go to their virgins!"

We spent the next few hours expressing a mixture of sadness and anger towards the murderous group we had been exposed to. The next morning we were up early to drive to Nashville and catch an early flight to Washington.

After we locked the house, Ashton walked to the front yard and picked three of her flowers. Walking back to the creek, she tossed the three blooms into the water, watching them float lazily downstream.

"Goodbye, pretty little flowers. I will never forget you," she said softly.

We arrived in D.C. about 10:45 AM, caught a taxi and headed to the vicinity of Mike's office. After a quick bite of lunch at a café nearby, we walked to Mike's office, arriving about 1:45 PM.

CHAPTER FIFTY-SIX

Just as we were walking into Mike's office, we met Bob Willoughby walking out.

"Ashton!" Bob hugged her. "Hi Dawson! And Darby, Thom and Steve—right?"

He shook all of our hands and seemed genuinely pleased to see us all.

"Mike told me about some of what happened to you in Tennessee," Bob continued after greeting us. "I know you all miss Lawrence. And Ashton, I've been so worried about you. Every time I'm able to get an update on the team, I get more frightened for your safety. Mike told me about you being in that ditch with bullets flying all around."

"Bob, I'm part of the team. And now, more than ever, they need me. We have to find the Laser! We've lost too many lives. And I'm scared to death that they might use it before we find them again. That would be horrible!" Ashton said, shuddering.

"Yes, I know, Hon. You just hang in there. You'll find it. I know how important it is to you to stop them. You've risked your life several times to do that. Just be careful—please?" Bob said, patting her on the shoulder.

"I will, Bob. I promise. But we've got to find it—soon," Ashton said.

We chatted a while longer, then Bob left and we went on into Mike's office. He was expecting us.

"Have a seat, guys!" he said jovially. "Let's get started. Did you find anything at the house or barn?"

Ashton handed him the piece of paper she had found.

"I'll send it down the hall. We can decipher the Arabic and get a rundown on Freightliner if that has any significance. It won't take long. We can have that info before you leave," Mike said, calling his secretary and handing her the paper, giving her instructions on the information we wanted.

"Now, first, I wanted to tell you that we have helped Larry's family make arrangements for his funeral. He's being buried in the Bronx, so you won't be able to go to his funeral. We have work to do. But I have the address of the funeral home if you want to send flowers," Mike started off.

"No one has a clue as to what the specific plans for the Laser are. But I checked the President's schedule over the next thirty days. He is visiting several countries in South America this week, returning Sunday, the 31st. He left yesterday. There will be heavy security provided for his visit, of course. But I don't think that would be the place the laser would be planned to be used. We know it was here in the U.S. just two days ago and we have had heightened security checks on anything going out of the country towards South America since your call. The logistics just wouldn't allow them to get it there and in position to use over there that quickly, I don't think," Mike continued.

"So that means we've got at least four days to try to find it," I stated.

"Right. In my opinion, that is correct," Mike answered.

"What is next on his schedule?" I asked.

"Well, he's going to be here working in the executive office the next week and a half. My intuition tells me that the strike might be planned after that---about two weeks from now," Mike said seriously.

"Why do you say that?" Steve asked.

"The FBI and CIA have been picking up a lot of traffic from known terrorist sources just in the past few day indicating that something will be happening September 11th. Nothing specific. And no indication of what or where. Just a lot of intercepted information that indicates something is planned for then. It could be a false alarm. It's happened before," Mike said.

"Wow! The anniversary of 9-11-2001! That would be a symbolic date for them to show us it can happen again," Thom commented.

"Right. We can't take it lightly. That doesn't give us much time to track the laser down again," Mike said.

"Where will the President be on 9-11?" I asked.

Mike hesitated a moment to let his answer sink in. "At the former World Trade Center site. As you know, there is a renovation project going on with a commercial development planned. But it's just in the foundation stages right now. When looking out across that area, it is still largely a flat, vacant piece of real estate, but soon it will be rising—with towers like the Trade Center—and a bustling two or three story shopping and commercial mall. A couple of years from now, except for a memorial to 911 that is being built in the center of the area, people will not be able to imagine what it has been like these past couple of years."

"What is planned for the President's visit?" Ashton asked.

"Well, he won't be there until evening. There will be a review stand erected from which he and other dignitaries will make short speeches in remembrance of 911, and for dedication of the new construction and the memorial," Mike replied.

"What do they have planned for this event?" Steve asked.

"The plans haven't been finalized yet as to exactly what the program will be. The planners just got word yesterday that the President could be there. All we know is that, in addition to the President, the Mayor, former Mayor, Governor, several Senators and Congressmen from New York as well as other states and a number of other dignitaries plan to be present. Some of them will take part in the ceremony. And, of course, the general public will be invited to attend. A preliminary estimate is that there could be 100,000 to 150,000 people there——maybe more. The Fire and Police Departments as well as various EMS will be a part of the ceremony. The President is expected to make a major policy statement regarding the continuing battle against domestic terrorism. It's even rumored that the British and Canadian Prime Ministers and the Mexican President will be there and will make short comments, but that hasn't been confirmed yet."

"Wow! We better find the Laser before then! This is it! Just think of the significance that an attack would take on if it occurred on that particular date and with those people involved. The security problem will be horrendous!" I exclaimed.

"Yes, I know," Mike said, shaking his head. "We have already been in touch with the Secret Service, CIA, FBI and the city police force and state police. The area will be cordoned off and no one will be allowed within 100 yards unless they are searched thoroughly. Also, all of the adjacent buildings will be vacated, closed and guarded prior to this event. But, with this kind of crowd and all the other factors involved, something could easily slip though the cracks. All of the above agencies and departments have been alerted that we have received troubling information about that date."

"We know the laser couldn't walk in with a person," Ashton said. "And it has an effective range of about 200 yards we think. How do you think they could get it close enough, Mike?"

"Well, Ashton, I don't see how they could with the security we will have in place. Obviously, it would be within range if placed in the window of one of the buildings close by. But, as I said, those buildings will be searched, locked and guarded before this event. I just don't know. Maybe that is not the date they plan to use it. But that date, with those people scheduled to be there, would represent an unarguable coup if they can pull something off.

And we can't ignore the signals we have been getting about 9-11-03. Nor can we ignore the obvious intent to do something with the laser," Mike replied thoughtfully.

We decide to immediately start checking out organizations around Manhattan that were known to have leanings sympathetic to Infama. All of those organizations were under some form of surveillance now, but we would get warrants to search the premises of the places they lived and worked out of.

We would also do our own survey of the site and see if we could detect any avenue of bringing the laser within range of the review stand that might not have been thought of. All of that activity would take the next ten days of our time and would take us to September the 6th before we finished. We would come up empty handed as far as finding the laser, any one who would admit to being involved or any clues that would help us in any aspect of our investigation.

Before leaving Mike's office today though, we would discuss numerous scenarios without coming up with any ideas as to how the laser could be moved into position, or what we could do to prevent disaster if somehow it was. It was like looking for a needle in a haystack to find a 12' cylinder in Manhattan that probably only weighed about 500 pounds and could be concealed anywhere and in uncountable ways.

"Well guys, I don't have any answers to any of the questions we all have," Mike concluded. "You all know how serious this is, and I know the frustration you have. None of us knows where to start. We and our agencies are supposed to be the brains behind our intelligence and counter terrorism efforts. But sometimes I just feel dumb. It's not something I like to admit, but these fanatic hoodlums have outwitted us. And your team has paid a huge price along the way. We just have to figure out a way to catch them before they use the laser for their murderous purpose."

"Yeah. And it doesn't help that these fools, when it gets time for them to pull the trigger, don't care if they die or not," Darby reflected.

"You're right, in more ways than one," Mike said. "You know, normally, one part of an investigation like this is to try to figure out ways that people could accomplish their objective that would provide an escape route. With these people, that doesn't even have to be a factor. Look at those people who flew the planes into the Trade Center and the Pentagon a couple of years ago. They did their job. Then they died. And they didn't care. That suicidal aspect of these people complicates the process of trying to figure out what they are going to do and how. It creates avenues to accomplish their mission that don't have to provide escape, and that greatly increases the possibilities we have to look into."

"Okay, Mike. We'll get out of your way and get to work," I said, rising to go.

"Alright. We'll stay in constant touch and feed you any new information we get. Hold on before you go, though. I'll see if Nancy has the information we wanted on the Arabic writing on that piece of paper Ashton found in the barn, or on Freightliner," Mike said, leaving to check with his secretary.

"It's on its way to us now—will be down here in about five minutes," Mike said after checking.

"While we're waiting, Mike, what was Bob Willoughby doing here? We met him on the way in," I asked.

I thought I saw Mike fidget momentarily but, if he did, he recovered quickly. His answer was somewhat evasive, however.

"Oh, we just stay in touch with each other. He has been continuing to work on his end to find how the information got out of his facility to begin with and has been consulting with us on how he can prevent future lapses in security of this nature. And I have been keeping him updated on the progress of your team's investigation. Plus, he has a strong interest in Ashton's safety and well being," Mike laughed. "We have been talking about your dedication and courage, Ashton, and how much your involvement has helped the team. And I know how much you miss your teammates that aren't here, and how you have risked your own life to accomplish our mission and protect the other team members."

"Well, here's the info we are looking for," Mike said as an assistant came in and handed him a sheaf of papers. "Let's look at this before you go."

Mike read the information that had been handed to him carefully, then passed it on to us. There were several pages of information, but most related to financial data and other facts that were most likely not relevant to our interest.

Freightliner LLC is a subsidiary of Daimler Chrysler Company, the world's leading manufacturer of commercial vehicles. Its headquarters are in Portland, Oregon. Freightliner is the number one heavy truck maker in the U.S. and is a top exporter to Central and South America, Asia and the Middle East. They and their subsidiaries make ambulances, fire trucks, school buses and heavy trucks. One of their subsidiaries is American LeFrance which manufactures almost all of the fire trucks used in the U.S. and many other countries. They also make Thomas school buses and Western Star and Sterling trucks—all of those brands leading products in the fields in which they are used. Nothing in the background of any of the principal officers even remotely suggested any connection with Infama. We were perplexed. None of this information gave us a hint towards finding the laser or the people who had it.

"Well, I don't see anything here that immediately jumps out at me," Mike said, coming to the same conclusion that the rest of us had come to. "Let's see what the Arabic means."

After looking at that piece of information, which was on a single page, he chuckled.

"It looks like this is a grocery or food list. The Arabic language describes hot dogs and other sundries, specifying that the hot dogs be beef, not pork."

"So you think the whole lot of the information is worthless—probably just a piece of scrap paper they found to write their lunch order on the back of for one of their associates to go pick up?" Thom asked Mike.

"Most likely. But don't let's jump to any conclusions right now. From what you told me, all of the paperwork that they might have used was either taken with them or destroyed in the house or barn. You mentioned that you found a couple of piles of fresh ashes that indicated they burned a lot of papers that they didn't want to take with them. This piece may have been from that bunch and been wadded up and thrown away in a corner of the barn without any thought of it later, or that it might be found. There may be a clue here, but I don't see it yet. Let's don't dismiss it. Think about it and I will, too. In the meantime, lets just do some gumshoe detective work to see if we can turn up anything of value. If we're right about the 9-11 date, we don't have much time," Mike replied.

After a little more discussion, Mike concluded the meeting and the five of us began to leave.

"Dawson, let me talk to you privately just a second before you leave," Mike said.

The rest went on out and I went back in Mike's office, closing the door behind me. It was obvious he wanted the conversation to be confidential.

"How is Ashton doing?" he asked when we were alone.

"Great. She's been a valuable part of the team. Why do you ask?" I questioned him.

"Just to confirm my observations from the reports I have gotten and the comments from your other team members. She seems to have fit right in and has the respect of the rest of your group," Mike answered.

"Yes, she does. We have all become close associates professionally, as well as good friends. We all miss Larry, Percy and Ernest," I said.

"Yes, I know. They were good people and your group is considerably smaller now. You know, Ashton has been fearless in your exploits and has made great personal sacrifices to work with you. Not just professionally. You know she is considered to be one of the brightest scientists on Willoughby's staff. But that awful experience she had with Alziddi in Indonesia and putting herself directly in the line of fire in several instances all shows that she is very committed to our task," Mike said.

"Yes, she is. She is truly one of us. I would like to cut her some slack in those dangerous situations, because, as you know, I love her. But she won't hear of it. She insists on being right with us in the thick of things," I said.

"Yes—you're right. She has certainly been an integral part of your team. You've been fortunate to have her, I think. Well, that's all I wanted to hear. Thanks for staying back, Dawson. You can join the others now and get to work. Good luck," Mike concluded our conversation.

As I left to join the others who were waiting on me down the hall, I was puzzled. What was that conversation all about? Mike wasn't the type to just have idle chatter. He always had a reason.

Maybe I knew.

CHAPTER FIFTY-SEVEN

Thursday morning, August 28th, we hit the streets of Manhattan. Mike had suggested we go undercover to try to find clues as to who was involved in the Laser scheme, where it might be and what the plan was for using it. As he had pointed out, the bad guys we had met knew us anyway. But, unless we ran into them, we might find someone who didn't know us who would talk.

We decided to start in Harlem, work our way down to midtown, on down through Soho and end up in the financial district. We had covered some of this territory earlier when we were chasing down Abdul Mahmud, Reza Pahlavi and their friends, Mohammed and Saeb. We would touch bases with some of the previous contacts, but concentrate on trying to get updated information from the street people and people associated with organizations that the FBI had pointed us to that were known to have sympathetic leanings towards Infama.

Most of these organizations were already under surveillance, but maybe we could pick up some tidbits of information by appearing to mix with them as they went about their daily routines. We were not optimistic, but had nothing else to do. Our time was running out and it was frustrating not to have anything substantive that we could get our teeth into. It was as if our quarry had gone underground. Our fear was, when they did pop up, it would be too late.

Darby was dressed like a pimp with earrings, chains, natty clothes, alligator shoes—the whole sub-culture thing. Ashton was posing as his 'lady'. The other three of us had beards, dirty baggy pants, and scruffy looking shirts. I doubted that the people we had run into in Indonesia or at the farm in Tennessee could even recognize us now.

The one thing we all appeared to have in common as we walked down the street was clear evidence through slogans on our T shirts, that we had no love for the U.S. government. We weren't intending to blend in with the Islamic community in the places we visited. In fact, most of the Islamic community would find us despicable. But those that mattered in our objective certainly would not suspect us of being sympathetic to their arch enemy—the U.S. government.

We had decided to visit six different communities, each of which covered about two city blocks. We would spend about a day in each. Our objective was to simply blend in with the New York city scene, and observe. We would hang around the neighborhoods where our quarry would likely congregate and find refuge. Maybe we would see something suspicious, sight one of the people we might recognize or see some unusual activity. Our odds of finding anything that would benefit our mission were indeed slim.

Mike had told us that the FBI had released additional agents and that they were canvassing some of the same areas. We would just be five additional sets of eyes and ears.

We didn't want to split up, but we did separate, keeping about forty yards between us on the same side of the street as we strolled through or loitered in the areas we had chosen. Steve was up front, alone. Darby and Ashton would be behind him with Thom and I bringing up the rear. We would all be close in case we were sighted by any of the Infama people we had met and trouble broke loose.

"Yo man! Nice chick you have! You want to loan her out a while?" a seedy-looking character approached Darby.

We were alert, but paused to light cigarettes so we could observe. Steve had paused down the street, also. Darby and Ashton had walked a little beyond earshot with the man continuing to follow them, conversing with Darby. He fit in quite well and the black man who had confronted him looked to be negotiating with him while they all three stopped in front of a little market. Finally after a few minutes, Darby and Ashton walked on.

The day wore on with nothing sighted that would raise our suspicions. We stopped and chatted with a few people, but most would have little to do with us. About 12:30 PM, we rejoined each other for lunch at a dirty little café.

"What was that all about—the guy that stopped you guys about an hour ago?" I asked Darby and Ashton after we had ordered.

"Oh, he thought I was a pimp and took a liking to Ashton. He wanted to know if she could go with him to his flat for about an hour. I said no, but he insisted and offered me money. He said some real flattering things about Ashton," Darby grinned.

"Shut up Darby!" Ashton kicked him under the table.

"What happened then?" I laughed.

"Well, I didn't want to blow our cover, so I asked him how much" Darby replied, Ashton still glaring at him. "He said he would give me $250 for a hot white chick like Ashton."

"Darby, shut up—" Ashton kicked him again sharply.

"Gosh, why didn't you take it? That's a lot of money for one hour!" Thom remarked, trying to feign seriousness.

"Well, I didn't want to appear to be cheap. I laughed at him and told him she would cost $500. Well, he must have been a drug dealer. He pulled a wad of money out of his pocket and started pulling off bills to pay me the $500."

"How did you get out of that?" Steve asked.

"I had to think fast. I said "Whoa! That's just for her. She's my lady. I get a thousand on top of that!" Darby answered. "The man just looked at me like I was crazy, put his money back in his pocket and walked off cursing and shaking his head. I heard him say something about that being a high priced Ho."

We all laughed, except Ashton. "It wasn't funny! What if he had pulled out another $1,000!?" she asked.

"Well, I guess you found out what your market value was. You're worth something between $500 and $1,500," I said, trying not to grin.

This time I got the sharp kick in the shin.

We spent that afternoon and the next five days walking the streets. We did have several conversations with people in the Islamic community but, in most cases, they would not talk to us until we identified ourselves. Those people would readily talk to us, but had no information that would help. Several did agree to become extended eyes and ears for us when we gave them numbers that they could reach us if they heard or saw anything. The ones who only talked to us because of the political leanings we portrayed in our undercover roles were more angry than informative.

One night we ate at the little restaurant where we had all had dinner together shortly after the team was formed. Being in that same place gave us a desolate reminder that three of our members who had been with us then were no longer with us.

Finally, late Saturday afternoon, September 6th, we had completed our survey of the areas which we had intended to look at. We had been down in lower Manhattan, close to the World Trade Center site the past day and a half, feeling that, if that was the place the laser would be implemented, there might be activity around there to position it close to the site of the upcoming ceremony. Just in case the Statue of Liberty was the target instead of the Trade Center site, we thought about checking the security out there, but Mike said when I called him that the Statue location was being taken care of with highest alert security. Mike wanted to see us early Monday morning.

"Well, it's about 5:15 PM. Let's call it a day and catch the subway back to the hotel," I said. We were staying at the Milford Plaza, about a block off of Broadway.

"Sounds good," Darby said. "I don't know how you 'private eye' types stand it. I like action. This last few days has really gotten me down. I don't feel like we've accomplished anything."

"That's because we really haven't accomplished anything. And, if Mike is right about the 9-11 thing, our time is running out. If we don't pick up a clue in the next four days, all we can do is join with all the other security forces that will be in place and try to be ready for whatever happens the night of the ceremony," I said as we began our walk to the subway station. We were all dejected.

"Damn, I sure would like a drink and I'm hungry enough to eat a horse," Steve said.

"Me too," Thom said.

"Oh, you guys should keep an anorexic body like mine. You wouldn't always be thinking about food," Darby said.

"Okay. We'll eat and you can wait for us," Thom said. "You've got enough pounds on you to live three months without food, big man."

"Okay, okay. I'm starving, too," Darby conceded. "I was just trying to talk for Ashton. If I had her figure, I would watch my calories. But I'm too far gone to worry about it."

"Oh, you don't need to talk for your high priced Ho, Mr. Pimp man. I can talk for myself, and I'm starving, too," Ashton said.

"Tell you what. I'll treat everyone to a steak dinner at Ruth's Chris. It's only a few blocks from where we're staying," I said as we got off the subway at our stop. I needed to do something to boost the morale. We would all need to be in top form mentally in the next few days.

"Great!!! That's a deal!" Steve shouted.

"Okay. It's 6:10. Let's go up to our rooms and we'll all meet in the lobby at 7:30. I'm going to have a drink in our room and relax a little, then we'll walk to the restaurant, have another drink and a great meal. I have a feeling we're going to be spending some long hours as we close in on the 11th," I said.

We agreed to do that and Ashton and I went to our room down the hall from the others.

"Sweetheart, I'm going to fix a drink and do a few pushups, stretches and sit ups while you take your shower, then I'll take mine. I need to unwind a little. Not accomplishing anything makes me tense. I know how the rest of you feel. I feel the same way. We'll just have fun tonight," I said, giving her a peck on the cheek.

"Okay. Fix me a little one, too. I'll be out in about ten minutes," she said, already starting to shed her shorts and blouse while heading to the bathroom.

I went down the hall and got some ice, poured a little gin from the bottle and stripped to my boxers and T shirt. I could hear the shower running in the bathroom.

I did a few pushups and stretches, sipped a little from the gin over rocks I had prepared, smoked a cigarette and got on the floor on my back to do a few sit ups. I already felt better and was looking forward to relaxing with the team tonight.

Ashton came out of the bathroom with a towel wrapped around her. She looked freshly scrubbed and her hair was damp, falling around her face in strings. Each time I saw her, especially like this just coming from the shower, I was newly amazed at how cute and sexy she was.

"Thanks for the drink, Love." She went over to the desk and took a sip from her drink, a gin and tonic. "What are you doing on your back on the floor?"

"I was getting ready to do a few sit ups before getting my shower. Now I'm out of the mood. I'd rather just look at you. You're beautiful, doll—and sexy, too," I said, still staring at her.

"Oh, I don't look sexy—or beautiful. My hair's stringing down my face and I'm dressed in a big white hotel towel. Now why do you think that's sexy?" she asked with a mischievous little grin.

"That's what is so sexy about you when I see you like this. You are always pretty, but, when I know you don't have anything on under that towel, my mind undresses you. And I know how nice you are underneath that towel," I said. I could tell that I was getting aroused and suspect she noticed, also.

"I guess I better take the towel off then. That way you won't stress your mind. You said you wanted to unwind. Do you want to help me unwind?" she asked.

She had dropped the towel and moved to where she was standing over me with her legs spread so that her feet were on either side of my waist. I was looking straight up into the thatch of damp hair between her shapely legs.

"Let me give you a closer look and let you unwind me, Love. Then I'll help you unwind," she said.

Then she knelt so that her love was now only inches away from my face. I could smell the fresh scent of her recent shower and the faint musky scent of what was hidden behind the damp clump in front of my face. She leaned forward slightly so that this part of her was pressed closer with the hair tickling my lips.

I took my fingers and gently spread her apart, making a path for me to insert my tongue into the now exposed pink flesh of her vagina. As I flicked in and out and around that little love hole, she moaned and pressed herself down so that I was deeper in her. I then started little short upward flicks with my tongue, caressing the sensitive part above the opening. She was now, ever so slightly, moving up and down, getting lost in the ecstasy of the feeling she was experiencing.

When I felt her shudder and sensed she was ready, I slid down to where the aching, throbbing part between my legs could enter her in the area I had been exploring with my tongue.

"Wait! Let me taste you first," she half gasped, quickly reversing her position and enveloping the part of me that was ready to enter into her in her mouth. She quickly ran her tongue around my shaft, then began a slow up and down motion.

As quickly as she had done that, she turned around again so that her now moist and steaming love hole was directly over the now steel-hard rod that was longing to be inside her. Before I could anticipate what she was doing she, still on top of me, sank herself down so that I plunged inside of her forcefully. She paused for a second with me deep inside her, slowly withdrew, then began a frantic up and down motion that quickly culminated in both of us exploding in a shudder of delight and ecstasy.

After it was over, she sank down cozily on top of me, limp from exhaustion. We lay that way for several minutes, then she softly kissed me and I returned the kiss tenderly.

"Love, it's almost 7:00. You better go on and get your shower and let me get dressed or we will be late," she said, reluctantly disengaging from our prone embrace.

"I know. I love you," I said, rising to head to the shower.

"I love you, too. A whole lot," she kissed me quickly and I went in to get my shower.

I came out at 7:15 and she was dressed in a straight skirt and blouse, had her hair combed and looked like the beautiful girl I had just made love to. My foremost thought was how lucky I was to be with her and have her love.

I didn't know what I would do if I lost that love. I began to get dressed.

"Hon," she said as I was dressing, "I'm scared about what might be happening in a few days. I just hope we can stop it some way. But tonight, after making love to you, I just want us to be happy with our friends and try, for a few hours to forget what's ahead."

"I know. I feel the same way, little girl. This is mine and your night to spend with the people we have been through so much with in a few short months," I agreed.

"I know I've told you this before, but our team is like a family to me. For the first time in my life, I feel like I am doing something important, like I'm needed—and loved."

I kissed her. "You are loved. By all of us. But you were doing something important before you met us."

"I know. But I was doing that to gain respect for myself and a meaning to my life. Now, I am involved in something, not just for myself, but for others— others that I like and that like me. And one that I love. Let's go," she smiled.

I was ready and she grabbed me by the hand and pulled me out of the room to catch the elevator and go down to the lobby and meet the others.

I would remember that night with love, and would remember her words with understanding. She was special—very special—and I would appreciate that even more than now, down the road.

CHAPTER FIFTY-EIGHT

Monday, September 8, 2003. The five of us were in Mike's office at 7:30 AM. The atmosphere was tense and charged. We all felt that we were just three days away from disaster, and we were no closer to finding out what the enemy had in mind and how they were going to do it than we were months ago. Where was the laser?

"Okay, here's the plan for the memorial and groundbreaking event" Mike started out, getting directly to business.

"The platform where the dignitaries, including the President, will be is being built on the East side of the former Trade Center area. Here. I'll show you on this layout of lower Manhattan." Mike proceeded to mark that point on the map he had hung on his wall.

"The main ceremony will begin just after dark. The President is scheduled to make his comments about 7:45 PM. Prior to that he will be, at our insistence, shielded by a heavy, bullet proof reflective glass, as will the rest of the dignitaries there to observe or take part in the ceremony. The President is expected to make a major policy speech further defining our war on terrorism. He can be expected to pretty much say that, no matter what success the terrorists might have on occasion, the U.S. will ultimately conquer them, they will not destroy our way of life or our freedoms—we are invincible," Mike continued.

"What perfect timing for an attack! The President states we are invincible, then he gets zapped!" Thom exclaimed.

"What kind of protection is being afforded to the President and other speakers once they get to the podium?" I asked.

"Well, that's where the problem lies," Mike said. "This event is going to be internationally televised to audiences in Europe, Asia, the Middle East—all over the world. The President's strategists want this speech to serve notice to our allies as well as our enemies, in no uncertain terms, that we will take the battle to the terrorists and the countries who harbor and support them—with or without our friends and regardless of the resistance we might meet from our enemies. The camera crews will be positioned in front of the podium.

The President insists that he should not be cocooned behind a protective, hard to see through, apparatus. He thinks that would send the wrong message to the people he is trying to reach. In other words—we're invincible, but our President has to hide behind a shield in his own country."

"Yeah, I can see that. Thick reflective glass would distort his image on the TV screens. The lights from the cameras would probably just reflect back to the point all you could see on TV would be a fuzzy image of a person standing behind the podium. Facial expressions would be totally lost, for example," Darby commented.

"Right. So it looks like the only opportunity to get the President will be when he is speaking. His talk is scheduled to last about fifteen minutes," Mike said.

"Will the British Prime Minister be there?" Ashton asked.

"Oh, yes. I forgot to mention that. The British and Canadian PMs and the Mexican President will all be there and each will make short 3 to 5 minute comments," Mike said.

"Well, they will not have but one shot before everyone else ducks for cover, but their presence lends PR to the terrorist's cause. It looks like, though, that the President will be the target," I said.

"I agree. They will have about a fifteen minute window between 7:45 and 8:00 PM to do their deed," Mike agreed.

"What else can you tell us, Mike?" I asked.

"A lot. Across the wide open space on each side of the speaker's stand, there will be a line of about 50 police cars on one side and, on the other, about 30 fire trucks. It will be dark. The vehicle lights will be trained to the center of the wide open area where the memorial statue has been constructed. It will be about 75 yards to the direct front of the speaker stand. The stand itself will have separate lighting designed to illuminate the speaker for the benefit of the cameras."

"The firemen and police will be there as a part of the ceremony due to their heroism when the Trade Center was hit I guess," Thom said.

"I'm sure that's correct. It will be impressive when they unveil the memorial statue illuminated by their lights," Mike said.

"Will all the participants—the firemen and police officers be checked out?" Steve asked.

"Absolutely! The trucks and cars will be identified by station and each person in the vehicles will be required to show positive identification. Their names will be relayed to the appropriate captains to ensure that they, in fact, are assigned to the particular unit scheduled to be there," Mike replied.

"What else, Mike?" I asked.

"At noon on the 11th , all buildings around the perimeter of the ceremony area will be evacuated and thoroughly searched. Even now, everyone entering any of those building is being searched to make sure no weapons of any kind, much less a 500 pound 12' laser, is brought in. We will have secured any site within a minimum of 300 yards from the speaker's stand," Mike responded.

"What about the crowd that will attend the ceremony?" Ashton asked.

"The whole area will be evacuated starting at noon. No one but approved security forces, FBI, CIA, U.S. Marshals and Secret Service people will be left inside. Then the entire area will be roped off with security people on the perimeter and only four entrance ways to the grounds. When they arrive that afternoon and evening, everyone will be thoroughly searched, carry ins limited to handbags which will be X-rayed and facial ID equipment will be used. Everyone arriving will be thoroughly searched, including camera crews, dignitaries and their staffs—everyone."

"It sounds like you have every base covered," Steve commented.

"We think we have. This affair, because of the implications it has, combined with the threats and the known intelligence about a strike directed towards the President before the end of this year, as well as the information relative to the laser, is probably the most security intense operation we have ever had for one function on U.S. soil. But, I know that Infama knows that the situation is likely to be what it is. And my gut feel is that they have a plan that they think will somehow allow them to slip through our security net. That's why I can't sleep at night," Mike replied.

"And we don't have a clue as to what that plan is," I said thoughtfully.

"No. And that's scary. The only remaining information I have to give you is no information. We have re-studied the piece of paper that Ashton found at the barn and rechecked everything we know about Freightliner, its parent, Daimler Chrysler and its subsidiary American LeFrance. There is absolutely nothing that jumps out that is meaningful in any way to our investigation. Our people think it was probably just a scrap piece of paper they found around there to write their grocery list on. But a nagging feeling tells me that it has more significance than that," Mike said.

"You mentioned in the last meeting that American LeFrance is the leading manufacturer of fire trucks in the nation. And there are going to be 30 fire trucks at the 9-11 ceremony. Could this have any kind of significance?" Steve asked.

"Perhaps. But I can't dream up a scenario that would involve this company or their product in any terrorist act on 9-11—or anytime for that matter. As I said, the trucks that are to be there and the people with them will be checked carefully. Surely Infama knows that. If they have a plan that has any realistic significance to American LeFrance, for the life of me, I can't think of what it might be," Mike said quietly.

"What do you want us to do the next three days, Mike—and the night of the ceremony?" I asked.

"Good question. For the next three days, and on up to close to the beginning of the ceremony, I want your team to double check our security surrounding the grounds where the event will take place. I want you to personally go recheck those buildings that are supposed to have been secured, especially after noon on 9-11. Make double sure they are, in fact, secure. I want you to review the policies and procedures that have been set up for crowd security and for the inspection of the people involved in the ceremony whether they are media people, dignitaries, fire, police personnel—whoever will be inside that 300 yard perimeter that night," Mike said.

"Your major focus will be to try to find a loophole in security or a vantage point that has been overlooked from which the laser might accurately be fired. It could be a janitor's storage room with a window that allows a direct line of fire within the 300 yard radius that our other people have overlooked. It could be a bell tower in a church, although I don't think that a church is located within that radius. It could be any place that all the other people may have overlooked," Mike continued.

"What about the evening of the ceremony?" I asked.

"I want three of you on the ground facing away from the speaker stand. That would be the most vulnerable area for an attack to come from because of the obstacle of getting around or through the protective wall of reflective glass that will be behind the review stand. If anything looks amiss, take action immediately! Steve, you and Darby and Thom need to be in that position," Mike instructed.

"What about me and Ashton?" I asked.

"I want you two in a helicopter circling the grounds doing the same thing—observing. We have a copter and two well trained pilots available to you. You all—the five of you—will be in constant communication with each other and will have a direct line of communication to the commander of the joint security forces for the event," Mike answered.

"Do I have authority to land if I see something?" I asked.

"Yes. As quickly as you can get down. And these pilots can put you on a dime in ten seconds. Just be sure you inform the command post before you decide to come down or someone may shoot at you," Mike replied.

After discussing a few more details, the meeting broke up. It was about noon. We left to begin the task that had been assigned to us. We were now entering the last inning of this critical ballgame and the last strike would be thrown between 7:45 PM and 8:00 PM four nights from now. We just didn't know who would pitch that strike.

I decided to start carrying a 9mm 15-round clip Berretta automatic pistol in a paddle holster, in addition to my Cobra, starting today. It would prove to be a wise decision because we would end up needing all the firepower we could muster on that night.

CHAPTER FIFTY-NINE

September 11, 2003. It was 4:00 PM and people were already beginning to stream in. The previous three days, we had done what Mike had asked of us, and had found only a couple of loopholes that portrayed a remote possibility of a vantage point. The people in charge of perimeter security had actually done an excellent job.

The five of us were observing the security in place for early arriving spectators, lighting and sound crews and others that had a need to be there early. Security was extremely tight. We were very pleased with what we had seen so far, but we shared Mike's intuition that something was being overlooked.

The event would start at 7:00 PM sharp with the Mayor of New York, the former Mayor and both State Senators making brief comments. Then the Governor would address the crowd and introduce the President of Mexico, the Canadian Prime Minister and the British Prime Minister who would each make short comments stressing North American and British solidarity in the fight against terrorism. Then the President would be introduced, at which time he would make about a 15 minute speech. Although the schedule of time spent by each speaker except for the President had been held very firm, the news media had been informed that, with introductions, the schedule could slide about five minutes. That was no problem for the media. The talking heads could begin to anticipate the President's remarks and analyze what had yet to be said.

At the end of the President's speech, he would stay at the lectern and preside over the unveiling of the memorial statue, heaping praise upon the brave firefighters, police officers and many other departments as well as civilians who gave their effort and, a number of them, their lives in that day of tragedy in 2001. Therefore, we would have a window of possible attack of 20 to 25 minutes total, when the President would be openly exposed.

"Well, this is it, guys. Something might be planned later in the year for the Laser, but all the intelligence we have indicates it will be tonight. And, once it is fired, it is gone. There is no way they could get away or get the weapon out. Probably they have kept the plans where they could develop another one over a period of months, but the technicians who know how to operate it will most certainly be behind the gun tonight. They will be caught or killed after it is fired. We have already disrupted the part of the organization that has been involved in its development and implementation enough that it very well could take over a year to train or find the people to build and operate another one, and they may well decide not to try this route again—whether they are successful or not," I speculated to the team.

"I agree," Ashton said. "This will probably be a one shot assassination attempt in this manner. Future laser weaponry by anyone will probably be designed for much larger uses, such as missile defense or large offensive weapons against big targets. This system doesn't really lend itself well to hand-operated use. Its force is so destructive, though, that what they have represents a unique way of individual attack that will probably become obsolete after the first time its used."

"So tonight is the night most likely. After that each of us will go off in different directions to our respective departments and jobs," Steve said.

"I hadn't really thought of that," Thom reflected. "You're right. Tonight could end with the dissolution of our Laser Team."

"Yeah. You know, I'm going to miss all you guys," Darby said.

"Yeah. Me too. Let's make a pact right now to stay in touch after this thing is over, and try to get together once in a while," Thom said.

We all shared the same feelings and agreed to do that. We all would be very relieved to see the Laser hunt brought to a conclusion. And we tried not to even think about the possibility that it could be a disastrous conclusion. But the other part of each of our minds hated to leave the camaraderie we had established with each other. None of us liked to think about tonight being the end of our association with each other, but we all knew that was likely to be the case.

"Well, its almost 5:00. Ashton and I better be getting over to the copter pad. Mike wanted us to be in the air by 5:30 so we could see if we detected anything developing on the ground from our vantage point," I said.

We all shook hands as everyone got ready to move to their positions. Darby, Steve and Thom would move to the right front of the speaker's stand so as not to interfere with the TV cameras. They would be on the side where the fire trucks would line up and try to observe the entire front.

"Be alert. And be careful. Whatever plan Infama has for tonight, you can bet the people here on the scene will be well armed and intent on firing the gun during that window of opportunity. If we or the other security forces don't detect it in time, they will engage us or whoever comes after them, hoping to kill as many as they can before being taken out. If we do detect it before use, their fallback will be to kill as many of us as they can before being overtaken. Either way, its going to be war," I cautioned.

"Good luck, guys. Call us if you see anything and we'll do the same," I said as Ashton and I departed.

We were in the air by 5:30 PM and began to slowly circle the area. Bob Klien and Joe LaFerge were the pilots. We reviewed with them what might be required of them if we sighted anything. They understood and were ready.

By six o'clock the grounds were near capacity with people. The sun was getting low in the sky. With less than an hour until the event started, we were getting taunt with anticipation and straining to see anything that looked suspicious. So far, nothing.

The police cars and fire trucks were not in place. They would come in during the closing remarks by the Governor, right before his introduction of the President. They would make a grand entrance with their overhead lights flashing and headlights on, but there would be no sirens. The silent procession of emergency vehicles arriving and lining up in place just before the President went to the podium would set the stage for an eerie, but emotional kickoff to his remarks. They would turn on their sirens at the moment the President ordered the statue to be unveiled and their headlights would already be directed towards the statue. It was going to be some ceremony. Those of us involved in security operations could feel the impact of this momentous occasion, but would not really be able to enjoy it in our constant state of tenseness and alert.

7:00 PM arrived and the event started precisely on time with the current Mayor of New York making his opening comments.

The procession of dignitaries making their comments went along smoothly. They were staying close to schedule. Finally, the President of Mexico was introduced, then the Canadian Prime Minister. Our stomachs began to tighten. We knew that our team members on the ground were experiencing the same feelings. We knew the British PM would be next, then the President would be introduced. The time was 7:43 PM. It was now very dark.

We had been circling for more than two hours, straining to see every minute detail on the ground below. The strain had taken its toll on us, but was now replaced by a shot of adrenaline. We were as ready and alert as anyone could possibly be at this moment.

"Love, this is it," Ashton whispered, reaching for my hand and giving it a squeeze. I leaned over and kissed her on her cheek, returning the squeeze.

The British Prime Minister came to the lectern amid loud cheers. Great Britain had always been our strongest partner and ally in times of trouble. He made a rousing speech and received applause that went on for a full four minutes. His presence and his speech, in addition to the crowd's anticipation of the President had the crowd in a frenzied state of emotion.

The time was 7:52 PM. After the applause died and the PM had returned to his seat behind the protective barrier, the Governor came to the podium just as the police cars and fire trucks started into the arena with their lights flashing through the crowd as they began to get in their respective positions. The impact of that scene brought quietness to the crowd as the vehicles slowly moved into position. The theatrical effect of what was going on was magnificent.

The Governor thanked the previous speakers for their comments, thanked the crowd for being there to witness this historic event, then cleared his throat for the introduction of the President. Before he even got the words out of his mouth, the crowd began to roar. From the air, even flying low with the side doors open, we could barely hear his words over the loudspeaker.

"And now, ladies and gentlemen—I am honored to introduce the President of the United States of America!!!"

CHAPTER SIXTY

Ashton and I tensed and, by reflex, checked our weapons for readiness. We did a low fly around the perimeter and could see Darby, Thom and Steve standing to the right side of the President's stand. Their very body language showed that they were as tense and alert as we were as they peered intently out to the front of the speaker's platform. The next 25 minutes would, we all felt, produce the Laser. And it was up to us to sight some sign of it prior to its being put to its devastating use.

When the President began his speech, the lights all went out on the police cars lined to his left and the fire trucks to his right. The spotlight was on him and there was no other distraction visible in the arena at that time. We had been told that, when the moment arrived to unveil the memorial statue, all the car and truck lights would be turned on and focused on the shrouded statue in the center of the open space in front of the President. The whole thing was very dramatic and, even in our state of anxiety, we couldn't help feeling the chills go up our spine as this momentous occasion for the American people began to unfold.

The President made a rousing speech and was interrupted eleven times by spontaneous applause and two prolonged shouts of "USA...USA...USA!!!" The speech was going to run over the allotted 15 minutes by at least five minutes. We strained futilely to see anything amiss and were close to exhaustion when it became obvious that he was approaching his closing remarks prior to unveiling the monument. I was drenched in perspiration.

We would only have about ten more minutes of his exposure between the end of his speech and the conclusion of the memorial ceremony. Hope against hope tried to make us believe that maybe nothing would happen after all. But the other part of all our minds begged for this thing to come to a conclusion with the detection and destruction of the laser and those who would operate it. We just felt so vulnerable because we didn't know of any additional precautions that could be taken, but— if they were here, we knew they had thought of something that we had not thought of. Mike had stayed in constant contact. I could tell by the tone of his voice that he was frustrated and worried also.

"In closing, friends and fellow Americans, I want to reiterate to the world—we will not be blackmailed, we will not be intimidated, we will not abandon our policies or our way of life to accommodate a bunch of brutal, evil, cowardly thugs whose only response to common decency or common sense is to spread their senseless, fanatical terror through our land and that of our allies in this war on terrorism. We will defeat them. We will find them wherever they hide. If there are those countries out there who sympathize with and support these criminals—beware. The United States will hold you responsible for their actions as well. We—will—not—tolerate any attack on any citizen of the United States of America here or abroad!! You—you who challenge our will and our determination—take notice. Your deeds will not go unanswered! Our brave citizens, soldiers and professional people dedicated to our safety will respond, just as they did two years ago. If any individual, group or country doubts that resolve, you will be making a big mistake. We are strong! We are united. We are free!"

There was once again thunderous applause. Then the President began the line that was to be the cue to start the unveiling ceremony.

"Thank you. And now, let us celebrate the lives of all those brave people who lost their lives here and in Washington and Pennsylvania on that infamous day. We are gathered here tonight especially to commemorate the selfless bravery of our New York City Fire, Police and Emergency Service workers who answered the call of duty."

This was the prearranged signal for all the vehicles to turn their headlights on, with the beams directed toward the veiled statue in the center of the arena. Again, another chill went up our spines and, I'm sure everyone in attendance felt the same way. There was a deadly silence that allowed the President to close with his succinct final comment.

"They went above and beyond what would be expected of them in attempts to ensure the safety of their fellow countrymen. And so many of them lost their lives in that effort. Let us take this opportunity, fellow citizens, as we unveil the statue that will honor their memory forever, to vow that we will not ever allow this to happen again—ever! Their deaths will be avenged. All who threaten us will pay the ultimate price for their arrogant and ignorant brutality. I personally make that promise as I ask you to join me in saluting those brave men and women who paid the ultimate sacrifice for our country. Your deaths were not in vain. Your memory will live on forever."

With that comment the shroud was removed from the statue and the

President sharply saluted the depiction of the firemen raising the American flag amidst the rubble of the destruction of that day. As the statue was revealed in the illumination of the vehicle headlights, a ghostly silence remained while many in the crowd held salutes and shed silent tears.

It was at that moment that I noticed it. The trucks were lined up in a precision formation—except for one. One of the fire truck's lights was not directed toward the memorial. The lights on that truck were directed towards the platform where the President was standing and the truck was actually angled in that direction! It must have quietly changed its position during the President's closing remarks. He was scheduled to remain there for about five minutes more and close the ceremony with a brief remark.

"Darby!" I shouted on the phone. "Fire truck number eleven on the right! I'm going down!!"

I shouted for Bob Klien to take the copter down and land right in front of that truck. I could see Darby, Thom and Steve on the ground racing toward truck number 11. They were only about 75 yards away. My cell phone rang as Klien immediately banked and headed down. I grabbed it frantically. It was Mike.

"Dawson!! A fire truck was found behind a vacant lot on the West Side about ten minutes ago!! It's crew had been murdered! It was NYFD # 610!!," Mike bellowed.

"I know!! We see it and its' water cannon is directed toward the President! Darby's group is on the way and I'll be on the ground in less than a minute!!" I shouted into the phone.

Now we knew what the connection to American LeFrance was. They had apparently utilized schematics obtained on the Fire Trucks to modify the water cannon so that it would adapt to the laser! Then they had painted it with the logo of the 610 unit, murdered the crew, stolen their identification and moved into position with the other units. Their plan had taken a lot of planning and coordination. Now the question was could we stop them in time from carrying out their objective. We probably only had seconds!! It may already be too late.

I shuddered with the recollection of the laser hitting the Mennonite buggy and fully expected to see the deadly beam shoot out from the cannon before we positioned ourselves in front of it. The crowd below fanned away from us beneath the prop wash as we hovered 30 feet above the ground, waiting until they got out of the way before dropping down in front of the truck. I could hear screams of terror above the sound of the rotating blades as we forced our way closer to the ground. And Ashton and I held our breath, expecting at any moment to be disintegrated by the beam of light as we came closer to obstructing their fire path. In a quick glance at the speaker's platform, I saw the President's security detail rushing towards the stand to push him back behind the shield. But they wouldn't make it in time.

It was no time to take chances. We may be wrong, thinking this truck had the laser and was on the brink of firing it. If we were, innocent firemen would be killed if we attacked. Darby, who was in the lead and now alongside the truck, made the right decision. He immediately opened fire on the visible occupants in and on the truck.

We set down and Ashton and I jumped off the copter. Dust from the rotor blades blinded us momentarily, but I heard the static sound of small arms and automatic weapons fire as the truck occupants opened fire on Darby, and Thom and Steve who were now just behind him.

The dust cleared just in time for me to see Darby lurch forward and fall face down on the ground alongside the fire truck. With weapons drawn and blazing, Ashton and I joined the fray. I could feel my 9mm jump each time a bullet left the muzzle. I was firing indiscriminately at any target I could see. The truck was exploding with armed men. We would learn later that there were nine of them on board, including the two technicians that were at the farm whose responsibility was to activate the laser.

Darby had taken one of them out in his initial charge. But the remaining one pulled the trigger and, with a silent, blinding blast, a beam of light shot toward the review stand!

We had our hands full and could not even check to see if the laser found its mark. I saw Steve at my right jump on the side of the truck and blast the side of one of the AR people's head off just as he was taking aim at me.

Ashton shot the driver when he tried to jump out of the truck with a pistol. He fell with a thud at my feet. In the meantime, Thom was wrestling with one of the assailants on the ground. He had grabbed him by the neck, forcefully pulling him off the truck. They both fell in a struggling tangle to my immediate right. Careful not to hit Thom, I held my Cobra right above his right ear and pulled the trigger. His head exploded into a bloody, mushy mass. I noticed a deep gash on Thom's cheek where a bullet had grazed him when he jerked his antagonist off the truck.

I grabbed the dropped AR and quickly was able to drop two men as they came around the side of the truck with guns blazing. In doing so, I felt a sharp sting in my left arm as a bullet pierced it just as one of my attackers fell forward, still squeezing off shots as he died.

Steve shot the other technician in the back while he was trying to run into the scattered and horrified crowd of people who were pushing and shoving to get out of the line of fire. I turned just in time to see one of the remaining two men bringing his rifle up to a firing position aimed right at my head. Instinctively, knowing I didn't have time, I ducked and saw him fall forward, landing at my feet. Ashton had seen him and shot just as he was getting ready to fire. Her bullet had hit him right between the eyes and stopped him cold before he could pull the trigger.

Steve and Thom simultaneously shot the remaining Infama assassin who was just standing there looking dazed with his gun dangling lifelessly at his side.

All at once it was silent in our little world. Close around us, but seeming to be in a distance, we could hear the sounds of the hysterical crowd still surging in pandemonium away from us to get out of harm's way, and the sounds of sirens and other security personnel on the grounds rushing to the scene.

For a brief moment though, we were alone, standing exhausted and wounded. The acrid smell off gunpowder wafted gently in the breeze around us.

Darby was lying ten feet away from me, his face still in the dust. I knelt beside him and touched the side of his face gently. I heard a groan but he wasn't moving. I leaned closer and called his name.

"Dawson—I'm hit bad. I can't move. I think the bullet hit my spine," he managed to weakly respond.

Emergency medical personnel rushed in and began to gently roll him onto a stretcher, making sure his back and neck were supported. I grasped his hand while they loaded him into an ambulance. He squeezed my hand slightly before they closed the door and rushed him to the nearest hospital.

Teary eyed and still bleeding profusely from the wound in my arm, I saw Mike rushing through the crowd.

"The President??" I asked when Mike got alongside me.

"He's okay, Dawson. They got him out of the line of fire just in the nick of time. I was watching the whole thing from the command post over there. If Darby had not opened fire when he did, it would have been a different story. You would have been seconds late, I think. They appeared to be ready to fire the laser just as the President brought down his salute," Mike said soberly.

"Let's go see Darby," I said.

"Right. First, let Ashton check the laser and make sure it is inoperable. We'll have it sent to the lab and have the NIF people evaluate it to see how advanced their practical technology was. Then it will be held for evidence if we can at some point apprehend Alziddi and his cohorts and bring them to trial. Okay, Ashton?" Mike asked.

"Sure. It shouldn't take more than five minutes to disconnect some wires to make sure it won't go off by accident in handling and transportation," Ashton replied. "Love, let the medics look at your arm and Thom's cheek while I'm doing that," she added.

"Good idea. I'll have a staff car brought over to take all of you to the hospital to see Darby and take care of your wounds as soon as Ashton does her thing," Mike said.

My arm wound was a clean flesh wound and had not broken any bones. Thom's wound was a crease. He was lucky. A few centimeters over, and he would have been dead. The medic said we would both heal easily, but Thom would have a deep scar on his cheek that would most likely require plastic surgery at a later date to hide.

The staff car took several minutes to wind its way through the skittish crowd. The President had come back to the podium and tried to calm the remaining people in attendance, telling them and the worldwide TV audience that we would be undaunted in our attempts to bring to justice all of those people responsible for this heinous incident. He also told them that our intelligence had been aware of this plot for several months and had been tracking the perpetrators all over the world. He revealed that a team of people drawn from the FBI, CIA, Secret Service and private citizens who volunteered to serve on this team with full knowledge of the risk involved had joined together to stop this latest threat to our security, proving that our agencies can work together to defend our country. And he heaped lavish praise on our secret small team who had sacrificed some of their lives to find the people directly responsible, foil their attempt at the last possible second and make them pay the price that all terrorists will ultimately pay for attacks on our nation, its' leaders and its' citizens.

While waiting on the car and listening to the President's remarks, Ashton and I held each other tightly, silently thankful that we had survived and reflecting with remorse the deaths of Ernest, Percy and Larry and the condition of Darby, at this time unknown, Ashton's pretty face was smudged and her hair was tossed loosely around her face. She looked like a beautiful little doll who had been tossed around by rough kids. Thom and Steve were close by.

Our Laser Team had survived and remained in place to accomplish the team objective. The cost had been great. But, along the way, two people had fallen deeply in love with each other, and we all had evolved into lifelong friends with a bond to each other that only experiences together like what we had gone through could forge.

Now it was over. But I knew—and I think Ashton knew—that it wasn't over. Not yet. The car finally arrived and we left for the hospital.

CHAPTER SIXTY-ONE

At the hospital, Thom and I got quick attention on our minor wounds. The bullet that hit me went through the fleshy part of my upper arm and exited out the other side. The wound was cleaned, a couple of stitches taken at the exit hole, a tetanus shot, then my arm was bandaged. It would be a little sore for a while. Otherwise, I would be okay. Thom's wound was cleaned and bandaged after application of an antiseptic ointment. It would heal quickly, but would require some work later to hide the scar. In 20 minutes we were all on our way to surgery to check on Darby.

When we arrived at the surgical department, Darby was being operated on. The bullet was removed, then a neurosurgeon was called in to examine him before closing the incision. He was taken off critical status and designated as guarded. The operating Doctor finally came out and told us there was no life threatening danger, but they were concerned with the damage to his spine where a fragment of the bullet had lodged. The neurosurgeon would remove that and give us a prognosis when he was finished.

We waited patiently for another hour. Finally, the surgeon came out and asked us to come back to his office. There he told us that Darby was strong and would recover from the wound quickly—except that he was 95% certain that Darby would be paralyzed from the waist down for the rest of his life. The fragment had destroyed two vertebra and severed a portion of the spinal cord. Technology did not currently exist that could repair or replace the damaged areas. There was still remote hope because miracles had happened in injuries such as this where the nerve had somehow, over time, healed itself. But, even partial recovery was extremely rare. He gave scant hope that Darby would ever walk again.

The four of us and Mike, who had come with us, were devastated. In our minds, Darby was the big, strong, tough guy that could handle any physical situation. We couldn't picture him being confined to a wheel chair. More importantly, we couldn't picture him accepting his condition.

The Doctors allowed us to all go in for a couple of minutes to see him before we left. He was still under heavy sedation and had not yet been told of his condition.

"You guys got the worst end of this fight," he grinned weakly. "I'm going to be okay as soon as I come out of this dream world they put me in. In the meantime, have you seen that pretty nurse who's been hovering around me? She's almost as pretty as you are, Ashton. You guy's are jealous now, aren't you?" he asked, looking at Steve and Thom.

"Hang in there, big guy. Since you're so dopey, we're going to leave now, but we'll be back to see you tomorrow afternoon," I said, squeezing his hand. The Doctor had motioned us that our time was up.

It was after midnight when we all finally got back to our hotel, tired, dirty and battle weary. Ashton and I said goodnight to Steve and Thom.

"We'll see you guys for breakfast in the morning—a late breakfast, okay? About 7:00. Then maybe we can go back over together to see Darby in the early afternoon. Then I guess we better talk to Mike about how we disband our team since the purpose has been fulfilled. We are going to all stay in touch though. Right?" Steve asked before we broke up.

"Right," I said. "See you tomorrow."

Ashton sat on the edge of the bed. She still looked disheveled, but so cute. She sat there quietly, just looking at me expectantly. I kissed her on the cheek and sat down beside her. It was time for us to be honest with each other. Our trip was over now. We both, I think, had been dreading this time.

"Well, Love. I guess we need to talk. You know, don't you?" she asked quietly.

"Yes," I answered.

"I guess when two people love each other, it's hard to hide secrets. When did you find out?" she asked, a tear coming into her eye.

"Hon, the knowledge was progressive. There were several things. First, I need to tell you that our initial meeting in Atlanta wasn't a chance meeting. I was sent to Atlanta to find you and establish a relationship with you which might lead to information regarding illegal transfer of secure information which you were suspected to be involved in. No other person at NIF would have had the complete knowledge of the entire system that we suspected had been leaked out."

"You were under suspicion from the beginning because you were one of only a handful of people who had access to this technology and, in fact, were a primary contributor to its development," I continued. "Along the way, I was able to pick up circumstantial evidence that you were the source of the information that ended up in Infama's hands."

"Like what?" she asked, her lower lip trembling.

"Well, the first thing was the name Cedric that was found among the fragments of scorched notes we found in Mahmoud's room after he blew himself up. One portion, if you recall, mentioned Cedric and the Laser Team. Our thinking from the interpretation of the fragments of info was that Cedric might be the code name of the contact at NIF who passed the info on to them. The last message we saw was, you remember, fairly legible. And it mentioned you as the Smyth bitch and your seven associates. They knew you had joined us and the message said you made a big mistake and would pay with your life."

"Yes, I remember," she hung her head.

"Then, remember a little later when we were still in Manhattan I went down and picked up the mail?" I asked.

"Yes. That was the day you got the letter from your ex wife telling you she was re-marrying."

"Right. And I also brought a letter for you from Skipper."

"I remember. Later, before we left Manhattan, we met Skipper for dinner," Ashton agreed.

"Yes. I enjoyed meeting him. He's as nice as you had told me. The letter, though, had his real name on the return address. I noticed it was a fairly unusual name—Cedric. His nickname is Skipper. And, at dinner that night, you two were joking about you always using his name on things when you were growing up together so he could get credit for some of your accomplishments."

Ashton's eyes dropped again. "There must have been more. What you have told me so far is circumstance and coincidence."

"Yes. The confirmation of my suspicions occurred in Jakarta. When we were leaving to visit Abduel Hassan, you said you were sick and couldn't go with us. You said you were having your period and had the cramps really bad. You planned on meeting us later after the meeting with Hassan. I saw no evidence that you were actually having your period at that time and got the feeling you were trying to duck meeting up face-to-face with Hassan. Was he the contact that the information was passed on to?"

"Yes," she said quietly. "But still, you had no facts, just suspicions."

"I know. I found the first fact in Hassan's office when I had the opportunity to scan his money transfer records to confirm that funds had been transferred to Reza Pahlavi's account. This was before the intrusion of the other guys that blew our cover as to why we were there. One of the notations on the same page as Reza's transfer was noted for the X-Ray project. It was a transfer to NIF at Lawrence Livermore in September, 2002. It referred to the Cedric Agreement. Ashton, your name was penciled in the margin of that document."

"So you've known for sure since then?" Ashton asked.

"Yes, and I noticed how Hassan, when he finally saw you down by the waterfront, gave you special attention and indicated he would save you for Alziddi and that you could help them," I admitted.

"Yeah. Special attention. He beat the hell out of me, then took me to Alziddi who did worse," she said wryly.

"I know, Hon. And I'm sorry for that. They were getting back at you for what appeared to them as a double-cross because you were working with us. I made Hassan pay for that abuse and hope I meet up with Alziddi some time."

"What else did you find out during our time together?" Ashton asked meekly.

"Well, there were some other little things along the way. But when we got back to D.C. you remember we met Bob Willoughby coming out of Mike's office August 27th?" I asked.

"Yes. Does he know?" Ashton asked fearfully.

"Yes. He didn't want to know. But like you told me one time, in the end, Bob usually does the right thing. He had found evidence at the facility that a small bit of the information that was given to Hassan was material that only you had access to. It related to some of the latest refinements of the system that you had worked on and not yet had the opportunity to share with the others at the time of the transfer."

"I know he's disappointed in me," Ashton said quietly.

"No. He reluctantly shared the information with Mike on the condition that how we used it would take into consideration your sacrifice and effort to recapture the information. Bob thinks the world of you, both professionally and personally, and is convinced that you didn't realize what you were doing when you passed the laser technology on to the Infama people."

"I did know it was wrong to share any of the facility's information with any outsider without the express approval of Bob," Ashton said. Her eyes were moist and her shoulders slumped in defeat.

"Why did you do it, Ashton?" I asked.

"Dawson, you are one of the few people who knows my background. All that I told you about that is true. I don't offer this as an excuse, merely a motivation. My self-esteem had been so low since I was 16 that I longed to do something important that would cause people to respect me. The job at NIF gave me that opportunity. As I told you earlier, I totally engrossed myself into the work. I had very little social life. And I was probably as excited as Bob and more than most of the others when we made the technology breakthrough. I was an integral part of the research and experimentation that achieved that heretofore unknown capability. It was somewhat by accident that the capability was revealed to us through experimentation along a more traditional line of thinking. But it was me that dared to try something a little different that resulted in the breakthrough. I didn't know exactly where I was going, but had this feeling that there was a potential out there that we had not found yet."

"And then the funding was cut off, before the project was completed?" I questioned.

"Yes. I was devastated. We all were."

"How did Hassan find you?"

"I really don't know. All I know is one night he visited me at my apartment. At first I was scared. I had no idea who he was. And I really didn't have a clue who he was until after the FBI got involved, after it was discovered that the information had been copied and left the facility. Maybe they picked on me because I was so young. They must have known I was heavily involved in the research for the project. And, somehow, they must have known that the project, on the verge of success, had been halted due to lack of funding. That much he did tell me that night. The rest I just don't know about."

"What did he offer that caused you to agree to do his bidding?" I asked.

Ashton looked up at me sharply with a defiant look. "I got nothing personally for doing it! Absolutely nothing. I didn't ask for anything and he didn't offer!"

"So, why?"

Her eyes teared again. "I don't know. I really don't know. I was so naïve. He told me that he represented a group of people who had a lot of money and that they could possibly greatly benefit financially from the completion of this project. I assumed that he was with a company that might have been involved in manufacturing defensive or offensive weapons for the government. He led me to believe that, because of the potential value of this development to his group, they would be willing to fund the completion of the project."

"How did you respond to him when he indicated that?"

"I was delighted! When he offered all that money, it fulfilled all of our hopes at NIF. We could get private funding to complete what we had worked on for so many months. My first reaction was one of appreciation and I offered to call Bob and ask him to come over right then to talk to him."

"What did he say to that?"

"He emphatically said no. He stated that a condition of making the funds available would be to be given the complete file of the information we had developed to date on the super laser. He said there was no way the government would let that information out of the facility and that bureaucratic restraints would continue to stall, and probably eventually kill, the project. That was the first inkling I had that this strange man was going to ask me to do something that I knew to be illegal."

"And how did you respond to that?" I asked.

"I was shocked. But I continued to listen. He outlined the mechanics of getting the information and Lawrence Livermore receiving the funds. He emphasized that by presenting the information to him, I would be single handily saving the project. The NIF people, the government, all the citizens of the U.S. and, indeed the world, would owe a debt of gratitude to me. But I would never be thanked, because no one would know but me. If Bob or anyone else knew, they would be inclined to report it to the bureaucrats and the result would be the opportunity would never be presented because it would surely be against some government policy or procedure. He said I would just have to do this for myself—for my own knowledge and self worth." She began to cry again.

"So you told him you would do it?"

"Not that night. I couldn't sleep that night. I wanted desperately to talk to Bob or someone, but I couldn't. Hassan made that clear. If I talked, the deal wouldn't go down."

"When did you agree?"

"He called two nights later. I agreed to meet with him at a specified location. He implied that his request was urgent, plausible, appropriate, and even patriotic. I knew it was against the law, but I wanted to see the project completed. I knew that everyone at NIF did, too. And I truly felt this technology would ultimately be of benefit to our country for domestic as well as military use. I had begun to feel that the fact it was illegal was a technicality similar to sitting at a red-light in the middle of the desert with no traffic visible in either direction for as far as you could see. And sometimes common sense overrules policy. Or at least that is how I was thinking at the time. Like I said, I was naïve."

"How did you feel when you discovered the probable use of the secrets you had given to Hassan?" I asked.

"I was scared. But it was too late to change what I had done. I was sorry I had been such a fool. My self worth went back down to zero. It was *dejuvu*. I had done what I had rationalized to think was right and was actually proud that I had the courage to do what few, if any, of my colleagues would have done. Then when I found out "the rest of the story" as Paul Harvey would say, I was so devastated I wanted to go hide somewhere."

"But you didn't."

"No. Part of my background taught me to survive and to try to make things that were wrong right. That's why I was so anxious to join your team. I was also mad that I had been taken advantage of. I wanted to be a part of the effort to get the secrets back and stop whatever devilish plan they had to utilize the information I had given them. But I didn't know how to start doing that until you came along. Joining your team gave me the opportunity to join with a group of people who had expertise in tracking down these kinds of things and people. And I felt I could contribute to that effort because I knew what we were looking for."

"You did."

"Thanks. I tried," Ashton smiled weakly through her tears. "Now, what are you going to do with me, Love? I guess we both were deceiving each other the whole trip. Was everything deception with you? It wasn't with me."

"Not everything. I'm going to have to have you arrested and stand trial. You will go to prison. The jail term could be life imprisonment but, under the circumstances, should be less," I answered evenly.

Tears flowed freely in Ashton's eyes now, but she held her head up and tried to compose herself. She only asked one question. "When?"

"It's almost 4:00 AM now. We may as well stay up the rest of the night. We need to talk. I asked the U.S. Marshals to come by at 6:00 AM. Thom and Steve wanted to meet for breakfast about 7:00. You will be gone before they stop in."

We did talk—for the rest of the night until about 5:30 AM.

"Do you mind if I take a shower and get cleaned up a little before the Marshals get here? I'm filthy and look a mess. It would feel nice to put on some nice clothes before I have to change to jailhouse orange. I guess I should look nice when I leave," she said, her lip quivering.

"Go ahead. You are beautiful like you are, but I understand. I'll wait for you," I said.

"Thanks. I'll be out in a minute," she smiled, gazing into my eyes as she picked out a nice skirt and blouse and started to the shower.

When she came back out about twenty minutes later she was the same pretty girl I had met so many months ago. Each time she came into the room, I renewed my admiration for her. The tears had made her seem so vulnerable and I was so sorry to be a part of what was just one more bad chapter in her life.

"You look beautiful," I said, kissing her on the cheek.

There was a knock on the door. It was the two Marshals. She quietly let them cuff her and they left, going down the hall toward the elevators where we were on the fourth floor. Before she left, she turned to me.

"I'm not afraid. I'm used to rain. There will always be sunshine. I'll try to find it when the rain goes away. I love you. I trust you. I still believe in dreams. I still believe in 'we'." She turned and followed the Marshals down the hall, never looking back again.

I walked to the end of the hall by the elevators after they had gone down and looked out the window to the street. The Marshal's car was parked just below and I saw them lead her to the car and let her in the back seat. I know she couldn't see me standing there, but she paused before getting in the car and turned and looked upward for a couple of seconds before the Marshals closed the door, got in and drove away. I wiped a tear from my eye and went back to the room.

I sipped on coffee and brooded the next 45 minutes. There was a knock on the door. It was Steve and Thom.

"Ready to go?" Thom asked.

"Yeah."

"Where's Ashton?" Steve asked.

"She won't be joining us," I replied.

"I hate that. But she never was much for breakfast. Boy, I'm starved!" Steve said.

"Me too," I replied.

"You look like you've been up all night," Thom remarked as we walked to the elevator.

"I have."

We got to the lobby and walked out the front door. It had rained earlier that morning, but now the bright sun was peeking out behind fluffy white clouds drifting across the blue sky.

"The sun's out!" Steve exclaimed as we stepped outside. "What a beautiful day!"

"Yes, it is. Didn't you know? The sun always comes out after a rain," I said.

EPILOGUE

Monday, September 15, 2003, the three remaining active members of the Laser Team —Dawson Kohler, Thom Henson and Steve Whitt— met in Mike Reilly's office and the Laser Team was officially disbanded.

Dr. Thom Henson returned to NASA and headed up a development team that ultimately was instrumental in designing a satellite system that would serve as a deterrent for any future Laser attack by groups or countries that would attain this technology to do potential harm to the U.S. The system was designed to immediately detect emissions from a super Llaser conductor much like a nuclear detonation can be detected. The super charged ions emitted anywhere in the world would register on a very sensitive receptor and locate the source down to four meters of error.

January 12, 2004, Dr. Henson along with, posthumously, Dr. Ernest Brown and Percy Thackett would all receive the Presidential Merit Award acknowledging their volunteer meritorious service and, in Percy and Ernest's case, their ultimate sacrifice made during a time of threat to the security of the United States of America.

Steve Whitt returned to the FBI and was assigned to counter intelligence. In April, 2004 he was sent to Indonesia to take custody of Walid Alziddi, who had fled there from the international manhunt that was instigated to find him after the 9-11-03 incident.

Thinking that Indonesia would be a safe haven, Alziddi slipped into the country and blended into the populace, hiding with trusted associates in that country. What he failed to consider was that the Indonesian government, in their effort to continue to warm relations with the U.S. and the international community, as well as their fear that Alziddi in their country would provide a nucleus for strengthening the radical Islamic element in their country that could challenge the current leadership, was willing to assist the U.S. in finding Alziddi. Their intelligence became aware of his presence in a suburb of Jakarta and, in a secret early morning raid, quietly arrested him and three of his closest associates. They informed the U.S. and agreed to turn him over, provided the four would be spirited out of the country as soon as possible.

His arrest was never publicly announced.

Whitt, along with three CIA agents flew to Jakarta to take custody of Alziddi and his three cohorts. On the way back, they landed at an undisclosed location. When they departed, Alziddi and his three associates where not on board. Neither the U.S. nor Indonesia ever announced Alziddi's capture, but he was never heard from again.

Steve Whitt also got a department citation from the FBI for his participation with the joint Laser Team, but no mention was ever made in Department files of his mission to take custody of Alziddi.

Lawerence Childress posthumously received a commendation medal with endorsement by the President for his heroic efforts throughout the Laser Team episode. The CIA placed his picture in the lobby at Foggy Bottom, alongside others from the Department who had distinguished themselves in service to their nation. A brass inscription beneath his photograph described his unselfishly placing himself at risk to protect his team members and advance the objective of their mission.

Darby Peters received the Medal of Honor for his bravery under fire and his initiative that probably saved the life of the President of the United States. In presenting the medal to Darby, the President thanked him for his quick and decisive action in an uncertain situation and commented that he probably would not be the one presenting the medal if not for Darby's brave charge at his assassins.

Darby, confined to a wheelchair, went through an initial period of depression and despondency, but quickly regained his energy and enthusiastic attitude. He learned to expertly manipulate his wheelchair, drive with a vehicle designed for the disabled and became a national advocate for employment of the disabled.

First Lieutenant Darby Peters was promoted to Captain and allowed to return to active duty in an unprecedented decision by the Department of Defense that allowed him to do so. He was assigned as an instructor at Fort Benning, Georgia where he taught a class to Army Rangers and Delta Force trainees on their new role in combating international terrorism.

Dawson Kohler returned to his duties with the Secret Service. In January, he was presented with a Department Achievement Award endorsed by the President of the United States for his effective leadership of the joint department Laser Team. Subsequently, he was promoted to head a new Secret Service department whose mission was to coordinate efforts and analyze information from all enforcement and intelligence organizations that might be critical to the Department's primary mission of protection of the President and other key leaders in our national government. His duties required him to maintain constant consultation and contact with representatives of the FBI, CIA, ATF, Coast Guard, State Department, INS, Department of Defense and, in some instances, state and local law enforcement contacts.

Through his constant efforts, along with the support of Mike Reilly, Bob Willoughby and all the surviving members of the Laser Team, Kohler was able to convince a sympathetic President to grant Ashton Smyth a Presidential pardon.

In the final two hours of that night on 9-11-03 when he and Ashton were together while awaiting the arrival of the U.S. Marshals, they both confirmed their continuing love for each other. Although a major aspect of their relationship had been based upon deception, along the way, they had fallen in love with each other. Dawson understood the events and the motivations that led to Ashton's divulging the NIF secrets to an unknown party who promised to provide the funding that would save the project. He, Mike and Bob Willoughby all agreed that she had been naïve and that she had sacrificed a great deal to rectify her mistake. Plus, Dawson acknowledged he had fallen deeply in love with her.

On Ashton's part, she understood that Dawson had to do the right thing relative to his employment responsibility. If they were to have a continuing relationship, which they both wanted, his action was necessary to clear the air of this lingering cloud in her past. And she trusted him to try to attain an early release for her. Dawson confirmed this trust by visiting her in prison every single day when he was in town and by writing her letters the times he was not there. He kept her updated continuously on their progress to attain a Presidential pardon. That gave her hope. She endured the prison life, kept her hope and retained her commitment and enduring love for Dawson, the first person other than Skipper, her Mom and Bob Willoughby , along with the other Laser Team members that had shown her love and respect, and had not taken advantage of her.

Ironically, the President granted the pardon to a person who, inadvertently, had started a chain of events that threatened his life. Afterwards, in recognition of her sacrifice and bravery while working with the Laser Team, he did something even more that was unprecedented in the history of the United States. She received a Presidential Merit Award. There had never been such an award presented to a convicted felon. It was even more remarkable when considering the felony of which she had been convicted. The President received some criticism, even within his own party. But he steadfastly defended his decision as a means to express his gratitude to her for her part in the affairs of the Laser Team. The pardon was granted 11-3-04. She had served a little more than a year in jail and was still not quite 30 years old.

Ashton decided, much to Bob Willoughby's disappointment, not to return to Lawrence Livermore. She did agree to make herself available on occasion for consulting advice to NIF. After her release, she felt she had everything in her life that she had ever dreamed of. She had finally found her way, through the man that she loved. And she knew he loved her.

On December 17th 2004, the second anniversary of the date they met, Ashton Smyth and Dawson Kohler were married in a little chapel in a remote area of East Tennessee. Darby Peters escorted her down the aisle. She was beautiful and her face was radiant. There were few dry eyes that day when she and Darby came slowly down the aisle with her hand clasping his elbow. Darby was beaming also and his broad smile offset the little tear of joy that escaped out of Ashton's eyes as she came down the aisle.

Steve Whitt and Thom Henson stood alongside Dawson as he nervously awaited Ashton to arrive alongside him for the ceremony. Also in attendance were Ashton's mother, her brother Skipper, who was all smiles, Bob Willoughby and Mike Reilly. It had been raining earlier that morning, but the sun now shown brightly through the clouds.

When the ceremony was concluded, Dawson kissed his new bride.

"Love, we will always be 'we'. I love you—lots!" Ashton smiled up at him, squeezing his hand.

"Yes, my beautiful little wife, we are 'we'. I knew we would be, I think, from the day I met you. And I know we will always be." He smiled at her, and grabbed her hand to start back down the aisle and begin their lives together.

The other guests, including the surviving members of the Laser Team, followed them out into the chill morning warmed by the bright sunshine.

THE END

Printed in the United States
1118400004B/159